44

THE PERFECT LIAR

BRENDA NOVAK

THE PERFECT LIAR

MIRA®

MIRA®

ISBN-13: 978-1-61523-273-4

THE PERFECT LIAR

Printed in U.S.A.

To Marcie, my niece. You're a sweet girl who's easy to be around. Keep up the good work and build a wonderful life for yourself—you can be anything you want to be.

Dear Reader,

Welcome back to The Last Stand, a fictional victims' charity set in Sacramento, California. If you've been following the series, you've already met several of the characters, but the hero and heroine in this book will be, for the most part, new to you. Ava took over at the charity when Jasmine married and moved to Louisiana. Ava's an interesting character, so cautious about avoiding emotional entanglements that she lives on a houseboat in the delta. She can pick up and leave at any moment, won't commit even to a location. But she's not quite as free as she thinks, especially after she meets Captain Luke Trussell, a pilot at Travis AFB.

One of my favorite characters in the story is, as usual, the villain. The study of abnormal behavior has long been fascinating to me, perhaps because it's often so self-destructive. I don't always understand why some people act the way they do, but I based the major tenets of Kalyna Harter's personality on a woman I once knew who sued just about every employer she ever had for sexual harassment. She lied and manipulated and used laws meant to protect women to punish the men in her life, not only her employers but also those with whom she had personal relationships. Some of my outrage at her actions has no doubt filtered into this story. Kalyna is very real to me because I've known someone very much like her.

When you get a minute, please visit brendanovak.com. There's a lot there—contests and giveaways, interviews with various professionals in the criminal justice world, 3-D screensavers you can download free, a virtual tour of the offices of The Last Stand, a short prequel to the whole series, and more. If you sign up for my mailing list, you'll be invited to my annual cyber Christmas party, which is a blast. At my Web site, you can learn more about my annual online auction for diabetes research, an event I sponsor every May (my youngest son suffers from this disease). Together with my fans, friends, fellow authors and publishing associates, I've managed to raise over $700,000 to date. Don't miss the auction in 2010. It's going to be amazing!

For a free pair of 3-D glasses, send an S.A.S.E. to Brenda Novak at P.O. Box 3781, Citrus Heights, CA 95611.

I hope you enjoy *The Perfect Liar!*

Brenda Novak

When the sun sets, shadows, that showed at noon
But small, appear most long and terrible.
                    —Nathaniel Lee, 1653-1692

Prologue

Travis Air Force Base
Fairfield, California
Sunday, June 7

"You're here *why?*" Wearing only a hastily donned pair of jeans, Captain Luke Trussell stood squinting at the man and woman, both from base security, whose knock had just dragged him out of bed.

"We're responding to a complaint filed by Sergeant Kalyna Harter."

There had to be some mistake. He didn't even live here. He'd lent the use of his off-base apartment to two female cousins visiting from out of state. In the meantime, he'd temporarily moved into a friend's place because it was empty while that friend and his family were on leave. "Against *me?*" He raised a hand to his bare chest.

One of the officers, Sgt. E. Golnick according to her name tag, let her gaze range over his upper torso. Although female attention had little to do with why he worked out, it was a fringe benefit. But her expression revealed more contempt than appreciation. He could tell she was taking note of his size and musculature, thinking how easy it would be for him to overpower a woman, any woman, even a woman like Kalyna, who was five-ten and lifted as regularly as he did.

"Yes, *you*," she responded, her eyes shifting to his face. "You know her, right?"

"Yeah, I know her. She's in my flying squadron, has been since she was transferred here three months ago." Which was how they probably knew where he was staying. She must've told them.

"She's claiming you raped her last night, Captain. From the look of her, it was a brutal attack."

A brutal attack? Kalyna had been perfectly fine when he left her apartment only—how long ago? He glanced at his wrist, then remembered that she'd removed his watch when he started saying how late it was. She hadn't wanted him to leave her bed. Was this her revenge for doing so, anyway? Or had she been hurt by someone else—badly enough that she didn't know what she was saying? "Is she going to be okay?"

"She's got some nasty bumps and bruises," Sgt. P. Jeffers, Golnick's counterpart, chipped in. "It's nothing life threatening, but she's spent the past five hours at Northbay Medical Center being examined for sexual assault."

Luke shook his head. "This doesn't make sense. If she was assaulted, someone else did it."

"That's not her story."

A rush of anger burned away his sleepy confusion. "She must be out of her mind, delirious."

"She's perfectly coherent," Golnick said.

"Then she's lying!"

One eyebrow slid up. "They've extracted semen from her body. Are you telling me it won't prove to be yours?"

"I don't see how it can."

Golnick folded her arms. "You didn't have sex with her?"

Luke rubbed his neck. He hated discussing such personal matters—especially when all he wanted to do was forget—but he had to explain fast and be frank. If he didn't, there could be more trouble. "We had sex, yes," he clarified. "But it was consensual."

"Consensual means you both agreed."

He gave her what he hoped was a withering look. "I know what it means."

She stood her ground. "The fact that you didn't use a condom might suggest otherwise."

"I *did* use a condom," he insisted. "I wouldn't... I mean, I'm not *that* reckless."

"Then how do you explain the semen?"

He couldn't. But it wasn't as if last night was a complete blur. It was just that he remembered some details more than others. And it didn't help that he was hungover. "Maybe it broke..." He hadn't noticed anything unusual, but he'd drunk more than he had in years. And once he started sobering up, he'd been anxious to get home. "I didn't hurt her. I can promise you that. I'm sorry if someone else did, but I've never struck or forced a woman."

"You keep mentioning someone else."

"Because it wasn't me."

"So what do you suggest happened? Are you assuming someone came in after you left?"

"That has to be the case," he said. "It isn't as if I'm some predator out trolling for women. *I* wasn't the one who wanted to hook up last night. Kalyna got into my cab and gave the driver her address. I thought we'd already said good-night."

"Some men might think that means she's asking for whatever she gets."

He could easily recognize the trap in that statement.

"Some men, but not me. Quit trying to twist whatever I say. I'm just telling you how we got together. If I was a rapist, don't you think I'd be the aggressor?" That was how *he* pictured rapists, but Kalyna had been chasing him for weeks. She managed to bump into him all over the place, even when they were off work and off base. He'd been able to feel her interest from the moment they were introduced, could still remember how her smile had widened at the sight of him, how she kept trying to engage him in conversation.

"She said you asked to go home with her and she refused but later relented." Jeffers added this with some doubt in his voice, so Luke appealed to him.

"That's a *lie!* I didn't even ask her to *dance* with me. I've never been attracted to Kalyna." In his opinion, Kalyna was too masculine—at least in the light of day. And he'd been able to tell from very early on that she was too controlling. He avoided her if he could, but it was impossible to avoid her entirely. She was his crew chief, which meant she performed preflight, through-flight and postflight inspections and fixed anything that went wrong with his jet.

"If you weren't attracted to her, why'd you have sex with her?" Golnick asked.

Luke hadn't planned on touching Kalyna. *She* was the one who asked him to dance and kept rubbing up against him, whispering in his ear: *You make me so hot... When you gonna show me what you've got in your pants, Captain?* Even then, he hadn't been tempted until later on, after he had a good buzz going.

"To be honest, I don't know," he admitted with a sigh. He'd just let the sultry promise in her voice overcome his better judgment.

Golnick peered behind him, into the Craigs' house, as

if she might see something there that would provide proof of his guilt. "Why don't you get dressed?" she said. "We need you to come down to the squad room to make a formal statement. We've notified your commander. He's meeting us there."

Formal statement rang like a death knell in Luke's head. They were taking him in. This was serious. After all the bad press such stories had received in the past, the military had grown very intolerant of any kind of sexual misconduct. A wink or a nod or even a smile could be termed sexual harassment and ruin a guy's reputation, maybe his career. And here he was, accused of much worse. It didn't matter that he was innocent. He'd *look* guilty. To anyone else, the chances of a second person coming in after he'd left Kalyna had to seem minute; he'd been with her until three in the morning. Beyond that, he was bigger and stronger than she was, which meant public support would remain firmly in her favor. This was the one situation where, even in America, a guy was guilty until proven innocent.

He opened his mouth to plead his case. But a neighbor who'd spotted the security car was watching to see what would happen next, and Luke was reluctant to put on a show. Still hoping this was a terrible mistake that would be resolved quickly if he cooperated, he ducked back into the house and yanked on the rest of his clothes.

He'd had a feeling Kalyna was bad news, but he'd discounted it. He hadn't realized how much damage she could inflict if she set her mind to it. He'd never had reason to fear a woman. What could *she* do to *him?*

Apparently, he was about to find out.

1

Sacramento, California
Three weeks later

Ava Bixby sat behind her desk, watching the large-boned blond woman twist the tissue Ava had just handed her. The blotchiness of her face and the puffiness of her eyes seemed out of place against the battle fatigues she was wearing. But she'd been relating a horrific incident, one that had happened only three weeks ago and would make any woman cry, even a tough military type.

"Take your time," Ava said soothingly. She knew the right tone to use. She dealt with victims every day. It was her job. They hadn't all suffered rape, of course, but most had been directly affected by violent crime. Her partners, Skye Willis and Sheridan Granger, had firsthand experience. Ava had experience with it, too—just in a different way.

Kalyna Harter had introduced herself as a staff sergeant E-5 in the air force and looked Ukrainian, as her first name suggested. But she spoke with no accent, leading Ava to believe she'd immigrated to the United States when she was a child. A light dusting of freckles covered her nose and she wore her fine blond hair straight down her back. She would've been beautiful, except that her features were a little large or incongruous or…something. Ava couldn't figure out what made her face such a near miss.

"I'm sorry, it's—" Kalyna sniffed "—difficult to talk about this."

"I understand." Although Ava had never been physically attacked, she'd felt the effects of criminal behavior. She knew from what her mother had done how badly it hurt everyone associated with it, even those who weren't the intended target.

"He—he seemed like a nice guy, you know?" Kalyna was saying. "I mean, I've flown with him for three months. He's never said or done anything that made me think he might be dangerous. Besides, why would any guy with a body like that have to resort to force?"

Ava's mind had wandered, as it always did when she thought of her mother. She was tired, had less control today. It was Monday morning, but she'd spent most of the weekend working, as usual. Sometimes she didn't allow herself enough of a break from all this and she became almost…numb.

Picking up her pen, she focused, trying to shake off the heavy sense of loss and betrayal that weighed her down when she least expected it. She missed her mother—and felt guilty for missing someone who could do what Zelinda had done. "Rape's not about sex, Ms.—"

"Please, call me Kalyna."

"Kalyna. It's about power. And rapists come in all shapes and sizes. But—" she dropped her pen again "—I'm not quite sure how to help you. This is a military matter. You've already mentioned that their investigators are working on it."

"It happened at my apartment, and my apartment is off base. That means the civilian police could prosecute, too."

A sharp knock interrupted.

"Excuse me." Ava lifted a hand. "Come in," she called.

Skye Willis poked her head into the room. With her golden tan and long, well-toned limbs, she didn't need makeup or fancy clothes, but she always dressed nicely. Today she was wearing a summer dress and had her blond hair pulled back. Sheridan was with her. She wasn't nearly as tall or toned as Skye—she was a little more voluptuous—but every bit as pretty. Her unusual, almost violet-colored eyes and dark hair drew attention wherever she went.

Ava felt very plain next to her partners. With dishwater-blond hair, eyes that were neither brown nor green—just a murky in-between—and a body that was thin to the point of boniness, she couldn't compare with their kind of beauty. Maybe that was why she settled for boxy business suits. She accepted what she was, didn't try to compete.

"We're heading over to Starbucks," Skye announced.

"Can we get you two some coffee?" Sheridan chimed in.

Ava glanced questioningly at Kalyna.

"I'm fine," she murmured.

"So am I," Ava told them.

Skye must've noticed Kalyna's blotchy face and realized they were in the middle of a serious conversation because she lowered her voice. "Okay, sorry for the interruption," she said, and Sheridan waved quickly as they left.

"Those people work here, too?" Kalyna asked.

"They started the charity." Ava had worked at The Last Stand for two years, but Skye, Sheridan and a woman named Jasmine Fornier were the ones who'd conceived of the idea and gotten it up and running. An excellent forensic profiler, Jasmine still did some consulting—for them and for others—but she'd since married and moved to Louisiana, which was why there'd been a job opening for Ava.

"So it's just the three of you?"

"Yes, plus a bevy of professionals from psychologists to bodyguards, most of whom donate their time. In addition, we have a handful of volunteers."

"I didn't know that. When I called, I was simply given an appointment with you."

"I'm single, so I put in a few more hours each week. And I focus mostly on casework and less on administration and fundraising."

"I see."

In an attempt to guide the conversation back to where they'd left off, Ava looked at her notes. "So…you were saying something about the civilian police."

"I was saying they could prosecute, too," Kalyna responded. "But they don't want to get involved. They don't think it's necessary to spend taxpayers' money to prosecute the captain twice, so they've decided to let the military handle it."

"You don't want the military to handle it?"

"I don't trust the air force. They'd do anything to avoid a scandal, even if it means letting Luke off. He's one of their best pilots, an officer. That's quite an investment. I'm just an enlisted airman—and a woman at that."

Ava could easily believe the military would rather keep this quiet. But would they really investigate less thoroughly than they should?

As she deliberated, fresh tears welled up in Kalyna's eyes. "That's what you're here for, isn't it? To help people like me—people who have all the cards stacked against them and can't get justice?"

"That's what we're here for." Ava used the same soothing voice she'd used before, but there were a couple of things that bothered her about this case. The air force wouldn't be happy to have a civilian organization looking over their shoulder. Even the prosecutors she'd be trying to assist would probably stonewall her. Maybe that wouldn't be so much of a problem if she knew how the military worked or had any contacts there, but she didn't. And neither did the others at TLS. She had to be careful where she allocated the charity's assets, had to make sure that she didn't waste any of the money they so painstakingly raised. There were far more people needing help than they had the resources to cover. With the economic downturn, she and Skye and Sheridan had decided they could get involved only in instances of dire need or potential threat. Otherwise, they'd put themselves out of business and wouldn't be able to do anything for *anyone.*

But this case was a classic David versus Goliath. Always a sucker for the underdog, Ava felt tempted to accept the assignment. Maybe it was the sight of this woman wearing battle fatigues—knowing she had to compete in a uniquely male world. Or maybe it was the memory of Bella Fitzgerald, her very first client, which haunted Ava to this day....

"So you'll help me?" Kalyna clarified.

Kalyna's situation qualified under both the need and threat tenets. But Ava still wasn't convinced The Last Stand could make a difference. Would it merely drain her time and TLS funds, resulting in no better outcome than if she hadn't jumped in? She had to be sensible, couldn't let what'd happened to Bella provoke her into taking every rape case, regardless of practical considerations.

After removing some pictures from her purse, Kalyna shoved them across the desk. "Look what he did to me."

The photographs showed Kalyna beneath harsh white

lights, wearing a hospital gown. Several bruises darkened her face, her eye was swollen almost shut and she had a fat lip. At that moment, Ava saw Bella, not Kalyna— Bella in a similar environment, lying pale and lifeless beneath a sheet.

"How did you get these?"

"There are several of each in my file. I insisted the E.R. doctor give me a set. She leaned forward. "Will you help me? Please, help me."

Ava swore, but only to herself. She couldn't say no, refused to risk letting another woman die the way Bella had. "I'll do what I can," she promised, then spoke up to counter Kalyna's immediate relief. "But you have to understand that I've never worked with anyone in the military before. I have no idea what we might encounter, but I'm sure the rules are different than I've dealt with in the past. The military is a whole other world."

"Just knowing you've got my back should keep them honest," Kalyna said. "You're always in the paper, and they're afraid of the media."

"That's how you found us?" Ava asked. "You read about us in the paper?"

"And I've heard you mentioned on the news."

That explained it. Sacramento had shut down its two air force bases years ago, and Travis was an hour's drive to the west, in Fairfield. Although Ava rarely even saw an airman, at least in uniform, she and her partners had worked some pretty high-profile cases. The publicity increased donations, as well as notoriety. But, if the air force intended to protect their captain, they'd be a formidable foe, especially if the civilian police declined to get involved.

It would all depend on the evidence, Ava decided. If she could gather enough evidence—a witness who saw

Luke leave just before Kalyna called for help, proof of injuries on him that Kalyna had inflicted while defending herself, a past history of date rape or other problems—*no one* could save Luke Trussell.

"Give me the spelling of his last name and anything else you know about him," she said, "right down to the color of his underwear."

2

It wasn't a mistake. After three weeks of spending long hours being interrogated by the police or meeting with the defense attorney he'd hired—the best civilian attorney he could find—Luke had come to the realization that the trouble Kalyna Harter had caused him wasn't going to go away without a bitter, drawn-out fight. It didn't matter that he was innocent. The Office of Special Investigations planned to prosecute, which meant he'd actually sit in a court-martial accused of raping a woman. It was so unreal, he couldn't believe it.

And he still hadn't told his family.

Determined to get off the couch, where he'd been busy kicking himself for going home with Kalyna in the first place, he prowled around his apartment. As much as he preferred to keep his folks ignorant of his predicament, he had to call them before they heard the news from someone else. So far, he hadn't seen a report of his "crime" in the paper, but his father was retired military, and military circles were tight-knit. It was only a matter of time. Judging by the number of questions and comments he was getting on base, word was spreading fast.

With a sigh, Luke checked the clock hanging on the wall. It was after eleven on a Monday night. Too late; his parents would be in bed. But suddenly he couldn't put off contacting them any longer. He needed their support—even more than he loathed admitting that he'd gone home with Kalyna Harter. That he'd made what she was doing possible.

He wished he could speak to them face-to-face. His folks lived in San Diego—only a seven-hour drive away. He could be there by morning. But he wasn't allowed to leave town. He was lucky E. Golnick hadn't locked him up in the Solano County jail. If not for his commanding officer, she would've tried. As it was, Luke had been grounded from flying, pending resolution of the case. He currently had a desk job, which he hated.

A phone call was the best he could do. And he needed to make that call sooner rather than later. He'd put it off too long already.

Taking a deep breath, he picked up the phone and dialed.

His mother answered almost immediately. "Hello?"

"Hey, Mom."

"Luke?"

"Yeah, it's me."

"You scared me. Getting a call at this hour, I thought your sister might've caused another fender bender."

"What's Jenny doing out so late on a weeknight?"

"It's not her curfew yet. Besides, it's summer and she only went to the movies. How are you?"

His mother's genuine concern made him choke up. Frustrated by his weakness, he swiped impatiently at his watery eyes. "I've been better. Is Dad around?"

"He's here with me, watching TV. Why? Is everything okay?"

Luke swallowed hard. "Any chance you could get him on the extension? I need to speak to both of you."

He felt his mother's trepidation. "You haven't been hurt…."

"No, it's something else." To him, something worse, because it defamed his character. He knew they'd feel the same way.

"Oh, no…" she mumbled. Then he heard her ask his father to get on the line. "It's Luke. Something's wrong."

"Luke?" His father's voice boomed in his ear, filled with protective anger, even though Ed had no idea— could probably never guess—what was wrong.

"Hi, Dad."

"You okay, son?"

The lump in Luke's throat grew larger, adding embarrassment to a list of other emotions. He had to wrestle with himself just to gain control of his voice. "I'm okay," he managed to say.

"Tell me what's wrong."

"There's a woman here, at Travis, a sergeant. She's actually my crew chief," he said with a disbelieving laugh. "She's claiming—"

"You haven't gotten her pregnant!"

"No, it's not that." He prayed it wasn't, anyway. As far as he was concerned, that was about the only way his situation could get worse. He'd worn a condom, although Kalyna had insisted she was clean and on the pill. But a condom seemed like meager protection now. They'd found his semen in her body. What would he do if she wound up pregnant? "This woman's telling the police I raped her."

His mother gasped, but his father met his announcement with stunned silence.

"Dad?" Luke said.

"What do *you* have to say about that?" Edward finally asked.

"I didn't do it."

"You're one hundred percent certain?"

"Of course!"

"I raised you to be a man, Luke. To take responsibility for your actions. If you're guilty, I expect you to admit it and pay the price, even if it means prison."

Edward's code of ethics demanded he be sure before throwing his support behind anyone. That included his son. Luke understood it, so his father's words didn't hurt. They offered him the opportunity to tell someone the truth—someone who might actually believe him. "I swear it on my life, Dad."

"Then that's all that matters."

Luke laughed without mirth. "To you, maybe. But it's not all that matters to me. She's already reported it. OSI is handling it."

"They're charging you?" his mother said.

"Yes."

She made a strangled sound. "What happened?"

Luke dropped his head into his hands. "I was an idiot."

His father responded before his mother could. "You need to expand on that answer."

"I wasn't thinking straight."

"Why not?"

He remembered the call he'd received from Lilly Hughes, his best friend's mother. Because his parents were no longer at Hill Air Force Base in Utah—they'd left when Ed retired—they probably hadn't heard the news he was about to impart. "Phil was killed in Iraq."

"No!" his mother cried.

Luke sat on the edge of the couch and stared glumly at the floor. "I'm afraid so."

"That's terrible!"

It was worse than terrible, so terrible Luke couldn't accept it. He stared at the shoes he was supposed to mail to the cousins who'd used his apartment. They'd left them and a few other things behind. But he'd been caught up in this mess and hadn't made it to the post office yet.

"I'm sorry, honey," his mother was saying. "I know how much you loved Phil."

It was Phil who'd first befriended him when they moved to Ogden, Utah, halfway through Luke's sophomore year. Phil who'd convinced him to play football their junior year. Phil with whom he'd double-dated and competed for valedictorian. Phil with whom he'd gotten into trouble for starting a food fight the day of graduation, after which he'd been barred from speaking at the commencement exercises. He and Phil had even loved the same girl—but Phil had declared himself first, so Luke had said nothing. He stood as best man and watched Phil marry Marissa. Then Phil had gone into the marines and Luke had followed in his father's footsteps and joined the air force.

"When's the funeral?" his mother asked.

"It's over. He died five weeks ago. Lilly was so grief-stricken she didn't think to call me. She apologized profusely, but…"

"Why didn't Phil's wife get in touch? She had to realize you'd want to know. The three of you were inseparable in high school."

He was the last person Marissa would call. About a year after she married Phil, she'd told Luke she'd made a mistake, that he was the one she really wanted. It had nearly killed him to do it, but he'd turned her away and insisted she never contact him again—for any reason. He wasn't about to let their love triangle end in tragedy, the way so many did. As much as he cared about her, as tormented with jealousy as he'd been every time he saw them together, he'd wanted them to be happy. Phil had gotten with Marissa first; Luke was the one who had to suck it up and move on. "I guess she didn't think of it, either."

"So you didn't get a chance to say goodbye," his mother said.

"No." Even worse, he and Phil had argued the last time they'd talked. About Marissa. As usual. Phil shouldn't have volunteered for that second tour. Luke had tried to tell him to go home and take care of his family. That Marissa needed a husband and their son needed a father, but Phil wouldn't hear of it. He was too pumped up on the war and patriotism. Before slamming down the phone, Luke had told his friend that he didn't deserve Marissa. But he hadn't meant it. He regretted that statement even more than he regretted going home with Kalyna.

"How does his death relate to this…Sergeant—what's her name?" his dad asked.

"Kalyna Harter. I went to a local bar that night to get my mind off the fact that I'll never see Phil again, and she showed up."

"Go on…"

"She kept hitting on me and…" Guilt bit deep. He hadn't raped Kalyna, but he'd made himself vulnerable to her. Now her accusations would reflect on his entire family. "I… It was a mistake."

"So you slept with her," his father said.

"I slept with her, but I didn't *force* her."

"Why would she lie?"

"That's what I can't figure out. I mean, I know she was angry that I wouldn't stay the whole night. When I left, she made some pretty ugly statements, but—"

"For example…"

Luke didn't want to repeat them. He hadn't been with her because he wanted to pursue a relationship, which was the only honorable reason to get that intimate with a woman. But then, he'd thought she understood it was strictly casual. If he'd been interested in her, he would've asked her out on one of the many occasions she'd hinted that she wanted him to do so. "She accused me of using her, that sort of thing."

Edward sighed loudly. "Sex means something to a woman. You can't sleep with her and expect it to be taken in stride. I taught you better than that."

His mother rushed to his defense. "Ed, he'd just heard about Phil! He was grieving, looking for a diversion."

"That doesn't give him the right to hurt others."

"This is the first call we've ever received like this!" she argued. "You know Luke's not a womanizer."

The last thing Luke wanted was for his mother to fight his battles. "Dad, I didn't think it would hurt anything, least of all *her*. She was the aggressor. Once we got to her place, she offered to…" He considered trying to explain what a three-way was and decided against it. Old-fashioned, religious and disciplined, his father would never understand a woman like Kalyna. "Never mind. She's unbalanced, okay? That's what I'm trying to tell you."

"You're going to need a top-notch lawyer," he said.

"I already have one."

"What can we do to help?" his mother chimed in. "Would you like us to come up there and be with you?"

"No, Mom. This is Jenny's last summer at home. She'll be miserable if you pull her away from her friends, and Lord knows you can't leave her there alone." Jenny hadn't been hanging with the best crowd. *Beach bums, all of them,* his father said. Luke thought she was too pretty for her own good.

"It might not be convenient, but we can make arrangements," his mother insisted. "We're your family. We'll do whatever it takes."

Luke leaned his head back. He was still in trouble, but his parents were standing behind him. For now, the moral support was enough. "Don't do it yet. It helps just to have you believe me."

"Of course we believe you!"

"I hate the thought of Jenny hearing about this," he grumbled.

"We won't tell her." It was his mother who made this promise.

"Someone else could. It'll humiliate all of you."

"No, it won't."

"I'm sure some of our friends will wonder if it's true."

"The only ones who'll wonder are the ones who don't know you very well," his father said.

Luke gazed up at the ceiling. "I think most people try to give the woman the benefit of the doubt. I always have."

"That shows you're a good man," his mother said. "What does this Kalyna look like, anyway?"

His stomach churned as he pictured her, naked and in bed, glowering up at him as he dressed. She'd been unhappy in the end. But she'd been very vocal about letting him know she liked everything before that point. And he hadn't used her. He'd been sincere in his desire to please her during the time they were together. He'd thought it was a give-and-take, a mutual escape from regular life.

He closed his eyes as if that might dispel the vision of her screeching obscenities at him. "I suppose some guys would say she's pretty."

"What do *you* say?"

"I can't see it. Especially now."

His call-waiting beeped. Surprised, he sat up straight

and held the handset away from him so he could check caller ID. It read *Unknown.*

"I'd better go. I'm getting another call."

His father caught him before he could hang up. "How are you for money?"

"I'm fine."

"The legal fees won't be cheap. Not for something like this."

No kidding. Luke had already written a ten-thousand-dollar check—what his attorney required as a retainer. Fortunately, he earned a decent salary and his expenses were low. He had a nice car, a BMW M3, which felt like a jet on wheels. He had a hefty monthly payment for the pleasure of driving it, but most of what he made went into savings. "I'll let you know if I need anything."

"Fight for your reputation, son," his father said.

Luke had every intention of fighting—for his freedom, as well as his reputation.

After telling his folks goodbye, he switched to the other line. "Hello?"

"Luke?"

It was a man. "Yes?"

"Pledge McCreedy."

His attorney. But why would McCreedy be calling him so late at night?

A surge of hope shot through him. Maybe the case had been dropped. He hadn't been violent, hadn't harmed Kalyna in the slightest. He couldn't believe she'd be vengeful enough to keep this going. "Tell me you have good news."

There was a brief hesitation. "The opposite, I'm afraid."

Luke braced himself. Was Kalyna pregnant? "What now?" he asked.

"There's a woman from The Last Stand—"

"The Last What?" McCreedy hadn't said "pregnant." Yet. Luke jumped to his feet and began to pace in an effort to disperse some of the nervous energy pounding through him.

"The Last Stand. It's a victims' charity in Sacramento. You haven't heard of it?"

"No."

"It's run by three women who investigate various cases, retest evidence, offer counseling, self-defense classes and money for attorney's fees—whatever they feel the victims who come to them might need."

This wasn't what Luke had expected. He would've been relieved, except that his attorney seemed so concerned. "What does that mean to me?"

"More than you might think. Sergeant Harter has enlisted their help. I just picked up the messages from my answering service. An Ava Bixby from The Last Stand has been trying to reach me."

"And?"

"Let me put it this way. She could go to the media. Any exposure you get there would almost certainly work against you. These women are viewed as champions of the weak and afflicted, which would add to the appearance of guilt on your part. They could dedicate time and resources to helping the prosecution build its case. From what I've seen, they're absolutely dogged once they have someone in their sights. They could even drag the local police into this, a possibility that brings the potential for a second trial."

Great. Kalyna winding up pregnant wasn't the only way his situation could get worse. "How do we stop them from getting involved?"

"I don't know that we can."

"But I'm innocent."

He'd muttered those words to himself, but apparently Mr. McCreedy heard him. "All my clients are innocent, Captain Trussell."

Yeah, right. McCreedy believed Luke was innocent because he was being paid to believe it. He looked no further. And why would he? Not all his clients could be innocent. Believing any of them to be guilty as charged would risk a conflict of conscience. Provided he had a conscience. "What is it Kalyna Harter wants?" Luke asked. "My head on a platter?"

"I don't know, but if you can come up with her motivation, I'm all ears. We have to provide a plausible reason she'd lie—something we can prove—or we won't have much of a case. It'll be your word against hers, and all she has to do is break into tears to appear authentic."

"I don't know why she hates me," Luke said. "I didn't stay as long as she wanted me to and it pissed her off. That's all I can guess." He also hadn't been able to repeat to her what she'd said to him before he got out of bed. *I love you...* He'd assumed she was joking. They worked together, but there was no love involved. "So what can we do about Ava Bixby?" he asked.

"Pray she runs low on funds and has to close her doors. Soon."

Luke shook his head. Now he had a victims' charity after him, hoping to see him swing for a crime he didn't commit. "Would it help if I talked to her?"

"Definitely not! That's why I'm calling. She may try to get in touch with you, but don't speak to her. She's on their side."

Luke massaged his left temple. He wanted to declare his innocence to anyone who'd listen, which made it difficult *not* to talk. But ever since base security had banged on his door, he'd found himself standing in a legal mine-field. It was best to listen to someone who knew how to navigate it.

Or he might not make it through.

3

"Ms. Harter, can you please state your full name?"

Kalyna smiled calmly at the female lawyer, a major from the Office of Special Investigations, who'd been assigned to prosecute Luke Trussell. She'd spoken to Rani Ogitani on the phone a few times, but this was their first face-to-face meeting. The woman seemed brisk and efficient—emotionally distant but certainly capable.

"Kalyna Boyka Harter."

Major Ogitani typed the date—Tuesday, June 30— and Kalyna's name into her laptop, which rested on the large rectangular table filling most of the on-base conference room. "Thank you. And your birth date?"

"May 18, 1983," she said, going through the details as she had in an earlier meeting with Ava Bixby. Kalyna wished Ava could just send major Ogitani a copy of the whole account, but she knew it didn't work that way. She had to explain it all again.

The prosecutor shifted her attention from her computer screen. "So you're twenty-six years old."

"That's correct."

"And were you born in the United States?"

"No, in Ukraine. My twin sister, Tati, and I were adopted by an American couple living in Phoenix when we were six-years-old. Their marriage fell apart shortly after—within months—and neither one of them wanted to keep us. So we were passed off to the neighbors."

"The neighbors."

"That's right. A mortician and his wife."

The clacking of the keyboard again. Despite what Kalyna had told Ava Bixby at The Last Stand during their initial conference, Major Ogitani seemed eager to do a thorough job. But even with a competent prosecutor, it wouldn't be easy to get a conviction against Captain Trussell. He had an impeccable service record, or so she'd been told since lodging her complaint.

"This was done legally?"

"Yes, but at first we were just foster kids."

"What precipitated the original adoption?"

Kalyna set her jaw so she could talk about the past without flinching. "My real mother could no longer afford to feed us. She felt we'd have a better chance here." In reality, Talia Kozak had wanted to be free to marry the man she'd fallen in love with, a man who refused to have anything to do with her two children, which he saw only as mouths to feed. Talia had gotten rid of them for him, and she'd done it in a way that made her some money on the deal. Kalyna had heard from her once, several weeks after she'd sent a letter pleading to come home. Her mother had said it was impossible, that her new husband would never allow it, and that was that. It was her second adoptive mother who'd mentioned the money the first couple had paid.

The sympathy that flickered in Major Ogitani's eyes both angered and relieved Kalyna. She understood the relief. She needed to elicit sympathy, needed Major Ogitani of all people to believe her. The anger was more complicated.

"I see," the prosecutor said. "So…you were raised by

this mortician and his wife in Phoenix from that time forward?"

"Actually, we moved from Phoenix to Mesa in what would've been my eighth-grade year, if I'd been attending school."

"You didn't go to school?" Major Ogitani seemed all business. Removed. Mechanical. But surprise leaked through her voice with this question.

"I was home-schooled."

"What were the reasons behind that?"

Control. And privacy. Her mother didn't want any teachers or administrators nosing around, telling her what she could or couldn't do. "My mother said she was afraid the other kids would be a bad influence."

"I see," she said slowly. "So...did you have friends?"

"Just my twin sister. We owned a mortuary on a fairly busy street, and we lived above it. It wasn't as if there were other houses with children close by."

Ogitani didn't approve. Kalyna could see that in her body language. "So your adoptive mother did the teaching?"

"It was more like independent study, especially in the later grades. We met with a teacher once a week who checked our work and gave us new assignments."

"Did you like being home-schooled?"

"I hated it." But it kept her from sharing information with others, from socializing with them and inviting them into their home, which was what her mother had wanted. And as long as they met certain curriculum requirements, the state didn't interfere.

"Why?"

"If you knew my mother, you'd understand."

Ogitani's voice became brisk again, **almost as if**

Kalyna was already on the witness stand. "So coming to America didn't improve your situation."

Only if the major considered hell an improvement. "That depends on how you look at it."

"What do you mean?"

"We had enough to eat. We had clothes to wear."

"But..."

"It wasn't an easy life. That's why I joined the air force, to escape." She remained purposely vague. Her story would be more credible and cause a stronger reaction if the information had to be pulled from her. She'd learned that from experience.

"You felt the need to 'escape'?" Ogitani rested her forearms on the table. "Why is that?"

Kalyna purposely avoided her gaze. "My home life was...unusual."

The major leaned closer. "In what way?"

"My sister and I were forced to work in the mortuary from the moment they took us in. I've had to handle more rotting corpses than most people have ever seen."

Lines appeared on the prosecutor's smooth forehead. "You mean, when you got older and started taking part in the family business?"

"No, I mean from the beginning. It was terrifying. Especially when I was younger, and Tati and I had to work alone."

Major Ogitani didn't bother to record this information. She was too shocked. "You and your sister had to work with corpses when you were *children?* And there was no adult present?"

It hadn't happened as often as Kalyna was leading her to believe, but it'd happened occasionally, and the mental picture her words created hit with the intended impact. "Sometimes."

"Isn't that illegal?"

"That depends."

"On what?"

"On what we admitted doing."

"Meaning…"

"We had to wash the blood and embalming fluid off the tables and mop up the floor. You don't need to be certified to clean up." She could still remember the smell. She'd always remember the smell.

The prosecutor grimaced. "Where were your adoptive parents?"

"My father was usually at the morgue, picking up another body, or driving the hearse to the cemetery. Or maybe it was late and he'd gone to bed. My mother refused to work in the preparation area or what we called 'the back end.'" That was why the Harters were willing to take over when the Robinsons didn't want them anymore. They'd been attracted by the potential for slave labor, not the joy of raising children. And they didn't want Kalyna and Tatiana to attend school and circulate in the community for fear they'd say too much about their situation, which might have brought attention and interference. Norma would never admit it, but Kalyna knew the truth.

"You were sometimes up later than your father?" the major asked.

"All the time. He'd get us out of bed, if necessary."

She rocked back. "That's terrible! And this continued until…when?"

"Until I joined the air force. But as we got older, we did hair and makeup on dead people, not just the cleanup. You don't need to be certified for that, either." Her sister was still stuck in Arizona, handling stiffs. They hadn't even been permitted to apply for college. When Kalyna joined the military, she'd had to leave Tatiana behind. The air force wouldn't take her sister. Tati had epilepsy. She was too timid, too fearful, to leave what was familiar to her, anyway.

"How old were you when you entered the armed services?"

"Eighteen."

"So you enlisted as soon as possible."

Feeling more confident by the minute, Kalyna nodded. She could convince anyone of anything. She didn't have to worry.

"Where's your sister now?" the prosecutor asked.

"Tati still lives with my parents."

Ogitani shook her head. "What a life."

Kalyna dropped her voice to a whisper. "I'm out of it now. That's all that matters."

The prosecutor straightened her skirt. "Kalyna, I hate to ask you this, but...would you mind if we talked a bit about your background in court?"

This was the most personable Ogitani had been. Maybe there was a human element to the android, after all, Kalyna thought wryly. Ava had struggled with her emotions, too, but Kalyna could tell she was a big softie. *Too* soft, which was why she'd tried to counteract the empathy she felt by maintaining some distance. "My background? Why? That doesn't have anything to do with Captain Trussell."

"It might explain why you acted the way you did with him. And the more the jury feels they know you, the more they'll invest in your life and challenges, and the better our chances of having them see the situation with Captain Trussell through your eyes."

"But I don't like talking about the past."

"I think it will be extremely helpful."

She remained silent long enough to convince the major she was wrestling with the decision. "Okay," she said at last. "If we have to."

"It might bring back some painful memories. I'll apologize for that now."

"It'll be okay." Especially if it would help the case against Luke. He deserved to be punished. She wouldn't be taken so lightly. By anyone.

"Do you have any contact with your parents?"

"Not much." She hated all three sets—her American parents and her Ukrainian ones, including the father who'd run out on her real mother before she and her sister were born.

"I can see why." Major Ogitani made a few more notes. "Now, what happened on the night of June 6?" she asked, looking up again.

Kalyna knotted her fingers in her lap. This was the tricky part. She had to be careful her story didn't change from what she'd already told the police, and Ava Bixby, had to be sure any new details she offered created no inconsistencies. "I ran into Captain Luke Trussell at the Moby Dick."

"What time was it?"

"About ten o'clock."

"Who were you with?"

"I was alone."

"Do you typically go out alone, Ms. Harter?"

When Kalyna glanced up, Major Ogitani made a placating motion. "I don't mean any censure with that question. It's just something we need to establish. Who was there. Why you were there. How you connected with Captain Trussell."

Kalyna nodded. "I don't go out alone very often," she said, but that was probably the biggest lie she'd told yet.

Now that she was no longer living with her sister, she did almost everything alone. Even when she was having sex she felt alone. Until Trussell... No one seemed to understand her or like her. But she knew it wouldn't be considered "normal" to say she preferred her own company to anyone else's, and she needed to appear as normal as possible.

"I was assigned to the base only three months ago. You know how it is after a recent move." She smiled as shyly as she could manage. "I needed a break from military life but I wasn't acquainted with anyone well enough to call and ask them to go out with me."

"I completely understand." Major Ogitani went back to her keyboard. "Had you been drinking, Kalyna?"

"Not a lot—"

The major interrupted by clearing her throat. "Actually, before you finish answering, let me rephrase that. If I went to the bartender and asked for a copy of your tab—which the defense will most likely do—what would it indicate?"

"Two or three drinks."

"Wine? Beer?"

"Jack Daniel's and Coke."

"In a matter of how many hours?"

"One."

Three JDs and Coke in one hour was no small amount of alcohol, but the major didn't comment on it. "And Captain Trussell? Was he also drinking?"

"Yes."

"How do you know?"

Kalyna resisted the urge to claim he was drunk. She wanted to imply that he was more inebriated than she'd been, but the bar tab would show exactly what they'd both had. "He had a beer when I saw him."

"Where was he when you came in?"

"At a pool table in back, playing a man I didn't recognize."

Major Ogitani entered this information in her notes. "So you saw him and then what? Did he approach you?"

"No, I walked over to say hello. I've been his crew chief for almost the entire time I've been here." That gave her a lot of contact with him, but that contact didn't stop at work. She'd copied his address from various papers she'd seen him fill out, had been to his place when he wasn't home, even taken the spare key from under the mat and made herself a copy. She'd watched him—and followed him more than once. "I was feeling a bit displaced and lonely, so I was happy to see a familiar face."

More typing. "You're both part of the 60th Air Mobility Wing?"

"That's correct."

"Was Captain Trussell as friendly as you'd hoped?"

"He was preoccupied with his game, but he was nice enough."

The major's eyes flicked her way. "Did you ever learn the name of the man who was with him?"

"Yes. Captain Trussell introduced him as Technical Sergeant O'Dell—Frank O'Dell."

Tap, tap, tap... "And how did Sergeant O'Dell treat you?"

"He was friendly, too." But not half as gorgeous as Luke Trussell. Short and stocky, with evidence of acne at an earlier point in his life, Frank paled in comparison to Luke, so much so that Kalyna had all but ignored him.

The typing stopped. "What happened after you went over to greet Captain Trussell and he introduced his friend?"

"I chatted with them while they finished their game.

Then I asked Captain Trussell to dance." Unfortunately, O'Dell could testify to this, or Kalyna would've tried to tell everyone that Luke had asked her. He *should've* asked her. But really handsome men were too selfish. They liked having women want them but never bothered to return the favor. *Wham, bam, thank you, ma'am.* That was the most a girl could expect from a guy like Luke Trussell.

But he wasn't going to get away with it. Not this time.

"How did Captain Trussell respond to your invitation?"

The prosecutor was watching her so closely Kalyna feared her expression was giving too much away and quickly controlled her features. "He agreed."

"Did he dance with anyone else?"

"No." She would never have allowed that.

"Can you tell me about his behavior as the night progressed?"

"He was fine at the Moby Dick. He was getting tipsy, but I didn't care. We were relaxing, having fun."

"How did you wind up taking him home with you?"

"Like I said, I was lonely. He seemed to be a nice man, and I wanted to get to know him outside of work. To make a friend." She remembered Ava's reaction to this, how readily she'd accepted it.

"Up to this point, he'd done nothing to suggest he might be dangerous?"

"Nothing at all. I never would've dreamed him capable of—" She stopped.

A hint of commiseration flitted across the prosecutor's face but she seemed to fight it. Kalyna had never known anyone so stiff, so formal. Ava had knelt before her with tears in her eyes at this point in the story. "You don't have to go on until you're ready," she said.

Kalyna hid a smile. This was going even better than she could've hoped, every bit as well as the first two times she'd gone through the details. "After we danced for a while, and drank some more, we took a cab to my apartment."

"What time was it when the cab arrived at the bar?"

"Just after midnight."

"I'll contact the taxi company to substantiate that," she said as an aside. "We want everyone to know that you got home very late, which meant that Captain Trussell didn't leave until early morning. If we can prove there wouldn't have been enough time for someone else to come in after he left, we'll have a huge advantage." She made another note. "And how were you dressed that evening, Sergeant? Were you wearing your uniform?"

"No. I was off base and tired of being a soldier. I wanted to feel like a woman, so I wore a dress." And she'd looked damn good in it. She'd turned a lot of heads that night.

"Would you say it was a modest dress?"

The hope in the investigator's voice tempted Kalyna to say, "*I* think so." Ava had asked the same thing and reacted the same way. But the police had taken the dress into evidence. Major Ogitani would see it for herself eventually.

At least it didn't look as provocative lying flat across a table as it did when Kalyna put it on. Right now—fortunately—the tear down the front stood out more than anything. "Maybe not by some standards," she admitted.

"Can you describe it for me?"

"It had a halter top."

"And the length?"

"It hit at midthigh." Actually, since she was so tall, it hit a little higher. When she'd decided to wear it that night, she hadn't been concerned with having to defend her outfit. She'd been focused on catching Captain Trussell's eye—at last. Lord knew nothing else had worked. He'd remained polite but…guarded, distant. He was much warmer to the rest of the squadron, but they'd been together longer.

"So you had on a pretty dress, you were having a good time and you invited a handsome man home for a drink." Major Ogitani had given her recap the perfect spin, exactly what Kalyna thought would work in court.

"Yes."

"Not so different from what happens at bars all the time."

"That's right."

"When did it get ugly?"

"When we were sitting on the couch at my place." To appear more traumatized, she began wringing her hands. "We were watching Season Five of *Sex and the City,* and he started to kiss me. I was okay with that. I was sorta interested in him. But when he slipped his hands under my dress, I got uncomfortable. He was too bold. And his attitude… It was as if he thought I had no right to refuse because I'd invited him over."

"Did you attempt to stop him?"

After getting lucky enough to gain his interest, only a fool would stop him. She couldn't have been more thrilled when he finally, *finally* touched her. "Yes."

"How did he react?"

"He laughed it off. But a few minutes later, he was trying to touch me again."

"What did you do the second time?"

"I shoved him away and asked him to leave."

"Did he listen?" Sympathy tinged the prosecutor's voice.

"No. He grabbed me by the neck and forced me to kiss

him. Then he tore off my dress and—" she gulped for air, thinking fast, trying to be consistent "—and I tried to run away. But he caught me in the hall, shoved me to the ground and was on top of me before I could even blink. As I struggled, he yelled at me, telling me I was a bitch and a tease and he'd take whatever he wanted to."

Major Ogitani didn't deal with emotion well. Kalyna had watched her trying to distance herself throughout the interview. Now she put some physical distance between them, as well, by getting up and moving to the window. "Go on..."

"I managed to wriggle out from underneath him while he was fumbling with his pants. I tried to run to my room, where I hoped to lock him out, but he grabbed my arm, slammed me into the wall and punched me in the face."

"With his *fist*?"

"Yes. You can see the black eye he gave me in the pictures."

She started to get out the photos she'd insisted the Emergency Room doctor give her, but Ogitani shook her hand.

"They're in the file I received." Her voice betrayed no disgust, but Kalyna knew she was feeling it. She had her hands clasped behind her so tightly her knuckles were turning white. "Did you fight back?"

"Don't you think you should be writing this down?" Kalyna was doing such a good job, she wanted to be sure Ogitani was getting it all.

"I plan to do a detailed recap as soon as we're done. You paint a vivid picture. Believe me, I won't forget." She took a deep breath. "Did you fight back?" she repeated.

"I couldn't. I was so dazed I didn't know what was happening." Which would conveniently explain why he had no injuries....

"And then?"

Apparently, Ogitani wanted the gritty details. Maybe she was secretly, getting off on it. "And then he was inside me, thrusting hard and fast, telling me how badly he wanted me and how he'd never met anyone else he wanted as much." Excited by the mere pretense, Kalyna squeezed her eyes shut so the major couldn't ascertain her true emotions. "I'll never forget his hot breath on my neck." At least that part was true. She'd never forget a second of it. Being with Luke had been the best experience of her life, even when they weren't making love.

Major Ogitani came over to crouch beside her. "Did you cry out, make any noise?"

"Yes." She'd moaned in ecstasy....

"Did anyone come to help?" Ogitani straightened as she asked this question.

"No! No one heard me. I still can't believe it."

The major's pat on her shoulder didn't seem very natural, but the prosecutor's effort to console her made it easier for Kalyna to conjure up tears. "Are you okay?"

Kalyna sniffed and nodded.

"How'd you get to the hospital that night?" Her manner became indignant. "Don't tell me you had to drive yourself in that condition!"

"No. After he left, I—I stumbled to the apartment next door. My neighbor drove me. And…and the pictures show the rest."

"I appreciate the detailed account. I know it can't be pleasant to tell that story."

"It's not." Kalyna sniffed again. "But…do you…do you think it'll be worth it? Do you think we'll win?"

Major Ogitani worried her lip. "These are difficult cases to prove. But…I plan to do my best."

Shrinking away from her because the closeness of

other women always made Kalyna uncomfortable, she slipped off her chair on the opposite side and stood. "Thank you."

Ogitani favored her with a smile. "You're welcome."

After they shook hands and Kalyna left, she allowed her smile to grow more self-satisfied. She had him. Luke Trussell would go to prison, where he'd be isolated and nearly forgotten by the outside world.

He'd need someone then. He'd need *her.* And that was when she'd forgive him. He'd finally realize they were meant to be together. There'd be letters and protestations of love. Conjugal visits. Maybe she could even have his baby.

Maybe she was pregnant now. The thought sent a thrill through her, the likes of which she'd never experienced. She doubted that what she'd emptied out of that discarded rubber would bring her the baby she craved, but there was always the possibility.

Either way, they'd be together eventually.

4

Late Wednesday morning, Ava spoke to the neighbor who'd driven Kalyna Harter to the hospital. They met at a smoothie place located just off base. Maria Sanchez was the first person to see Kalyna after the attack, so Ava was eager to speak with her. But Maria didn't want to get involved. When Ava had first contacted her, she said she was too busy. After several calls, she'd allowed Ava to talk her into meeting, but only for a few minutes. She'd come late, and she wasn't smiling when she approached the table.

"Hi." Her expression wary, she removed a pair of sunglasses to reveal wide-set brown eyes. "Are you…"

Ava held up the smoothie she'd bought while waiting. "Your juice date? Yes, I'm Ava Bixby from The Last Stand. You must be Maria Sanchez."

She nodded.

"Thanks for coming." Hoping to get Maria to relax, Ava offered her hand. Kalyna's neighbor clasped it reluctantly, briefly, and Ava indicated the empty side of the booth. "What can I get you?"

"Nothing, thanks," she said as she sat down.

"You don't want a smoothie?"

Maria didn't even glance at the list of drinks posted on the wall. "No, there's a lot more sugar in fruit smoothies than you might imagine."

The airman looked as if she took exercise as seriously as diet. Short and stocky, she had enough muscle mass to rival most men. "You're into health food?"

Ava could tell Maria didn't want to be drawn into a friendly conversation. She preferred to get through their meeting and be done with it. But she mumbled an explanation that was partially drowned out by the high whine of the mixers. "Everything I eat is organic."

"My friend Skye is constantly at me to improve my eating habits. I thought I was doing well by adding wheatgrass juice to this," she said with a laugh.

Maria fidgeted with the keys she'd carried in with her. "The wheatgrass juice is healthy, all right. It's the sugar you gotta watch."

"My problem is coffee. I'm too busy to slow down and eat properly."

She glanced at the door as if she couldn't wait to escape through it, but she didn't bolt. "Caffeine will kill you."

Making another attempt to put her at ease, Ava indicated the cooler next to the cash register. "Are you sure you wouldn't like *something?* Maybe some plain juice?"

Maria relented enough to get a bottle of water, and Ava paid for it.

"You've probably guessed why I want to speak to you," Ava said as they returned to the table.

"Kalyna mentioned that you might be calling. But Major Ogitani already met with me. So did a man named Pledge McCreedy."

"McCreedy's the defense attorney."

"He was kind of a jerk."

Ava had never been particularly interested in the smoothie she'd ordered. Now that it didn't sound as healthy as she'd thought it was, she was even less interested. "It's his job to protect the defendant."

"He acted as if he didn't believe what I had to say."

"I'm not surprised." Notorious in Sacramento, Pledge McCreedy rarely lost a case, which made Ava more than a little defensive of her client. The moment she'd heard that Captain Trussell had hired Mr. *McGreedy*, as they referred to him at The Last Stand, she'd become that much more determined to increase her own efforts.

"But I don't have any reason to lie. Like I told him and Ogitani, I don't know Kalyna very well," Maria said. "She lives in the apartment next to mine. We bump into each other in the hall, keep each other's spare key in case we ever get locked out, and she feeds my cat when I'm out of town. She doesn't have a pet so I don't have to return the favor, but I have her over for a drink now and then to thank her. That's about it."

Ava studied her. Why was Maria so anxious? "I just want to hear your version of what happened the night you drove Ms. Harter to the hospital," she said. "Did you hear a ruckus going on next door?"

Maria put her car keys on the table. The key chain held her driver's license with some bills rolled up under the plastic; she wasn't carrying a purse. "No, but it was very late. And my job is physically demanding. When I sleep, I sleep."

"Not much wakes you."

"I could sleep through an earthquake. And I told McCreedy that, too."

"This close to San Francisco, you might be tested on that someday," Ava teased, still working to calm her, to gain her confidence. "What about the other neighbors? Have you talked to them?"

"A young couple lives on the opposite side. They were gone. Someone in the family was getting married. I doubt anyone else knew until the next day."

Ava kept her voice conversational, as if they'd been friends forever. "I'll bet they were surprised. This type of thing doesn't happen in Fairfield very often, does it?"

"The neighbor across the hall, Petra, wasn't too surprised," she said.

"Petra?"

Her gaze lifted from her keys. "Lewis. She's in the air force, too."

"Why wasn't she surprised?"

"She said Kalyna probably deserved it."

Ava spooned up some of her smoothie, let it melt on her tongue. "For what?"

Maria blew out a sigh. "For the way she acts around men, I guess."

Although Maria didn't seem eager to explain, Ava continued her questions. "How does she act?"

Again, more hesitancy.

"Is she a little too friendly?" Ava guessed.

"You could say that. But it's not the only reason Petra doesn't like Kalyna," she hurried to add. "She says Kalyna's a lazy slouch. That she has an excuse for everything."

"Do you agree with that statement?"

"It's airmen like her who give women a bad name in the military." She fiddled with her keys. "But I try to mind my own business."

Ava was more concerned about Kalyna's behavior around men than her work ethic. "Does she have a lot of men over?"

"Not really."

"Then how can you tell she's too…friendly?"

The way Maria shifted in her seat suggested she was searching for the perfect answer, one that would back up her statement but get her out of more questions. "I've seen her flirt with guys on base. And she stays out late quite a lot. It's pretty often that I see her dragging in when I'm getting up."

"This bothers the other women?"

"Only because it makes it difficult for her to perform well," she said. "Sometimes she's late for her shift or shows up smelling like a bar. Or she talks about her exploits, which can be uncomfortable."

"Did you see her with anyone on the night in question?"

"No."

Ava had another taste of her smoothie. "What's the first thing you remember about that night?"

"I heard what sounded like a moan, and maybe some sobbing, coming from next door."

"So you got up to investigate?"

"No, I was too tired. I convinced myself it must be the television and drifted off."

"What time was it?"

Maria flipped her license over, then flipped it back. "I have no clue."

"What happened next?"

"I woke to Sergeant Harter beating on my door."

Giving up on actually eating it, Ava stirred her smoothie. "What did you think when you saw her?"

"What would anyone think? I could see she'd been hurt. There was blood on her face and her hands were all scraped. She was sobbing that she'd been raped. Definitely not a scene you expect to encounter, you know?"

"What time was this?"

"Three-twenty. I glanced at the clock on my microwave when I got the keys to my car."

"Did Kalyna tell you anything about her ordeal?"

Maria seemed to be loosening up. "No. She sat shivering and rocking in the passenger seat as I drove. I had to put her seat belt on for her because she was, like… dazed. It was scary."

"Did she say who'd raped her?"

"She said it was Captain Trussell."

"Are you familiar with the captain?"

"I've seen him on base, but we've never been introduced."

"Then how do you know who he is?"

Her lips curved in a slight smile. "Word travels fast when you're as good-looking as he is. The single women all talk about him. Besides, he's friends with another officer, Weston Anderson, who's married to a girlfriend of mine." She twisted off the cap to her water. "And…"

"And?"

"Kalyna mentioned him to me one time."

Maria seemed reluctant again. "Do you remember when that was?"

"A week or two before the incident."

"What'd she say?" Ava felt as if she was tugging the information out of Maria, but at least Kalyna's neighbor was still with her, still responding.

"She was on her way out when I met her in the hall. I asked her if she had plans for the evening—you know, the regular chitchat you do with neighbors—and she said she had a date with a pilot. I asked her who it was, and she said Captain Trussell."

A *date?* Kalyna had given Ava the impression that they'd never been out together prior to meeting up at the Moby Dick. "So she had some interest in him before that night?"

"Definitely. And she was giddy with the thrill of letting me know she had what so many other women want." She grimaced. "But the fact that she was excited about being with him—proud, even—makes what he did to her all the worse."

"You believe Kalyna, then. You have no doubt she's telling the truth?"

Maria tapped her fingers against her water bottle. *Ba-ba-bump. Ba-ba-bump.* "Of course I believe her, don't you? I mean, why would she lie about something like that?"

"It happens."

She shook her head. "No, I saw her. She was definitely traumatized. And somebody beat her up."

"You don't think she could've done it to herself?"

Her jaw dropped. "What? No!"

"That's what I needed to hear. Thanks for talking with me." Ava handed her a card. "This is where you can reach me if you have anything to add."

"That's it? We're done?"

"We're done. Unless there's something else you'd like to tell me...."

"Oh...no. Nothing else. Thanks for the water." She grabbed her keys and started out in a hurry, but her footsteps slowed as she got to the door, and she turned back. "Ms. Bixby?"

Ava had been watching her, wondering about her true feelings toward Kalyna. "Yes?" she said hopefully.

Maria stared at her feet, then frowned. "There's one thing that sort of bothers me."

"What is it?"

"I—I didn't mention it to the prosecutor or the defense lawyer because, well, I keep telling myself it doesn't have any bearing on the case. But—" biting her lip, she moved close again and lowered her voice "—I feel sort of guilty about keeping it to myself."

At last, they were getting somewhere. Ava waved her back into her seat. "What is it, Maria?"

She sat down and leaned halfway across the table. "What I told you about Kalyna and men?"

"You said she was too friendly."

"I might've understated it a bit. She...she sleeps around *a lot*."

Ava pushed her smoothie aside. "You know that even though she's not bringing men to her apartment?"

Maria sighed. "Yeah, I know—because she's not ashamed to admit it. She's a self-proclaimed nympho who brags about her exploits."

"What kind of exploits?"

She hadn't bragged to Ava. She'd acted quite innocent.

"Kinky stuff."

"Are you sure it's not all talk? Something to get attention? To shock you?"

"I don't think so." She wiped the condensation from her water bottle. "One time I invited her over for a drink," she explained. "We got to talking, and she asked if I'd ever been with another woman." She checked behind her, as if she was afraid she'd be overheard, even though they were the only customers in the shop and she was already whispering. "When I said no, she asked if I was ever tempted to see what it would be like."

"You think she's gay?" If Kalyna was a lesbian, that would explain why she'd tried to put on the brakes with Trussell. Maybe she showed interest in men as a front; maybe she overcompensated with the whole nympho routine.

"I doubt it. It's definitely men she likes. This was just a way to get me intrigued, show me how daring she is."

Their conversation was doing little to build Ava's confidence in Kalyna Harter, which was a disappointment. She didn't want to be faced with a difficult dilemma. If Kalyna had really been victimized, she'd need Ava's full support. But Ava couldn't ignore this. She had to see her client realistically. "Why do you feel this is relevant?" she asked.

Maria held up a hand. "I'm not done yet. When she asked me if I'd ever…you know…I joked that the only way I could get interested in another woman was if there was a man involved."

"A threesome."

She blushed. "Yeah."

"And what did Kalyna say to that?"

"She said she'd like to include me sometime." Maria tore at the label on her water bottle. "I didn't believe Trussell was all that interested in her, so I asked her if she could convince him to join us. I wanted to see if she'd been lying about him before."

"And?"

Her chest rose as she drew in a deep breath. "She smiled as if she was eager for the challenge and promised me she'd do it."

"Is that what she was attempting to arrange on June 6?"

"If so, she never called me. Maybe she knew I wasn't serious. Maybe she wasn't serious, either." Maria held her long hair off her neck and fanned herself. The day was so hot, the air-conditioning wasn't helping enough, and this was a conversation she clearly didn't want to be having. "But when the whole rape thing came up and Trussell's name was brought into it—that gave me a funny feeling. I knew Kalyna would love to be with him. So why would she invite him to her apartment and then tell him no? I honestly can't imagine him having to force her. Not the way she was talking."

"There could be a lot of reasons she changed her mind." Ava managed a smile. But the fact that Kalyna had been discussing Captain Trussell in such a light—and well in advance of the incident—troubled her, too. The defense would certainly make an issue of it if they found out.

"I didn't mean it, so she probably didn't, either," Maria said again.

Ava fell back on the pictures she'd seen and the fact that there wouldn't have been time for someone else to enter Kalyna's apartment after Trussell left. Kalyna's testimony had been convincing, too. They'd gone over the incident in two separate meetings, and Kalyna had cried during both. "It doesn't matter if she was the pursuer, Maria. At some point, she wanted to bail out, and he resorted to violence. There's no excuse for that."

"Right. I agree. So...I don't need to tell anyone else about...about that embarrassing discussion? I mean, if someone were to interpret it the wrong way, it could ruin my career. You know how the military is, the whole 'don't ask, don't tell' thing."

"If someone in authority questions you about it, you need to be honest."

"But what if I'm *not* asked? I haven't been asked about it yet."

And she'd only spoken of it once. Now.

Ava felt a twinge of conscience, but she had no intention of helping the defense. She'd been through this before and allowed her loyalty to be shaken. Bella had taken her own life when she couldn't get anyone to believe her. Ava wouldn't let that happen to another soul. Kalyna's sexual habits and preferences didn't matter, not if she'd tried to say no to Trussell and he'd ignored her. "I don't see why you'd need to volunteer the information."

Smiling in relief, Maria tossed her keys in the air and

caught them, finally relaxed. "Thank God. I wish I'd never been stupid enough to have that conversation. Imagine what the other airmen would make of it," she said with an awkward laugh.

They'd wonder, as Ava did, if Maria wasn't hiding more than she wanted to admit. But Maria's sexuality had nothing to do with this case or anything else. No reason to drag that into it.

"Don't worry," she said, and waved goodbye. Then she sat at the table a while longer, contemplating what Maria had shared. Obviously, Kalyna wasn't someone with an impeccable reputation. Her image was tainted, and she wasn't particularly well liked. That might be a challenge to the prosecution. But even those who were less than perfect deserved justice when they were wronged.

Wanting to discuss the situation with someone else, she took her cell from her purse and called Jonathan Stivers, the private investigator who helped out with so many of their cases at The Last Stand. He did a lot of pro bono work but they used him so often they paid him when they could. Fortunately, like them, he cared more about the people who needed his help than he did about living in luxury, so he kept his charges in the survival range.

"Hello?"

"Jonathan, it's Ava."

His voice warmed. "What's up?"

"I have a job for you."

"You always have a job for me. Do you *ever* have any fun?" he teased.

"No."

"That's what I would've guessed."

"Just because I act like an adult and you don't?"

"You don't have to work around the clock to be an adult," he said.

"A lot of people are counting on me. I have a responsibility to them."

"Did you ever think you might be letting *yourself* down?"

Perhaps. But she didn't really know how to remedy that, and there was so much to do each day. Besides, the more she worked, the less time she had to think about herself. She'd been busy trying to wrap up a few older cases so she could concentrate on Kalyna Harter's, or she would've called Jonathan about Captain Trussell sooner. "I'm happy the way I am," she insisted.

"So what do you need?" he asked. "Proof that your boyfriend spends more hours at work than you do?"

A mother and her young son came in, and Ava lowered her voice. "Quit it. Geoffrey's an up-and-coming land developer. That takes time and dedication."

"He's not right for you."

With a fleeting smile for the child who glanced at her, she turned away. "And that friend you've been trying to set me up with is?"

"Justin's a good guy. I think you'd like him."

"I met him at the Christmas party."

"You need to date other people before you do something stupid, like marry Geoffrey."

"I'm not going to marry Geoffrey." A permanent commitment couldn't be further from her mind. She'd witnessed her mother's marriages, feared she was just as incapable of sustaining a long-term relationship.

"You might do it by default," he said.

"No chance."

"Then why are you wasting your time?"

Because she was lonely enough to settle for comfortable and because she hadn't met a better candidate—and that included Jon's friend from the gym. "Enough already. I need you to do a background check for me."

He hesitated as if reluctant to let her change the subject but ultimately took the bait. "What's the name?"

"Captain Luke Trussell. I don't know where he was born, but he's a pilot stationed at Travis Air Force Base."

Jonathan whistled. "Sounds impressive—an officer and a gentleman. What're the charges?"

Bowing her head so no one would be able to hear her, she said, "Rape."

"Okay, so maybe he's not a gentleman."

"We'll see," she said, and dumped her melted smoothie in the garbage as she headed for the door

"I'll look into it."

"The sooner the better on this one, huh?"

"You say that on *every* case," he complained, and hung up.

"Because *every* case is important," she grumbled. And this one promised to be more difficult than most.

5

Luke was just walking out the door of his apartment on Wednesday afternoon when the phone rang. He turned back to pick it up but hesitated when his caller ID showed *The Last Stand.*

That was the name of the victims' charity his attorney had warned him about.

Nervously swinging his keys around and around his finger, he let the answering machine pick up. It kicked in on the sixth ring. A few seconds later, a woman's voice reverberated his living room.

"Captain Trussell, this is Ava Bixby. I'm with The Last Stand, a victims' charity in Sacramento. I've been contacted by Sergeant Kalyna Harter. She told me an unsettling story about the time you spent together on June 6. Before I get too involved in this case, I'd like to hear your version of the encounter. If you can spare a minute, please call me."

She left her cell-phone number, as well as her office number.

Luke's hand hovered over the handset. Ms. Bixby sounded open-minded, as if she hadn't yet decided to go after him. But he couldn't pick up. The best defense lawyer in Sacramento had warned him against talking to her.

After he was sure she'd hung up, he called McCreedy.

"It's Luke Trussell," he said when his attorney came on the line.

"Hello, Captain Trussell. How are you today?" McCreedy responded.

It was easy to be pleasant when you weren't the one on the hot seat, Luke thought. "Anxious."

"How can I allay your fears?"

"I'm not sure you can. Ava Bixby, from The Last Stand, just called."

"You didn't give her any details, did you?"

"None. I didn't even answer."

"Good."

Luke kept twirling his keys. "Why is that good? She said she wants to hear my side, and I'd really like to tell her."

"It's a trap. She's hoping to catch you in a weak moment, get you to say something that can be used against you later. Trust me, Captain Trussell, she's called a victims' advocate for a reason."

But McCreedy was dispensing advice based on a false premise—that Luke might be lying. Most defendants lied, didn't they? They *couldn't* be honest, not if they expected to stay out of prison.

"This case is different," he argued. "I'm not like most of your other clients. I have nothing to hide, so I don't see how it can hurt to talk to Ava Bixby."

"All my clients are innocent until proven guilty. And you could do a world of damage."

"But if I didn't rape Kalyna, how can anything I say hurt me?"

"Depending on her level of motivation, Ms. Bixby could misinterpret a comment or two, or even misrepresent what you said."

"But if I don't respond, she'll assume the worst. Anyone would."

"No, she'll assume you have good representation," he said. "Because you do."

At that point, Luke gave up trying to convince McCreedy. He was paying the man for a reason. He needed to trust his advice.

Fifteen minutes later, driving to the gym, he was telling himself he'd done the right thing. But it didn't make any difference. He couldn't stop thinking about Ava Bixby and her message, so he turned around and went home. He wanted to learn more about The Last Stand, and he was too impatient to put it off a couple of hours.

Tossing his keys on the counter as soon as he walked through the door, he went directly to his computer.

Google provided a whole list of links on the charity, mostly newspaper articles citing how various individuals from the organization had found missing persons, helped convict sex offenders and murderers, protected abused spouses.

The praise lavished on them made Luke nervous. McCreedy had said they were "dogged"; that seemed to be true. But would they go after an innocent man with the same dogged determination they'd go after a guilty man? Would they bother to notice the difference?

One link that came up went to the official Last Stand Web site—TheLastStandVictimsCharity.com. There, he saw their mission statement posted on the home page: *To help victims of violent crime find justice, safety and peace of mind.*

It sounded noble. Several other paragraphs detailed the need for such an organization and made a plea for financial support. There was even a way to donate directly through the site via a secure server.

Luke would probably have given them a couple hundred bucks had he stumbled upon the site at another time, but right now he was afraid his money would end up being used against him.

Surfing through a few of the other pages, he pulled up information on the staff. According to what was posted, only three people, all of them women, worked full-time in the Sacramento office. Unfortunately, the Web site didn't include pictures of these "directors," as they were called, but he found a short bio on each one. Ava had been born and raised in Northern California. She'd graduated Phi Beta Kappa from Stanford University with a B.A. in psychology, and she'd gotten involved with The Last Stand through volunteering.

Luke stared at the short paragraph he'd just read. She seemed smart. But could he trust her? Would she have an ear for the truth or even care about it? Or had she been so convinced by Kalyna that she'd care only about chalking up another conviction?

He needed *someone* to listen, to stop this travesty of justice before it went any further. He wanted to resume his life, get back to flying.

He called the office number Ava had left on his machine.

A pleasant voice answered. "The Last Stand."

"Is Ava Bixby in?"

"She's on another line. Can I take a message and have her call you back?"

Don't talk to her. She's on their side, McCreedy had warned. Why wasn't he listening?

"No, no message," he said, and hung up.

6

"You got a minute?"

Ava glanced up as Jonathan Stivers poked his head into her office on Thursday afternoon. "Of course," she said. "Get in here. I've been trying to reach you."

"Sorry, my phone's dead and I lost my charger."

Just shy of six feet tall with a wiry build, brown hair and brown eyes, Jonathan was definitely handsome. Although Ava had never been attracted to him in a romantic sense, the interns and volunteers gushed over him all the time—to no avail. He was engaged to Zoë Duncan, a woman he'd met while he was working to locate her kidnapped daughter.

"Then I'm glad you stopped by." She shoved some phone records she'd been studying for another case off to one side. "I've been dying to talk to you."

He ambled in and took a chair across from her desk. "Fortunately, you're still here. I didn't want to drive all over the place looking for your houseboat."

She rolled her eyes. "Don't start, okay? It's not *that* hard to find."

"It's at least a forty-minute drive."

"But I dock it in the same place every night. Well, every night so far this month," she corrected.

"When are you going to buy a real house?" he asked.

"It can't be convenient driving out to the delta every night."

"Skye's house is farther." She shrugged. "Anyway, a houseboat has its advantages."

"And they are..."

"I'm not sure I want to live in Sacramento forever. If I had a regular house, I'd have to sell it in order to leave."

"So you're saying you can pick up and go whenever you want."

She opened her top drawer to get a package of gum, then slammed it shut. "Exactly."

He arched an eyebrow at her. "Like right now."

"Yup. I could if I wanted to." She unwrapped a piece of gum and tossed the paper at the wastebasket, but missed.

"You can't simply abandon the houseboat."

"I'd call my father and tell him to take care of it himself. After all, it's his, isn't it?" She popped the gum in her mouth.

"You couldn't do that. Because then he'd have to sell it, dispelling the illusion you've helped him create that he hasn't gotten too henpecked to steal away on a fishing trip now and then." Jonathan jerked his head toward her desk. "I'll have a piece of that."

She threw a stick of gum *at* him instead of *to* him, but he managed to catch it. "His illusions are not my problem."

"Now you're dissembling."

"*Dissembling?* Where'd you come up with that word?"

He wadded up his wrapper and tossed it in the direction of the wastebasket—it went right in. "I have a good vocabulary. I just try not to use it. I don't like to intimidate those around me."

She had to laugh. "Well, I'm not *dissembling* or *prevaricating* or *fabricating*."

"You've been holding back, too," he said with a whistle. "I'm impressed."

"I'm glad. Does that mean we can stop arguing?" There was no point in trying to convince him she was right, because she wasn't. She couldn't hand the houseboat back to her father, not without plenty of notice. Now that her mother was in prison, Chuck Bixby was all she had. Distant though he'd always been, at least in an emotional sense, she was taking it upon herself to bridge the gap between them, to build what she could out of the tattered remnants of her family. That meant she couldn't rock the boat—in her case, the houseboat.

"We're not arguing. We're *ratiocinating*," he said.

"Ra...what?" She got up to put her gum wrapper in the garbage.

"Ratiocinating." He offered her a smug smile. "It means to reason methodically and logically."

She raised one hand as she returned to her seat. "Fine, smart-ass. I've got one for you. Quit being a polemical asshole, okay? *Now,* can we get on with business?"

He scratched his head. "The asshole part I definitely understand...."

"Forget it!" She opened her file on Kalyna Harter. "What have you learned about Captain Trussell?"

Jonathan made a clicking sound with his tongue. "I hate to tell you this, babe, but you've got the wrong guy."

"What?"

"The Luke Trussell you had me run could be a Boy Scout. I don't know what more there is to say."

"His record is *that* clean?"

"Two speeding tickets in three years. That's it."

"No previous arrests? No DUIs?"

"No assault and battery. No domestic abuse. No disturbin' the peace. No freakin' skateboarding in the park."

"Have you talked to his friends, enemies, previous lovers?"

"I couldn't find any enemies. I got hold of two women he's dated in the past. One said he took her out a few times, but never tried to sleep with her. When I asked why, she told me he didn't want to make a commitment. He was only twenty-four at the time, wasn't ready."

"And the other one?"

"Paris Larsen. Captain Trussell dated her for more than a year. And she admitted right up-front that he was the best lover she could imagine. Kind and gentle. Those were her words. He broke off the relationship eighteen months ago, but if I had my bet, she's still in love with him and would take him back in a heartbeat. And this woman is a clothes designer who's now living in San Francisco and making a name for herself. Completely credible, very sharp."

"He's a kind and gentle lover?" Ava echoed. "My client claims he used his fists on her, and then he raped her. Does that sound kind and gentle to you?"

"You're forgetting the alleged part."

"Why would my client lie?"

"I don't know, but Trussell has a flawless service record. And get this—he was valedictorian at his high school."

Ava wasn't sure what to make of this information. So far, she'd heard her client portrayed as a tramp, and the accused as a model citizen. "So, what's up? Did he drink too much and let his libido get out of control?"

"This wasn't about libido, Ava. Whoever attacked Kalyna Harter was angry."

The phone rang, but it was after-hours so Ava let it go to voice mail. "Maybe she really pissed him off. She could've hit him first or belittled him in some way." She tilted her head quizzically. "Maybe she made fun of his package."

"From what his ex-girlfriend had to say, I'm guessing his package is nothing to be embarrassed about. I doubt it's as impressive as mine, but you know…not bad."

"You're too much." She grinned in spite of the serious nature of their conversation. "He was drunk the night he attacked Kalyna. Alcohol alters behavior."

"Bar-hopping isn't a pattern of conduct. None of the places I visited recognized his picture."

She could've argued that anyone could get drunk and act up, even if it wasn't a pattern. But something Jonathan had said caught her attention. "You have his picture?"

He pulled a photograph from his back pocket. "Courtesy of Paris Larsen," he said, and slid it across her desk.

She studied the clean-cut man staring back at her. He had nice, even features and a great smile, but it was difficult to make out the finer details of his face because he was outdoors at a baseball game, wearing a ball cap, a pair of sunglasses and a windbreaker. "What about steroids? Is he into weight lifting?"

"He lifts, but he hasn't been to a civilian doctor or pharmacy in six years. He gets regular checkups at the military hospital, and that's it."

"I would imagine, because of his job, there's some mandatory drug testing going on."

"There is. He's tested randomly. All his tox screens have come back clean."

Ava refused to give up so easily. Kalyna's past exploits meant she'd have a very small chance of obtaining justice. *If Trussell was actually guilty,* she thought, but she didn't want to consider the possibility that she'd been played. She hadn't believed Bella, either, and Bella had been telling the truth. She'd left Bella friendless and depressed enough to resort to the most desperate of measures... "There are other ways to get steroids."

"Trussell lifts to stay in shape, like he plays basketball," Jonathan said. "He's not a bodybuilder."

She drummed her fingers on the desk. "Why would such a smart, successful, clean-living guy suddenly flip out and rape a woman—especially so violently?"

"That's my point," Jonathan said. "I don't think he did."

But he *could* have. And if she hoped to help Kalyna— hoped to avoid another tragedy like Bella's—she needed to know for sure.

"Then there's Technical Sergeant O'Dell," Jonathan went on.

She set Trussell's picture aside. "Who's Technical Sergeant O'Dell?"

"According to the bartender, Trussell was hanging out with him at the Moby Dick."

"What about him?"

"He says our supposed victim is nothing but a two-bit whore out to hurt someone. He was furious when I told him she's accusing Trussell of rape."

"Whores can be raped, too. They have the right to say no if they want to," Ava said, clinging stubbornly to her belief in Kalyna's tears, to her own determination to protect the weak and powerless. Because Bella was a stripper, no one would believe she'd been raped. It wasn't until two months after she'd killed herself that the truth came out. That was when the man she'd accused struck again—and strangled his next victim.

Bella had deserved more than she'd been given, more than instant acceptance of brief character sketches.

"O'Dell didn't go home with them, did he?" Ava said. "He can't know for sure what really went on."

"No, but he's pretty familiar with the defendant. He'll testify if this case goes to court. And he'll say Kalyna sidled up to the captain wearing a skimpy dress cut low on top and high at the bottom. That she kept bending over to give him an eyeful. That she repeatedly insisted he dance with her. That she wouldn't let him out of her sight. What does that sound like?"

"It sounds like she was more interested in him than he was her." Kalyna's version had the captain acting decidedly more aggressive. But that could be a matter of perspective. It didn't prove she was lying.

"She was pursuing him, Ava," Jonathan said. "Maybe she was even setting him up."

"Why would she do that?"

"There could be a lot of reasons. Revenge is one of them."

Ava didn't answer.

"She's part of his flying squadron," he continued. "Maybe she's got some sort of grudge against him."

"But look how handsome he is! Isn't it possible that she was honestly interested in him and had no idea he was dangerous?" she asked. "The fact that she was pursuing him is no excuse for what he did to her."

"Only the two of them know what really happened in those early morning hours."

"Exactly." She straightened a few things on her desk. "I wish he'd talk to me."

"You've tried to reach him?" Jonathan asked in surprise.

"I left him a message. Why?"

"Because there's no way he'll call you back. His lawyer would never let him. Surely you know that."

Bristling at his skepticism, she stiffened. "He could. If he's innocent, he *should*."

"Why? You think he owes it to us to relieve our curiosity?"

"I'm neutral. I just want the truth."

Jonathan got to his feet and crossed to the desk. "Ava, you're not neutral, and he knows it. You're working for the victim—the alleged victim. But whether the captain returns your call or not has no bearing on his guilt or innocence."

She sat up. "Maybe he thought he could get away with it because she *is* a whore and he can easily prove it. Maybe he considers her expendable." A cast-off—like Bella. "*Someone* beat her up, Jon."

Straightening, Jonathan folded his arms. "Why does it have to be him?"

"Because he left her place at 3:00 a.m., and she was admitted to the hospital thirty minutes later. The neighbor said Kalyna was hysterical, completely out of it, when she knocked on the door. His was the only semen collected with the rape kit. No one else was seen entering or leaving the premises."

"Maybe she injured herself."

That was what Ava had been afraid he'd say. And, after talking to Maria Sanchez, she was more than a little worried that he could be right.

Damn, she didn't want an ambiguous case, a case that would force her to act on mere guesses. Those cases could haunt you for a lifetime....

7

"Surprise!"

As Kalyna's sister opened the door, her eyes went wide. "Kalyna!" she screamed. "What are you doing in Arizona?"

Kalyna dropped her luggage so she could return her hug. I came for a visit."

"Mom and Dad didn't say a word about it!"

"I didn't tell them. Where are they?"

"The hearse has been running a bit rough. They took it over to the garage to have it checked out."

"*Mom* rode in the hearse?" Normally Norma wouldn't go near it, not since her own child had drowned at two and been transported in a similar vehicle. She avoided anything to do with her husband's business.

"No, Mom followed Dad over in the Oldsmobile," Tati clarified. "The garage is closed. They're leaving it there and dropping the keys in the slot."

"Oh, right." Relieved to find her adoptive parents gone, Kalyna breathed a little easier. She'd have to face them eventually, but this would give her time to settle in before she had to answer their questions.

"How long can you stay?" Tati asked.

"I'll be here tomorrow and Saturday." As Kalyna dragged her bags into the foyer, she appraised the inside of the Victorian her father had bought when they moved to Mesa. It had once been a restaurant, but the conversion was a good one. The viewing rooms were in front; the embalming stations and the kitchen were in back. The walk-in cooler, where the corpses were stored until they could be embalmed, was downstairs next to the service elevator, along with the room she'd always shared with Tati. Her parents lived upstairs.

"This place hasn't changed a bit," she said. Even the selection of urns in the front parlor, and the caskets on display, were largely the same.

"Business has been slow," Tati admitted.

"Anderson Brothers Mortuary undercutting your prices again?"

"Yep."

"They can't do hair and makeup nearly as well as we can. They never could. Their stiffs look like…well, stiffs," she said, laughing at her own joke.

"I'm not as talented as you were, but…I do my best. Anyway, I thought you were out of leave. I thought you used it all to go to Santa Cruz with those guys you met last month."

"I did, but something came up."

"What?" Tati watched as Kalyna fell onto the settee reserved for clients.

"You're not supposed to sit on that," she cautioned. "You know Mom and Dad won't like it."

"They're not even here." Kalyna propped up her feet, too, exploiting her new status as the world-wise wanderer. She'd broken free while her sister remained firmly under her parents' rule.

Tati frowned. "Why can't we just go in back?"

"Because we're as important as anyone else. Sit down." Kalyna waved at the one chair that was a real antique instead of a replica. "You work hard around here—a heck of a lot harder than Mom. Don't you think you've earned the right to sit in front if you want?"

Tatiana wasn't the type to argue. She perched on the edge of the chair Kalyna had indicated but looked uncomfortable. "Tell me what made it so you could come home," she said.

Eagerly anticipating her sister's horrified reaction, Kalyna lifted her chin. "I was raped."

The horror she'd expected to see didn't register on Tati's face. Tati didn't even seem surprised. "No, you weren't."

Her sister's skepticism caused a flash of irritation, but Kalyna tried to shrug it off. She was free of the air force for a few days—and the fake weeping and tortured expressions she'd had to conjure up since June 6. Why let this get her down? Who cared what Tati thought? "It's true." Planning to leave it at that, she leaned back and relaxed, but when her sister didn't respond, she couldn't help adding, "He beat me up and everything."

Tati peered at her more closely. "You look okay to me."

"Because it's been a few weeks, stupid! I didn't come home right away."

"That's why they let you out of the air force? Because you were raped?"

"They didn't 'let me out.' My master sergeant wouldn't grant leave and he should have, so I left."

Tati's voice finally showed concern, but not the kind Kalyna had been hoping to elicit. *"That means you're AWOL!"*

"So? They can't expect me to stick around after such a horrific ordeal." She hadn't given even Ogitani the chance to object to her departure. The prosecutor wanted

Kalyna available at all times. But Kalyna had already spent hours and hours with her and, separately, with Ava, chronicling every detail of the supposed rape, and the constant pretending was growing tedious. She needed a break. She was afraid she might slip up under such intense questioning. Why not relax in Arizona?

"Who says they can't expect it?" Tatiana asked.

"I do! Besides, disappearing for a few days will only prove I was suffering too much to stay."

"Once you sign on the dotted line, you belong to the air force, Kalyna. They were very clear about that."

"The air force doesn't *own* you. I have more freedom there than I did here. At least I get to go out at night." She flipped her hair. "Anyway, I'm not worried. It's not a desertion unless I'm gone longer than thirty days."

"You'll still get in trouble!"

"I'll get an Article 15 for being absent without leave." And, if possible, she'd figure a way out of that.

"What's an Article 15?" Tati said.

"In this case, most likely a forfeiture of pay, but it can be other things."

"Like what?"

"Like a reduction in my rank. But that's not going to happen. It's a few days. No big deal. And it's my first infraction." For being absent without leave. She also had an Article 15 for failing to obey an order to report in before departing work, but that was because her superior officer hated her and went after anything he could.

"Why risk it? Why not stay if you're supposed to stay?"

"Don't worry about it. I'll take care of it." She scowled. "What's your problem, anyway?"

Tati blinked. "I don't know what you mean."

"You're acting like Mom and Dad. And you look like hell. Why'd you let yourself gain so much weight?"

Her sister winced. "I haven't gained *that* much."

"Yes, you have. You're frumpy. It's disgusting. And your hair!" Her twin's appearance was like gazing into a mirror and seeing the worst possible version of herself. She couldn't imagine Captain Trussell ever being attracted to a woman who looked like Tatiana.

But we're not the same. Kalyna tanned, weight trained and ran. She had her nails done every week. She was assertive and friendly, not shy and unassuming. And she no longer smelled like formaldehyde. Maybe she wasn't as attractive as she'd always dreamed of being; she had to deal with her own limitations. But very few men turned her down. She knew how to make the most of what she had. After weeks of fantasizing about him, she'd gotten Captain Trussell, hadn't she?

"Did they catch the guy who raped you?" Tatiana asked, changing the subject.

"They did. They're bringing him up on charges. We'll be going to court soon."

Suddenly acting self-conscious about her appearance, Tati tugged her skirt down so it covered more of her. "You're not afraid to testify?"

"Not in the least. I'm looking forward to it."

"What if he gets out and comes after you?"

Kalyna examined her recent manicure. "He won't."

"How can you be so sure?"

Because Luke wasn't violent, the way she'd claimed. He was one of the most honorable men she'd ever met, and by far the best pilot. "I know how to protect myself."

Tati didn't state the obvious—that she hadn't done a very good job of it so far if she'd been beaten and raped. "How'd it happen?"

Kalyna was tired of telling the story, tired of worrying about how she was coming across. Her sister already doubted her, so she preferred not to discuss it anymore. "I don't want to talk about it." Kalyna shrugged. "It happened, and I'm dealing with it. That's all."

Tati made no comment.

"So what *have* you been doing around here?" Kalyna asked.

Her sister jerked her head toward the back, where they did the embalming. "Guess."

"God, I'm so glad to be out of here. You should've come with me. California's amazing!"

Tatiana shifted her gaze to the flowered rug covering the hardwood floor. "You know the military won't take me."

"You could've gotten a job, lived with me."

"A job doing what?" her sister countered.

"Anything! Maybe you wouldn't have been surrounded by men who are all in great physical shape the way I am, but it'd be better than working like a slave for Mom and Dad. They're using you. That's all they've ever done. You're wasting your life."

"I'm not wasting my life! Dad needs my help." She stood as if the mention of Dewayne made it impossible to continue disobeying his orders by sitting on the antique chair. "He can't run this business by himself. And I'll be compensated. When he retires, I'll take over. He told me that."

"That could be twenty years, Tati. Do you plan to scrub stiffs for the next two decades? And what if he dies before Mom? How will you put up with the old bitch?"

"She's not a…a bitch. Anyway, I'll cross that bridge when I come to it."

Thinking she heard a car pull up, Kalyna checked the driveway, but they were still alone. "Don't you want to get out of this place, meet a man, *have sex?*" she asked.

Her sister's cheeks flamed bright red. "I'd like to fall in love and start a family, but—"

"*Ugh!* You're such a loser. You can't sit back and wait for Prince Charming to sweep you off your feet. Since when has *anything* we've ever wanted come to us? You have to go out and get it."

"And be raped, like you?"

Tati was finally showing some spirit, but Kalyna couldn't allow her sister to think the decision to leave had been a bad one, couldn't have her gloating that she'd been wiser to stay. "If you could see the guy who raped me, you'd stand in line to be with him," she said with a taunting smile. "He's the most gorgeous man I've ever seen. And it wasn't as if I didn't have fun."

"Fun!" Tati's jaw sagged. "You said he beat you!"

Kalyna assumed a long-suffering manner. "You don't understand what it was like."

"Explain it to me."

"You wouldn't understand even if I tried. You don't know squat about life or love. So just drop it, okay?" She got up. If her sister was so damn nervous about sitting in the "parlor," they might as well go. "You've changed," Kalyna said with a frown.

"No, I haven't."

"Yes, you have. You take the joy out of everything."

Tati stiffened. "You'd rather be somewhere else, getting raped?"

"Don't knock it till you've tried it," she muttered. But she didn't want to think about the intimacy she'd shared with Luke. Recalling those special moments made her want to be close to him again, to see him and touch him and smell him. That yearning caused her to wonder how he would've treated her if she hadn't reacted so hastily. Would he have called?

No, she couldn't have risked it. She had to go after what she wanted, just as she'd told Tatiana. "What's there to eat?" she asked. "I'm starving."

Her sister gave her an incredulous look. "Sometimes I don't understand you at all."

Kalyna would've laughed it off, but the noise of a car brought her up short. Her parents were home.

Hearing the engine, Tati fell silent, waiting anxiously. "What are you going to tell them?" she asked at length.

"The truth," Kalyna said, and forced a smile as her mother charged into the house.

"What are you doing here?" Norma demanded.

Kalyna raised her chin. "What, I can't come home?"

Her father entered behind her mother and spoke before Norma could respond. "What'd you do?" he asked.

"What are you talking about? I didn't do anything," Kalyna said.

His labored breathing told Kalyna he'd seen her car and moved faster than normal to get inside the house. "Why'd they kick you out?"

"They didn't kick me out!"

"Thank God." Her mother sank into the seat she'd just vacated. "So when are you going back?"

8

Ava stood at the railing of her houseboat, gazing at the sinking sun, which resembled a giant red fireball sitting on the water. Uncontained brushfires—seven hundred of them—raged all over California. They weren't close, but they still made the air acrid and hazy, which probably explained the unusual color of the sun. Ava had never seen it quite so red before.

We need rain, she mused. This time of year, Sacramento had little chance of getting any moisture—April through October were dry months—but at least the gentle delta breezes cooled the area, especially in late evening. She hated how hot it was without them.

A bird swooped low, barely skimming the surface of the water. Ava watched it dip, twirl and pull out of its dive. Jonathan didn't approve of her living accommodations, but she wasn't staying on the houseboat just to please her father. She loved it. She'd never known a more tranquil place than the delta. Only an occasional car navigated the narrow roads that wound through the sloughs and the many single-lane bridges; some islands weren't even accessible by car.

Wind chimes tinkled behind her. It was so quiet she could hear the water lapping at the pontoon. The two other houseboats that often docked there had gone on a fishing excursion together. It could get lonely without them, and the delta could get foggy and gray during the winter. But it wasn't winter now, the others would be back soon and she had her work to keep her busy. She generally toted home a heavy briefcase and put in a few extra hours before bed.

Inside the cabin, she turned on the TV to fill the silence. She hadn't heard from Geoffrey today—not since last weekend. But that didn't matter. She had another set of phone records to scour on the Georgette Beeker case, some computer searches to perform on Willie Sims and she needed to make a few calls on Kalyna Harter, beginning with Kalyna's parents. Jonathan had provided their phone number. Ava could've asked Kalyna for it, but she wasn't ready to inform her client that she had some misgivings about her veracity. Letting Kalyna know might change what she'd hear from the people closest to her. Besides, Ava was still trying to give Kalyna the benefit of the doubt, although she had to wonder if she was overcompensating because of Bella.

She needed to find out if Kalyna was capable of telling such a terrible lie. That was what she hoped to learn from the Harters—if they'd talk to her.

The ice clinked as she drained the glass of iced tea she'd left on the dining-room table, next to her briefcase and files. She had no idea how Mr. and Mrs. Harter might respond to her questions. It was possible that Kalyna hadn't told them what had happened on June 6. Some rape victims were so humiliated they didn't want to talk about it to anyone, even family or friends.

Ava frowned. She wasn't eager to be the one to break the news. It wasn't her place. But the context of Kalyna's life would be too valuable to either the prosecution or the defense, depending on what that context proved to be. So, with or without her interference, Kalyna's folks wouldn't remain in the dark for long.

Before picking up her cell phone, Ava checked the clock. Nearly eight. Arizona and California were in the same time zone. If she was lucky, she'd catch the Harters well after they'd finished dinner.

She dialed, the phone rang and a recorded greeting began.

You've reached the Harter Family Mortuary, a male voice said. *Our office hours are nine to six, Monday to Friday, ten to six on Saturday. We're closed on Sunday. If your call is business related, please leave a message after the beep and we'll get back to you. If you'd like to speak to a member of the Harter family, press "1."*

Glad she hadn't hung up as soon as the recording came on, Ava did as instructed.

Almost immediately, she heard a female voice. "Hello?"

"Is Mr. or Mrs. Harter there?"

"This is Mrs. Harter."

"Hello, Mrs. Harter. My name is Ava Bixby—"

"If you're looking for the mortuary, it's closed for the night," she cut in. "I'm afraid you'll have to call back in the morning."

"I'm not looking for the mortuary." Ava pulled out one of the heavy dining room chairs and squeezed around the arm of it so she could sit down. "I'd like to speak with you regarding your daughter, Kalyna."

There was a silence, then Mrs. Harter said, "Oh, boy, what is it now?"

Ava felt her eyebrows go up. "Oh, boy" was a rather inauspicious beginning… "I'm with a charity called The Last Stand. We help victims of violent crime who—"

"You're calling about the supposed rape."

"Yes." *Supposed* wasn't a word she would've expected

Mrs. Harter to use, either, but at least the woman had been told. That was a relief.

No longer worried that she'd be breaking a confidence, Ava relaxed and started doodling on her steno pad. "Your daughter came to me for help last Monday."

"What kind of help was she after? *Money?*"

Ava's pen carved a deeper imprint on the paper. "No, not money. She wants to make sure the man who hurt her goes to prison, as he should."

"Do you have any *proof* that he raped her?" she asked.

"We have your daughter's testimony," Ava replied.

"I'd be careful basing anything on that—especially a man's freedom."

Ava dropped her pen, which rolled off the table and hit the floor before she could catch it. "Excuse me?"

"Just tell me this, what's in it for her?"

Ava stiffened. "I don't know that there's anything in it for her."

"There has to be. There always is."

How was she supposed to respond to this? She'd expected a *little* more from Mrs. Harter. Some sympathy, perhaps. Some concern. "Kalyna was beaten up, too," she said.

News of the beating didn't seem to make a difference. "Do you think that means anything?"

"I have pictures."

Kalyna's mother laughed at this. "Oh, I'm sure the injuries were real enough, but they couldn't have been *too* serious because every last bruise is already gone."

"You've seen her?" she asked in surprise.

"She showed up out of the blue just today."

Kalyna hadn't mentioned that she'd be visiting Arizona, but it wasn't as though she had to check in with Ava. "I guess it's natural to want to be with family at such a time."

"Ms. Bixby, her visit has nothing to do with any desire to see us. She's getting as much mileage out of this as she can."

"I don't understand."

"She's playing the poor, injured victim. Did you know she's AWOL?" she asked, as if that proved Kalyna wrong in every respect.

Ava opened Kalyna's file and flipped through her summary of their first meeting. "She couldn't get leave?"

"She says they wouldn't grant it to her. Claims her superior officer is out to get her. But anyone who stands in her way is out to get her. Chances are she didn't bother asking like she should have. She had a good excuse and she used it."

Kalyna's mother was *so* negative it was off-putting, and that created the reverse effect, making Kalyna seem more credible rather than less. "Her situation with the air force doesn't have anything to do with me," Ava explained. "I'm only interested in what happened—or didn't happen—the night of June 6. To be honest, I'm shocked you're not more concerned about her injuries."

"Obviously, you've never seen what she can do to herself when she throws one of her tantrums."

"You're saying she's injured herself before?"

"That's exactly what I'm saying."

Shit. This had been Ava's fear, and yet she was tempted to tell Mrs. Harter about Bella, whose death had been a painful lesson about using past behavior to judge a particular incident. Every situation had to be judged on its own merit. But what was the point in trying to share what she'd learned? The most she could hope to get from Norma was clarification.

Slipping out of her chair, she wandered over to the window. "Tantrums? At age twenty-six?"

"I don't know if she's thrown one lately, but she did it all the time she was growing up, whenever she didn't get what she wanted."

"What did these tantrums consist of?"

"She'd start screaming and crying and hurting herself. That's a tantrum, isn't it?"

It sure sounded like one. "How bad would it get?"

"Bad. So bad that a few bruises are nothing to her. I caught her sneaking out one night when she was...oh, probably seventeen, so I told her she'd be doing cleanup duty for the next month. And you know what she did? She started banging her head against the wall! We had to tie her to the bed to stop her from bashing in her stupid skull."

If that was true, Kalyna was a very troubled woman. But Ava had already suspected that. "Has she ever received counseling?"

"No, we knew she'd only manipulate the therapist, have her thinking we were ogres. She tried turning us in for child abuse a few times, nearly got herself put in foster care. That would've been lucky for us. I don't know why we fought it."

Ava wasn't a psychologist, but she was well aware that self-mutilation was a big danger sign. They should've sought help. "What about hospital visits?" she persisted. "Surely there's some proof of this behavior. Even a single documented case?"

"Her injuries were never so serious that we couldn't look after them ourselves," her mother said.

"You're kidding, right?"

"Why would I kid about that? What can a doctor do for a bruise?"

Ava drew the drapes against the deepening dark. "How did you know she hadn't given herself a concussion with the head banging? You never had her checked by a professional?"

Mrs. Harter didn't react well to censure. Her voice cooled considerably. "Do you realize how much that would've cost?"

Didn't most people care more about their kids than money? "But—"

"We own a small business, Ms. Bixby. We can't afford health insurance. Besides, it would only have given Kalyna the attention she craves. She's an actress, that one."

Ava pictured the young woman who'd sat sobbing in her office. She'd seemed so normal that day, at least for someone who'd been recently traumatized. "What if, in this one instance, she's telling the truth?"

"How would you ever know?" her mother asked.

"That's what I'm trying to determine."

"Listen, Ms. Bixby, I'm sure you have plenty of other people to worry about. Don't waste your time with Kalyna. Some people are just bad eggs—and she's one of them."

A click signaled the end of the conversation.

Ava tried to call back, but the mortuary message came on, and this time when she pressed "1", no one responded. "Damn it!" she grumbled, and called Jonathan to blow off steam.

"You won't believe this," she announced as soon as he said hello.

"What's up?" he asked.

"I just hung up with Kalyna Harter's mother—she's a piece of work, let me tell you."

"Unfriendly? Eccentric?"

"More than unfriendly." Ava rubbed her tired eyes. "Callous, uncaring—hardly the stuff most mothers are made of. I feel sorry for Kalyna."

"Well, before you shed too many tears, I've found

more proof that Kalyna isn't what you'd call an exemplary citizen."

Just what she needed. With a sigh, she returned to the table. "Proof in the form of what?"

"LexisNexis shows that she got a couple of Visa cards as soon as she turned eighteen, charged them to the limit the very first week and never bothered to pay."

Ava pulled the pictures from Kalyna's file and studied her injuries again. This wasn't head banging. She'd have to have punched and clawed herself. *Could* she have done that? "I guess she was under the mistaken impression that goods purchased with Visa are free?"

"They were free for her," he said. "But she won't get that chance a second time. Not for a while, anyway."

"Okay, so she's an irresponsible nymphomaniac who was a problem child. I think we've established that. *But is she lying about the rape?*"

"I can't say. I can, however, tell you that Trussell's credit is perfect. Not one late payment."

"We're not judging these people based on their credit scores, Jon."

"We check for a reason, babe."

Because it was a fairly accurate indicator of the way people lived their lives. He was right….

Ava eyed the files that represented her other clients— all of them credible victims. Was she wasting her time with Kalyna? This case was getting more convoluted by the second. But the memory of Bella wouldn't allow her to let go until she was absolutely certain she wouldn't be abandoning someone who desperately needed her. "Anything else?"

"Nothing. Zip. Nada. Weird, huh?"

She nibbled on a strawberry from a bowl of strawberries she'd rinsed earlier. "Why would that be weird?"

"It's as if her life didn't start until she joined the air force. Well, that's not *strictly* true," he said, correcting himself. "I came up with proof that she and a twin sister were adopted out of Ukraine at six years old and then again—by new parents—three years later, but that's it. There's no record of either of them ever having attended school. They weren't immunized as children. As far as I can tell, they never even visited a doctor."

"Their mother home-schooled them. And she considers doctors an unnecessary drain on the family coffers," Ava explained.

"Interesting take for a parent."

"My thoughts exactly." Bringing her laptop out of sleep mode, Ava looked up Harter Family Mortuary and watched as a picture of a yellow-and-white Victorian appeared on her screen. She knew she had the right place when she checked the address. It was located in Mesa and had the phone number she'd just called. "The Harters own a mortuary. Check it out," she said, and gave him the URL.

"Looks like a bed-and-breakfast," he said a few seconds later.

"Close—minus the breakfast part and the fact that the bed is permanent."

"Why are we looking at this? What does the family business in Arizona have to do with the alleged rape in California?"

"Maybe nothing, at least no more than Kalyna's credit score. It's just an interesting background, don't you think? Especially when you put that together with such an uncaring mother?"

"Burying the dead is a dirty job, but someone's got to do it," Jonathan replied. "What I want to know is whether or not you're finally convinced Captain Trussell is innocent."

"I'm convinced he's a good credit risk," she said. "But I'm not interested in giving him a loan."

"So you're sticking with it? God, Ava. What's it going to take?"

Once again her eyes shifted to the files littering her table. She had limited time and resources, and this case wasn't going to be an easy one. If everything she knew about Kalyna came out, she suspected the prosecution wouldn't take it to court. Certainly, a jury of military personnel wouldn't be highly sympathetic to a woman who ran up Visa bills, didn't make a single payment, had a history of self-mutilation and slept around.

"*Everything's* going against this girl," she said.

"That's why you can't let it go. She's the underdog."

"What if she's a hurt, confused woman who was abused by her parents, joined the air force as her only escape, reached out for love in all the wrong ways and ended up getting beaten and raped by a man who was so sure he could get away with it he didn't bother to cover his tracks?" The mere thought enraged her. No human was expendable. If Captain Trussell had raped Kalyna, he should be brought to justice.

"I think you're better off getting out of this one," Jonathan said.

And she hadn't even told him about the tantrums.

"Look at the other side," he went on. "What if you help put an innocent man behind bars? How would you feel about that?"

"Terrible."

"And it'll hurt the charity, ruin our credibility, cost us everything we've worked so hard to build."

"You're right," she said. "But I want to talk to my client one more time. I feel I should give her a chance to address my concerns before I call it quits."

"Fair enough. Meanwhile, is there anything else you want me to do?"

"No, that's it for now. Thanks."

"Is Geoffrey coming over tonight?" he asked before she could hang up.

"Is Zoë?" she countered.

"Zoë's in L.A. She took her daughter down to visit her father."

"He still clean and sober?"

"So far."

"Great news." She leaned down to retrieve the pen she'd dropped earlier. "When's your wedding?"

"We're thinking August, before Sam has to go back to school."

"I know Zoë's a wonderful woman, but I still can't believe you're going through with it."

"Why not?"

"Getting married is so...*permanent*."

"That's the strange part," he said. "That's how I used to feel, but with Zoë I *like* the idea of permanent. Permanent sounds good. It's all about meeting the right person, Ava."

She found her pen but bumped her head on the way up. "Ow!"

"You okay?"

"Fine." She rubbed the sore spot. "How can you be so sure Zoë's the right one, Jon?"

"Because I'd rather die than live without her."

For once he wasn't joking; he'd made that statement as if it was the irrefutable truth. But Ava couldn't imagine feeling that strongly about anyone, least of all Geoffrey. He couldn't make or break her day, let alone her life. And she considered her ambivalence to be a blessing. Marriage required so many compromises, so many sacrifices. And for what? Most ended in divorce, which screwed over any kids who were involved.

Look at what she'd been through with her own step-father. Look at where "till death do us part" had led her mother....

"I'm glad you feel that way, truly," she said. "But don't think I want the same thing, okay?"

"You don't know what you're missing, Ava."

"Marriage isn't for everybody, Jon," she said. "Good night."

After she'd disconnected, she tried to forget how envious she was of his happiness, and how quiet her own house was even with the TV on, as she gazed at the mortuary pictured on her screen.

Just tell me this, what's in it for her?

I don't know that there's anything in it for her.

There has to be. There always is.

Was it true? Ava could've believed Mrs. Harter—could've believed her and walked away from this case without a second thought—if only Kalyna had gone to school and visited a doctor at least once or twice in her youth. An education and medical help were considered bare essentials, what any normal parent provided for his or her children, weren't they?

9

"They didn't mean it," Tatiana murmured.

Kalyna nearly snapped at her to close the door and go away, but she couldn't afford a fight with her sister. Since she'd left home, her folks had boxed up her belongings and shoved them in a forgotten corner in the detached garage. They'd also sold her bed and dresser to give Tati more space—a not-so-subtle hint that they wouldn't appreciate having her back. Now that she was here, anyway, she had no choice but to sleep on the trundle bed in her sister's room. No way would they relent and let her use one of the couches upstairs. She wasn't good enough for that. In their minds, she'd never been good enough for anything except cleaning up blood and embalming fluid and dressing dead people.

"They *did* mean it," she said, and continued to search for any money she might've overlooked in her purse. She'd been so excited about this trip, so anxious to show her parents and her sister how well she was doing. And for what? They'd treated her like shit!

Tati came closer and touched her shoulder. "They're just...upset. They're worried about you going AWOL. But don't let them get you down. They'll get over it."

"How can I not let them get me down?" Kalyna said. "They don't even want me here! They'd be happier if they never heard from me again."

"That's not true."

"Yes, it is." She thumbed through her wallet, but found it as empty as she feared. She'd never been good with money, couldn't seem to hang on to it longer than a day or two.

"Did you think they'd be happy to hear you deserted?" Tati asked.

"I didn't desert! I'm going back. I just took a trip to see my family."

"Without permission."

"It wouldn't matter to Mom and Dad even if I had permission." She should've figured that out before she ever crossed the state line into Arizona, but she'd imagined her homecoming so differently. Why couldn't they be proud of her for a change? She had a job, was making money. And she looked a hell of a lot better than her sister. "They don't care about me."

Tati sat on the edge of the desk chair. "Sure they do. They...well, you know what sticklers they are for rules."

"I was *raped,* Tati. You think they'd care more about that than the fact that I left the base without permission." Kalyna tossed her wallet aside. As usual, Tati was trying to smooth things over, but it didn't help. Kalyna wanted to flip off her parents and walk out. But she'd have to sleep in her car if she did. She'd spent the last of her pay on a cool pair of sunglasses for the trip and wasn't even sure how she'd buy the gas to get home.

"I think they just... Never mind," Tati said.

"What?" Kalyna kicked her purse off the bed and let its contents spill across the floor. "If you have something to say, spit it out!"

"Forget it." Tati eyed the picture that'd tumbled from Kalyna's purse. It was of Luke. Kalyna had snapped it at the Moby Dick while he was playing pool and had it printed the very next day. "Who's *that?*" she asked, pointing.

"A friend. He's in my squadron." Kalyna got up to retrieve the photograph before her sister could ask any more questions about it. If Tati realized who Luke was, she'd be even more suspicious of Kalyna's story. Not many rape victims carried around a picture of their attacker. "Whether you want to admit it or not, I know what you're thinking," she said, going back to their conversation. "You don't believe me any more than they do."

Tatiana slid off the chair and knelt on the ground, where she began gathering up Kalyna's belongings. "I *want* to believe you."

Kalyna put the picture upside down on the dresser. "Then why don't you?"

A pained expression appeared on her sister's face. "It just doesn't ring true to me. So I can't really blame Mom and Dad for distrusting you. Sometimes *I* don't even know whether to believe some of the things you say."

Kalyna moved close enough to stab a finger at her sister's chest. "Are you calling me a liar?"

Tati ducked her head and busied herself, shoving the makeup, hairbrush and gum wrappers back into Kalyna's purse. "No, of course not. But *rape?*" She paused when she came to Luke's watch and held it up. "This isn't yours, is it?"

"It belongs to another friend. I was holding it for him while he played volleyball and he forgot to get it back."

Tati set Kalyna's purse safely on the desk. "You've been with so many men. You use them and let them use you. It's a game to you. How can I be sure you were raped, considering everything you've done?"

"How dare you!" Kalyna retorted. "You don't know anything about me. I haven't been with *that* many." At least, not that her family knew about. They'd once caught her screwing the son of a client. Shane. He'd come with his mother to make funeral arrangements for his grandmother, and while the adults were talking she'd taken him into the basement to show him the cooler. She'd done it to freak him out, to make him quiver in discomfort and fear at the sight of his poor, dead grandmother. But it turned out he didn't scare that easily. He said he was bored. So she pulled off her shirt and tossed away her bra—and almost laughed herself to tears when his eyes nearly bugged out of his head.

Wh-what are you doing? he'd cried.

Have you ever had sex in a cooler? she'd asked.

Not a cooler full of dead people, he'd said, but she knew he'd never had sex anywhere.

Now's your chance. Or are you too scared?

I'm not scared. I'd do it in a heartbeat, but…not while my grandmother's in here. Put your clothes on.

It's not your grandmother that's making you nervous, she'd scoffed and begun touching herself.

That had distracted him, but he'd still been terrified. *I can't do it with* you. *My parents would have a coronary.*

Why would they have to know?

What if they found out?

Take a chance, scaredy-cat.

I would if you were any other girl, but—

But what? What's wrong with me? Look. How many girls do you know with tits this big?

He'd looked, all right; he wasn't afraid to do that. She could tell he wanted her. But he'd still argued. *It's not your body. It's your screwed-up mind. Everyone says you and your sister are weird.*

That comment had made her feel like a leper. But it wasn't her first snub. She wasn't blind. She saw the way people watched her whenever she went to the library or the drugstore, how they whispered behind their hands. *Is that what* you *think?* she'd asked.

I don't know, Shane had hedged.

He was a year younger than she was. Where did he get off acting as if he was too good! And that was when she'd decided to enslave him, to make him think of her constantly, to crave her. *I'll show you weird,* she'd said and backed him into a corner.

He hadn't had any complaints about her after that. Ten minutes later, he was sighing in ecstasy and telling her she was the only girl he'd ever love. But then her father had walked in and ruined everything. Shane was never allowed over again. And if she bumped into him in town, he wouldn't even look at her. He'd turn bright red and stare at his feet.

Then, when she was seventeen, there was the twenty-six-year-old her father had hired to help out around the grounds and drive the hearse. Mark Cannaby. He'd loved her, would do anything for her. But she couldn't forgive him for what happened with that hitchhiker chick. She'd only stuck with him because it upset her parents.

Mark gave her quite an education before her parents caught on and put a stop to it. They played "hide the salami" everywhere—in the yard, in the coffins, on the embalming table. It was Mark's fault she'd had to have her first abortion. When she was a couple months along, her mother had heard her on the phone, trying to find an abortion clinic close to home and had dragged her across town, where no one would know them. She'd had to claim she was a runaway without the means to pay or Norma would've thrown her out. And her relationship with Mark had stalled shortly after. Why she'd gotten involved with him, she had no idea. At least he'd kept quiet about the hitchhiker they'd secretly killed and cremated.

He *should* have kept quiet. It was his fault. She never would've done it without him.

"I know of at least two guys you slept with," Tati said.

"That was it," Kalyna responded, but there'd been a number of sexual conquests after Mark, including the postman. She still laughed when she remembered him showing up at the door on any excuse, hoping she'd bring him to her room. She couldn't remember why she'd bothered with that old man in the first place. It wasn't as if she didn't have better candidates, especially once her e-mail address started circulating among the football players at the local high school. During what would've been her senior year, she met a group of boys at the cemetery down the street almost every Friday night and did them all. One time she had ten different boys taking turns with her. She'd wanted to do the whole team for homecoming, but someone spread the rumor that she had herpes and only a few showed up.

She got pregnant for the second time during those two months. She'd had no idea whose baby she carried, but she still wished she'd told Logan it was his. Logan was the quarterback, but he never joined the group. He couldn't show up at the cemetery or someone would rat him out to his prude girlfriend, who'd barely let him kiss her, never mind get her naked. He'd have Kalyna come to his house every few weeks, instead; he'd sneak her in through his window while his parents slept.

She liked being in his room, his bed, his space. Liked pretending *she* was his girlfriend. It made her feel as if she belonged with him, as if she was part of something good. His family was just an average middle-class American family, but he and his siblings went to public school, played sports, had lots of friends. She'd envied them and everyone associated with them.

Being pregnant and not using it to snag Logan was definitely a missed opportunity. She realized that now. But she'd been young and naive and so afraid of her mother finding out. She'd thought there'd be other opportunities, but she hadn't gotten pregnant since her second abortion.

"Anyway, the number doesn't matter," she told her sister. "Just because I've had sex with a few guys doesn't mean I wanted to have sex with this one."

Tatiana had reseated herself in the corner. "But you told me yourself that he was handsome. You said if I saw him, I'd stand in line to be with him. What was it about him you didn't like?"

Nothing. That was the problem. Luke Trussell was everything she'd ever wanted. Luke was Logan, only better. The way he'd made love to her had been different than all the others. He hadn't been quick or rough or selfish. He'd treated her with respect, made her feel like he cared about her. And that was the worst cruelty of all because his gentleness made it so difficult to settle for less.

"I wasn't in the mood for sex and he forced it, okay?"

"Fine," Tati said with a sigh. "Forget I said anything. I— You're my sister, and I love you regardless. So, come on. I have to prepare a lady who came in yesterday for her funeral on Monday."

"I think I'm going to leave." Kalyna fingered the frayed hole in her blue jeans. What kind of vacation was this? Taking shit from her parents again, helping her sister work. Besides, she really wanted to see Luke again, wanted to see how her actions were affecting him.

"Leave when?" Tati asked.

"Tonight."

"No!" Her sister got up and came over to take her hands. "Not so soon, Kalyna. I'll be sad if you go. Talk to me while I work. Then we'll go out to dinner, my treat, and you can tell me what it's like in California."

"What about Mom and Dad? Will they let you out of their sight?" The Harters were so worried she'd somehow corrupt Tatiana that they wouldn't be happy to see them go out alone. *You're nasty,* her mother had once told her. *Weird. Don't you dare put evil thoughts in your sister's head. She's a sweet thing, got a chance of being normal.*

"They can't object if we invite them," Tati said.

"I don't want to invite them." Kalyna wasn't sure how much more of her parents she could tolerate. *Do you know what a court-martial is?...Damn it, girl, we should've turned you over to the state when we had the chance... Oh, for crying out loud! You weren't raped! You can't rape the willing, Kalyna... How many abortions have you had, anyway?*

"Give them another chance," Tati coaxed. "They'll be nicer. You've driven all this way."

And she didn't have the money yet to get herself home. Maybe she'd been wrong to let her parents upset her. Norma and Dewayne had never liked her, not from the beginning, so nothing had changed. She'd come mostly to see her sister.

So she should stay for the weekend, as originally planned.

"Okay," she relented.

Tati smiled and clasped her in a quick embrace. "Let's go," she said, but Kalyna stayed behind long enough to slip Luke's picture back into her purse.

10

When Kalyna's phone rang, she was with her sister at their favorite Mexican restaurant on Main Street, enjoying an after-dinner margarita. Her parents hadn't joined them because they'd bought some fast food when they dropped off the hearse, or so they said. Kalyna didn't believe them. She knew they didn't want to be around her. It was a miracle they'd agreed to let Tati have dinner with her at all. Chances were they wouldn't have if Tati hadn't pulled them aside for a whispered conference.

"Don't you want to answer that?" Tatiana asked when Kalyna merely silenced the ringer.

"Not right now." Caller ID showed a Sacramento area code, and Kalyna wasn't sure she wanted to talk to anyone in California. Why deal with the backlash of leaving just when she was finally beginning to have some fun? But when the call came in again fifteen minutes later, she reconsidered. It didn't matter who found out she was gone. Her disappearance from the base wouldn't remain a secret for long. Major Ogitani had probably already been notified that she hadn't reported for work today.

She pressed the Talk button. "Hello?"

"Kalyna? It's Ava Bixby from The Last Stand."

Kalyna had suspected it had to do with the case. She

didn't know very many people in Sacramento, other than a few guys she'd met at various dance places and bars.

Taking another sip of her margarita, she relaxed. There wasn't as much at stake with Ava as Ogitani. "What can I do for you, Ava?" she said.

"Who is it?" Tati wanted to know.

Kalyna covered the mouthpiece. "My caseworker at the victim's charity in California."

"Did I catch you at a bad time?" Ava asked.

"No, it's fine."

"Good, because I think we need to talk."

Something was up. Kalyna could tell by Ava's tone. In case this developed into a conversation she didn't want Tatiana overhearing, she started to get out of the booth. "Hang on a sec." She covered the mouthpiece again. "It's about the rape," she explained. "I'll just be a few minutes."

She felt Tati's gaze follow her as she walked through the restaurant. It wasn't until she stepped outside and the door closed behind her that she had the privacy she needed. "I'm back." She picked a spot at the corner of the building, under the eaves, where she had a clear view of the door and the walkway from the parking lot.

"I got off the phone with your mother a little while ago," Ava announced.

A surge of anger made Kalyna grip her phone tighter. She hadn't expected this. Not from Ava. "You called my *mother?* Why?"

"To be honest, I'm a little confused."

"About what?"

"I'm getting conflicting stories, Kalyna."

Kalyna's stomach knotted painfully. "Then why didn't you come to me?"

"Because I wanted her perspective."

"Do you always investigate the victim instead of the perpetrator?"

"I investigate both. I can't look at a crime separately from the people involved—on both sides. That'd be like taking a controversial comment out of context. And a man's freedom could be at stake. We can't get this wrong."

Kalyna smashed a beetle scurrying across the concrete near her foot. "I still don't understand why you had to talk to my mother. If you'd asked me, I could've told you she hates me."

"So far, all I have is your account of what happened on June 6, Kalyna. What I need is another witness, some evidence, something to corroborate it. Can you help me out with that?"

"It's not just my account," Kalyna argued. "What about Luke's semen? They swabbed my—"

"That proves you had sex," she interrupted, "not that he forced you."

"And the pictures? They prove force. You saw what he did to me."

"Again, we have only your word that he's the one who gave you those injuries."

"There wasn't time for anyone else to come in. You said so yourself."

"Your mother suggested another scenario."

Kalyna wrapped her free arm around her middle to control the nervous feeling in her stomach. Her mother had betrayed her once again. From the time Kalyna had moved in she could remember her mother pulling her father aside to complain about her. *That child's not right, Dewayne,* she'd say, and he'd click his tongue against his teeth and shake his head as if he agreed. "My mother wasn't there. How would she know what happened?"

"She raised you. She knows your history."

"You can't listen to her! Do you have any idea what it was like growing up with *her* as my mother?"

Ava's slight hesitation encouraged her.

"She kept us locked up in that morgue, day and night. If we did anything wrong, left a smidgeon of food on our plates or…or forgot to pick up a toy, she'd put us in the cooler with the dead bodies and turn off the lights."

"Do you have any proof of that?" Ava's voice was less strident. Kalyna had managed to evoke some doubt. But how could she prove her words? She couldn't.

"No, of course not. We didn't dare tell anyone or she'd do worse."

"When you say *we,* you're talking about your twin sister?"

"Yes, Tatiana."

"Will she corroborate these events?"

Kalyna began to chew on the ends of her hair like she used to do as a child. She wasn't completely certain of her sister anymore; maybe it hadn't been smart to drag Tati into this. "I don't know," she muttered. "She might have blocked it all out. Besides, it wasn't quite as bad for her."

"Why not?" Ava sounded doubtful again.

"My parents liked her better. They still do."

"Do you have any other siblings?"

The heat was causing her clothes to stick to her. It was nearly nine o'clock but it didn't cool off in Arizona the way it did in California. "No. My adoptive parents had fertility problems. They did have one son, but he was only two when he drowned in a neighbor's pool."

"I'm sorry to hear that."

"I didn't know him. That was before my first set of American parents gave us up. But my mother never got over his death. I could never measure up to her own precious child." She added some extra bitterness to her voice for good measure but secretly smiled at how she'd tormented her mother over Robert's death. She used to get his little shoes out of the attic and place them on Norma's bed, shove his blanket between the sheets, knock his picture from the wall.

"Why didn't you go to school, Kalyna?" Ava asked.

"My mother wouldn't let me or my sister. She homeschooled us. I told you that already."

"Yes, you did. You said you followed the curriculum just enough to keep the state off your backs."

"That's true."

There was another pause, then Ava said, "Your mother told me you sometimes used to hurt yourself."

"You think that's where I got those injuries?"

"I'm wondering."

She wiped the sweat from her upper lip. It wasn't only the heat; it was nerves. She felt like she was melting. "That's ridiculous! How many people do you know who purposely cause their own injuries?"

"I don't know any," Ava conceded. "But I've heard it happens."

"With psychos, maybe. But I'm not psycho. How could my own mother say such a terrible thing?" The tears that began to fall were real. Kalyna felt hemmed in on all sides. First her parents had let her know they weren't happy to see her. Then Tatiana had played the intermediary, making it plain that she held far more sway with them. And now this. Kalyna couldn't take much more. *Everyone* was turning against her. "She's always lied about me. She wants to make sure I have no one I can talk to who'll trust me. She enjoys hurting me, enjoys alienating me from any friends I might make."

"Kalyna, calm down," Ava said.

But Kalyna couldn't calm down. If she allowed Ava

to believe she was lying, Ava would feel obligated to tell Major Ogitani, and then Major Ogitani would very likely drop the case. After that, Kalyna would have no hope of ever speaking to Luke again. They'd assign her to a new flight squadron or possibly transfer her off the base. Or worse...bring her up on charges. Even if she stayed at Travis and managed to avert legal trouble, he'd go out of his way to avoid her. He'd get with another woman who was just as eager to be his lover, and she'd be left as she was before—with a craving only he could fulfill.

At that thought, she released a racking sob.

"Kalyna, stop," Ava said, growing more insistent.

"I was raped! And because Luke has more friends and better parents, he'll get away with it." She hiccuped in her effort to draw enough breath to continue. "My own mother's ruining my chances for justice!"

"Why would she do that?"

"I told you, she hates me. And she knows if this goes to court the truth'll come out. Don't you understand? Major Ogitani plans to establish what my childhood was like. My mother could go to prison herself for what she did to me!"

"Shutting you in the cooler was bad, but...are you talking about more than that?"

"Yes! She backhanded me at every opportunity, pinched me really hard, bent my fingers back, kicked me. Once she shoved me down the stairs and broke my arm!" Kalyna had told this story so many times she couldn't remember what parts of it were true. Although her parents had used corporal punishment, she was pretty sure they'd never broken her arm. But it didn't matter. Their cruelty went beyond spanking.

"Is there a record of that? Did she take you to a doctor or hospital?"

"No. It had to heal on its own. Luckily it was probably only a fracture."

The gritty feel of the bricks behind her seeped into Kalyna's consciousness, and the temptation to bang her head began to well up like bile. Sometimes the desire to destroy herself stole over her, a kind of madness so consuming that once it took root, she couldn't overcome it. She wanted to knock herself senseless, claw at her arms and face, pull out her hair. *I hate you. I hate you,* she kept saying in her mind. But she wasn't sure if she was addressing Ava Bixby, her adoptive mothers, her birth mother or herself.

"Kalyna, listen to me! Calm down so we can talk."

"What?" She was already yanking on her hair, pulling out a fistful.

"Did anyone ever see the bruises your mother left?"

"Of course. But she'd tell them what she told you. That I hurt myself."

Tatiana poked her head out of the restaurant. "Kalyna—" She fell silent when she saw Kalyna crying. "Are you okay?"

Her sister's appearance made Kalyna let go of her hair. She couldn't bang or scratch or pull, not in Tati's presence. She'd promised her family she'd stopped all that, that it was a childish compulsion she'd outgrown. They wouldn't believe she was what she said she was if they knew she was still injuring herself. "No, I'm not okay!" she told Tati. "I need you. I need you to come here."

Tatiana rushed forward. "What is it?"

"They're going to let him off. They're going to let him go."

"Who?"

Kalyna made no attempt to hide or wipe her tears. "The man who raped me!"

Her sister began to stutter. "They—they won't do that if—if there's enough evidence to convict him."

"They won't if you tell this lady the truth."

"*What?*"

"My sister will tell you what it was like," she said into the phone. "She saw it all—went through it, too." She thrust her cell at Tati.

Tati tried to swat it away. "No! What are you doing?"

"You have to tell Ava what Mom did to us. You have to tell her about the beatings."

Her eyes as round as silver dollars, Tati made a second attempt to refuse the phone, but Kalyna was having none of it. "Do it," she whispered.

"But I don't want to get involved!"

"Come on. You're my sister!"

The misery that registered on Tati's face revealed how torn she felt. What the hell was happening that even her twin sister would hesitate to help her? Was *everyone* in her life bound to disappoint her?

"If you won't do this for me, I'll leave, disappear, and you'll never see me again!" Kalyna threatened.

"But, Kalyna—" Tati pleaded.

"Mom beat us!"

"No worse than most moms. And only when we acted up."

"I don't care. All I'm asking is that you say it." She pressed the phone on her again. "*Say it!*"

Keeping her hand over the mouthpiece, Tati opened her mouth to argue some more, but the murderous look Kalyna gave her quelled further protest. She put the phone to her ear. "H-hello?...Who's this?...I'm Tatiana...Yes...Kalyna's sister."

Kalyna held her breath.

"It was difficult at times..."

"Speak up," Kalyna prompted, but Tatiana didn't even glance at her.

"We—we sometimes struggled to get along with our new parents... What'd you say? Did Kalyna ever *harm* herself?" Tati's eyes finally sought Kalyna, and Kalyna shook her head.

Tati licked her lips. "N-no. Of course Kalyna would never do that...My m-mother doesn't like outsiders to know about our private lives...Yes...Yes, that's true... Mmm-hmm..." She closed her eyes. "Of course... You're welcome."

By the time she finished the conversation, her voice was so small, Kalyna wondered if Ava could hear her, but she accepted the phone when Tati handed it back.

"What have I done?" she heard Tati mumble, but she ignored her.

"Hello," she said to Ava.

There was no answer.

"Hello?"

"Oh—sorry, I was thinking."

"About what?"

"Your sister seems like a very nice person."

Kalyna watched Tati slide down the wall and bury her face in her arms. "She is. We've always been as close as two sisters can be." Or so she'd thought until recently....

"I'm sorry your original adoption didn't turn out as you'd hoped—as anyone would hope. It's a tragic story."

"As long as you know my current mother's lying about me," Kalyna said.

"This isn't an easy case," Ava responded.

Sensing another chance to convince her, Kalyna spoke even more earnestly. "I know. But it'll be fine if you'll help. Stick by me, okay? I need you."

There was another pause, then Kalyna heard Ava sigh. "I'll do my best."

At this, Kalyna pulled her sweat-dampened blouse away from her skin. "Does that mean you're keeping the case?"

"I guess," she said, but she sounded resigned rather than dedicated.

"Thanks, Ava. You won't regret it."

"Just tell me one more time that you're not lying to me. Because if I get involved in this and we put an innocent man behind bars..."

"Luke isn't innocent. I'm telling you God's honest truth, Ava. I swear it on my life."

"Okay. I'll move forward, for now. Meanwhile, you'd better return to the base as soon as you can. Desertion is a serious offense, and we'll need you to look repentant. That's our only intelligent approach to this. Everyone can sympathize with a desire to reform, even strict military personnel—if we're lucky."

"Is Sunday night soon enough? There's no point in returning earlier. I couldn't get back before the weekend, anyway."

"If it won't make a difference."

"It won't make a difference. Thank you. Thank you so much." After she hung up, Kalyna crouched and gave her sister's shoulders a squeeze. "I knew you wouldn't fail me."

11

Ava set down her phone and leaned her head against the back of the chair. Why did she just agree to keep working on this case? She didn't have any more proof of Kalyna's veracity now than she'd had fifteen minutes earlier. Not really. Who was to say Tatiana was any more credible than Kalyna? Or that the woman she'd spoken to on the phone was even Kalyna's sister?

Ava hadn't wanted to say yes, but it was so difficult to resist those tearful entreaties. She couldn't stand the thought of turning away someone who might really need her. She kept asking herself, "What if I was that lost soul? What if something like this had happened to me and no one believed it?"

That empathy made her a good caseworker—but she could see how it might also make her too gullible. Was she being conned? Maybe...

The television suddenly sounded far too loud. Irritated by the noise, she got up to switch it off and noticed the picture of her and Geoffrey propped on her bookshelf. It'd been taken when they visited San Francisco a year ago. Twelve months had passed and they weren't seeing any more of each other than they had then. No wonder Jonathan made fun of their relationship.

But she missed Geoffrey tonight. Didn't she?

She couldn't decide if she missed *him* or if she was just lonely, but she picked up the phone to call him.

"Hey, I was wondering what you were up to," he said when he heard her voice.

He could've checked in with her just as easily, but she didn't complain. At least he was always congenial. That was one of the traits she liked about him.

"How's work?" she asked, carrying her empty sandwich plate into the kitchen.

"Busy." While she cleaned up the small mess she'd made preparing her dinner, they talked about a big meeting he had on Monday with another wealthy developer who wanted to do a joint venture in the Natomas area.

"I could make a quarter mil on that deal alone," he said.

"That's great." They talked about some of his other projects and a recent acquisition of a hundred acres in Roseville, where he hoped to do some commercial development. She was just starting the dishwasher when the conversation turned to her.

"What about you?" he asked. "What's going on at TLS? Anything new?"

"A strange case I'm not quite sure what to do with," she said.

"What's strange about it?"

She finished wiping the counters. "One minute I think my client's lying and I'm determined to dump her. The next I think she's one of the most tragic victims I've ever met." *My mother used to lock us in the cooler with the dead bodies....*

Ava shivered. How would that affect a young mind?

"So what are you going to do?" Geoffrey asked. "Take it—or let it go?"

"Give her the benefit of the doubt, I guess, and do

what I can for her. Trust in the due process of law to take care of the rest."

"Do you want me to talk you out of it?"

"No, I want you to come over." She'd said it on impulse, but after the invitation was out, she realized it was true. She wanted his company, his reassuring presence.

"Now?"

"Why not?"

"Because it's ten o'clock."

"So?"

"So...why would I come over this late? Just to say good-night?"

"You don't want to drive out unless you know up front that you're going to get laid?"

Obviously aware that didn't paint him in the best light, he tried to backpedal. "I didn't mean it that way. It's not like you have to reward me for the drive or anything. It's just...I'm tired and I have to get up early in the morning."

"So it's too much trouble." Gee, maybe she'd be more tempted to sleep with him if he wasn't so practical, if he was willing to be impulsive now and then.

"Do you have to put it like that?"

"Isn't it what you're saying?"

"You haven't slept with me in months. Why would tonight be any different? And if tonight *isn't* any different, we could hang out on the weekend."

"I thought you were going to the Bay Area to be with your kids on the Fourth."

"Is it the Fourth already?"

"Day after tomorrow. It's on Saturday."

"Damn, you're right." He hesitated. "Okay, what about next weekend?"

"That's fine. If it won't put you out too much."

He didn't seem to pick up on her sarcasm. "It won't put me out at all. Let's grab a movie."

She nearly burst into laughter. With him, it was sex or a movie, and she always chose the movie. "Sure, give me a call."

The ringing of his cell phone woke Luke from a fitful sleep. He blinked, realized he was bound by blankets and not iron bars as he'd just dreamt, and breathed a sigh of relief. Then he checked the alarm clock on his nightstand. It was three in the morning. Who'd be calling him at this hour?

His mind immediately went to his younger sister and the trouble she'd managed to find lately, and the relief at being awakened from such a terrible dream disappeared. Was it his family? Had Jenny been hurt?

His arm shot out before the call could transfer to voice mail. Once he had the phone, the glowing LED screen enabled him to read his caller ID despite the dark room. It said *Restricted* but that did little to calm him. His parents weren't very conversant with recent technology. He'd given them a cell phone for Christmas and shown them how to use it, but they still hadn't incorporated it into their daily lives. Knowing them, they could be calling from a pay phone in the lobby of some hospital because they'd forgotten to charge it.

Swinging his legs over the bed to sit up, he punched the Talk button. "Hello?"

"Luke?"

It was a female. But he didn't recognize the voice. "Yes?"

"It's Kalyna."

A surge of righteous indignation made him clench his jaw. But he didn't hang up. He couldn't help hoping she wanted to apologize, to fix the mess she'd created. Before he'd hired his attorney and been told in no uncertain terms that he was not to contact her, he'd tried to reach her several times. He'd been convinced that having a conversation would solve everything. He'd never meant her any harm. But she wouldn't pick up or return his calls.

Until now. At last he had a chance to figure out what went so terribly wrong the night of June 6.

"What do you want?" he asked cautiously.

"To hear your voice."

"Excuse me?"

"I miss you."

After what she'd done to him? Where the hell was this coming from? "Kalyna, how can you say that?"

"Because it's true. I want to feel you inside me again. I want your hands on my body and—"

"You're trying to ruin my life!"

His outburst caused a sulky silence. He was afraid she'd hang up if he didn't calm down, so he took a deep breath, fighting for control. He had to think, be careful. "I don't understand why you're going after me," he said, his voice as level as he could make it.

She responded as if any idiot would understand. "So we can be together."

"You've got to be joking." He had too much adrenaline flowing through his blood; he couldn't stay seated. Getting to his feet, he began pacing the length of the room. "If you don't stop, I'll be in prison, Kalyna. How does that enable us to be together?"

"It doesn't *have* to end with you in prison," she said.

He froze. This whole time, he'd held on to the remote possibility that someone else might've broken into Kalyna's apartment and beat her up after he left, that she'd been confused and didn't know it wasn't him or else blamed him for not being there to protect her. But the truth, and all its staggering implications, hit him with the force of kick to the gut. She knew he was innocent. She was *trying* to hurt him.

"What is it you want?" he breathed.

"I told you—"

"I didn't rape you, Kalyna. You and I both know that."

"You raped my soul, Luke. You hurt me worse than anyone ever has."

"How?"

"You know how."

"No, I don't. You're not making any sense. We were never close enough for our *souls* to be involved. And I'm not the one who hit you. I don't know where you got those injuries, but it sure as hell wasn't from me!" Damn, he wished he had a tape recorder, some way to capture her words, her tone of voice, her…weirdness.

Just in case he did have such a device and had forgotten about it, he strode to his dresser and pulled out the top drawer. Shoving his M9 to one side, he pawed through his gun license, extra bullets, his iPod, pocket change, checkbook and earplugs but found no recorder. *Shit!*

"Please, Luke. I don't want to argue."

"So why did you call?" He dashed into the living room and replayed the messages on his answering machine. He needed Ava Bixby's number.

"Why do you think?"

His chest rising and falling with each breath as if he'd run five miles, he turned down the volume so she wouldn't be able to hear what he was doing. "I don't want to play games. Will you drop this, Kalyna? Will you tell the truth?"

No answer.

"Kalyna, talk to me. Please, stop what you're doing. There's no point in it. I don't know what you've conjured up in your mind, but June 6 was a one-night stand, nothing more, and you knew it when you took me home with you."

"No, I didn't."

"Yes, you did!" He pushed the fast-forward button to skip a message from his mother. Ava had called after that, hadn't she? He was so frantic it was hard to remember.

"How could you make me feel like that and then say it means *nothing?*" she said.

"It was a climax, Kalyna. A physiological reaction to stimulation. I was trying hard not to be the selfish jerk you're accusing me of being. But that's different from love." Where was it? Why couldn't he find it?

"You just don't get it."

He skipped another message, this one from a friend wanting him to play racquetball. "*You're* the one who doesn't get it," he said. "I was an idiot to go home with you."

"So now you regret it."

Could she expect anything less? "Of course!"

"All you care about is yourself!"

Finally! Here it was. As Ava's voice came softly into the living room, he jiggled his leg, waiting for the number, then jotted it down. "I hope that's not true," he said, still trying to maintain the conversation, "but if it is, I'm sorry. I'm not asking for a lot here. I just want this to go away. I just want you out of my life. So what's it going to take? Money?"

There was a lengthy pause during which he grabbed his landline and dialed Ava. If only she could hear Kalyna. If only *someone* could hear this...

Never had it seemed to take so long for a connection to go through, but eventually her phone started ringing.

"Money?" Kalyna repeated. "Do you think I'm stupid? You're not going to get off that easily."

"Why not? You have to want *something*," he said, "or you wouldn't be doing this."

Answer, damn it. Answer the phone. He'd been in such a hurry, he wasn't sure if he'd written down the number correctly. When he got a voice-mail response at The Last Stand, he realized he'd called the office instead of her cell, and it was asking him for an extension, which he didn't have. *Son of a bitch!*

"You're nothing but a selfish bastard, you know that?" Kalyna was saying.

"Maybe that would upset me if it wasn't coming from a deranged, vindictive bitch." He knew he shouldn't let her incite him, that it would only make matters worse. But he was so focused on trying to get the right number, he wasn't completely sure of what he was saying. Nothing he said or did seemed to improve the situation, anyway.

"You're going to pay for that," she said.

He ignored the threat. "If you don't want to work this out, why are you calling?" he asked. "To gloat? To rub my nose in the fact that I can't work because of you? That I have to worry about how this is reflecting on my parents, who don't deserve the humiliation? That I have to suffer strange glances from my female friends, knowing that they're wondering if I'm dangerous—if I'd hurt them if we were ever alone?"

While he talked, he listened to Ava's message with one ear. *Now* he had the right number.

"That's what you're worried about?" Kalyna screeched. "How this looks to *other women?*"

How had she isolated that from everything else he'd said? "I want my life back!" he shouted.

"Well, you can forget it! You're obviously not ready."

Dial, come on. He was trying to go too fast. As a result he'd made a mistake and had to hang up, start again. *Damn it!* "For *what?*" he said, trying to keep her talking.

"You'll see. You'll come crawling to me on your hands and knees before I'm done with you, Luke Trussell," she said. And then she was gone.

Ava's cell phone was finally ringing, but it was too late. Calling her now would prove nothing.

With a curse, Luke slumped onto the couch and hung up.

12

"Why are you still awake?" Tati mumbled, yawning loudly.

Kalyna felt the pressure of Luke's watch against her, held tightly to her body by her underwear. But the excitement of placing it in such a sensitive spot had long since disappeared.

"Kalyna?" Tati persisted.

She'd just returned to the bedroom, after calling Luke from the bathroom, and sat on the floor, rocking back and forth. "I can't sleep."

Her sister punched her pillow but sounded just as drowsy as before. "What's wrong?"

Kalyna dug her nails into her palms so deeply that she almost drew blood. But it wasn't enough. She needed to do more, do *something* to punish herself for being so stupid. So she'd remember. So she'd learn.

It's my fault. I blew it. I called him too soon because I couldn't wait. I'm so stupid. She forced her nails deeper. *I'm* so *stupid!*

"Kalyna!"

It took her a moment to realize that her sister had called her name yet again. *"What? What do you want?"*

The snarl in her response made Tati hesitate. "Can't

you go to bed? I'd like to get some sleep. I have to work in the morning."

Jumping to her feet, she whirled on her sister. "Sorry if I'm keeping you up. I wouldn't want to *inconvenience* you just because I'm dying inside!"

Tati propped up her head. "*Dying* inside? Kalyna, what are you talking about?"

"Never mind. You don't care."

"Of course I care," her sister said, but her carefully engineered tolerance grated on Kalyna's nerves.

"No, you don't. You've been mad at me all night, ever since I asked you to talk to my caseworker. Don't try and pretend otherwise."

"I haven't been *mad*. It's just—" She blew out a long sigh. "Kalyna, I don't agree with some of the things you do. And I don't like getting dragged into them. Surely you can understand that."

"You'd rather take Mom and Dad's side? You make me sick! You're as much of a weakling now as when we were kids!"

Tatiana didn't answer right away. When she did, her voice was barely audible. "Whatever you think of me, I'd rather not lie for you again."

"When did I make you *lie?* Mom was horrible to us while we were growing up. Have you forgotten, Tati? Have you forgotten how she shut us in the cooler for hours at a time? How she'd tell us the dead bodies in there were zombies that were going to come to life and eat us for being bad little girls?"

"There were those times," Tati conceded. "But they didn't happen often. And there were decent times, too. She kept us and fed us and took care of us. That's more than our birth mother did, or Mrs. Robertson, either. Aren't you the least bit grateful?"

Kalyna couldn't believe Tati had used that word in association with the Harters. *"Grateful?"* she echoed. "Did you just say *grateful?* She used us to work in this damn mortuary so she wouldn't have to. So Dad would have someone to help him because she couldn't stomach the thought of death. So she could lie in bed all day, mourning her poor little Robert."

"She lost a child, Kalyna."

"We were children, too!"

"It could've been worse."

"And it could've been a lot better. If she'd cared half as much about us as she did Robert."

"It wasn't all her. Let's face it, Kalyna, you provoked her. You did anything and everything you could to torment and upset her."

Kalyna started laughing. "Because I hated them both from the beginning."

"See? Why? It wasn't their fault our real mom gave us up!"

"Don't talk about our birth mother! As far as I'm concerned she doesn't even exist."

"I'm just saying Mom had her own issues to deal with. And things are better now, a lot better."

"For you! And that's all you care about. I don't mean anything to you anymore."

"That's not true."

"Yes, it is." She stalked closer. "You've changed. You're not the sister I knew, the sister I grew up with."

Tati didn't move. "Would you *stop* saying that? I'm trying to put the past behind me, Kalyna, and make peace with who I am and where I come from. And I'm trying to plan where I'm going. I'm happy for the first time in years. *Is that so bad?"*

"If it changes who you are."

"Maybe it only changes who you want me to be."

With the lights off, Kalyna could hardly see her sister, but she concentrated all her hatred on that dark amorphous shape. "You're not better than I am. You never will be."

Throwing off the sheet, Tati sat against the headboard and drew her knees to her chest. "I never said I was. You're purposely misinterpreting everything I say. We're adults now, Kalyna. I want to decide who I am. I don't want you to decide for me. Not anymore."

Kalyna propped her hands on her hips. "I don't know why I'm even bothering to talk to you. You're just like he is."

"*He?* Who's *he?*"

"Never mind." So what if her sister no longer admired her? Luke was the only person Kalyna cared about. And she'd have him. One way or another, he'd be the father of her children.

She pressed a hand to her stomach, remembering, hoping. "Do you have a pregnancy test?" she asked.

"A *what?*" Obviously taken aback by the sudden shift in topic, Tati gaped at her.

"You heard me."

Scooting down, her sister curled up on her side. "Of course not. I haven't even slept with a man yet," she grumbled.

"How pathetic! And you think there's something wrong with *me?*"

"It's *my* choice, Kalyna. I'm saving myself for marriage, and I don't want to hear what you have to say about it."

"Oh, good grief!" Kalyna felt like slapping her sister. "You've seen too many Disney movies. Life isn't a fairy tale, Tati. If you're waiting for a knight in shining armor to come and rescue you from this dump of a mortuary, you might as well embalm yourself because you'll wind up rotting here, just like the corpses in the cemetery down the street. That's all that'll happen."

"I'll take my chances," Tati said.

"Oh, yeah? Well, I'm not taking *any* chances. I'm going to get what I want."

"And how are you going to do that?"

"Any way I can!" she snapped.

"That's what scares me," Tati muttered, and pulled the covers over her head.

Luke continued to pace long after Kalyna hung up. He wanted to call his attorney, but he didn't have an after-hours number. Instead, he made circuit after circuit of the room, struggling to come to grips with his anger. If only he'd gotten hold of Ava Bixby. If only she could've heard what a terrible liar Kalyna Harter really was.

He was tempted to call Ava back, hoping she'd pick up so he could tell her about it, even though he couldn't provide proof. He hated waiting for the legal process to unfold, and longed to help himself. But he was afraid he'd come across like some kind of madman, phoning Ava in the middle of the night without a more pressing reason than his panic and impatience.

He spent several minutes arguing with himself but finally realized there was nothing to do but wait until morning. He decided to watch TV, hoping it would distract him enough so he could stop fuming.

It didn't work. He was just as angry when the sun began to lighten the sky.

At exactly eight o'clock, he called in sick. Then he called McCreedy, Eisner and Goran, but he wasn't able to speak to his attorney. McCreedy was already on his way to court, he was told. He should be back after one.

Luke watched the clock for most of the day, but his attorney never called. At three, the law firm's secretary informed him that McCreedy had left for the Fourth of July weekend directly from the courthouse and would have to call him on Monday.

"Of course!" he snapped as he slammed down the phone. And that was when he decided he couldn't sit back and bide his time anymore. He was going to effect some change. He was going to fight back.

He was going to call The Last Stand to see if he could meet with Ava Bixby before she left for the weekend, too.

The Last Stand wasn't located in a high-crime area, but because of the kind of work they did, and the kind of people it angered, Ava, Skye and Sheridan kept the offices locked at all times. Meetings were always by appointment. So Ava was a little surprised when someone rang the buzzer just before five o'clock on Friday afternoon. She was the only one working late—in the summer they closed at four on Fridays—and she wasn't expecting anyone.

Assuming it was a volunteer returning to pick up the box of envelopes he'd forgotten thirty minutes earlier, she skirted her desk, grabbed the work Greg Hoffman had left behind and hurried to the front. But it wasn't Greg standing on the other side of the glass door.

Although the glare of the sun made it difficult to see her visitor's face clearly, she saw his body. He was at least six-three—and definitely a man. His broad, powerful-looking shoulders, pectoral muscles and biceps filled out a plain white T-shirt that appeared to have been ironed. Judging by the contours of his well-worn jeans, which had a slight crease as if they, too, had been ironed, his long legs were just as muscular as his upper body.

Whoever he might be, he was obviously in excellent physical shape....

When Ava drew closer, his head blocked the sun and she caught sight of his face. It was Captain Luke Trussell. She identified him from that photograph Jonathan had brought her. But his skin was a lot more tanned than it'd been in that snapshot, and the bony ridge above his eyes was slightly more pronounced. As a matter of fact, every feature seemed more rough-hewn—from his long straight nose that flared slightly at the nostrils, to his strong jaw and stubborn chin, to his high forehead and well-defined cheekbones.

"Wow," she muttered to herself. He was handsome, all right. Just as Kalyna had said. But he also looked as if he could tear her in two with his bare hands.

Wishing she was holding the can of mace she kept in her top drawer instead of a box of envelopes, she hesitated in indecision—and he removed his sunglasses, revealing a pair of troubled blue-green eyes.

Slowly, she lowered the box into a nearby chair. She'd told Kalyna that rapists come in all shapes and sizes, and it was true. Maybe she'd never seen one *this* perfect, but she wasn't about to let a flash of straight white teeth and an intense but hopeful expression dazzle her into being stupid.

"I'm sorry, we closed at four," she called through the door. "You'll have to make an appointment."

A V formed between those dark eyebrows. "I phoned for your hours before coming," he called back. "A man named Greg told me you were open weekdays from nine to five. And—" he consulted his cell phone "—it's not quite five." He turned it to show her.

Ava sighed. Because they worked by appointment and

often stayed late, sometimes well into the night, Greg hadn't noticed the change in their official hours.

"Did Greg also tell you that we don't accept walk-in visitors?" she asked.

"No. He said Ava Bixby was on the phone at the moment but she was around today and I'd be able to catch her if I hurried over."

Another sigh. They needed to have a meeting. The volunteers were getting careless about security, no doubt because everything had been going smoothly of late— no bomb threats, no altercations, no crank phone calls. Skye was so preoccupied with her family, she'd been spending less time at the office and wasn't as vigilant about reminding everyone of the safety issues as she used to be. Because Ava hadn't picked up where Skye had left off, she was faced with a potentially dangerous situation....

How should she handle it?

By being firm, she decided. "We're closed," she said again.

"Are you Ava, by any chance?"

Was it safe to admit that she was? She had to. It'd feel too silly to deny it. "Yes."

"I only need a few minutes of your time," he said. "Please. I'm Captain Luke Trussell. You wanted to speak to me. You called me a few days ago."

"I know who you are. I also know that you're accused of rape, Captain Trussell."

His lips formed a straight, unhappy line. "Believe me, I'm well aware of that."

"What I mean is, I won't be alone with you."

His forehead rumpled. "I didn't rape Sergeant Harter. I've never raped anyone, and I'm not going to hurt you. We could go somewhere public, if you want." He glanced up and down Watt Avenue as if searching for a solution. "I'm not that familiar with this street. But...name a place, any place, and I'll meet you there."

She would've been willing to meet with him had he set this up over the phone, so she could've made arrangements for Jonathan or someone else to join them. "Come back on Monday," she said. "First thing in the morning."

"Don't put me off," he pleaded. "I fought ninety minutes of traffic to get here." He lifted his hands, large hands that were callused enough to prove he'd done some hard work in his life. "I won't come within three feet of you, I swear."

"Not now. Not today."

"Please?"

Ava sighed once again, this time in resignation. Oh, hell...why not? He was already here, wasn't he? And she probably had nothing to fear. She'd been over and over his record. It was impeccable. Only Kalyna had anything negative to say about him. Even Jonathan believed in him, citing the fact that he'd been a popular, well-adjusted boy all the time he was growing up. Besides, she needed to hear what he had to say. It might put her uneasiness and indecision on this case to rest.

"Meet me at the Starbucks just down the street." She pointed to indicate the direction.

"Thanks." His scowl dissolved into an expression of relief, and Ava went back for her mace.

13

Luke tried to relax as he waited for Ava Bixby to join him, but he couldn't. He had too much riding on this. At the very least, he hoped to talk the victims' advocate out of weighing in on Kalyna's side. At best, he hoped to solicit her help for himself. He doubted The Last Stand had ever come to the defense of someone who'd been wrongly accused. That wasn't really part of their definition of "victim." But it was worth a shot. His attorney had a great deal of respect for Ava and her partners, which meant others might listen to them, as well.

The door opened, and a blast of heat from outside entered the coffee shop, along with Ava. She was slightly taller than average—close to five-eight he guessed—and too thin, her face more interesting than pretty. Rather angular, in fact. But the dramatic A-line cut of her blond hair suited it well. She carried herself a bit too stiffly, but there was confidence in her bearing and she had nice eyes. Clear and intelligent, they missed nothing.

He'd already brought her a drink. He tried to wave her over, but she stopped to order anyway, and, while her back was turned, he let himself take in the rest of her. He doubted she would've attracted his attention had he met her under different circumstances. He typically liked his women a little softer, in looks and manner, but her no-nonsense figure seemed to fit her personality.

He glanced away before she could catch him checking her out. He didn't want her to assume he was the sexual predator Kalyna accused him of being. But he was so curious about the kind of woman it would take to do her job—and what she already thought about this case—that it was difficult not to study her.

Leaning back in his chair, he drank one of the two iced mochas he'd ordered when he first came in, staring out at the passing cars while he waited.

Not until the chair opposite him scraped the floor did he allow himself to focus on Ava again. At that point, he found her eyeing the drinks he'd bought with smug suspicion.

"Was one of these intended for me?" she asked.

"I thought you might like it," he said with a shrug.

Her lips, just full enough to balance the abundance of angles everywhere else, curved into a smile. "Very polite, Captain."

"Anything wrong with polite, Ms. Bixby?"

"Of course not," she replied, but he got the impression that his attempt to be courteous had somehow backfired. She definitely wasn't impressed.

Someone behind the counter called her name, and she got up to retrieve a glass of iced tea. While she was gone, Luke tossed the mocha he'd purchased for her into the garbage.

When she returned, he waited for her to position her purse at her feet and place her drink on the table before speaking. Then he said, "So you can't accept a coffee drink from a suspected rapist. Anything else I should know?"

Just the way she sat down—knees together, feet tucked under her chair, posture rigid—told him she was on guard. "I don't like iced mocha. I buy my own drinks.

And, no offense, but I won't base your guilt or innocence on your looks or your charm."

"To be honest, I wasn't expecting that much out of a four-dollar drink." He grinned, hoping to win her over, but her expression didn't change.

"Why are we here, Captain?" she asked.

He wasn't sure what he'd done wrong. He typically got along well with everyone, especially women. But he could tell that Ava Bixby disliked him on sight. "You called me." He let his smile disappear. That approach clearly wasn't working.

"You took a while to respond to that call. May I ask why?"

"I have a lot on the line."

"And you don't trust me."

He folded his arms. "From what I can tell, the feeling's mutual."

"Just because I haven't melted at the sight of you?"

"Friendly would've been nice."

"We're not here to become friends. I'm looking for your side of the story. That's it."

He let his eyebrows slide up. "You don't believe your client?"

"I'd hate to think Kalyna Harter would tell lies that could destroy a man's life, but…"

"But?"

"She's not my friend, either. Put it this way—I've learned that it's always better to be open-minded."

If only she meant it. "How can you say that when you've already decided I'm guilty?"

"I *haven't* decided you're guilty. I'm just letting you know I'm not your typical female admirer."

He leaned close. "Are you really that attracted to me? Because I'm not having the same problem."

He'd only been as frank with her as she'd been with him, but he had everything at stake and she had nothing. He was afraid she'd be angry, maybe even stomp off, but she inclined her head as if she finally felt she owed him some respect. "Point taken."

"Great. Now that we're back on an equal footing, I need to tell you something. Kalyna called me last night."

Ava didn't show a great deal of surprise, but a slight tightening around her mouth told him she hadn't expected this. "Why would she do that?"

"I'm not sure. Especially if she's as terrified of me as she's pretending to be. Why would any little piggy call the big bad wolf?"

"Is that how you see yourself?" she asked.

He clasped his hands loosely between his knees. "That's how I'm being portrayed, isn't it?"

She took a sip of her tea. "What did she have to say?"

He shook his head. "Nothing that made sense."

"Give me an example."

"She said she *misses* me. As if we were ever dating. As if we even knew each other well enough for her to miss me." He was tempted to add the part about her wanting his hands on her body. That proved she'd been an equal participant on the night of June 6. But he was afraid repeating that remark would sound false.

"Interesting."

"You're skeptical?"

"Open-minded, remember? Do you have a record of the incoming call?"

"Of course." He took his cell phone from his pocket to show her. "See here? Three a.m. That was her."

"It says *Restricted*," she said pointedly. "Anyone could've made that call."

Again, he lamented being unable to record his conversation with Kalyna. "Of course she's going to block her number. She's not stupid."

"Just crazy."

He set his phone aside. "That's what I think."

"Did she say anything else?"

"She said she wanted us to be together. That she..." He told himself to state it baldly. He didn't like Ava. She was part of the nightmare into which he'd fallen. But he couldn't bring himself to be that crude. Not in the presence of a woman wearing a business suit. "Let's just say she made some sexual innuendos."

Ava crossed one leg over the other. "Captain, thanks to the nature of my career, it's very likely I've heard more graphic descriptions than you have. Just give me the facts. I'd rather you were straightforward than trying to protect my sensibilities."

"Fine." He lowered his voice so no one else in the restaurant could hear. "She told me she wanted to feel me inside her again."

Their eyes locked and Ava's lips parted, but nothing came out of her mouth. Then she blinked and cleared her throat, and he figured he must've imagined that spark between them.

"Let's back up," she said. "Why don't you tell me in your own words what happened on June 6."

He focused on his drink in case that little sizzle returned. He didn't want to feel anything like that right now, least of all for this woman, who was someone he couldn't envision as a friend—even if she wasn't Kalyna's advocate. Talk about uptight. "I ran into Kalyna at a bar, and I went home with her. It was a typical one-night stand."

"Just a sec." She dug a pad of paper and a pen out of her purse.

"You're going to take notes?" he asked.

"Do you have a problem with that?"

Because he was here against his attorney's advice, it made him nervous. *Depending on her level of motivation, Ms. Bixby could misinterpret a comment or two or even misrepresent what you said.* But he supposed recording what he said wasn't any riskier than meeting with her in the first place. He didn't want to act as if he had anything to hide. "I guess not."

"Thank you." She scribbled on the page to make sure the pen was working. "Do you pick up women at bars very often?" she asked, getting back to business.

"No."

She glanced up.

"Ask anybody."

"I've already asked Paris Larsen," she said.

Luke hadn't heard Paris's name since they'd broken up. "How do you know about Paris?"

"Actually, I didn't speak to her myself. A friend of yours mentioned to my investigator that you used to go out with her, so he met with her to see what she had to say."

Ava Bixby was certainly thorough. "And?"

"She told him you picked her up in a bar."

"That isn't true," he said. "We met at a restaurant."

"A restaurant better known as a bar."

"But I was there for dinner. She was sitting at the table next to mine. And I took her out a number of times before…anything happened. That's not the same as a one-night stand. We knew each other, trusted each other, before we made love. There was a commitment involved." He shook the ice in his mocha just to hear it rattle. "Why, what did she tell your investigator about our relationship?"

Ava didn't answer. She was writing again.

"She said I was never rough with her, right?" he persisted, ducking his head to catch her eye.

Ava put her pen aside. "Actually, she said you broke her heart."

"That wasn't intentional. I was ready to end the relationship, and she wasn't ready to let go. That's all. I'm sure you've been in similar situations."

"No, I haven't," she said. "I'm careful to avoid it."

He used his index finger to move the change he'd dropped on the table. "You've never broken anyone's heart?"

"Not that I know of."

Was she serious? "Have you ever been in love?"

"Not deeply," she said without a second's hesitation.

He shook his head. "Somehow that doesn't surprise me as much as it should."

She set her jaw at a stubborn angle. "You don't hand your heart to every girl you meet, do you?"

"No, but at least I know what love feels like."

"Are you sure about that, Captain?"

"Positive."

"Have *you* ever been hurt?"

"Yes. My senior year in high school, I fell hard for a girl who wound up marrying my best friend. I've never been more miserable."

It took her a moment to come up with a response to that. "You seem to have survived," she said. "But back to Kalyna."

"We were talking about Paris."

"We were done with Paris."

"Not yet. Did she or did she not admit I was never violent with her?" He wanted an answer and he knew what that answer would be.

"Fine. If it'll allow us to move on, she said you were never violent."

There was more. Ava was holding out on him; he could tell. "What were her exact words? Your investigator asked, 'Was he ever violent with you?' And she said..."

Ms. Bixby blew out a sigh. "'Never. He was an amazing lover.' Happy now?"

"I'd be happier if you believed her," he said.

"I'll take that part on faith because whether or not you were *amazing* in the sack isn't really the issue here. Just because you never hit Paris doesn't mean you've never hit anybody."

He hung an elbow over the back of his chair. "If what Paris had to say has no bearing, why'd you track her down in the first place? Her testimony only counts if it's dirt?"

She frowned. "She's still in love with you. That doesn't make her praise very reliable."

"You can talk to *any* of the women I've dated. They'll *all* tell you I'm an amazing lover." He laughed at his own joke. But she didn't even crack a smile. "What, you have no sense of humor?" he asked.

"I'm not sure that was a joke."

He splayed his hands. "I was kidding. You know I was kidding."

Her eyebrows arched.

"Forget it." He made a dismissive gesture. "I'm not a sexual predator."

"Can you back that up with more than your word and a couple of character witnesses?" she asked.

He tipped his cup to get at the ice. Ava was looking for hard evidence, but what evidence there was seemed to support Kalyna's side. "The cabdriver who took us to her place can tell you I got into his cab alone and gave him my home address. He'll also tell you that Kalyna climbed in at the last second, of her own volition, and insisted he take us to her place instead."

"You didn't mind having your vehicle commandeered?"

He put his cup back on the table. "I was pretty preoccupied."

"Doing what?"

Their eyes met again, and this time he refused to glance away. "Use your imagination."

When the color in her cheeks heightened, he hid a smile. For all her tough talk, Ms. Bixby wasn't nearly as world-wise as she pretended. And that was good to know, because it finally gave him an advantage. "Did the cabdriver see what was going on?" she asked.

"He couldn't have missed it."

"Did he ask her to buckle up or do anything else to acknowledge the fact that he'd witnessed this behavior?"

"No. But I could feel him watching us in the rearview mirror. That's why I tried to convince her to back off until we got to her apartment."

Ava asked him for the name of the cab company and the approximate time and wrote it down, but he got the impression she could easily have remembered that information. She was using her pen and paper to regain her bearings. The conversation, and the visual images it aroused, was affecting her more than she wanted.

"You asked her to stop but she couldn't wait?" she said when she looked up.

He nearly cracked another joke about his sex appeal. She already thought he was arrogant, which tempted him to play it up. But he knew it wasn't in his best interests to make himself look bad. So he overrode the impulse by getting far more specific than he would have otherwise. If she wanted answers that wouldn't spare her sensibilities, he'd give them to her. "She wouldn't. She was moaning and talking dirty to me, telling me she'd never touched a man who was bigger and thicker than I am. She was putting on a show."

He'd expected to see her writhe in embarrassment. But she didn't. She was on to him. "Apparently, so are you," she said dryly.

He tried an innocent scowl. "I'm just telling you what happened."

Her gaze remained steady. "Sounds like you have an excellent memory of the night's events, including word-for-word snippets of the conversation."

The cab ride was mostly a blur. He knew Kalyna had been all over him, because he'd tried to stop her, but that was it. "Well, I'm guessing she said something like that," he told her. "But to be honest, I don't remember much more than her grinding against me while trying to stick her tongue down my throat."

Ava's face reddened, but her emotions had nothing to do with embarrassment. "You think it's funny?" she snapped. "You're accused of rape!"

The desire to laugh disappeared as the *R* word scraped through Luke's brain like broken shards of glass. He managed a careless shrug, but he was sick inside and doing everything he could not to show it, especially to this particular woman. He had no idea how his life had come to this. One bad decision—that was all it had taken. "I might as well have a good laugh at your expense, Ms. Bixby, because you're not going to believe me no matter what I say."

This seemed to bring her up short just when she was about to let him have it. "That's a rather fatalistic view, wouldn't you say?"

"You've been biased since I introduced myself."

"If I didn't want to hear your side, I wouldn't be sitting here."

"You're sitting here, but you're not really listening. You're merely searching for tidbits to support what you've already heard from Kalyna."

"That's not how it is," she argued. "Anyway, I can't form a fair opinion if you won't cooperate with me."

Muttering an unintelligible curse, he pressed a thumb and finger against his closed eyelids. What was wrong with him? He was panicked, frantic, furious—and when she'd provided a target, he'd gladly gone after it. But he was only hurting himself.

"Fine," he said, sobering. "I get it. You're right. I'm sorry." He didn't give her the chance to accept or reject his apology; he immediately went on, hoping to get this over with as soon as possible. "What else do you want to know?"

If she was surprised by his sudden reversal, she didn't comment on it. She remained very much in control—calm and cool. But then, she wasn't the one whose life hung in the balance. "What happened after you reached the apartment?"

He moved the money around some more. "We had consensual sex."

"That's it?"

"That's it."

"It couldn't be that she decided she'd had enough, but you were so turned on you wouldn't let her quit?"

"No."

"From your own description, she was extremely forward. It's natural that a man might become frustrated if she backed off. Some might even insist she deliver on the promises she'd made."

A gaggle of teenagers came in, laughing loudly and

taking an occasional swat at one another. They drew Luke's eye, but his thoughts remained firmly anchored on the discussion. "*Some* might, but I didn't."

Ava added yet another packet of sugar to her tea. She'd spent more time stirring it than drinking it. That indicated how uncomfortable she felt. But he was uncomfortable now, too. Had he really made that "big and thick" comment? He might've laughed at himself, except he knew his behavior had been a childish reaction to her surliness.

"Still, a scenario like that would be understandable," she said.

"To *you?*" he asked in surprise.

She toyed with the empty sugar packet. "To a jury."

His eyes narrowed in suspicion. "Meaning I'd get a lighter sentence."

"Exactly."

Here was the trap his attorney had warned him about. Ava was piecing the encounter together in such a way that rape sounded like a logical conclusion. "I don't care," he told her. "Maybe your version makes more sense than what really happened, but it's just that—your version."

"If you can't prove what happened, you might be better served to look at other options."

That comment convinced him Ava Bixby was every bit as dangerous as Kalyna Harter. She was trying to make him feel as if he'd have a greater chance of surviving this ordeal if he confessed. She was leading him right to the noose.

"I'd be dishonorably discharged," he said. "As far as I'm concerned, that's not a minimal sentence. And it isn't the truth. I didn't force her. Period. As a matter of fact, I was the one who almost called it off—twice."

"Why?"

"Because she offered me…" Now that the desire to punish Ava was gone, he found himself reluctant to lay out the gritty details.

"What?" she prompted.

He swallowed a sigh. "Options I wasn't interested in."

"Like a three-way with her neighbor?"

"She told you about that?" he asked, sitting up straight.

Ava shifted her purse next to her feet. "No."

"Then how do you know?"

"I've been doing my homework."

"It appears so." His attorney hadn't gotten nearly this far. Luke had to admit that Ava Bixby was good at her job. He wanted to press her for more details, wanted her on his side, but he knew that wasn't going to happen. She was working for the prosecution, and although he and Ava had called a truce, that was all it was—a truce.

Her knowledge of Kalyna's offer did help in one way, however. It proved to him that at least part of what had occurred could be corroborated. That was something, wasn't it?

"Was there an argument when you turned down her offer of an additional partner?" she asked.

She was fishing, trying to find a reason for the bumps and bruises. "Not at all. I got the impression she was showing off by suggesting it in the first place. That she was trying to prove how adventurous and fun she was— sort of like what she'd been doing in the cab."

"Why weren't you interested?" she asked.

For the first time, he stared at her openly, assessing the contours of her face, and found a simple yet elegant beauty there. What with the suit and that starchy bearing, he would've missed it entirely if he hadn't had reason to look closer.

She began to fidget under his regard. "What?"

"Are you asking to satisfy your own curiosity or because you think it pertains to the case in some way?"

She rolled her eyes. "Your conceit is really appalling."

"It was an honest question."

When she didn't answer, he knew. Her problem wasn't that she didn't like him. It was that she didn't *want* to like him. "I'm satisfied with one partner at a time," he explained. "It's pretty tough for sex to have any meaning beyond physical gratification if it's a party, you know?"

"Now you're saying you were investing in Kalyna emotionally?" she asked.

"Not in the way you think. But…yeah, I was interested in connecting with someone. I was upset, didn't want to be alone."

Seemingly eager to lead the conversation into safer territory, she clasped her hands in her lap. "Why were you upset?"

Phil. He grimaced at the fresh onslaught of grief and remorse. "It didn't have anything to do with her. It was something else."

"Like…"

He glared into his cup. "I'd just gotten word that my best friend was killed in Iraq." Embarrassed by the cracking of his voice, he scowled and forced himself to continue as his stoic father would. "We went to high school together."

"In Ogden, Utah."

Shoving his cup away, he rested his elbows on the table. "Evidently, you've contacted people besides Paris."

"My investigator has, yes."

Had he spoken to Marissa? Could she tell him how Marissa was doing? Luke had thought about calling her over the past few weeks, but couldn't let himself. He was in too big a mess, for one thing. And it felt too disloyal to Phil to contact her now. "Is that why you called me?"

"Excuse me?"

"You've studied my background, had your investigator talk to my friends. You know something like this is out of character."

"That doesn't make you *incapable* of it."

"But it makes the scenario as Kalyna's describing it unlikely."

She tucked a few tendrils of hair behind ears that were small and delicate and adorned only with simple pearl earrings. "You admit you weren't yourself that night."

He stretched out his legs and slumped lower in his seat. "But I wasn't *violent.* I was looking for escape, and Kalyna offered me a night of mindless sex when I needed it. Had I been thinking, I would've passed. I've never been interested in Kalyna. But...I wasn't thinking, and getting drunk made it worse."

"You said you almost bailed out on her *twice,*" she reminded him.

He shook his head. "Let's not go into that."

"The devil's in the details," she persisted.

"It won't be a comfortable conversation."

"My job seldom allows for comfortable conversation. Necessary but not necessarily comfortable, Captain."

"Fine." He angled his chair away from the teenagers. "The second time was when she didn't want me to use a condom. I insisted on it. I always insist on it."

Ava smoothed a few strands of hair out of her eyes. "She claims you *didn't* use any birth control."

"That's a lie!"

"Then how did they find your semen?"

Briefly closing his eyes, he ran his fingers over his

eyebrows. "The condom must've broken or leaked. Or she retrieved it after I threw it in the trash."

He knew from the lines forming on her forehead that the mental images he'd created were as vivid in her mind as they were in his and somehow that bugged him. He didn't want to be sitting here talking so explicitly with a stranger, especially a woman, especially *this* woman. She'd probably never made a stupid mistake in her life.

"That's going to pretty great lengths on her part, don't you think?" she asked.

"I know it sounds…unlikely, but I'm not playing you. She was egging me on, trying to spice it up far more than I found appealing. She…she stopped me from going into the bathroom when it was all over—she wanted to do something…different. Otherwise, I would've flushed the condom, instead of just tossing it in the bedroom garbage."

"What different thing did she want to do?"

"There's no way in hell I'm going to describe that for you or anyone else. It was gross. She's…depraved."

At the decisiveness in his response, she backed down. "Fine. I get it. And now she's lying."

"Yes." The teenagers chose a table nearby, so he lowered his voice even more. "But we should be able to prove that I used a condom. And if we can prove she's lying about that, maybe someone will believe me about the rest of it."

"How do you plan to prove you used a condom?"

"The wrapper had to go somewhere."

"They went through her trash the morning after."

He knew from her manner what was coming next.

"But there was no wrapper," she said.

He dropped his head in his hands. She'd taken the condom and used it, just as he'd thought, and then flushed it.

"You going to be okay?" she asked.

"It doesn't feel like it," he said but raised his head, anyway. "The wrapper was there when I left. So was the condom. She must've gotten rid of both after putting my semen inside her."

Ava drew circles in the condensation from her glass. "Why? Why would she go to so much trouble to set you up?"

"I don't know. All I can tell you is that she was angry when I left."

"Over what?"

"She wanted me to stay and I wouldn't."

"That's it?"

"For the most part." He shrugged. "Out of nowhere, she started professing her undying love. It made me really uncomfortable to hear her talk like that. I hadn't made any promises, but she got so clingy. She was acting as if she expected us to spend the rest of our lives together. I tried to extricate myself, to explain that she might've misunderstood, but she refused to hear it. She begged me to stay, kept telling me she'd make me happy if I wouldn't leave her."

He tried to read Ava's reaction, but her face was more shuttered than ever. "It was…awkward, upsetting, odd," he said. "So I insisted on leaving before it could get any worse. But when I began to dress, she went berserk. She kept saying I'd tricked her into believing I actually cared but that I'd used her the way I use all women."

"So she's in love with you, and you don't feel the same way."

"This isn't about love," he said. "It's about…infatuation, or obsession, or revenge, but it's not about love."

"So what did you tell her when you left?" Ava asked.

"I said I was sorry for the confusion and she could

call me later if she wanted to talk about it. Otherwise, I'd see her at work. The next thing I knew, the cops were at my door."

Ava tapped the side of her cup with one slim finger. "What about the pictures she showed me? The ones where she's sporting a black eye and a fat lip?"

The police had shown Luke those photographs, too, hoping to elicit a telling reaction. "I can't explain those. She wasn't injured when I left."

Ava remained silent.

"So what do you think?" he asked.

She smoothed those wayward strands of hair again. "I'm not sure."

"Come on. You believe me now, don't you? You don't want me to be telling the truth, but you think I am."

"I don't know what to believe."

"You know *something* isn't right with Kalyna. I can tell. That's got to be part of the reason you called me in the first place. I'm guessing you don't meet with every man who's been accused by one of your clients."

"Not every man who's been accused by one of my clients has your track record." She stood and slung her purse over her shoulder. "Thank you for your time, Captain."

"Wait!" He wanted to catch her by the wrist but didn't dare touch her. Fortunately, she turned. "Will you be out there, trying to help Kalyna convict me?" He definitely didn't want this woman working against him. She was tenacious, methodical, smart and seemed to be investing a lot more hours in this case than his own attorney was.

"No."

"Because…"

She tossed her nearly full cup in the trash. "I'm going with my gut on this one."

"And your gut tells you I'm innocent."

She located her keys in her purse. "My gut could be wrong."

"Does that mean you won't help me?" he asked.

"You think I'm going to switch sides?" she said with a laugh.

"I'm the one you should be helping."

"You don't need me. Maybe the investigator—Major Ogitani, isn't that her name?—is gung ho right now. From what I've seen, she's hoping to make an example of you. But I doubt the charges will stick. Anyone who really looks will find exactly what I found—a woman who's less than credible pointing a finger at a man she desperately wants but can't have. I doubt they can build a strong enough case to go to trial."

He was feeling a lot better. This was the first good news he'd received since before E. Golnick wrinkled her nose at him as if he was slimier than pond scum. "What makes you say Kalyna's not credible?"

"Your defense team should be able to answer that for you."

"They're weeks behind you," he complained.

"But they're good."

"McCreedy told me not to meet with you." Luke flashed her an appreciative grin. "I'm glad I didn't listen."

"I suggest you take his advice in the future," she said as she left.

14

How was she going to do this—for the second time?

Ava sat in her car even after she reached her houseboat. She had the windows down to take advantage of the perfect sixty-five-degree weather and was staring out at the moon. She'd expected to see the Myerses and the Greenleys, the two couples who owned the houseboats that so often docked where she did, back from their fishing trip, but her boat remained a solitary hulk upon the water.

"Where are they?" she muttered, but she knew she was only trying to distract herself from what she needed to do. She'd been going back and forth on the Kalyna Harter case the entire ride home. She wanted to be sure she was dropping Kalyna as a client because she thought Kalyna was lying and not because she was attracted to the accused. But she wouldn't have had such a positive reaction to Luke if she truly believed him to be a rapist. Everything she'd felt when she was with him told her he wasn't. So she had her answer, didn't she?

Bracing herself for Kalyna's disappointment, she finally picked up her cell phone and dialed. Kalyna wasn't Bella; this was different. It had to be different.

"Hello?"

"Kalyna?"

"Yes?"

"It's Ava Bixby." *Calling to sever ties...again.*

"Oh, hi." She sounded surprised and a little wary. "Is...is something wrong?"

"No, not wrong exactly."

"Then why are you calling?"

Ava's car door creaked as she opened it. She shoved it wider with her foot, but made no move to get out. "I'm afraid I have some news you probably won't want to hear."

There was a brief silence. Then Kalyna said, "What is it?"

"I've decided I can't take your case, after all."

"*What? But...why?*" she cried. "Just last night you said you would. You said it wouldn't be easy but you'd be there for me. How can you break your word?"

"It wasn't a promise, Kalyna. I was hesitant even then, and you know it."

"But what changed your mind?" Her tone became accusing. "Did my sister call you back?"

This question made Ava feel even more convinced that she was making the right choice. "No, she didn't. What would she have said if she did?"

Another pause. "Nothing."

"Then why'd you ask?"

"She's afraid she might've gotten Mom in trouble because of what she admitted to you last night and she feels guilty about it. She doesn't want to be drawn into a family feud. She still lives at home, has to put up with the backlash. And she doesn't like talking about the past to begin with. Neither of us do."

Except when there was some advantage to doing it, Ava thought. Then Kalyna seemed plenty ready to talk— in great detail. "Kalyna, I have no doubt you had a difficult childhood. I feel terrible about that. But if you're lying about Luke Trussell, you'd better stop, because you could be prosecuted yourself."

"I'm not lying!" she snapped. "How can you accuse me of that on top of what I've been through? You have no idea what it was like when he attacked me. I thought he'd *kill* me! I have nightmares about it every night."

Ava couldn't help herself; she had to ask. "You *honestly* feared for your life, Kalyna?"

"Yes! He was so…angry and violent. And the brutal way he held me down and forced my legs apart…"

Ava squeezed her eyes shut. She didn't want to think of Luke with Kalyna, was glad she wouldn't have to now that she was taking herself off the case. "You already told me what happened. There's no need to go into it again."

"But you don't believe me!"

Ava wanted to accuse her of lying, to demand the truth, but she knew that would only make this call more difficult. The case would get sorted out without her. "I just don't see how I can be of any value to you."

"What does that mean? You're looking for an excuse—*any* excuse—not to do your job."

"That's not true."

"Then what went wrong? Are you giving up because you don't like me? Is that it? Is it personal?"

"It isn't personal at all, Kalyna." Ava began gathering up her briefcase, purse and the bag of groceries she'd bought on the way home. "It's a business decision. I have to be careful with the charity's assets."

"I'm not good enough for the charity's assets?" she shouted. "I haven't suffered enough? You're useless, you know that? You couldn't help anyone if you tried!"

Ava was tempted to come right back at her, but if she wasn't going to be involved, what was the point? It was better to avoid an argument. "I'm afraid we take on only a select number of cases, and there isn't sufficient evidence here to determine guilt, that's all." Proud of her restraint and professionalism, she drew a deep breath. She wasn't going to let Kalyna get under her skin.

"You don't know that," Kalyna said. "We were just getting started. Come on, stick with me!"

"No, definitely not." Ava's arms were too full, so she set the groceries back in the seat. "I've made up my mind, Kalyna. I'm sorry."

"What good is a victims' charity if it won't help when you really need it?"

"We assist those we can."

"So what do you expect me to do?" Her voice rose to a whine. "Let him off?"

"That's not your decision anymore. It's up to the prosecutor. But there isn't enough evidence to convict him, so I'm guessing they'll drop the charges at some point."

"You're wrong! He deserves to be punished. And Major Ogitani will see to it."

Ava considered explaining that unless something else came to light, Major Ogitani wouldn't have a choice. But she bit her tongue. Sooner or later, Kalyna would find out for herself. "Good luck."

"That's it?" Kalyna said. "I come to you, beaten and bruised and crying for help, and you turn me away? What kind of person are you?"

Despite the little voice in her head that warned her to keep her mouth shut, Ava couldn't resist. "What kind of person are *you?*" she replied.

"What do you mean by that?"

"Did you call Luke Trussell last night, Kalyna? Did you tell him you wanted to feel him inside you?"

"No!"

"What if I told you part of that call was recorded?" She held her breath, wondering if Kalyna would fall for it.

Dead silence suggested Kalyna assumed she'd been caught.

"And how did you *really* get those injuries?" Ava asked.

"You're an evil bitch," Kalyna screamed. "I hope you burn in hell!"

A click signaled that she'd hung up.

Trembling, Ava turned off her phone. The venom in Kalyna's parting words had surprised her. She hadn't expected the call to go smoothly, but such palpable hate was beyond anything she'd ever experienced.

Was this irrational anger what Luke had encountered with Kalyna?

Ava was willing to bet it was.

Luke was in touch with Ava Bixby. He'd called her, or she'd called him. Maybe they'd even met.

Somehow that bothered Kalyna more than the fact that Ava had decided to take herself off the case.

What had happened between Luke and Ava that had made Ava's decision so absolute? Would it poison Major Ogitani's good opinion of Kalyna, too? Would the prosecutor drop the case as Ava had hinted?

If so, Luke would get away from her.

Kalyna's heart thumped at the thought. It felt as if he was slipping away already....

"Hey, there you are!" Tati approached from the other side of the bar, where she'd been playing darts. "Where'd you go?"

"I had to step out," Kalyna said. "I had a call." She hadn't wanted Ava Bixby to know she was partying.

"Oh." Tati didn't ask who it was or if everything was

okay. She probably didn't want to know. Since last night, she'd been careful to avoid any topic that might cause friction. Which was just as well. Kalyna was tired of her disapproval.

"Are you ready to play darts?" Tati jerked her head toward the two burly guys, obviously brothers, who were waiting for them in the corner. Their barrel chests were stuffed into Van Halen T-shirts with the sleeves ripped out. Dirty jeans, black boots and wallets attached by chains added to the biker-wannabe effect. They didn't interest Kalyna, not after someone like Luke. But on the positive side, they were younger than most of the men in the bar. "They keep asking when you're going to join us," her sister whispered.

Because they could see she was more attractive, Kalyna thought. Too bad they weren't good enough for her. "Not right now," she said. "You go ahead without me."

"Are you sure?"

"I'm sure." Knowing Tati was out of her element, Kalyna smiled. "Go. Flirt. Have fun."

Tati hesitated, but eventually went back and started another game. Soon, she was laughing as if this was the best time she'd ever had. Kalyna was just thinking how pathetic that was when a middle-aged man carrying fifty extra pounds around the middle approached.

"What do you say, beautiful? Will you let me buy you a drink?"

The gray in his whiskers and the lines in his face made her want to tell him to get lost. How dare he think he could hook up with her? He was twice her age. But she was tempted by the free drink. And if he could still get it up, she might be able to use him for something more. The pregnancy test she'd begged Tati to buy for her and taken before coming to the bar had been negative—a bitter disappointment. But if she got pregnant right away, she could still pass the baby off as Luke's, couldn't she? She'd have nine months or so before he could prove otherwise. And wouldn't she look pitiable in court with an extended belly?

Picturing herself pregnant, she smiled as she studied the rest of the men in the bar. Surely someone here had to be virile enough to make a baby with her. And wouldn't it be funny to have sex with each and every one of them while her sister played darts, completely unaware of it all? If Tati thought these men were taken with *her,* she knew nothing about the real world. In a mere five minutes, Kalyna could make sure they never looked at Tati again.

"Tell the woman I came in with that I had to take another call," she said. "Then meet me in the alley. You can buy me a drink later."

He seemed confused. "You want me to meet you outside?"

"Only if you're hoping to get lucky."

His lips parted in surprise, then that gleam of excitement entered his eyes—the gleam that made her feel like the most desired woman on the planet—and her breasts began to tingle with anticipation. It didn't matter that he was one of the ugliest men she'd ever met. He wanted her with the singular focus she craved. "How much is it going to cost me?" he asked.

Obviously, he was aware of his shortcomings. And she did need gas money to get back to California. "If you'll send a few customers my way once we're finished—and if you can do it without my sister catching on—I'll give you a discount."

"How much of a discount?"

"I'll do it for forty dollars."

"I don't have that much," he said. "But I know most

of the regulars in here. And I can be subtle. Will you take twenty?"

Twenty bucks was cheap, even for a bargain basement streetwalker. But Kalyna wasn't doing it exclusively for the money.

She glanced over at Tati, caught her sister's eye and waved. "Fine, twenty bucks," she said. "But that doesn't get you anything kinky. And you can't wear a condom."

Distrust dampened the man's eagerness. "You're not one of them weirdos who try to spread diseases, are ya?"

"Nope, I'm clean."

"So what's up?" he asked.

"I'm on the pill. I don't need to worry about birth control. And I think a rubber ruins all the fun, don't you?"

He moved close, so Tati wouldn't be able to see what he was doing, and cupped her left breast. "You wouldn't lie to me, would you?"

Watching her sister over his shoulder, Kalyna unsnapped her bra and moved his hand inside the collar of her shirt. "Does it matter?" she asked as his fingers curled around her breast.

He didn't answer.

"Just imagine what I could do to you," she whispered, and walked out, knowing he'd be in the alley.

On the way home, Luke called his parents and got his mother on the line. "I just wanted to tell you not to worry. Things are looking up for me—I think."

"Why, what's happened?" she asked, her voice filled with relief.

"I met with a woman named Ava Bixby tonight." He adjusted his Bluetooth. "She was actually Kalyna Harter's victim advocate, but she said she's going to drop the case. I'm pretty sure she knows Kalyna is lying."

"Does that mean they'll be dropping the charges, as well?"

He wished. "Not necessarily. But there'll be one less person working to put me in prison. And I get the impression she would've been formidable."

"Well, I wish it was more, but I'm happy to hear it, Luke. Your father and I have been so worried."

"That's why I wanted to tell you."

"I can't believe the nerve of this Kalyna woman," she fumed. "Your father's been talking about hiring a private investigator to take a look at her background. Do you think we should? People like this don't suddenly start lying. They typically have a history of it. If we could prove she's unreliable, it might help."

Luke checked his speed and slowed his BMW so he wouldn't get a ticket. "My attorney will be working with some investigators," he said.

"But this one would answer directly to us, independent of your defense. It can't hurt to have an extra pair of eyes on the job. Maybe he'll find something your attorney won't."

"Maybe." Ava's image appeared in Luke's mind—the wide mouth, the intelligent eyes, the blush that rose to her cheeks at various moments during their conversation. "I wish I could hire the woman I just met."

"Why can't you?"

"I doubt she'd do it. She works for a victims' charity, and I'm not technically considered a victim."

"Charities always need money. Tell her we'll make a generous donation."

"That might not be the only problem."

"What other problem could there be?"

"I don't think she likes me." And he hadn't done a lot to change that. She'd assumed the worst, so he'd behaved like a conceited asshole, just as she'd expected. Probably not the smartest move he could've made, but the frustration and anger he'd been feeling were taking their toll.

"Everyone likes you, Luke."

A grin spread across his face. This was the reason God had created mothers. "A completely unbiased opinion, I'm sure."

"Give her a call," she prodded. "The worst she can say is no."

He'd already asked for Ava's help. But he hadn't offered to donate. Would it make a difference?

"We've never hired a private investigator before," his mother went on. "Who knows what we might get? We could end up with someone who's a total waste of money. This woman is local, she's familiar with the case, she believes Kalyna is lying—"

"And she's good at what she does," he finished.

"Exactly. It's worth a shot, isn't it?"

"I'll think about it." He wasn't sure he had the nerve to contact Ava again. *Are you really that attracted to me? Because I'm not having the same problem.* Had he actually said that? He was never rude to a woman. And then there was the comment he'd made about his penis... That one was *definitely* over the top.

"Okay, you think about it," his mother said. "And if you don't want to call her, your father will."

"Mom," he warned. "You have to let me handle this."

"But I have a good feeling about it, Luke. We were just discussing this before you called, so it's serendipitous that you've mentioned someone who'd be ideal. Anyway, let's discuss it some more tomorrow. If I don't get our movie started now, it'll be too late."

"No problem." He said goodbye, then he considered calling Ava to see if he could enlist her help. The fact that she'd started out on Kalyna's side and then switched over to his would speak volumes. That in itself would lend him credibility, wouldn't it?

Positive that it would, he went so far as to scroll through his call list and highlight her number. But too many things he'd said echoed back to him. *You can talk to any of the women I've dated. They'll all tell you I'm an amazing lover.*

God, what had gotten into him? He wasn't going to call her. He hoped he never had to face her again.

She was dropping the case. Maybe he should just leave well enough alone.

15

Nearly three hundred and fifty dollars wasn't a bad take. And because she'd made a quick trip to the Quick Stop next door and insisted on charging for a condom if her partner was set on using one, only two of the men had bothered. That meant she had a good chance of getting pregnant. What more could it take? At least *one* of those guys had to be virile enough. And Tati was none the wiser. It was all Kalyna could do not to laugh in her sister's face. How stupid could she be?

Tati had come outside looking for Kalyna once, but someone in line waylaid her until Kalyna could straighten her clothes. At that point, Kalyna had acted as if she'd just stepped out for a smoke and some conversation, and because there were so many men with her, Tati never questioned it.

After that close call, the guys who'd already been outside kept Tati busy, flattering her with compliments, games of darts and invitations to dance, and she didn't bother to check again.

"What are you smiling about?" Tati asked. They were in Kalyna's car, but Tati was driving. Tati had only had one beer; Kalyna could barely stand.

"I had fun tonight," she said.

"I did, too." Tati smiled shyly. "Those guys were nice, weren't they?"

Kalyna thought of her bulging wallet. *"Very."*

Tati stopped at a red light. "Guess what?"

"What?"

"Danny asked for my number." Excitement lit her face. "And I hope he calls. I *really* like him."

Kalyna noticed the flush on her sister's cheeks. "Which one was Danny?"

"The cute one with the red hair."

"I don't remember him," Kalyna lied, but she did. He hadn't come out back. None of the other guys knew him well enough to invite him. But she'd taken him into the women's restroom once she'd seen his interest in her sister. He'd said he didn't want to have sex with her, but after they shared a few lines of coke she'd gotten from another guy in lieu of payment, he'd been eager enough.

"How could you miss him?" Tati asked. "He was the best-looking guy there. And he danced with me a few times."

Kalyna adjusted her seat belt, which was so confining she couldn't get comfortable. "I remember now."

"He was hot, don't you think?"

"Not so much. I wouldn't go out with him if I were you."

She scowled. "Why not?"

"He's not your type."

"How do you know? You spent all your time outside, smoking."

Oh, well. If Tati wouldn't listen, she'd have to settle for Kalyna's leftovers. Kalyna imagined seeing Danny with her sister at Christmas dinner, both of them knowing what they'd done, and her smile grew wider. Maybe they'd do it again. Maybe *he'd* be the father of her baby.

"Suit yourself," she said, and slid lower in her seat to stop her head from spinning.

The light turned green, and Tati gave the car some gas. "Since when did you start smoking, anyway?"

"I don't smoke. Not really. Just when I'm drinking and having a good time. And even then, only occasionally."

"I wish you wouldn't. It's not healthy."

Her sister was worried because she'd smoked a few cigarettes? Tati's complete naivete made Kalyna giggle.

"What's so funny?"

"Nothing. You're...sweet, you know that?"

Obviously pleased, Tati squeezed Kalyna's hand as if she'd meant it as a compliment. "I'm glad we got to go out tonight. This is the first time I feel we've really connected since you came home."

"I'm glad, too. The way things were going, I was afraid we wouldn't have *any* fun."

Tati glanced at her. "I love you. You know that, don't you?"

The gravity in her voice pierced through Kalyna's buzz, and suddenly the memory of the game she'd played at the bar wasn't quite so enjoyable. She remembered laughing at Tati's ignorance while the men stood in line, and wished she hadn't done it. At least with Danny.

"Of course you do. I love you, too." She turned to the window so her sister couldn't see her face. "That's why I don't want you to go out with that Dan guy."

They were close to the mortuary. "What are you talking about?"

"I hesitated to say this before, because I didn't want to disappoint you, but he came on to me, too."

Her sister deflated like a balloon. Even her shoulders slumped. "Oh," she said. "I didn't notice."

"I don't think he wanted you to know. That's why he shut up the second he realized I was around."

Tati pulled into the driveway and parked off to one side. "I should've known," she mumbled.

"Known what?"

"That someone cute wouldn't want me."

"Don't talk like that. You just need to lose a little weight. And there are other men out there," Kalyna said. "What's the big deal with this one?"

"There's no big deal." Tati managed to pull herself together, but Kalyna was pretty sure there were tears in her eyes when she got out.

Because it was the Fourth of July weekend, Mother's Country Kitchen Café was even more packed than usual, but Ava didn't mind the bustle. She, Skye and Sheridan had been meeting here for breakfast on the first Saturday of every month since she'd been promoted to full-fledged director. She enjoyed getting away with them for a few hours. It gave them all a chance to go over their cases and make decisions for the organization without the interruptions that typically occurred at the office.

"So what do you think?" Skye asked as the waitress who'd filled their coffee cups walked away. "Should we hire Jane?"

Ava waited for Sheridan's response. She didn't have the seniority they did. She'd first met Skye when she showed up in response to an ad in the *Sacramento Bee*. Shortly after her mother had gone to prison, TLS had offered a free seminar for victims and their families. Little did Ava know when she attended that it would result in an entirely new vocation for her, but it had. Bored with her job as a bank teller, she'd started to volunteer at TLS—and that was when she'd gone back to school three nights a week to get a masters in criminal justice.

She'd graduated last spring but was still the new kid on the block and careful not to come across as too presumptuous or pushy.

"I guess it's okay, if that's what you want to do," Sheridan said.

Ava put down the spoon she'd been using to stir her coffee. She didn't want to be the sole dissenting voice. She knew what Jane Burke meant to Skye. But she had some concerns about bringing her on staff. "I'm not sure it's our best move."

Skye glanced up at her. She sat next to Ava wearing a pair of khaki shorts, a simple white tank and little white loafers—nothing fancy and yet she looked as glamorous as any model. "Why not? Maybe Jane doesn't have a police background or a degree like yours, but she could work alongside me until she's trained." She took the last bite of the multigrain pancakes she'd ordered. "You had no experience with criminal investigations when you started, and look at you now."

"The only real prerequisite is a genuine desire to help," Sheridan concurred. "The rest can be learned."

"I'm not saying Jane needs a degree," Ava told them. "But she was married to a serial killer who all but ruined her life *before* he attacked and nearly murdered her. That kind of experience could warp a person, make it difficult to remain objective, that's all."

Skye turned her orange juice glass around several times. "Oliver Burke nearly murdered me, too. Twice. Does that mean I'm too warped to do my job?"

Ava flushed. Sometimes she spoke her mind before considering all the implications. "What happened to you is different. You didn't live with him. You didn't **trust him** the way she did. She believed him while he was in prison and still tried to make her marriage work when he got out. She's the mother of his child. Talk about betrayal! What Jane went through has to have left some deep scars, and they might make her prone to see only one side of a situation."

"You're afraid she won't be fair?" Skye clarified.

"It's more that I'm afraid her experiences will affect her judgment." Ava's thoughts reverted to her meeting with Luke Trussell and her decision to drop the Harter case. She felt sure she was doing the right thing, but if he hadn't come forward and given her the chance to see what he was like, she might've stayed in Kalyna's corner simply because of her experience with Bella. "Not every situation is as it appears," she said. "Sometimes people lie."

Skye shoved the hair that'd fallen from her ponytail out of her eyes. "The victims don't lie nearly as much as the offenders."

"But some victims aren't victims at all," Ava countered. "They're master manipulators."

Sheridan scowled. "That's got to be a very small percentage, Ava."

"Even one is too many. We don't want to punish the innocent. Ever."

"Where is this coming from?" Skye asked.

Ava smoothed the front of her sleeveless black dress. "A woman came into my office on Monday claiming she'd been raped a month ago. She showed me pictures of herself bruised and battered, and she was accusing a man whose semen had been collected with a rape kit. At first, it seemed like a cut-and-dried case. As she sat in my office sobbing, I wanted to cry with her. I was indignant, filled with a righteous anger, eager to help her obtain justice."

"Probably *more* than eager because of what happened to Bella," Skye said.

Ava flinched. "Exactly. But when I had Jonathan do the research, I learned that the accused has more credibility than the accuser."

Sheridan slipped a credit card onto the table. "Even people with credibility commit crimes, Ava."

"I almost missed the truth because I was so busy trying to make up for...the situation with Bella. We're shaped by what we experience, that's all I'm saying."

Skye slid the syrup back into its place near the laminated menus. "I wasn't aware that you knew Jane."

"I don't but I talked to her when you brought her to the office."

"Last week?"

"Yes. I got the impression she wants to work at The Last Stand to vent the anger she feels toward her late husband and any other men she thinks are like him. She was telling me she's learned so much, that she knows what to look for, how to read behavior others might not notice." Ava shook her head. "No one can tell the difference between a good person and an evil person, not every time. Especially someone like Jane, who has reason to doubt even the people closest to her. I think she would've missed something like this."

"We all have scars, Ava. They're what keep us motivated." Sheridan adjusted the strap on the blouse she was wearing with a loose, flowing skirt and sandals. "We can't be perfectly objective because we deal with every case from our own perspective. I don't see how we can avoid that."

"We can if we recognize our prejudices." The waitress stopped to pick up the check, and Skye gave her a polite smile before continuing. "I understand that you're rattled by the fact that you were almost taken in. It's disconcerting to realize how easily we can be duped—and that there are people out there who would try to take advantage of our good intentions. But I highly doubt Jane would be any more susceptible to going after the wrong person than the rest of us. She's come a long way in the time I've known her. And—" she toyed with a plastic cream container, then tossed it back in the bowl that held the rest "—oh, shoot, I guess what I'm trying to say is that…she needs this. It's been almost four years since Oliver died, and she's still struggling to get past it. And now the salon where she's been cutting hair is closing down…" Skye appealed to them with a frank expression. "She'll be without work."

So this wasn't really about doing what was best for the charity; it was about helping another victim. If Ava had known that, she wouldn't have bothered expressing her reservations. "You couldn't have led with that?"

Skye shrugged sheepishly. "I wanted you to agree without my having to ask it as a favor."

"She can learn, just as we have, that not every victim who walks through the door is someone we can support," Sheridan said.

Ava tried not to be irritated. She wanted to help as many people as possible, but they had to consider the practicality of each decision. "Can we afford another full-time employee?"

The waitress returned with the credit slip. "It'll be tough," Sheridan admitted as she signed the bill. "There's never enough money for everything we'd like to do, but we can use an extra set of hands. We've been buried for months."

"Jane plans on pitching in with the fundraising, too," Skye said. "I've already prepped her for that."

Ava still felt negative about it, but if she was the only one of the three, she was outvoted, anyway. "Okay, I'm willing to give it a try."

Skye squeezed her arm. "Thanks."

After saying goodbye, Ava sat in her car and watched her two partners drive out of the lot. She'd intended to head to the office, as usual. She worked more Saturdays than she took off. But that suddenly seemed excessive. It was a holiday weekend. Why wasn't she celebrating Independence Day like everyone else?

Because she had no one to celebrate with. Her father had gone camping in Yosemite with Carly, his young wife. No matter how hard she tried to get closer to him, their relationship never improved because Carly stood between them. Her mother was in prison. Skye and Sheridan were hurrying home to their husbands. Jonathan hadn't mentioned his plans, but she was sure they included Zoë and her daughter. And Geoffrey was in the Bay Area seeing his two kids. Even the Myerses and Greenleys weren't back from their fishing excursion as planned. They'd left her a message saying they'd met up with another group and decided to stay an extra week. The joys of being retired....

She sighed. The day stretched before her with absolutely nothing except work to fill it. But work was usually enough. What was wrong with her today? Why was she feeling so dissatisfied?

She found herself thinking of Luke Trussell again. She couldn't seem to put him out of her mind. *She was moaning and talking dirty to me, telling me she'd never touched a man who was bigger and thicker than I am.* He'd been trying to exact a bit of revenge when he'd made that statement. So why was it the line that kept coming back to her?

It's obviously been too long since I've been with a man. And Luke Trussell's blatant sexuality had affected her more deeply than she wanted to admit. She was only thirty-one. It was natural that her body would try to assert its needs, especially when she encountered a man as attractive as he was.

Part of her wished she could call Geoffrey and tell him she was ready to be intimate again. Maybe if she started sleeping with him she'd be able to forget Trussell. But she hadn't found that kind of relationship satisfying before and doubted that would change. Besides, she knew it wasn't Geoffrey she'd be seeing when she was in bed with him—and that hardly seemed fair.

"Damn. I've only met him once," she grumbled. And that first meeting hadn't gone particularly well. She'd been bitchy and rude in her attempt to remain unaffected. And he'd retaliated. *Are you really that attracted to me? Because I'm not having the same problem.*

Yeah, she was really that attracted to him. Which meant she needed to keep her distance before she did something stupid, like become infatuated with him. But after last night's conversation with Kalyna, she was absolutely convinced he was innocent. And that obligated her to share what she'd discovered. She kept telling herself that those details wouldn't make a difference. As she'd explained to Kalyna, the case would probably never make it to court. But...what if it did? Or what if the information she possessed could put an end to it sooner—give Luke back his life? McCreedy was a talented attorney, but he was paid by the hour and might not be in any hurry to end this. And just because he was good didn't mean he'd make all the right moves. Whether Kalyna's neighbor Maria was homosexual, bi or straight, she wasn't likely to repeat the fact that she and Kalyna had spoken of a three-way. The implications could ruin her career. Ava had given her permission to keep her mouth shut, hadn't she? And no one but Ava knew about the conversation with Tatiana Harter or Kalyna's response on the phone last night—the panicked *Did my sister call you back?*

Ava drummed her fingers on the steering wheel. She could wait until Monday and contact Luke's attorney, pass along a copy of his file. But she occasionally came up against McCreedy on other cases and didn't want him thinking he had an ally at The Last Stand just because she'd helped him with this one case. And the prosecutor refused to call her back. She'd tried to get in touch with Major Ogitani several times, to no avail. Just as she'd assumed, the military didn't want her involved and were doing their best to ignore the intrusion.

"Call Luke and get it over with already," she muttered.

After digging through her purse, she located her phone and ran through the notes attached to her calendar. Luke wasn't in her address book because she hadn't expected to call him again, but he was in her notes. She scrolled farther down, and found his number in a memo she'd recorded the day she'd tried to get in touch with him regarding Kalyna.

She held her breath as the phone rang....

But she'd screwed up her courage for nothing. He didn't answer.

You've reached Luke Trussell's mailbox. Leave me a message and I'll call you back.

Squaring her shoulders, she waited for the beep. "Captain Trussell, this is Ava Bixby at The Last Stand." She knew he'd recognize her name without any mention of the charity, but she was determined to behave more professionally than she had at Starbucks. Last night, they'd somehow crossed boundaries she normally kept very rigid. *Are you asking to satisfy your own curiosity or because you think this pertains to the case in some way?*

That was the second time he'd seen through her.

She was determined there wouldn't be a third.

"I have something I'd like to discuss with you," she said. "If you could give me a call at your convenience, I'd appreciate it." With that, she recited her number and hung up.

Like almost everyone else in America, he was probably busy with Fourth of July activities. Figuring she'd hear from him on Monday, she headed over to the office.

But it was only a few hours later that he called her back.

16

Luke hadn't checked his phone when he left the gym so it wasn't until he was getting out of his car to go into Outback for a steak that he realized he'd missed a call— from Ava Bixby. Intrigued, and just a little nervous about what she might want, he listened to her voice mail.

She needed to talk to him. But she gave him no clue as to why. He hoped his parents hadn't called her.

He punched in her number and she answered on the third ring. "Hello?"

"Ava?"

There was a slight hesitation. "Yes?"

"It's Luke."

"Captain Trussell."

He would've chuckled at her starchy response, except that he wasn't sure what it signified. "That would be my formal form of address, yes."

"Thank you for calling."

As he gazed across the lot toward the busy street fronting the restaurant, waves of heat rose from the asphalt to mix with smoke from all the forest fires in the state. The air quality was always at its worst in the late afternoon, especially on days like today when the temperature rose to triple digits. "You haven't changed your mind and decided to help Kalyna put me behind bars, have you?" he asked bluntly.

"No."

Good news. His shirt was already sticking to his back, so he got out of his BMW and started toward the restaurant entrance. "So...what did you need to talk to me about?"

He was expecting to hear that his parents had made her an offer, but that wasn't it. "I'm going to give you copies of what I've collected on your case so far."

He stopped walking. "Really?"

"Yes. It's not a huge amount, but some of the information could prove useful. At the very least, it'll save you some money because it's work McCreedy and his investigators won't have to duplicate. It might even highlight the best places to focus your resources as you go forward."

She could've told him this last night, but hadn't. "I don't have my parents to thank for this, do I?"

"Your parents?"

Apparently not. "Never mind. I appreciate your help. Should I pick up the file?"

"That might be simplest. Or I could save you the drive and ship it to either you or McCreedy."

"No, that's okay." If she had anything useful, he wanted it right away. But it was nearly five o'clock on the Fourth of July. Not exactly the optimum time for a business appointment. "Is it too late to meet up tonight?"

"Don't you have other plans for the evening?"

His only plans were to have dinner alone. He had friends who were at the lake playing beach volleyball and riding Jet Skis; they'd invited him but he'd begged off. The last thing he wanted was to face a crowd. "Being accused of rape has a way of dampening your desire to take part in group activities. My situation isn't something I want to explain a dozen times, if you know what I mean."

"I understand. Sure, you can come by. I'm at the office."

"It'll take me an hour, without traffic."

"I'll wait."

Was he inconveniencing her? "This won't make you late for your own celebration, will it? I mean, I could stop by on Monday if—"

"No, today's fine."

He noticed that she didn't mention whether or not she was under time constraints. "Okay. I'll see you soon." He searched for a way he could thank her or repay her for her help. "Have you had dinner? Can I bring you anything? No iced mocha, of course. But maybe some take-out wouldn't be considered too manipulative?"

"You don't owe me dinner," she said. "But..."

"What?" Was she already having second thoughts?

"There's no need to have you drive all the way into Sacramento. I live in the delta, which is closer."

"Would you rather meet there?"

"We might as well. I was thinking of heading home, anyway. Are you familiar with the area?"

"Not at all, but I've got GPS."

"It won't help with this because I can't give you an exact address. But there's a fish-and-tackle shop in Penrington that shouldn't be too hard to find."

"Penrington?"

"It's a town of only three."

"You mean three hundred?"

"No, I mean, three *people*," she said with a laugh. "But it'll be easier to locate than my houseboat, so I'll meet you there."

"You rented a houseboat for the Fourth?"

"No, that's where I live."

"Every day?"

"Every day."

"With just the three people in Penrington for company."

"No. I've met some friends who usually dock where I do."

"How many friends?"

"Two other houseboats."

Somehow he wouldn't have imagined her in such an environment. Her manner suggested an efficient downtown condo. "Sounds interesting."

"I like it. Are you ready for directions?"

"I'm ready." He returned to the car and jotted down what she told him on an envelope he dug out of the jockey box. "I think I can find that," he said.

"Good. See you in about thirty minutes."

"I'll be there." Luke had skipped lunch because he was working out. He was ravenous. But he wasn't about to risk missing this opportunity. With a parting glance at his favorite restaurant, he got back in his car and peeled out of the lot.

Ava was wearing a sundress and a pair of sandals. At first, she looked too young to be the woman he'd met last night. But as Luke drew closer, he recognized her dramatic haircut and willowy body. He didn't see a car—any car—so he guessed she lived within walking distance.

The bait shop was closed. More of a shack than an actual store, it had peeling white paint and a padlock on the door, which was too warped to shut completely. A homemade sign out front bore the picture of a crudely drawn night crawler. Another sign in the window read Back at... A clock indicated 6:00 p.m. Luke wondered if it was merely a remnant from summers past. The place felt as if it had been shut up for some time.

Ava stood next to a rusty gas pump with a third sign— Out of Order. She stepped forward when he drove up, and he immediately saw the envelope in her hands. There it was. Copies of what was in his file, as promised.

Letting his engine idle, he lowered his window. "Nice place," he said, taking in the weeds that grew in clumps around the building and the shiny bits of colored glass that littered the broken asphalt.

She seemed surprised by his words. "You don't like it?"

"It's fine, I guess. Just an unlikely place for a single woman to live."

"How do you know I'm single?"

"You told me you've never been deeply in love. I'm hoping that would keep you from getting married." And she wasn't wearing a ring, but he didn't mention that, didn't want her to think he'd checked.

"Oh, right. I forgot we discussed that."

And she obviously didn't want to talk about it now. "What brought you out here?" he asked.

"It's got character."

He bent forward to take another look around. "I'd have to agree with you there."

"You should see the old guy who owns this place. He's as decrepit as his shop but really nice."

"He's not around?"

"Not this month. He's traveling from state to state, visiting family."

"And the other two people who live in Penrington? What do they do for a living?"

"They're a married couple, both of them environmental scientists. They're currently studying how ammonia from Sacramento waste can hurt the delicate ecosystem."

"Where do they live?"

"You can't see their house from here. They're not at home. They told me they were going into town for dinner and fireworks."

He realized his radio was playing rather loudly and turned down the volume. "Why didn't you stay in town so you could see the show?"

"I needed to give you this." She handed him the envelope, and he put it on his passenger seat.

"We could've met in Sacramento."

"I didn't plan to see the show, anyway." She backed up and tossed him a quick smile. "Good luck!"

He stayed where he was, trying to think of a way to make the offer he'd discussed with his mother.

"Is there anything else?" she asked when he didn't drive off.

He slung his arm out the window as he studied her. "Why are you helping me?"

"Because I believe you're innocent."

"You thought I was innocent last night, too. You could've had me follow you to the office and given me a copy of the file then."

She squinted into the distance, then approached the car. "I talked to Kalyna after I left you."

"And?"

"And I think you're right. She's crazy."

"What did she say?"

"You mean, besides calling me an evil bitch and telling me she hopes I'll burn in hell?"

Apparently, Ava had caught a glimpse of the Kalyna he knew. "Welcome to the dark side."

"No kidding. She changed so fast I thought she was possessed."

He chuckled. "It only comes out when she doesn't get what she wants."

"There's something missing in her. I'm afraid she might be dangerous."

"Physically?"

Ava's expression grew contemplative. "You never know. We've seen that she's vengeful."

"Those couples you mentioned, who dock near you?"

"What about them?"

"They're there now, right?"

"Actually, they're on a fishing trip. Why?"

Because if Ava got into trouble there'd be no one to help her. Maybe it came from his military training, but Luke immediately recognized her vulnerability. "Does Kalyna know where you live?"

"No."

"That's good."

"I wasn't thinking of me," Ava said.

"She's not going to hurt *me*," he responded. The very idea seemed preposterous. But then he hadn't expected Kalyna to do any of the things she'd already done.

"You can't protect yourself against some weapons." Forming her fingers into the shape of a gun, she pulled the imaginary trigger. "And I'm guessing she knows where *you* live—or she can find out."

"At this point, I think *I'm* more tempted to shoot *her*," he admitted. "She's already got me by the b—er, throat. What more could she want from me?"

Ava's smile was mocking. "Are you kidding? She's never touched a man who's bigger and thicker than you are."

She was teasing him, rubbing his nose in his bad behavior. Luke's neck and ears burned, but he grinned. "I might've been exaggerating."

"A lot or a little?"

She was pressing her advantage, so he put her in her

place. "Are you hinting that you'd like to see for your-self?"

When her eyes widened, he knew he'd turned the tables on her, as he'd planned. But the spark that'd flashed between them last night suddenly flared up again, surprising him. The instant tightening in his groin re-minded him how quickly a man could bounce back from a bad experience like Kalyna.

But *Ava?* Was he out of his mind? She wasn't his type at all. Maybe she was cuter than he'd first thought. She looked a lot more feminine in this dress than that non-descript suit she'd been wearing before. But she was in-dependent to a fault, fussy, bossy and stubborn. And that was just what he'd learned about her so far.

Fortunately, she laughed and raised her hands in the classic halt motion, which eased the tension. "Okay, I asked for that," she said. "But I think we should stop there. Have a nice life, Luke Trussell. And watch your back. You never know what Kalyna might do next."

That was goodbye. Telling himself to get the hell out of there, he waved and gave the car some gas. But he felt sure that Ava's personal weaknesses would be profes-sional strengths. She knew Kalyna and had lost faith in her. She could make a big difference to his case. And he'd never have a better opportunity to enlist her help.

At the edge of the lot, he threw the car into Reverse.

When she heard the whine of the engine, she waited, letting him drive up beside her.

"This has absolutely *no* reference to our earlier con-versation, so please don't get the wrong idea, but is there any chance you'll have dinner with me?" he asked.

She didn't take even a second to consider it. "No, thanks."

Slightly offended that his invitation hadn't tempted

her at all, he glanced pointedly around. "You don't seem to have any better offers. Not for tonight, anyway."

"I don't need any. I'm fine as I am."

"Doing what?"

She began to walk away, but he kept pace with her. "I brought some work home with me."

"You're going to work while everyone else is out watching fireworks? Where's your patriotism?"

"Were *you* planning to do any flag-waving tonight?" she countered.

"My life's a bit upside down right now. Yours, on the other hand, is business as usual."

"People are depending on me."

Here was proof of those professional strengths, he thought.

They reached some gravel along the bank of a canal, and he raised his voice to speak above the crunch of his tires. "It doesn't mean you'll be letting anyone down if you take time out to have dinner, Ava. You have to eat."

She raked her fingers through her hair, which immediately fell back into place, brushing her chin as she walked. "That's not what I'm worried about."

"Then what *are* you worried about?"

She came to an abrupt halt. "Let's just say I prefer a more direct approach. You want me to go to dinner with you for a reason. What is it?"

"I have to have an ulterior motive?"

"You made it very clear yesterday that you're not attracted to me, so I know you're not asking me out."

Embarrassed yet again by his bad behavior, he flinched and stopped trying to charm her. "I was...frustrated when I made that statement."

She resumed walking. "That's what makes it so refreshingly honest."

It wasn't *exactly* honest. In his right mind, he wasn't attracted to Ava. But there were those odd moments when she got to him. Why, he couldn't say. "Can't we forget about that and all the other stupid things I've said and start over?"

"No problem. But the answer's still no."

"You don't even know what I was going to ask."

"Yes, I do. I'm not switching sides."

He steered around a clump of trees as he followed her down a dirt road that branched off the gravel one. "Why?"

"It doesn't seem ethical."

"How can it be unethical if you believe I'm innocent?" He managed to stay even with her despite several deep ruts.

"I don't *know* that you're innocent."

The road began to narrow. He had to maneuver the car among various obstacles, but she didn't alter her course. "You think I raped Kalyna?" he called out to her.

She stared straight ahead. "All I'm saying is that I wasn't there. I can't be one hundred percent certain either way."

"You saw what she's like."

"Doesn't matter."

A large pothole forced him to slow down but he accelerated the second he got around it. "It should!"

"The charity's funds are reserved for cases of dire need."

He snapped off the radio. "My need feels pretty dire to me."

"I'm talking life and death." She paused to remove a small rock from her sandal, which drew his attention to her feet. They were slender, just like the rest of her—but unlike her unvarnished, neatly trimmed fingernails her toenails were painted bright pink and there was a line of tiny diamonds sparkling across each big toe.

Somehow that made him wonder if Ava wasn't quite as she appeared to be. Was she wearing frilly, sexy or practical panties beneath that dress?

Why he'd even ask himself such a question, he had no idea. Except that he was a man. "You just said you thought Kalyna might be dangerous. You told me to watch my back," he reminded her.

The road was about to end. If she passed through the wooden gate, onto a walking path, their conversation would end with it because he couldn't drive down there, and he wasn't about to get out of his car to follow her.

"She hasn't made any threats, has she?" she asked.

"She said I'd come crawling to her on my hands and knees before this was over. Does that count?"

Stopping again, Ava bent to adjust the strap on her sandal. She held her dress off the ground as she did so, and Luke caught himself hoping she'd raise it a little higher. She had nice legs—lean but shapely. "Robbing you of your pride isn't fatal," she said.

"For someone as conceited as I am, it could be."

She shot him an amused look. "I think you're more resilient than you realize."

"What if I pay you?"

"McCreedy will cost you enough as it is."

"Don't you ever work for hire?"

"I haven't yet, but my partners sometimes do. If we need the money badly enough."

"Could be time for you to follow their lead."

"No, thanks."

Maybe he needed to sweeten the pot. Inching forward the last few feet, he yelled out to her as she opened the gate. "Okay, what if I donated a large sum of money instead?" It was essentially the same thing, but if her switching sides made as big an impact as he thought it could, she'd net a lot more.

The latch of the gate clanged as it swung shut before she passed through. "How large?" she asked, turning to face him.

He scrambled for a figure. "Ten thousand?" Could he even afford that much? His parents had offered to help, but he didn't really want to go to them, and his defense could cost him as much as seventy or eighty thousand. Definitely more than the fifty thousand dollars he had in savings. But at least this ten thousand would be tax deductible—unlike the money he'd given McCreedy. That made it more attractive than hiring her.

"A significant amount," she breathed.

So significant he'd probably have to sell his car, but he didn't complain. Saving his ass came before saving his car. "Can we discuss it over dinner?"

She didn't respond right away, but she was obviously thinking about it.

"Ava?" he prompted.

"What?" Her answer was sullen enough to tell him he'd won.

"I'm starving." He reached across the seat and opened the passenger door. "Get in."

17

"Where are you from originally?" Luke asked.

Ava set down her wineglass. She hadn't officially agreed to work with him yet, but she knew she would before the evening was over and so did he. No way could she could pass up a ten-thousand-dollar donation. Skye and Sheridan would kill her if she did. It was a constant struggle to raise the money they needed to keep their doors open. "I was born and raised in Sacramento," she said. Like everything else about her, that wasn't very exciting.

"Do you have any siblings?"

"No. Well, a half brother, thanks to my father. My parents' marriage didn't last long enough to create baby number two." They'd already placed their order, but the food seemed to be taking forever. Although a lengthy wait was typical in a steak place, Ava wasn't too thrilled about being sequestered in a booth at the back of the restaurant with this man. Sitting there, she had nothing better to do than admire all the details that came together to make him so handsome.

He swallowed some wine. "What does your father do?"

Great. They were going to continue talking about her background. This wasn't a topic Ava generally enjoyed, but it seemed prudent to keep her mind occupied. Otherwise, she might be tempted to let her gaze wander over Luke's lips, the muscles in his arms, his eyes, which were the nicest color she'd ever seen. And then there were the long lashes that framed those eyes....

It had definitely been too long since she'd been with a man. She could hardly remember what it felt like. But her imagination was more than ready to step into the gap. And the wine didn't help. She'd eaten her salad and a sourdough roll, but the alcohol still seemed to be going straight to her head. "He's a high-school football coach," she said.

"So he remarried after the divorce?"

"Three times so far."

"Four marriages in total? You're kidding."

"Women can't resist him." She figured Luke could probably relate. Kalyna was a case in point. "The first time, he married the substitute teacher with whom he'd been cheating on my mother, and they had one kid, Neal, who's now a card dealer living in Las Vegas."

Luke added more olive oil and balsamic vinegar to the plate they'd used to dip their bread and pushed the basket of rolls toward her. "Do you have any contact with Neal?"

"No. He wants nothing to do with my father or anyone connected to him." She glanced toward the kitchen, hoping to see the waitress carrying out their plates so they could eat and head home, but...no luck. "He and his mother are pretty bitter about the way that marriage ended."

"Your dad cheated on her, too?"

"This time with the mother of one of his students."

Luke made a face. "*Nice.* Any kids with wife number three?"

"No. They were married very briefly, but only because they were still seeing each other after the divorce and she turned out to be pregnant. When a paternity test proved the baby was her ex-husband's, they split."

"Messy. How'd he get to wife number four?"

She helped herself to another roll and dipped part of it in the oil. She didn't want any more, but she was feeling so jittery… "That's even worse. Are you sure you want to hear the rest?" she said with a laugh, glancing toward the kitchen again. *Please, bring the damn food.* She was about to say she needed to use the ladies' room so she could escape for a few minutes, but he said he could handle anything, which left her in the middle of their conversation.

With a shrug, she ate the bread. "I guess we've got time. They're really slow in the kitchen tonight, don't you think?"

He acted surprised. "Not really. We just ordered ten minutes ago."

Somehow it seemed longer. "Oh. Well, after wife number three, my father got involved with a former female student. Or maybe he was having an affair with her *before* the split. With his track record, who knows?"

"How long did that one last?"

"He's still with her. It's been five years."

"Any more children?"

"No. Fortunately, somewhere in between wife three and wife four, he got himself fixed." Or she could've had a whole horde of half siblings. One who wouldn't speak to her was bad enough.

"Probably a good thing," he said.

"Absolutely a good thing." Although, the last she'd heard, her father's latest wife was coaxing him to have his vasectomy reversed….

Luke shifted in his seat. "How much longer do you give it?"

"Give what?" The shape of the dog tags that hung beneath his T-shirt, between his pectoral muscles, had distracted her.

"This latest marriage."

She dragged her eyes away from the appealing contours of his chest. "Hard to say. I know he's not cheating this time, so that should help."

Long, tapered fingers with wide, blunt-cut nails cradled his wineglass. "How do you know he's finally broken the pattern?"

"Because he doesn't have any choice. Carly—that's her name—watches him like a hawk. And he's too afraid of losing her to try anything. He won't even see me because it upsets her to have to share him."

Why she'd added that, Ava didn't know. She hadn't meant to get so personal. Maybe it was the wine, or the way she was scraping for conversation....

Fortunately, Luke didn't pounce on it, and for that she was grateful. "How old is she?"

"Twenty-six."

He blinked several times. "Did you say *forty*-six?"

Ava frowned. "No."

"That's two years younger than me!" he said with obvious distaste.

And Luke was three years younger than *her.* "They look ridiculous together," she admitted. "Especially now that Carly's having him dye his hair blond and is making him go to the tanning salon."

"You must hate watching your father turn into a caricature."

"I do. No one wants to see her father lose his dignity, but...I'm not sure mine ever really had any."

"It can't be easy to keep the attention of a twenty-six-year-old when you're...what? Fiftysomething?"

That was a practical consideration she figured a woman would be more prone to recognize than a man. "Fifty-nine. He's on the desperate side, and it's beginning to show."

Luke gave a low whistle. "He must've been something in his prime."

He was. Something like Luke. Ava's mother had once told her there'd never been another man who'd made her heart flutter the way Chuck did with just a smile. And this was years after their divorce, after Zelinda had remarried the loser who'd become Ava's stepfather. "Some men have a way with women, I guess. And some women are too stupid to avoid them."

Luke studied her for a moment. "Not you, though. You'd never let that happen."

"Never," she said.

He offered her more bread, but she refused. "Is Carly attractive?" he asked.

Ava tried to be objective with her answer. "She's not bad."

"So you like her."

"No. I tried, at first. But it's impossible. She hates the fact that I even exist. I'm not welcome at their place and can't join them for holidays. My dad has hell to pay if he so much as calls me." More personal stuff she hadn't meant to divulge. Somehow it kept seeping out, as if she were some kind of leaky container. But Luke was as easy to talk to as he was to look at. She hadn't expected that.

He shook his head. "That's not fair."

She'd thought the same thing many times. But she couldn't figure out how to change it. "There's nothing I can do if my father won't take a stand." Uncomfortable with the pain that statement inadvertently revealed, she deflected Luke's sympathy before he could extend it. "But I'm sure it'll all work out in the end."

He took another piece of bread. "Now I get it."

"Get what?"

"You."

She rolled her eyes. "I'm not interested in your psychoanalysis, but thanks, anyway."

Fortunately, the waitress interrupted with their food just then, and he didn't bring it up again. Once they were alone, he said, "What about your mother?"

There was no way Ava was going to talk about her mother. She could make fun of her father's stupid choices and complain about her nemesis—the dreaded stepmother who was younger than she was. Zelinda was a different story entirely. Ava had always known better than to count on her father. But what her mother had done had come as a complete surprise—and been a leveling blow.

She waved away the curl of steam ascending from her plate. "Looks good."

"Was that a dodge?"

"Just my way of saying, 'Enough about me—it's your turn.'"

He was cutting his steak. "What do you want to know?"

"Where do you come from?"

"I was born in San Antonio. Although he's retired now, my father was in the military, so I went to more than ten different schools in a number of states."

She took a bite of her sweet potato and had to admit he'd been right to recommend it. "Never overseas?"

"Never overseas."

"Have you ever been to war?"

"Not yet, but it's always a possibility."

"You wouldn't mind?"

"I knew what I was signing up for when I joined."

He motioned to her plate with his fork. "How do you like it?"

"With butter, brown sugar and pecans on top, I can't imagine it's very healthy, but—"

He cocked an eyebrow at her. "Let go for one night, Ava."

"Let go?" she echoed.

"Just enjoy yourself."

She opened her mouth to tell him she was perfectly relaxed, but why bother? He knew she was too serious, too driven. Most people recognized that shortly after meeting her. She was too much of a lot of things. But she was pretty sure she couldn't be too *cautious* around him. "I'll try."

"That's the idea."

"How'd you handle all the moving?" she asked.

"It wasn't that bad. But I think it's easier on boys. The second you join a sports team, you're part of a group and you have instant friends."

"You're lucky you were always good enough to make the team."

"I suppose."

"Is that desire to belong to a team the reason you joined the air force?"

"Trying a little psychoanalysis yourself?"

"Perhaps. How'd I do?"

"Not too well. I joined the air force because I've always wanted to fly."

Somehow she'd already finished her entire sweet potato—giant slab of butter and all. She switched to her meat, a filet that nearly melted in her mouth. "Are you glad you did it?"

"Definitely."

"I'd love to see what it's like up there, in a jet-fighter," she said.

"It's the most incredible experience in the world."

"Is it frightening, too?"

"It can be. It's definitely an adrenaline rush. You feel like you're traveling at the speed of light. Flying requires absolute trust in yourself, your plane, your commanding officer and flight crew. It's more of an act of faith than anything I've ever done."

She wanted him to go on, but he didn't. He smiled and lowered his voice. "You've got really pretty eyes."

Ava hadn't expected the compliment. Straightening, she swallowed. "Thank you."

"How's your steak?" he asked.

"Perfect."

"Would you like another glass of wine?"

She shouldn't. She was beginning to relax, to feel warm and comfortable and even a little sleepy, but she said *yes,* anyway. "Sure."

"I'll flag down the waitress when she comes by."

"What about siblings?" she asked. "Are you an only child or…"

"I have one younger sister. She'll be a senior in high school."

"Are you close?"

"As close as we can be, considering the age difference."

"Has all the moving been more difficult on her than it was on you?"

"Yeah, she's had a few problems with it. Fortunately, my folks have been settled in one spot for a while now."

The waitress came to check on them, and Luke ordered her another glass of wine. "Aren't you going to have one?" she asked.

"No, I'm okay."

When she heard that, she almost canceled her own, but

the waitress had already left, and she didn't want to have to hunt her down. Besides, she didn't have to drive, and he did. It made sense. "Was your baby sister a surprise?"

"More like a much-wanted blessing," he said. "My parents had been trying to get pregnant for years, but couldn't manage to conceive. Then, the month after they stopped taking fertility drugs—*wham.*"

"So a surprise *and* a blessing."

"Definitely."

Ava took a swallow of water. "Where's your family now?"

"In San Diego."

"Do they know about…what you've been going through?"

He was nearly finished with his own steak. "Yeah, I told them."

The waitress arrived with her wine, and Ava thanked her. "How did they respond?" she asked when the woman was gone.

"They're supportive. I have great parents."

"You're lucky," she said, and she meant it. But she would've expected nothing less. This man had it all.

"How did you come to be living on a houseboat?" he asked.

She tasted her steamed vegetables and found them bland after all the other flavors. "It belongs to my father. Carly doesn't like to fish, and since she won't let him go anywhere without her, he doesn't have much use for it right now. I suggested he sell it, but I think he realizes this marriage might not make it, either, and then he'll want it back."

"He's planning for failure?"

She rested her knife on the edge of her plate. "Just keeping his track record in mind."

"I see." He dipped some more bread in the oil-and-balsamic mixture. "Meanwhile, you take care of the boat for him."

"Yes, but I benefit from the arrangement, too. As you might've guessed, the work I do doesn't pay a lot, so it helps to have free rent. I consider it his contribution to the cause."

"Living alone and in such a remote location doesn't bother you?"

"I'm not alone all that often."

"Right. You've got those two couples who dock their boats near yours some of the time."

"Most of the time."

The waitress came by, carrying a tempting array of sweets. She told them to save room for dessert. Luke promised her they would, then when she moved on, he said, "How close is your boat to that gas station?"

"About a mile."

He wiped his mouth with his napkin. "You walked a *mile* to meet me?"

"The delta's a maze. You never would've found it, otherwise."

He offered her another piece of bread, but she declined. "Where are all the rest?"

"Rest of what?"

"Houseboats. I didn't see a single one after I turned off Highway 12."

"Various places."

"Then why not dock yours with some of them until your friends return?"

"I don't mind being alone occasionally. I get to see more wildlife that way."

"Sounds romantic," he said.

"It *is* romantic. You should watch the sun come up through my bedroom window." She'd said it impulsively and, thanks to the wine, probably a little too passionately. Sunrise really was her favorite part of living in the delta and on the water. But her words sounded like an invitation. He raised his head and stopped chewing.

"Sorry, that came out wrong," she said with an awkward laugh and focused on cutting another bite of her steak.

"You didn't mean it in a personal way."

"No, of course not."

"Right," he said. "I understood that." But she got the feeling he'd wondered, just for a second—that the image of them together had zipped through his brain—and it reminded her why she shouldn't take his case. If she wasn't careful, she'd wind up in bed with this man. Not only did that break the charity's cardinal rule about not getting involved with clients, it threatened Ava on a whole new level. Because, for the first time in her life, she'd met someone capable of breaking her heart, and she knew it.

18

Ava wasn't going to take Luke's case. She'd made the decision. Now she just needed to figure out how to tell him. Maybe she could ask Skye or Sheridan to work with him instead. That would be a reasonable compromise, wouldn't it?

But she knew part of the reason he'd offered such a large donation was because she'd already shown him how single-minded she could be. Her job was her life. Skye and Sheridan were equally devoted, but these days they split their time between work and home. They had husbands, families. Last week Sheridan had announced that she was pregnant, so she wouldn't be putting in as many hours as she was now. Skye and Sheridan had all the cases they could handle, anyway. Hadn't they, just this morning, discussed the fact that they needed help?

They'd chosen Jane to be that help, but Ava couldn't turn Luke's case over to Jane.

"What are you thinking?" Luke asked. Although they'd talked a lot during dessert, mostly about what he'd find in his file, they'd ridden in silence since getting back in the car.

"Nothing," she said, but she remembered Luke walking her out of the restaurant with his hand lightly touching her back, the envious glance she'd received from the waitress, the way he'd opened her car door and handed her the leftover steak she'd had the waitress box up. He did it all so smoothly, so naturally, as if he'd do it for anyone. And he probably would. Which was what made it hard to object. She'd tried to pay for her own dinner, but the waitress listened only to Luke and wouldn't take her money. Ava had also tried to sidestep his hand at her back and open her door, but he kept her so busy talking that before she knew it she was letting him put her in his car as if this had been a date.

It wasn't a date. It was a business meal, she told herself. But it sure felt good to let a man take charge for once. Especially a man this capable. Of course, it would be even more enjoyable if she wasn't so preoccupied with how to get him out of her life.

"You're not going home to work, are you?" he asked.

"No, I'm too tired." They'd eaten so much she was sure she wouldn't be hungry for a week. But it had tasted better than her usual fare. Because she spent so much of her time immersed in her cases, she rarely cooked. She usually settled for an energy bar or a sandwich.

Not long after they'd left the restaurant, he noticed some fireworks in the sky and suggested they pull off the main thoroughfare to watch. He'd teased her that she could afford the time if she wasn't going to work, and she was feeling too good to resist the suggestion.

Careful not to stand too close to him, she leaned against his car, just as he was doing, while the finale of some Independence Day show exploded overhead. The spectacular display capped an enjoyable evening.

Despite her initial reluctance, Ava felt so satisfied and mellow that she had difficulty summoning the courage to tell Luke she didn't want to take him on as a client. But she was about to broach the subject when he noticed the goose bumps on her arms and insisted she put on a sweatshirt he took from his gym bag.

As she pulled it on over her head, she was enveloped in soft fleece that smelled exactly like him. And when he rolled the sleeves past her hands, she finally gave up on the idea of backing out. She didn't relish the thought of dealing with McCreedy—or even being perceived to be on the same side—but for ten thousand dollars she could make it work. In any event, she couldn't refuse Luke. Not when it came to taking his case. And, judging by the flutter in her stomach as his fingertips brushed her wrists, maybe not if it came to other, more personal requests.

Apparently, she was as much of a fool as her mother, her father's other wives and the millions of women who'd ever let a handsome man convince them to forgo their better judgment.

Good thing Luke wasn't attracted to her. If her feelings weren't reciprocated, she didn't have to worry about the situation getting too far out of control, did she?

Ava climbed out of Luke's car almost before he could bring it to a complete stop. "Thanks for dinner," she said. "I'll be in touch on Monday. I can't stand your attorney, so you'll have to—"

"Whoa!" he interrupted. "What don't you like about McCreedy?"

"I came up against him on a Murder One case a year ago and he tried everything in the book to get his guy off. When that didn't fly, he convinced his scumbag defendant to cop a plea, which got them a very favorable deal. So basically, because of McCreedy, a cold-blooded killer will soon be out on the streets, where he'll probably hurt other innocent people, like my client, who now has to live in fear."

"I can see where the two of you could be at odds," he conceded.

"I'm not used to working for the defense. So you'll need to be the go-between. I don't want anything to do with McCreedy or his investigators. Make sure he understands that he's not to contact me."

"Okay." Luke gazed at the large, mountainous shape at the end of a rickety pier. Ava's houseboat looked old, but it was hard to tell much about it beyond that. There wasn't a single light on. They'd gone to dinner before dark, and she hadn't planned to stay out so late.

"We'll start by trying to document the self-abuse Kalyna's mother told me about," she said. "If we can prove she injured herself in the past, it'll take away the whole timing issue. We won't need to look for someone who could've come in after you left. A half hour is long enough for her to give herself a few bumps and bruises."

He had trouble imagining Kalyna beating herself up, but Ava had assured him there were plenty of documented cases of people engaging in such behavior. And when he thought about it, he realized it wasn't so different from cutting, which had become a problem among teens in recent years. "Good idea."

"Are you sure you can find your way out of here?" she asked.

"I think so."

"Drive safely."

She shut the door and began to walk away, but he lowered the window. "You really won't let me walk you to the door?"

"There's no need," she called over her shoulder.

"You're all alone in the middle of nowhere." He was pointing out the obvious, of course, but at this time of night he was reluctant to leave a woman in such a remote location, especially without seeing that she got in safely. Maybe it was because he functioned, for the most part, in a protected environment, but this seemed…risky. Anyone could break into her boat, go aboard and rob her, rape her, kill her, and there wouldn't be a soul to come to her aid. Even the bait-and-tackle guy was away.

"This is my home. I'll be fine," she said with a laugh.

"Where do the scientists live?"

"A mile from the bait shop, on the other side."

He saw no buildings and no lights, just the glow of a half-moon grinning eerily overhead. "I don't have to go inside. I can take a peek through the door."

She pointed in the direction from which they'd come. "The highway's that way."

Damn, she was stubborn. Ava Bixby believed she could cope with anything.

Luke thought she should know better. Considering her job, she must have heard some real horror stories. He could understand why she might refuse to live behind barricades and locks, but this was right out in the open. Sure, it wasn't easy to find, and there weren't many other people around—none at the moment, as far as he could tell. But if the wrong man stumbled across her when her friends were gone…

He didn't leave. He sat with his engine idling so she'd at least have the benefit of his headlights.

Her footsteps echoed on the wooden planks of the wharf, fading as she moved away from him. Then she stepped onto the boat and was lost in the murky shadows.

The cicadas seemed to grow quiet as the wind picked up. Luke could almost hear the water lapping against her boat. It was a perfect night, and there'd probably be a glorious sunrise. *You should see the sun come up through my bedroom window,* she'd said. Somehow, that sounded more appealing than he would've expected. Maybe Ava wasn't beautiful in the classic sense, but she had… something. Exactly what that quality was he couldn't say because she was about the prickliest woman he'd ever met.

A light went on. She was in. Putting the transmission in Reverse, he wheeled around and headed home. But he'd barely reached Highway 12 when his phone rang. He thought maybe Ava was calling him with some detail she'd forgotten to mention, but when he checked caller ID, he knew it wasn't her.

Ava rested her head against the inside of the door. Dinner was over; Luke was gone. Thank goodness. Now she could put him out of her mind and get on with her regular life, at least until Monday when she'd have to delve into his case again. Then he'd be front and center for a while. But she'd make quick work of it. Prove Kalyna's injuries were self-inflicted and use that to convince the prosecutor to drop the case. Easy. She'd be a hero. Luke would have his life back. And McCreedy would lose out on a lucrative fee. Then she wouldn't have to face any more of Luke's devastating smiles. And maybe after a few months she'd forget him altogether.

Suddenly she realized that in her haste to get out of the car, she'd walked away wearing his sweatshirt. He hadn't said anything, hadn't even tried to get it back, which was nice of him. But she didn't particularly want to think of him as "nice." Hard enough to battle "drop-dead gorgeous" and "sexy as hell."

Turning toward the mirror in her entryway, she gazed at herself. AIR FORCE was emblazoned across her chest in big block letters. She was infatuated with a rock-hard military guy. Who would've guessed?

She told herself to take off the sweatshirt and put it somewhere safe so she could return it to him. But as she pulled it off, she couldn't help pausing for a few seconds to breathe in the masculine scent that lingered.

At least now she knew she was normal. At least she hadn't grown old before her time as she'd feared. She had the same sexual appetites and desires as other women her age. It was worth meeting Luke just for that, wasn't it?

Or maybe not. Was it better not to crave—or to crave and not be satisfied?

"Luke?"

The sound of Kalyna's voice came through his Bluetooth and put Luke's teeth on edge. He'd never hated anyone in his life, but he was pretty sure he hated her.

"What do you want?" Ignoring his sudden tension, he thought of the sack in his trunk. He'd purchased a recorder this morning, but it wouldn't do any good to stop and get it because the store he'd got it from had been out of AA batteries. He'd planned to pick some up from another store, but he'd taken Ava to dinner instead, and now he had Kalyna on the phone again and no way to prove that she'd called or what she said.

Except for the possibility of a witness. Swerving around, he headed back to Ava's. Maybe he could get there before she went to bed and before Kalyna hung up....

"I have something to tell you, something important," she said.

He went right through an intersection that had a stop sign. Thank God for the absence of other traffic. "You're dropping the case?"

"That depends on how you react."

Perhaps Luke should've felt hope, but he didn't. He

could tell this wouldn't be good. Kalyna's voice was too smug, too excited. Dread sat in the pit of his stomach. "What is it?"

"I'm pregnant."

"No." Suddenly incapable of driving, he slammed on the brakes. "I don't believe it. You're lying."

"I'll send you proof if you want."

"Shit. Tell me it's not true. Tell me this is one of your vindictive games." No wonder she'd dared to call him back. She had an excuse, a very sympathetic excuse.

"Are you *that* unhappy?"

Now he knew she was insane. How could she even dream he might be anything other than completely distraught?

"Because…I'm thinking maybe we should make the most of it," she went on.

He sat in the middle of the road at a dead standstill. "Make the most of it?" He could barely get the words out. He knew that if he raised his voice, he'd be yelling his head off.

"Right. You know, for the sake of the baby."

He'd been so relieved to enlist Ava's help, so sure she'd be able to make a difference. But no one could save him from *this*. So what did he do now? His worst fears had been realized, what he'd been worried about ever since he'd learned of the semen they'd found at the hospital. Until this moment, he'd thought there might be a chance the condom had simply failed. But he knew better. Kalyna had sabotaged it. She'd tried to talk him out of using it in the first place, and when that didn't work, she took other steps. She'd obviously hoped for this outcome all along. "You told me you were on the pill."

"I must've forgotten to take it that day."

"One day probably wouldn't matter."

"It could. That means this is God's will. Every baby's a miracle, Luke. Every single one. Even a rape baby."

"I didn't rape you!" And this baby was no miracle. This was worse than any nightmare he could imagine. He'd rather be caught behind enemy lines, alone and un-armed with his plane in ashes, than facing a lifetime of dealing with Kalyna as his child's mother. "You did this to me on purpose!"

"That's not true."

"Yes, it is. You targeted me."

"How can you blame *me* for this?" she said. "You're the one who forced me, Luke."

"Quit saying that! It's a lie."

"I'm just trying to accept it. In my mind, a baby changes everything. A baby means we should set our conflicts aside and try to get along."

He wasn't sure it would do him any good to reach Ava. Kalyna wasn't telling the truth. What she was saying was crazier than hell. But he continued driving to the houseboat because he had no better plan. "That's impos-sible."

"No, it's not. You could love me if you'd give me a chance."

"Why me?" he asked. "There are other guys out there. You can't want to be with me that badly. You know me in a professional sense, but not personally. Not really."

"I know how you touch a woman when you want to bring her pleasure," she said, talking in a seductive whis-per. "I know the expression that comes over your face when—"

Eager to stop her before she could conjure up any more bad memories, he broke in. "Because we slept to-gether once. That's it. That's *not* knowing me!" He pushed the accelerator to the floor. It wasn't safe to go so fast on these dark narrow roads. He wasn't familiar with them and didn't want to hit a possum or a deer. But making sure Ava heard Kalyna suddenly became all-important. She had to understand how grasping and desperate the woman was.

Kalyna's voice grew more strident, almost challenging. "I know lots more than that. I know you always buy your gas at the Chevron station near the base. I know you buy a pack of sunflower seeds and an energy drink before you go to the park to play ball on Monday nights. I know you're a great catcher because I've watched you behind the plate."

Shocked by the details she'd been able to provide, he racked his brain, trying to remember when he might have mentioned the Chevrom station or sunflower seeds or baseball. "When? It's not as if I've ever invited you to the park, or even told you I was playing."

She didn't answer. She was still rattling off various facts about him. "I know you love egg burritos from Del Taco, that you carry sports equipment in the trunk of your car and that the girl in your wallet is your little sister. I know your parents live in San Diego and would be thrilled to hear they're going to be grandparents—"

"Stop it!" He couldn't listen anymore. He was about to be sick.

"I have your watch," she whispered. "It's in my panties."

He grimaced. "That doesn't excite me. Just…throw it away."

"You're not making this any easier."

Come on, come on. He had to get to Ava's. Gravel flew as he skidded around a turn and almost landed in a canal. "I'm trying to be clear about this. I'm not interested, Kalyna."

"You won't even give me a chance!"

She couldn't really expect him to—not after everything she'd done. She had to be after something else. "I'll pay you," he said.

This seemed to bring her up short. "For what?"

He could see the light of Ava's houseboat. He was almost there. "To get an abortion." He knew his parents would die at the thought. He wasn't sure how he felt about it himself, but he was desperate. He couldn't bring a child into the world under these circumstances, with this woman.

"An abortion?" she echoed. "You want me to get an abortion?" She broke into tears. "How can you ask me to *kill* our child on top of everything else you've done to me?"

It didn't even feel like a child, didn't feel real. "Okay." He was still reeling as he skidded to a stop at the end of Ava's pier. But now that they were talking about the baby, he didn't want to get out of the car. Ava couldn't solve this; this was something he'd have to solve himself. "You're right, I don't want that. I don't think I could live with that, but…I'll take the baby. I-I'll raise it myself." Yes, that was the only option that would work. "Just— just name your price. If I've got the money or I can borrow it, it's yours. All you have to do is admit I didn't rape you and hand the baby over to me once it's born."

She sniffed. "Will I be able to see you through the pregnancy?"

He couldn't stand the thought of her in his life. But if she'd admit he didn't rape her, it'd be worth it. Wouldn't it?

"Maybe."

"And after the baby comes?"

Again, he wanted to say no. But would that be fair to his child? To her? Did he have to worry about what would be fair to a person like that?

God, this was so far from anything he'd ever dreamed he'd have to face. "Er...maybe. Probably. I guess," he said, and stared out at Ava's houseboat as he awaited her response. This was a good offer. There wasn't any more he could do. She had to accept it, didn't she?

"So we could make something positive out of all this negativity? There'd be a chance for you and me?"

They were back to *this?* "Come off it, Kalyna. There is no you and me. There never has been."

Her tears grew into full-fledged sobs. "You're going to prison if it's the last thing I do!" she screamed, and the line went dead.

Luke was shaking when he turned off his phone. He'd never felt such rage, especially against a woman. How did she know so much about him? *I know you love egg burritos from Del Taco. I know you always buy gas at the Chevron station near the base. I know you're a great catcher because I've watched you behind the plate.*

She'd been following him. That pretty much constituted the definition of stalking, didn't it? How was that for a switch? A female stalker. He'd never thought it could happen, never once glanced over his shoulder. He'd "bumped" into Kalyna often enough that he should've wondered, he supposed, but he hadn't thought twice about it. And here he'd been feeling guilty for having sex with her, had even been tempted to believe his father was right about *all* women taking sex more seriously than men, which meant he sort of deserved what he was getting for crossing that line. But she wasn't some tragic figure he'd mistakenly hurt. She was crazy.

And now she was even more determined to destroy him.

Pushing his door open, he got out. He wasn't sure

what Ava could do about what'd just happened, but he wanted to tell her about it while it was fresh in his mind.

A moment later, he was glad he'd acted on that impulse because Kalyna called back.

19

Ava was at her computer in the dining room, checking e-mail, when Luke appeared out of nowhere. She'd heard a soft knock above the music she had playing, but it was almost midnight, so she thought she must've imagined it. Then the door swung open before she could get out of her seat.

"What's going—" she started, but he pressed a finger to his lips, indicating silence, and beckoned her toward the phone he had pressed to his ear.

"Kalyna?" she mouthed.

He nodded.

She could understand why he'd come back, but that didn't make her any more comfortable about the fact that she wasn't wearing any clothes except his sweatshirt and a pair of thong panties she'd bought because they made her feel sexy. She almost didn't get up, but the intensity on Luke's face overruled more practical considerations, and she decided it didn't matter. The sweatshirt covered her to midthigh. And even if it hadn't, he'd probably seen a lot of women in their underwear.

When she met him in the middle of the room, he didn't seem to notice her state of undress. He was too engrossed in his conversation. Turning the phone slightly, he leaned close so she could hear.

"I'm just saying that's a big part of your case, and now it's gone. You caused your own injuries," he said.

Obviously, they were engaged in a heated argument.

"Who told you that?" came the response. The voice sounded a bit tinny and edged with panic, but it was Kalyna, all right.

"Someone I know spoke to your mother."

"Ava Bixby? You think I'm not aware of that?"

Luke pulled Ava onto the couch with him; sitting made it easier to share the phone. "Your own mother won't support you in this, Kalyna. That's the point I'm trying to make."

"My mother won't support me in anything. She never has. And I don't care. What I want to find out is how you know Ava."

"She called me."

"Have you met? Have you been together?

"What difference does that make?"

"It explains a lot. You've been seeing her, haven't you! That's why she dumped me."

Uneasy with that accusation, Ava bit her lip.

"She dumped you because she knows you're lying," he said. "She's working for me now."

"What?" Kalyna cried. "You're not a victim!"

"I'm more of a victim than you are."

"That's bullshit! She just wants to jump your bones, like every other woman you meet."

Ava wished she could deny it, if only to herself, but she felt a little conspicuous having donned Luke's sweatshirt—and nothing else.

"Go to Ogitani and tell her to drop the charges," he said.

"It's too late for that."

"Then why'd you call back?"

"Because I think it's only fair to warn you."

"About what?"

"Now that I'm carrying your baby, I won't take kindly to being cheated on. You'd better not be seeing anyone else."

Ava and Luke exchanged glances. The baby remark stunned Ava, but Luke didn't make any reference to it. "I can see anyone I want, and there's nothing you can do to stop me."

"Wanna bet?" she challenged.

"What are you talking about, Kalyna?"

"I'll tell you what I'm talking about. If you so much as *look* at another woman, *I'll kill her.*"

Luke didn't respond right away. If Ava had her guess, he was at a loss for words. "I hope you don't mean that literally," he finally said.

"Oh, I mean it. I know how to do it, too."

Ava had heard enough. If she'd had any remaining doubt that Kalyna had lied from the outset, it was gone now. "Kalyna, stop threatening people, or you'll end up in serious trouble yourself," she said into the phone.

This met with shocked silence. Then there was a click and Kalyna was gone.

Waiting for the adrenaline pumping through her system to abate, Ava shifted to the opposite end of the couch.

Luke rocked back and stared at her. "Do you think she was serious?"

A chilling sense of foreboding told Ava that she was. Kalyna was unconcerned about the pain she inflicted on others, a liar—probably pathological—completely narcissistic. "Maybe."

"But people get upset and say stuff like that all the time." He didn't want to believe it. He hadn't come up against anything like this before. Although he'd never gone to war, all the enemies he'd imagined facing were properly labeled and wearing a different uniform. Kalyna was part of his flight crew, a comrade, a woman.

"Are you seeing anyone right now?" she asked.

"No."

"Good thing."

He sank lower. "What kind of consequences would she face for making these threats?"

"Nothing serious or long-lasting enough to render her incapable of acting on them."

"You mean, there are no consequences until she actually hurts someone?"

"Nothing that's going to be effective if her mind's made up." That was the problem Ava ran into all the time, especially with domestic disputes. But the police couldn't start throwing people in jail on speculation.

He rubbed a hand over his face. "Damn, where's this going to end?"

"Do you think it's true about the baby?" she asked.

"At this point, I don't know." He set his cell phone on the coffee table. "They collected my semen at the hospital, so it's possible."

That had to scare the hell out of him. "What will you do if it's true?"

"Try to gain custody."

"There's an example of family planning."

"No kidding."

Ava got up and crossed to the kitchen. "Can I get you a drink?"

Blowing out a sigh, he dropped his head on the back of the couch and gazed up at the ceiling. "Right now I could drink an entire bottle."

Everyone was asleep.

Now that she'd finished packing, Kalyna took a last

look at her sister and felt a strange pang. She doubted she'd be coming home again. There wasn't anything for her here. Her parents were even less tolerant, less accepting, of her than they'd been before. She'd hardly exchanged a civil word with them since she'd arrived. But she'd never gotten along with them so she could've dealt with that. It was her sister who broke her heart. Tatiana was the only person Kalyna had ever loved and yet…she didn't know this version. These days Tatiana was so influenced by Dewayne and Norma she felt guilty about letting so much as a cussword slip out. And she said she was finally happy. What she meant was that she was happy with *them,* happier without Kalyna.

This was the worst betrayal Kalyna had suffered so far. Now she had no one. No one to act as an anchor when she felt as if she was about to spin out of control. No one to save her from the void that threatened to consume her in the long, dark hours when she couldn't sleep.

She was truly alone.

Never had the memory of that girl she and Mark had tortured ten years ago felt closer. Maybe this was that stranger's revenge. She'd never done anything to Kalyna. Kalyna had killed her just because she could, because Mark was egging her on. And she'd enjoyed the power it gave her. That was why she hadn't wanted to spend time with Mark anymore. He'd made her too much like him.

Kalyna checked her wallet for what was left of the money she'd earned at the bar last night. She'd spent most of it at the mall earlier today, flashing it around for Tatiana's sake. After borrowing the money for that pregnancy test, she'd told Tati that her paycheck had been electronically deposited, even though it wasn't due for a week. She hadn't wanted her sister to think she was absolutely broke. She spent too much time trying to convince her she'd done the right thing when she joined the air force, that she had plenty of whatever she needed. It wasn't as though she'd spent it all on herself. She'd bought Tati a cute pair of jeans to make up for screwing that Danny guy. Tatiana didn't know about it, but Kalyna had made it up to her, anyway. That was nice, wasn't it?

Of course. The money was well-spent. But now Kalyna wasn't sure how she'd get home.

Dropping to her hands and knees, she looked behind the trundle for Tati's purse. It wasn't on the desk or anywhere else she could see. Nor was it under the bed. But it had to be somewhere. Maybe up in the kitchen.

Careful not to make any noise, she opened the bedroom door and hefted her suitcase through the opening. She was about to climb the stairs when the door to the cooler caught her eye.

When she was little, she'd been frightened of that cooler. She didn't like the waxy skin, the blotchiness, the bloating that made it so obvious that the people in there weren't just sleeping. And yet…those corpses sort of appealed to her at the same time. They couldn't hurt her. They'd never be able to hurt her. They were powerless. It was the living she had to fear.

Crossing to the heavy door, she unlatched it and heard a small whoosh as the seal was broken. The cool air swirled around her, welcome as an embrace, while she eyed the four gurneys that awaited Tati's attention. One contained an old man, shriveled and already skeletal in appearance; another an old woman with liver spots; the third a middle-aged woman, and the fourth the woman's teenage boy. They'd both been killed in a drunk-driving accident. She'd never met any of them, and yet they were her friends, the only people who'd never rise up against her.

If Ava were here, she'd be as powerless as they were, Kalyna told herself. And, unlike that hitchhiker from years past, Ava deserved to die. Not only did she pretend to be something she wasn't, she thought she could stab Kalyna in the back and get away with it.

It was time to eliminate Ava as a threat.

The stairs creaked as she climbed them, but she couldn't hear any other sound, except the *rat-a-tat-tat* of the automatic sprinklers outside. Her father watered at night so the hot Arizona sun wouldn't scorch the lawn. A mortuary had to have curb appeal, he said. Perfectly manicured grass had a soothing effect.

Once she reached the kitchen, Kalyna moved more quickly. Leaving her suitcase by the door, she began searching for Tati's purse—and came across her mother's instead.

"Even better," she muttered, and carried it into the pantry, where she could safely turn on a light.

Bingo! Her mother had nearly five hundred dollars in her wallet. She'd also put her wedding ring in her coin purse. Norma couldn't wear it anymore. Her hands were too swollen from the water retention caused by some of the meds she took for depression.

It was a pretty ring with a large, square-cut diamond. Kalyna shoved the money in her pocket, then slid the ring onto her wedding finger to see how it looked. Not bad. It was much more attractive on a young hand—

A noise drew Kalyna's attention to the doorway. Her mother stood there, bedding lines scoring the cheek with the mole, her dark hair, normally ratted in a fixed "do," flat on one side.

"What do you think you're doing?" Norma wasn't yelling. Her voice was low, but the look in her eyes suggested serious trouble.

It was more than obvious what she was doing. She'd been caught in the act. So Kalyna decided to shrug it off as if it wasn't a big deal. She pulled the ring from her finger and returned it to her mother's coin purse. "I couldn't sleep, so I figured I'd get a jump on the drive home."

"You've got my purse." Favoring her bad knee, Norma stepped forward. Her weight was wreaking havoc with all her joints and had been for some time. "You were stealing from me."

"I wasn't *stealing*," Kalyna said. "I was just borrowing a few bucks to get me home. I'll send it back to you as soon as I get my next paycheck."

"And my ring?"

"I was admiring it. What more would I want with it?"

"That's what I'd like to know. Give me my purse." Her tentlike nightgown billowed around her as she limped forward to grab it. "What else did you take, huh?" she asked, rummaging through it. "Where're my diamond earrings?"

"I don't have them. I didn't even know they were in there."

"They're gone."

"I didn't take them!"

"Like hell! They can't disappear on their own." She snatched her wallet and opened it to find it empty. Then her face contorted with the seething hatred Kalyna had sensed all along. "You little bitch! You took my money. You were planning on cleaning me out, weren't you!"

Her mother was starting to raise her voice. Kalyna knew the scene that would ensue if her father got wind of this. Tatiana would jump in, too, trying to calm everyone down—but she'd ultimately take Norma and Dewayne's side. She wouldn't see getting up in the middle of the night to pilfer from Norma's purse as borrowing, either. She would've forgiven her for stealing from her own purse; she'd done it before. But not Norma's. *Why didn't you tell me you needed money?* she'd whisper, wearing that disappointed expression she'd perfected in Kalyna's absence.

"Stop freaking out!" Kalyna said. "I was planning on paying you back, like I said. I'm just a little short on cash right now."

"I saw those packages you brought home today. What about all the money you spent at the mall?"

"I was trying to show Tati a good time."

Her mother couldn't even take her makeup off properly. Her eyebrows, normally penciled in, had been washed away, but mascara smudges beneath both eyes made her look like a raccoon. "And that means it's okay? You can spend your money however and whenever you please and then take money from me when you run out? You're unbelievable, you know that? Just when I think you can't surprise me anymore, you do something like this."

"There's a woman in California who's trying to sabotage my case," Kalyna explained. "She was supposed to be helping me, but now she's gone over to the other side. If I don't get back, she'll convince the prosecutor to drop the charges against the man who raped me."

"Oh, stop going on about being raped!" she cried. "You weren't raped. That's the biggest farce I've heard yet." Dropping her purse, she went into the kitchen. "This is it, the last straw. I'm calling the police."

Kalyna followed hot on her heels. "To tell them what?"

"That you're a thief, a whore and a liar, that's what! You're not worth the air you breathe, Kalyna, and you never have been."

The anger Kalyna felt toward Ava and Luke and even Tatiana mingled with the hatred she felt toward her mother and quickly boiled down into a steely determination. "Stop saying that! I'm tired of hearing it!"

"I'll say whatever I want." She had her hand on the phone. Kalyna knew that if the police arrived it'd all be over. Even if they didn't put her in jail, they'd send her back to the base, and she'd pay whatever penalty her commanding officer decided to levy. She wouldn't evoke any sympathy when she'd just been busted for stealing. She'd lose favor with Ogitani, too, and Luke and Ava would get away with teaming up against her.

"Put the phone down," she said.

Her mother lifted her face, causing her double chins to wag. "Like hell I will." Then the tenor of her voice changed, and Kalyna knew someone had answered. "Hello? Yes, I'd like to report—"

Kalyna grabbed the phone and slammed it down before Norma could say any more. But she wasn't prepared for the hand that whipped around to slap her across the face. Stunned to think her sick, aging mother had actually struck her, she stood there with her ears ringing.

And then she snapped.

Lowering her shoulder, she shoved Norma into the counter. Norma grunted and opened her mouth to call out, but Kalyna grabbed her by the throat. Before she knew it, they were both on the floor and she was choking her mother for all she was worth. "This is how you make me feel. This is how you've always made me feel. How do you like it, huh? *How do you like it?*"

Her mother's eyes bulged from their sockets, her face turned blue, and her mouth opened and closed, but Kalyna kept squeezing, using the weight of her body when the strength in her hands gave out. She wouldn't let her whale of a mother cost her Luke. She wouldn't let her whale of a mother cost her anything. Finally, Norma would pay for what she'd done.

20

When Luke woke the next morning, he found himself on Ava's recliner with a blanket tossed over him. She was on the couch, curled up and facing in the other direction. Her blanket had slipped onto the floor, leaving her uncovered and revealing her shapely legs. But it was the curve of her bare bottom beneath her sweatshirt—*his* sweatshirt—that really caught his attention.

She made such a pretty sight he didn't move right away. If he stirred she'd probably jump up, realize she'd been running around the house half-dressed and shove him toward the door. He remembered how she'd nearly leaped out of his car rather than invite him in. She did that when she got defensive. But she wasn't defensive now....

Was she still wearing that thong he'd glimpsed last night? If not, he wasn't the one who'd removed it. He hadn't drunk that much. After what'd happened with Kalyna, he wasn't stupid enough to let go to that degree. He'd only wanted someone to talk to. And Ava had given him that. But she didn't have his body weight—or any tolerance for alcohol, apparently—and had gotten buzzed while they were still sitting on the couch. From that point on, she'd treated him like a girlfriend, as if it didn't matter that she was in her underwear. But it did. The image of her small buttocks, the scrap of lace that covered her in front, her bare legs and those painted toenails was indelibly imprinted on his brain.

If he leaned slightly to the left, he'd be able to see more, he realized, but he didn't allow himself the liberty. She'd trusted him enough to let him stay over, and he didn't want to betray that trust. He liked her, had enjoyed spending time with her, especially once she lowered her guard and was simply herself. At first, they'd talked about Kalyna and the possibility of a baby. But then they'd put on an old movie and played poker, and the conversation had drifted all over the place. Ava was actually a funny drunk. Luke wasn't sure what surprised him more—that or the thong.

The sun climbing over the horizon reminded him of what she'd said about watching the sunrise from her bedroom. He wasn't seeing it from that vantage point, but there was a window close by and it was beautiful all the same. Although not beautiful enough to compete with what was peeking at him from beneath that sweatshirt....

She rolled over, and the sweatshirt rode even higher so he got up to cover her. He was just pulling the blanket over her hips when she opened her eyes and stared up at him with such a sexy, sleepy expression he was glad the blanket concealed his lower half.

"I think you owe me money," she mumbled.

"Money?" he repeated.

"Didn't I win last night?"

She was the worst poker player he'd ever met, but he'd let her win a few hands because it meant so much to her.

"Oh, yeah. Fifty bucks."

"Bummer," she said, covering a yawn.

"Why is that a bummer?"

She shoved the hair out of her face. "I thought it was more. I had a dream I was driving your car."

Luke laughed. He was nice, but not that nice. "Sorry to disappoint you."

"Didn't we gamble on who had to make breakfast?"

"We did."

Tucking her hands under her chin, she closed her eyes. "Shouldn't you get started?"

"You lost that one."

She opened her eyes just a slit. "You're sure?"

"I wasn't drunk. I remember it very clearly."

"I wasn't drunk, either."

"Then why are you still in your underwear?"

Her eyes went wide and she sat up. "When did I take off my pants?"

"You never had them on." He didn't know why he'd brought it up. Possibly because he was fixated on what she looked like in that thong. And possibly because he wanted to let her know he'd seen her so he wouldn't feel like such a lecher for gawking. "But I'm not complaining."

Avoiding his gaze, she stood and wrapped the blanket around her, and he knew he'd seen all he was going to. "I'll get dressed so I can make breakfast." She started toward the back part of the cabin, but a knock at the door brought her up short.

"Are you expecting company?" he asked.

"No."

When she didn't move to answer it, he stepped toward the door himself. "Want me to get it?"

"Is it as early as I think?"

He checked his cell phone, which was lying on the coffee table. "Six."

"You *can't* get it." Dragging the blanket behind her,

she tiptoed to the door and peered through the peephole. "Shit," she whispered. "It's my stepfather."

Luke immediately straightened his clothes. "Maybe you should go put on some pants."

"Maybe you should hide." She glanced around as if searching for a place, but he shook his head.

"I'm not hiding. We haven't done anything wrong. I say we play it straight. Pants are a better idea."

"What good will pants do? We obviously spent the night together."

"But we didn't sleep together. And even if he thinks we did, we're both adults. How angry is he going to get?"

"He's not going to get angry. I just...I don't want to hear his snide comments. And he'll shoot off his mouth to my father. It's weird, but he and my father have struck up this unlikely friendship."

The knock came again, this time more impatient. "Ava? Hey, quit stalling and open up. I know Geoffrey's in there. I can see his damn car."

"Geoffrey?" Luke echoed. "Who's Geoffrey?"

"Just play along," she said, and drew the bolt.

It was over. Kalyna had taken Norma's wedding ring and her money—she never could find the earrings—and left her dead on the kitchen floor. And now it was daylight and she was flying along the highway with her windows down and her radio up.

She expected to feel some remorse. Or at least fear. This wouldn't be easy to hide, not like that hitchhiker. But it'd been hours since she'd driven away and all she felt was relief. It wasn't as if she'd *planned* to murder Norma. She'd been forced into it by Ava and Luke and Norma herself. All she'd done was finally stand up to the person who'd hurt her the most.

And now she was free. She'd never go back to Arizona. She wouldn't go back to the base, either. She was done with the military. She'd go into hiding until she could give Luke and Ava what they both deserved, and then she'd go back to Ukraine and disappear. That was her real home, anyway, wasn't it? She should never have been taken away in the first place. This life she'd lived was not *her* life. She deserved better.

She pulled off the road when she came to a truck stop. In case the police were already looking for her, she was taking the long way to California, and the lack of sleep was beginning to take its toll. At some point, she needed to ditch her car and get some rest. But she hadn't come across the right opportunity. And she doubted she'd find it here.

The mini-mart was empty except for a pimply-faced boy at the cash register. Never one to underestimate a potential benefactor, she offered him a bright smile. "Hi."

He blinked several times. "Uh, hi," he said, and stumbled backward into his stool.

Kalyna sidled up to the counter. "You old enough to drive, handsome?"

Righting his stool, he sat down, but the blinking accelerated. "Yes, ma'am. I-I'm nearly eighteen."

"Almost grown up."

"Yes, ma'am."

"You got a car?"

He seemed to struggle with this answer. When she reminded him that it was a *yes* or *no* question, his gaze fell to his tennis shoes. "No, ma'am."

"Then how'd you get to work today?"

His face turned red. "My, um, my dad dropped me off. But I'm saving up for this super sick Trans Am. My uncle owns it. We've been working on it all summer."

"Oh. Cool." If he didn't have a car, he couldn't be much help to her. She couldn't keep driving her own. It would make her too easy to catch.

No longer interested, she let her smile fade. She hung around for a while, hoping to meet someone else, but it was early and no one came in. She'd just resigned herself to buying an energy drink—to help her stay awake so she could forge ahead on her own—when the bell over the door signaled a new customer.

"Hey, Jerry," the boy said. "What're you doing back so soon?"

A gruff voice answered. "Just passin' through on another run, kid."

Kalyna stood on her tiptoes to see over the racks. The salesclerk was talking to a tall, weather-beaten cowboy, probably in his forties, who'd thrown a pack of cigarettes onto the counter.

"Where you goin' this time?" the boy asked.

There was a semi parked out at the far pump. Kalyna could see it through the window. This "Jerry" had to own it. He was the only other person getting gas in this Podunk place located somewhere in southern Utah.

"Reno."

Reno wasn't exactly California, but it was only two hours from Sacramento, and it had a bus station.

Kalyna dropped the NoDoz she'd picked up back on the shelf and went to the front counter, where she set a package of ribbed condoms next to Jerry's cigarettes.

When the cowboy saw it, he glanced at her in surprise and she offered him a seductive smile. "Nice day we're havin', isn't it?"

Obviously more experienced than the boy, he tipped his hat back and gave her a leisurely once-over. "Yes, ma'am, that it is."

"But it is a little...*hot,* wouldn't you say?"

"Don't you have any AC in that vehicle?" His eyes twinkled with lascivious interest as he nodded toward her Ford Fiesta.

"I'm having a bit of engine trouble. But even when the damn thing runs, the air conditioner isn't very powerful. I'm looking to put the fire out, if you know what I mean."

"Too bad about your car," he said. "If you have somewhere to leave it, my truck's working fine. It has an air conditioner that's mighty powerful indeed."

"That's what I was hoping." She winked, and he put a package of breath mints on the counter, too.

Something was going on and the boy knew it, but he couldn't figure out exactly what. His eyes bounced between them. Then he cleared his throat to get Jerry's attention. "Just the cigarettes and breath mints for you?"

Jerry stood taller. "Hell, no, son. Jerry's always a gentleman."

When the kid's eyebrows went up, Kalyna knew he had to be wondering why being a gentleman included purchasing products for a complete stranger. But he was smart enough not to ask. At Jerry's request, he added a couple of cold drinks to the tab and a can of whipping cream. Then Jerry paid, and Kalyna walked out with her new ride.

When she got her suitcase out of the trunk, the boy stood in the doorway and called after her. "Hey, you can't leave your car here."

She tossed him a smile as Jerry took her case. "Don't worry. Someone will be along to pick it up."

Ava forced a smile for Pete Carrera, her stepfather. Fortunately, he didn't come by often. Although he was much nicer now than when she was a teenager in his home, it was only because he couldn't get away with the old behavior anymore.

"Good morning." Stepping back to admit him, she gritted her teeth, trying to hide her irritation at his unannounced and ill-timed visit.

An abundance of hair gel fixed the long strands of his salt-and-pepper hair so firmly in place a hurricane couldn't muss it, and he smelled like he'd bathed in cheap cologne. Ava could barely refrain from wrinkling her nose as he came inside and eyed Luke, who moved forward to greet him. "Hello, sir."

Pete wasn't much taller than Ava. He had to tip his head back to take in all of Luke's six-foot-three frame. "Very polite," he said as he accepted Luke's hand. "I like that. Nice to finally meet you, Geoffrey."

Luke slanted a quizzical glance at Ava. "It's Luke."

Her stepfather scratched under his chin. "Your name's not Geoffrey?"

"It's Geoffrey *Luke*," Ava clarified. No way did she want to explain what she was doing at six in the morning, only half-dressed, with a client in her house.

Luke cleared his throat to let her know he didn't approve, but she ignored him. This was the only time he was going to come into contact with her family, so it didn't matter. One white lie would save her untold grief.

"Well, whatever your name is, you're a pleasant surprise. With all of Ava's talk about getting you on Weight Watchers and out in the sun a bit—"

"Pete! I've *never* said that!" Ava protested.

"You said he works a lot, needs to relax more. Anyway, I expected a soft, pasty-faced office type." He whistled as he shook his blockish head. "But you are *in shape*. How often do you work out?"

"Almost every day," Luke said, but Ava quickly steered the conversation away from him.

"To what do I owe the—er, pleasure of this visit?" she asked Pete.

"Do I need a reason to come by and see my only step-daughter?"

"I'm not your stepdaughter anymore."

"Come on, Ava. You know I wouldn't have filed for divorce if your mother hadn't tried to kill me."

"Metaphorically speaking," she muttered for Luke's benefit but couldn't resist addressing Pete's personal responsibility in the whole affair. "And you two would have gotten along fine if you hadn't been insufferable in the first place."

"Hey, I'm easy to live with," he said. "Just give me a cold beer, and I'm happy. She was the one trying to collect on my life insurance. Have you heard from her lately?"

"Of course not." Ava had refused every letter until they stopped coming.

"Well, she wrote *me*. Can you believe that? She wants me to forgive her. How do you forgive someone who tried to *poison* you?"

He kept talking simply because he knew she didn't want him to. That, and he liked telling anyone and everyone what'd happened because it instantly made him the center of attention. *Your wife tried to kill you?*

Fortunately, Luke said nothing.

"They're moving her to a different prison," he added, "in case you haven't heard."

Ava didn't want to hear. She preferred to forget that her mother existed, preferred to pretend she didn't feel an acute pain in her chest every time she thought of Zelinda behind bars. "I *never* want to talk about it, *never* want to hear her name. And Luke—um, Geoffrey—doesn't want to talk about it, either, so quit grandstanding."

Her stepfather rubbed stubby, grease-stained fingers over his wife-beater T-shirt. "Boy, *someone* got up on the wrong side of bed this morning."

Ava wrestled with her temper and lost. "Did you come for a reason, Pete, or—"

"Hell, yeah, I came for a reason. You think I'd drag my ass out of bed just to catch you two screwing around?" His laugh sounded more like a hoot as he slapped Luke on the back. "Your dad said I could use the boat today. Didn't he tell you?"

Ava's heart dropped to her knees. "You don't mean my *house.*"

"It's a house*boat,* right?"

"But…you've never borrowed it before." He couldn't be serious. She needed her house right now. It was her haven, her place to recover after trying to drink away her fascination with Luke. "What do you want it for?"

"I'm taking my new girlfriend and her boy fishing." He winked at her. "Gotta get in good with the kid, you know?"

The excess gel and cologne should've warned her. Her stepfather was on the make, hunting for another woman to take care of him, and he'd found a new target.

Ava felt sorry for the poor, unsuspecting soul. "But I was planning to hang out at home. It's Sunday."

"Liz doesn't have to work *because* it's Sunday. This is the perfect time."

For him, maybe. "I— Dad didn't tell me. I haven't even showered. And I have company."

Pete favored Luke with a knowing grin. "Come on, Geoffrey's not company. You've been together for over a year." He lowered his voice and nudged her with his elbow. "And so much for acting like you two don't get it on."

His chortle grated on Ava's nerves. She could tell Luke didn't like it, either. He stood a little closer, as if he wanted to interrupt but was too polite to get involved.

"Stop it, Pete."

He ignored her. "I'm actually kind of glad to see it," he confided to Luke. "Her dad and I've been worried she might be frigid. You're the first—"

"Are you for real?" Ava cried. "I can't believe you show up at dawn and start telling my...my boyfriend, who isn't really my boyfriend by the way, that—"

A car door slammed by the pier and what she was about to say was lost as Pete whipped around to stick his head out the open door. "Oops. There she is. Now smile and be nice, Ava. I'm trying to make a good impression," he said, and hurried out to meet his new love interest.

Ava turned to Luke. "There are days when I almost understand why my mother did it." Now that he knew about Zelinda, she needed to cover for it, make light of it, but he didn't follow up on the comment. He didn't even return her smile. He seemed angry as he jerked his head toward her room.

"Get dressed. I'm taking you to breakfast."

21

Exhausted from her long night and an energetic early-morning interlude with Jerry, who was now driving, Kalyna was asleep in the bed at the back of his cab when her phone rang. She roused herself to glance at the screen, saw that the call was coming from the mortuary and silenced it. She couldn't use her cell phone. She'd seen enough true crime shows to know that the police would be able to locate her via a method called triangulation if she did. She should actually turn it off. She wasn't positive, but she suspected they could track down any phone that was on.

But as she lay awake for several minutes afterward, she realized that it was too soon for the police to be involved. More likely, Tatiana or Dewayne had just stumbled on Norma's body and were trying to piece together what had happened. And even if she was wrong and the police had already been called, she was traveling in the cab of a semi. If she tossed out the phone, they'd never find her.

Entering the code to reach her voice mail, she listened to her sister's panicked message.

"Kalyna, where are you? Please, call me. Mom's dead. We just...we found her on the kitchen floor. I'm hoping she had a heart attack, that you had nothing to do with this. But her purse is right here, and all her stuff's scattered beside her. And Dad is…Dad's on the phone to the cops. I—I don't know what to think." She broke into a sob. "I'd assume somebody hurt you, too, but your bags are gone, and so is your car."

Kalyna considered her options. She could remain silent, get rid of her phone and let the police start searching for her. Or she could call her sister back and throw up a few smoke screens.

She decided to go with the smoke screens.

Tatiana answered on the first ring. "Kalyna?"

"I got your message. What's going on?"

"I don't know!" Tati wailed. "Dad thinks you killed Mom. But you didn't, did you? Someone else must've done this."

"Mom's *dead?*"

Tati gulped for the breath to speak. "You didn't know?"

"How would I? I couldn't sleep. I was too worried about getting back to the base, so I left around midnight. Mom and Dad were in bed as far as I could tell."

Her sister paused, sniffed and sounded more hopeful. "You left before it happened, then."

"Unless she was lying there and I didn't see her. I didn't turn on any lights. I didn't want to wake anyone."

"Thank God. It must've been a robbery."

"I guess so. I feel terrible. Mom and I didn't get along, but…I never would've wished for something like this."

"Of course not."

If someone else had done it, that person would've needed a way in, so Kalyna supplied this information seamlessly. "I did find it a little odd that the house wasn't locked up…."

"It wasn't?"

"I must've forgotten when I came in from the car. I feel *so* bad."

"It wasn't locked when we got up, either."

"See? I'm terrible about being cautious. I never dreamed anyone would break in. To a mortuary? Give me a break!"

"Some people will break in anywhere."

"I'm surprised I didn't bump into whoever it was. Was Mom shot or—"

"No, not shot. She wasn't stabbed, either. We don't really know what killed her. Maybe she hit her head when she fell but Dad thinks she was strangled. She's all…blue, Kalyna. And her money's gone."

"Why would I take her money? That should've told you it wasn't me!"

"That's what I said to Dad. I told him you had plenty of your own money when we were at the mall yesterday. And you wouldn't take her wedding ring. What would you want with that?"

Kalyna held her hand in front of her to admire the sparkle of that square-cut diamond. She wasn't sure how much she could get for it, but she planned to visit a pawn shop as soon as possible. "Who could've killed her?" she asked.

Tatiana lowered her voice. "I think it was Mark."

"Mark who?"

"Mark Cannaby."

Kalyna shoved herself into a sitting position. "Mark hasn't worked for Mom and Dad in a long time. They fired him before I went into the air force. We don't even know where he is."

"Yes, we do. He's running the cemetery. He's been doing that for over a year."

For once, knowing Mark as well as she did might be

an advantage. "Have he and Mom been having problems?"

"She's hated him ever since she caught him...you know...with that corpse. She says he's a necrophiliac, that he shouldn't be free to circulate in society. Two weeks ago, she ran into the woman he's dating at church and told her all about him. He wasn't happy when he found out. He called here a few times and left some threatening messages, telling her she'd better mind her own business and stay out of his."

Kalyna smiled as she considered this. Poor Mark. "I guess he decided to get even."

"That's what I'm thinking." Tati broke into tears again. "It's so sad to imagine her gone. I—I can't believe it."

"Tati, I have a terrible confession to make," Kalyna said.

As the silence stretched on, Kalyna could sense her sister's fear. "What's that?"

"I'm not sure I should tell you. I've kept it secret for so long. But you're right. It has to be him. He's the only one I know who's capable of murder."

"I don't want to think that of him, but—"

"I can almost guarantee it. He killed a hitchhiker once, Tati. Then he stuffed her body in the crematory."

Tatiana gasped. "How do you know?"

"Because he—he made me help him." She added a quaver to her voice. "He told me he'd go to Mom and Dad and tell them I was having sex with him again if I didn't. After that, I was afraid to tell anyone—I was afraid he'd blame it on me. Mom and Dad have always thought the worst of me, and I was terrified they'd disown me. But now that he's done this to Mom...I don't have any choice but to speak up."

"No, of course not! But how do we prove he killed this hitchhiker?"

"The girl's name was Sarah. She was about fourteen. The police will probably find her listed as a missing person. I think she said she was from New Mexico. I—I have her necklace. Remember that floating diamond on the gold chain that I kept in the bottom of my jewelry box?"

"The one you said the quarterback gave you?"

"That's the one. It belonged to her. I've hung on to it in case this ever came up, so I'd have proof she existed."

"I wondered why you never wore it. Why you wouldn't let me wear it, either."

"Now you know."

"Oh, God, this is even worse than I thought," Tatiana cried. "But at least it wasn't you, Kalyna. That—that really scared me."

Kalyna feigned a few tears of her own. "How could you ever believe I'd do such a thing?"

"I didn't, not really. I mean, I was just so shocked. It looked like…well, you know how it must've looked. But I knew you were planning to head home early. You often have difficulty sleeping. And Mark was so angry about what Mom did… It all makes sense now."

It did make sense. Perfect sense. Kalyna reveled in her good fortune. She'd blame both murders on Mark and walk away scot-free.

"Are you coming back?" Tati asked.

"I can't come right away, but I'll see if I can get leave," Kalyna said. After she'd protected her interests in Fairfield. "I'm already in enough trouble."

"The police will want to talk to you."

"They'll have to call me."

Kalyna heard voices in the background. "I've got to get off the phone," Tati whispered. "The police are here."

"Let me know how it goes," Kalyna said, and hung up.

"Who was that?" Jerry called from the driver's seat.

"My sister. There's been an accident in my family. Can you let me out at the next stop?"

He tilted up his hat. "Of course. But will you be okay if I do?"

"I'll be fine. I have to go back and get my car." Now that Mark was going to take the fall for her, she had no reason to give up such a convenient mode of transportation.

"How will you get back? You've got your luggage, too."

"Are you kidding? The same way I got here," she said with a laugh.

Luke chose his favorite breakfast place—Hog Heaven in Davis. Slightly west of Sacramento, Davis was a college town and had several mom-and-pop-style restaurants. Because he came to Hog Heaven fairly often, he was recognized by the hostess, who greeted him with a warm smile.

"Hi, Captain. Welcome back. It's been a few weeks since we've seen you."

"Too long," he said. "I'm craving one of your famous omelets."

"I'm sure we can cook one up for you." Her gaze shifted to Ava and a hint of surprise registered, probably because he generally came with a group of friends.

"Right this way," she said, and he motioned for Ava to precede him.

Ava had combed her hair and donned a pair of sunglasses but wasn't wearing any makeup. Luke didn't mind. She had pretty skin, an expressive mouth and he liked her "just tumbled out of bed" look. He wasn't too impressed with her clothing, however. She'd put on the most godawful pair of shorts and blouse he'd ever seen.

The shorts rode high on her waist and went to her knees and seemed to be made of the same wrinkle-free material his mother admired. Somehow she'd taken a popular style—he'd seen a lot of women wear shorts the same length—and made it…frumpy. Even worse, her top had a ribbon threaded around the neck that would've been more fitting on a kindergartener. Luke doubted there was another guy in the place who'd give Ava a second look in that getup. But he'd seen her wearing only a pair of panties and a sweatshirt—and if he'd witnessed a more tantalizing sight, he couldn't remember it.

"Will this table be okay?" The hostess touched his arm to gain his attention, and he realized she'd just caught him staring at Ava's behind.

Grinning to cover the gaffe, he said, "It's fine," and slid into the booth.

Ava sat across from him and immediately stuck her nose in a menu. Since her stepfather had shown up with his new girlfriend, she hadn't said much. She'd insisted on bringing her briefcase and a stack of files, but he wondered where she expected to work.

"You might want to take off those sunglasses," he said.

She didn't glance up; neither did she remove them. "I'm perfectly capable of deciding when to take them off, thanks."

Chuckling at her stubbornness, he opened his own menu. Poor Ava. She had a lousy family situation. She couldn't dress worth a damn. She couldn't flirt any better, at least not when she was sober. And she couldn't completely hide the vulnerability beneath the dark glower that'd descended when her stepfather motored off with her houseboat.

"So maybe we should talk about it now and get it over with," he said.

This time her gaze lifted. "Talk about what?"

"Your stepfather. Your mother."

The waitress came with two glasses of water; Ava didn't respond until she'd walked away. "I don't want to talk about them. What makes you think I want to talk about them?"

"I'm just saying that once we lay it all out, we won't have to avoid the subject. Then we can forget about it."

"We don't need to lay it all out. This is a business relationship. Once your case is resolved, I'll probably never see you again."

Why was she always reminding him of that? He wasn't interested in her. He'd told her as much, and he'd meant it. Sure, there were moments when he was tempted to take on the challenge she posed, to prove she wasn't as aloof as she pretended. But those thoughts usually centered on getting her naked, and he knew that wasn't an honorable goal.

"I don't see any reason we can't be friends," he said.

"I'm not in the market."

"I said *friends.*"

"I know." Turning her menu so he could see the front, she pointed to a picture of an egg scramble. "Have you ever had this? It looks good."

He ignored her question. He'd never had a woman—anyone, really—refuse his friendship. "Why don't you want to be friends with me?"

She was once again shielded by her menu. "Because you have too many friends as it is."

Taken aback, he pushed her menu down so he could see her face. "What makes you think that?"

"I can tell."

"Simply because I happen to know the hostess?"

The menu went back up. "It's just how you are."

He forced it down again. "I don't collect friends. I like a lot of people. There's a difference."

"If you say so."

"I say so. And there's nothing wrong with that." Although her accusation echoed something his mother had said before the mess with Kalyna—that he didn't seem to have strong feelings about any of the women he dated. She'd said he was too affable, too easygoing, always somewhere in the middle, and she was right on-target. Only Marissa had penetrated to the heart of him, and she'd married his best friend.

"I can't argue," she said with a shrug.

"Then why did you say it?" he asked.

"I'd rather be one in a million to someone, that's all."

Now she was pissing him off. "Are you one in a million to Geoffrey?"

She took a sip of water. "I don't want to talk about Geoffrey, either."

"Of course not. You're not even sleeping with him. How much can he mean to you?"

"Maybe I'm just more selective than you are."

"If you're suggesting I sleep around, I don't. I made a mistake that night with Kalyna, I'll give you that. And I'm paying the price. But don't assume that's normal behavior for me, because it's not."

She raised one hand. "That's your personal business. You don't have to explain your habits."

The fact that she didn't seem to care bothered him. "And for the record, you're not being selective, Ava. You're hiding behind your work. You won't let anyone really get to know you. And you want me to tell you why?"

"No."

He told her, anyway—and leaned halfway across the table to do it. "Because you're scared."

"Can we decide on breakfast?"

"You don't have anything to say about that?" he asked.

"I'm not scared. What would I be scared of? You?"

"Maybe."

She finally set her menu aside. "It's not fear, Luke. I'm not stupid enough to fall for someone who's prettier than I am, that's all. Especially someone who can't fall as hard as I can."

He gaped at her. He could've argued about the pretty part, but she was right about the rest. He *couldn't* fall as hard as she could. He was afraid he couldn't fall, period. No matter whom he dated—no matter how attractive, nice, intelligent—he couldn't seem to feel that all-consuming passion his father felt for his mother. Not since high school.

"You don't know that," he said, but it was a feeble response and she suddenly seemed ashamed, as if she realized she'd struck a nerve.

With a sigh, she removed her sunglasses. "She used antifreeze, okay?"

"What?"

"My mother. She tried to poison Pete with antifreeze. She put it in a diet drink she concocted to help him lose weight."

This was her apology for being upset and taking it out on him. He knew that. He also knew he should let her off the hook by telling her she didn't need to talk about it. But she wouldn't share what had happened with just anyone. If she'd trusted him with the details of *this,* they were friends, even if she denied it, which put him back on more familiar—and comfortable—ground. "How long ago?"

"Five years."

"How was it discovered?"

"By chance, really. He got so sick he drove himself to

the hospital while my mother was at work. The doctor who treated him had seen this kind of poisoning before. When my mother showed up and kept asking if Pete would survive, he found it odd and decided to run the tests. The toxicology report showed proof of ethylene glycol, and she was the only one who could've administered it."

"Wouldn't he have tasted it?"

"It's clear and odorless and tastes sweet. At least it used to, until the manufacturers changed it. She put it in his diet drinks, and he thought that was just the way they tasted. Then it came out that she'd recently purchased another life-insurance policy in his name—with herself as the sole beneficiary—and that was all it took."

"How'd you find out about the poisoning?"

"I received a call at work. I didn't have the money to continue my education the way I'd originally planned, so I'd gotten a job at Bank of America as a teller."

"*She* called to confess or—"

"No, it was my father. My real father. When they arrested her, she didn't reach out to me. She turned to him." She frowned. "*That* should've told me something."

A wave of sympathy caused Luke to lower his voice. "The whole thing must've come as a terrible shock."

She flinched despite an apparent effort to conceal the depth of her hurt. "I refused to believe it until I heard what she yelled out in court as they took her away."

"What?"

"'He owed me that money!' The guilty verdict had already been read, but it was that line that convicted her in my mind. Until that moment, I'd stood by her regardless of the evidence."

"I'm sorry," he said.

"Don't be. I'm fine now. I'm past it."

She wasn't even close, but he let that go. "Why'd she do it?"

"I don't know exactly." She shook her head. "She was miserable. I don't think she ever got over my father. She had a hard time seeing him move on to one woman after another without giving her a thought. So she finally quit waiting for him to realize he'd lost the love of his life and married again. And, well…you met Pete. It was a disaster." She toyed with her sunglasses. "My father had fidelity issues and he was shallow, but he was also dashing, debonair and full of life. Pete is a slug. He gave her nothing emotionally or financially. He claimed he had an injured back and couldn't work, so he sat in front of the TV all day while she worked at the neighborhood elementary school, in the cafeteria, and sold Tupperware on the side. They got behind on their bills, argued constantly. Then she began cleaning houses on weekends. He claimed he had a settlement coming for a worker's comp injury, but that never materialized. She was really counting on the money and when she found out he'd been lying all along just to avoid work, she decided he'd pay up one way or another. His life insurance was how she'd get a fresh start and—" she winced again "—help me afford school so I could finish."

Ava obviously felt some personal responsibility for the situation. "How old were you when they got together?"

"I was in high school but left for college soon after. That's why I didn't know their relationship was as bad as it was. Although I mostly put myself through college, my mother would send me money every once in a while. She'd insist she was doing fine. And of course I'd visit on weekends and holidays. But…" The slight tremor in her voice told him she was close to tears. He'd broken down her defenses because he couldn't stand to be shut out and now he felt guilty for dredging up a subject that was so painful for her.

Reaching across the table, he took her hand. He expected her to pull away. She was determined not to need anyone, to shoulder her burdens on her own. But she allowed him to move his fingertip lightly over her palm. "Sometimes people get desperate," he said. "Sometimes they make bad decisions."

"Bad *decisions?*" she echoed. "She tried to kill him!"

The anger and bitterness she carried inside were more than apparent. But so was the longing she felt for the mother she'd once had. The attempted murder had occurred when she was probably at her most self-absorbed, focused on her schooling and the hope of a good career. From what he could sense, she didn't blame her mother as much as she blamed herself—for not seeing her mother's desperation, for not being there to relieve it before it cost them each other.

"It might be easier if you'd forgive her—and yourself," he added and, just like that, she closed up again. Yanking away her hand, she got up and stalked to the restroom and Luke was left with the sensation of her fingers slipping through his.

Ava didn't want to leave the restroom. She hadn't known Luke long but he had a way of making her feel as if there was nowhere to hide. She kept trying to convince herself he was as shallow as her father, nothing more than a handsome face, but then he'd catch a nuance her father would've missed, and that forced her to respect him. Even Geoffrey took what she said about her mother at face value. It was Luke who'd immediately driven to the heart of the matter. And he was right. She couldn't forgive

Zelinda, but she held herself more accountable than anyone. She'd let her mother down; because of that Zelinda
had become so needy and desperate she'd committed a
terrible act, and now their lives would never be the same.

Could she have changed the situation if she'd been
more observant? More supportive? A better daughter?
Those were the questions she asked herself time and
again, but the answers never came. There was no way to
go back and rectify the situation. That was the worst part
of all.

Knowing she had to go out and face Luke again, she
stared at herself in the mirror above the sink. When
they'd walked into the restaurant, the hostess had looked
her up and down as if she couldn't quite believe they
were together. And Ava didn't blame her. They were a
mismatch. That was clear to everyone. But it didn't stop
her from craving his touch. This morning, when she'd
opened her eyes and found him standing over her, every
nerve had come to life.

The door opened. "Ms. Bixby?"

Ava turned to see the hostess. "Yes?"

"Are you okay? Captain Trussell wanted me to check."

Taking a deep breath, she nodded. "I'm fine. Tell him
I'll be out in a minute."

What the heck was wrong with her? She couldn't
stand there in the restroom mooning over Luke. She had
work to do.

If only Pete hadn't shown up today. Then Luke
would've left and she'd be home by herself....

After splashing some water on her face, she walked
out, but her cell phone rang before she could cross the
restaurant. Staying near the restrooms so she wouldn't
disturb the other diners, she pulled it from her pocket and
touched the Talk button. "Hello?"

"Ms. Bixby?" It was a male voice calling from a 480 area code—Arizona. The rest of the number she didn't recognize.

"Yes?"

"This is Detective John Morgan from the Mesa Police Department in Arizona."

The only person she knew from Arizona was Kalyna. Had something happened to her?

Flashbacks of the call she'd received the day Bella Fitzgerald hanged herself hit with startling impact, and Ava's knees went weak. Had it happened again? Had she completely missed the signs that a second human being was living so close to the edge?

She could see Luke watching her from across the room, noted the concern on his face as he got up and came toward her, but she stayed where she was. "Don't tell me you're calling about Kalyna Harter," she said, scarcely able to breathe.

"I'm afraid so," Detective Morgan responded. "How well do you know Sergeant Harter?"

Trying to concentrate despite the worst-case scenario that had instantly appeared in her mind, Ava pressed the fingertips of her free hand to her temple. "I work for a victims' charity in Sacramento. She came to me last Monday, claiming she'd been raped. That was the first time I'd ever met her."

There was a brief pause while he absorbed this information, but Ava couldn't wait for him to formulate his next question. She had to know what was going on. "Please tell me she's okay."

"I have no idea," he said. "I haven't seen her, although I'd like the chance to speak with her. It seems she left early this morning. Just about the time her mother was murdered."

22

"What is it?" Luke asked when Ava had finished her conversation.

She hit the End button and glanced up at him. "Kalyna's mother is dead. Someone killed her early this morning."

He grew even more alert. "You're kidding me."

"No. Her husband found her on the kitchen floor when he got up at nine. There were signs of a struggle. Her money was gone. So was her wedding ring."

"Was it Kalyna?"

Ava slipped the phone into her pocket. "They don't know yet, but...she's a suspect. She was there last night."

"She's not there now?"

"No."

"Oh, God." He pinched the bridge of his nose. "She's psycho, completely nuts."

"You may be right."

"Who called to tell you?"

Two diners kept looking at her, so she pulled Luke farther into the alcove by the restrooms. "A detective from the Mesa police. Kalyna's sister, Tati, told him I was working with Kalyna. He thought she might've tried to contact me. That I might be able to tell him where she is."

"The air force sure as hell can't tell him."

"No."

"What does he think happened?"

"He doesn't know yet. He said Mr. Harter insists it had to be Kalyna. Tati claims it could be someone named Mark Cannaby."

"Who's Mark Cannaby?"

"From what I was told, he used to work for the Harters. He hasn't for several years, but he only lives three miles away and works just down the street at the cemetery."

"The detective told you all this?"

"Yes."

"Aren't they usually pretty tight-lipped?"

"Professional courtesy. He's familiar with TLS. He once met Skye at a forensics seminar in Scottsdale."

"Why would Tatiana blame this Mark Cannaby? Did she see him skulking around the house or yard or—"

"She didn't see him. She had no clue there was anything wrong until her dad cried out. But there's plenty of animosity between Cannaby and the Harters and has been ever since he was let go. When Kalyna was sixteen, they suspected he was messing around with her, so they started watching him very closely."

"And caught the two of them in the act."

Ava lowered her voice. "No, they caught *him* in the act. But he wasn't with Kalyna. He was having sex with one of the corpses."

Luke blanched. "That's too sick to even contemplate. I hope they turned him in."

"No, they were afraid the negative publicity would adversely affect their business, so they simply fired him and agreed to say nothing so long as he kept his distance."

"But it didn't end there."

"Detective Morgan said that, according to Mr. Harter, things settled down for a while. Cannaby was gone, out of sight. But then he got a job at the cemetery, so the Harters would bump into him now and then. When he started dating a girl from Mrs. Harter's church, it was too much. She couldn't stand to see him every Sunday, acting as innocent and normal as everyone else. So she went to the girl privately and warned her."

"I don't blame her, but..." Luke gave a low whistle. "I can't imagine that went over very well."

"No. He called up, ranting and raving, saying she was a bitch who deserved to die. And then he threatened her—told her to keep her mouth shut or he'd make her pay for trying to ruin his life."

"When was this?"

"Sounds as if it was just a few weeks ago."

Luke shook his head. "Wow. Does Cannaby have an alibi?"

"I don't know. Morgan hasn't talked to him yet."

He stroked his chin, scraping the stubble. He hadn't been able to shave. It wasn't his usual look, but Ava liked seeing him a little rough around the edges. "If Kalyna goes to jail, I can't imagine my case will proceed to court," he said.

"What happens with your case will depend on whether or not the prosecutor believes there's enough evidence to proceed. But I'm betting Ogitani would drop it instantly. The military has too much invested in you."

"*And* I'm innocent," he reminded her with a slightly wounded expression.

She managed a smile. "That, too."

He stared at the floor. "Part of me hopes she goes to jail."

This statement surprised Ava. Since Kalyna's incarceration would very likely make the rape charges disappear, she would've expected him to be *all* for it. "And the other part?"

"I don't like the idea of her being in prison while she's carrying my baby."

Ava knew it was silly, but she experienced a twinge of jealousy at the thought of Kalyna having such a permanent and very personal tie to Luke. "It would solve any custody issues."

That seemed to offset his concerns. "Good point. What else did the detective tell you?"

"Nothing. That's all he knows. Except that he believes Kalyna might be on her way to California. He'll get in touch with the air force, just in case she shows up for work, and he asked me to give him a call if I hear from her."

"They can't reach her on her cell?"

"She's not picking up. But Tatiana spoke to her earlier."

"And?"

"She acted surprised by their mother's death."

"If she just learned that her mother's been killed, wouldn't she be on her way back to Arizona—not here?"

"It didn't sound like they were expecting her."

"Wouldn't *most* people turn around, considering the circumstances?"

"You already know Kalyna isn't like most people," Ava said. "She and Norma were estranged. Besides, she's absent without leave so she has a very good excuse to continue on to the base."

"I don't care if she has a good excuse or not. To my mind, that makes her look even guiltier."

"I agree. I'm just telling you how the police see it."

Luke leaned one shoulder against the wall. "She said she'll kill anyone I'm involved with."

"You told me you're not involved with anyone."

He tilted up her chin. For a second, she thought he might kiss her. But he didn't. "She thinks I might be involved with you."

And she'd done nothing to destroy that assumption when she'd spoken on his cell phone last night. "No... she's got to realize that can't be."

"Why not?" He grinned. "I *have* seen you in your underwear."

"It doesn't matter."

He leaned closer. "Does it matter that I want to see you that way again?"

"Don't joke about this."

"What makes you think I'm joking?"

Their eyes met, and Ava felt butterflies. "You're a client," she said to cover her reaction.

"That's not what concerns me."

"What does concern you?" she asked.

Putting his hand on her waist, he guided her back to the table. "The fact that there might be a homicidal maniac out to kill anyone I touch."

Tatiana Harter stared at her mother's bloated body. At least two or three times a week, her father picked up a corpse from the morgue. It was routine, part of the business. Today, however, that process would happen in reverse—a body would be taken from the mortuary to the morgue. And it wouldn't be a member of someone else's family. It would be Norma, one of the central figures in Tati's life. After the autopsy, they'd be able to bring her home—here, where she'd spent the past thirteen years—but only to dress her for burial.

Her artist's eye already dictating what she'd use, Tati imagined applying Norma's makeup as she did every Sunday before church. Maybe she wasn't the best makeup artist in the area, but she knew what Norma liked. She'd apply a thicker foundation than normal to hide all the bruising. Then she'd go with a pretty pink blush and matching lipstick, and pencil in her eyebrows with a high arch the way Norma preferred. From there she'd create some definition around the eyes using brown shadow and a touch of green at the outside corners. But first she'd dye her hair to hide the gray. Norma hated going gray.

Tati had done her mother's makeup for years. But now that Norma was dead, this would be the last time she'd perform this service, and she wasn't sure how she'd get through it. She'd finally established a relationship with the woman who'd adopted her at the age of six, finally gained an appreciation of her strengths and some tolerance for her weaknesses.

And now Norma was gone. It wasn't fair. How could Mark, or anyone else, have done this?

"Hey, you okay?"

Tati glanced up to see her father watching her closely. As skinny as Norma was fat, he looked more shrunken than usual, the lines on his face etched more deeply than before. Wearing the same black polyester slacks and button-up shirt he'd had on yesterday, as if he'd scooped them off the chair next to his bed, he'd slicked his dark hair into place but somehow still looked disheveled, bewildered, *old*. Someone else might never have noticed the change. But to Tati he seemed to have aged a decade in a matter of hours.

"I don't know," she said. "I don't know what to think. This seems…unreal, like a nightmare." Realizing that he probably felt as lost as she did, and just as robbed, she conjured up a smile. "What about you?"

"I always thought I'd be the first to go. I never dreamt it would be like this."

The deputy coroner had just pulled the van around to the loading area. He threw open the back doors and strode in to get the gurney, and Dewayne followed, obviously planning to help.

The phone rang. Tati's eyes shifted to the counter, but she hesitated to answer for fear the police had discovered who'd done this terrible thing, and it wasn't someone as far removed from her as she hoped.

When she made no move, Dewayne switched directions, but somehow Tatiana found the energy to intercede. "I've got it," she mumbled, and motioned him back toward the van. "You go with Mom."

"Are you sure?"

"I'm sure."

"Okay, call me on my cell if it's important," he said.

She nodded as he left. Then she forced her wooden legs to carry her across the room. "Hello?"

"Is Tatiana there?"

She'd been hoping it would be Kalyna. That her sister was calling to say she was driving back, after all. Tati *wanted* to believe what Kalyna had told her earlier, but the way the police had acted, and her father...she was beginning to have some serious misgivings. If only Kalyna would arrive soon and prove that she'd had nothing to do with whatever happened this morning. Then Tati could focus her pain on the tragedy of losing her mother and stop worrying that the situation was about to get worse. But it was a man's voice on the other end of the line. "This is Tatiana," she said.

"Tati, this is Mark Cannaby."

Tati's first thought was to catch her father. Maybe Mark was going to confess. Maybe all their questions would be answered right here, right now, and she could feel good about her sister again. But something in his voice made her cautious. She walked toward the door, even opened it, but didn't rush out to stop the van. Instead, she waved her father off. "How dare you call here!" she said into the phone when Dewayne was gone.

"I don't know what the hell Kalyna is telling you, but I didn't do it," he responded.

"Then how do you even know what 'it' is?" she challenged.

"How do you think? The police were just here! Detective Morgan said someone murdered your mother and asked me where I was last night. But I was home sleeping, where I always am that late at night. They're coming after the wrong person."

"No. Kalyna told me, Mark." Tati had been mostly dry-eyed since talking to Kalyna. But the confusion and loss she felt now brought a fresh flood of tears.

"She told you what?"

"About the hitch—" her voice snagged on a sob "—hitchhiker you—you killed ten years ago. The one you cremated after you were d-done."

"It's not true!" he insisted. "Even if you believe I'm capable of such a thing, do you really suppose Kalyna would keep quiet about it all these years?"

He had a point, but Tati didn't want to acknowledge it. Kalyna loved to shock others, loved to gossip. And she trusted Tati with everything. At least, she used to. "She has the girl's necklace," she said. "I've seen it in her jewelry box."

"Oh, yeah? What does it look like?"

This took her by surprise, but she was determined to convince him she knew what she was talking about. "It's a floating diamond on a gold chain. A piece of jewelry she could never afford herself."

"You saw her with it?"

"I saw it in her jewelry box. No way would she wear it. She watched you take it from a girl you murdered!"

"I have something to show you," he said. "Can I come over?"

"No!" Tati wouldn't feel safe. She'd never liked Mark to begin with, didn't trust him.

"Then give me your e-mail address, and I'll send it to you."

"What is it?" she asked.

"You'll see."

Tati was sitting in front of her parents' computer when his e-mail arrived. "Here's your sister showing how horrified she is by what *I* did," it read.

"What?" Tati downloaded the attachment. It turned out to be a picture. But it was so large she couldn't see the entire image at once, or even figure out what it was.

After typing in a few commands, she got it to fit her screen. Only then could she tell what she was looking at. It was a picture of Kalyna at maybe…seventeen. She was sprawled on a bed, completely nude, laughing as if carefree. And she was wearing that necklace.

23

Ava was at Luke's apartment. He'd dropped her off so she could get some work done, then he'd left to get groceries and run errands. But even with him gone she couldn't concentrate. Just being in his space was enough to distract her.

She forced herself to finish checking the phone records on the Beeker case. Then she opened her laptop, typed out a few letters she planned to print later and tried to return some e-mail. But after reading one particular message three times without comprehension, she gave up. She was no longer getting anything done.

With a sigh, she got up and wandered around the room. Luke's apartment was plain but clean, and she had to smile at the various masculine touches that put his stamp on the place—a bike propped against the wall behind the couch, skis in the corner, *Sports Illustrated* magazines on the coffee table and a giant TV against one wall. There was a picture of him with his family on a shelf—taken at Christmastime—and several other photographs, mostly snapshots of various buildings or landforms as seen from the air. Luke obviously loved being a pilot. She'd bet he was a great one.

She went into the tiny kitchen and checked a few cupboards. He'd told her to help herself if she wanted anything to eat but she wasn't hungry; she was bored.

He had canned goods, a whole shelf of vitamin supplements and a large container of protein powder. The fridge wasn't any better stocked. The fruit-and-vegetable bin contained one apple and a few carrots. On the shelves, she found milk, sour cream, jelly and a package of hot dogs. He probably ate out a lot.

From there, she walked down a short hall to his bedroom and poked her head through the doorway. His bed was made, of course. His closet door was shut but she didn't need to see inside to know that his uniforms would all be neatly ironed, with his shoes shined and organized beneath. Remembering the first time she'd seen him at the door of The Last Stand wearing jeans and a T-shirt that'd been pressed, she chuckled.

Some free weights lined the wall and a giant model plane took up most of the space on his dresser—what was left by a second flat-screen TV. There was another bathroom off the master bedroom. She knew it would be as clean as the one she'd used when she arrived—

A knock at the door brought her immediately back to the living room. "Hey, Trussell. You home? Open up!"

Ava answered to find two men there. One was every bit as tall as Luke, the other only five-nine or so, but both were dressed in muscle shirts, gym shorts and tennis shoes and were sweaty enough to suggest they'd been exerting themselves. Their haircuts would've told her they were military, even if she hadn't been able to see the dog tags hanging around their necks.

"Who're you?" the tall one asked.

"Ava Bixby," she said. "I'm a friend of Luke's. And you?"

The short one spoke up. "I'm Sergeant O'Dell. This is Captain Fewkes. Also friends of Luke's."

Ava recognized the sergeant's name. He was the one

who'd gone to the Moby Dick with Luke. She was glad to meet him. "Would you like to come in?"

They stepped into the living room and Fewkes closed the door, but they didn't sit down. "Where's Luke?" O'Dell asked, glancing toward the bedroom.

"He's running some errands."

"Oh." The two men looked at each other. "He knows you're in his apartment, though, right? You're not friends with Kalyna Harter or anything."

She laughed. "No. I'm with The Last Stand, a victims' charity in Sac. I'm trying to help him with the Harter situation."

"Oh, I remember now. He's mentioned you. So what do you think of Kalyna?"

"I think she's trouble."

"You know I was with Luke at The Moby Dick, don't you?"

"Yes. Jonathan Stivers is my investigator. He spoke with you this past week."

"That was your guy?"

"He has his own agency, but he works with us a lot."

"Did he tell you I said Kalyna's lying?" O'Dell asked.

"He told me. Now we just need to prove it."

"This might help." He jerked his head at his companion. "Fewkes ran into her in mid-May. That's why I brought him over. She said some weird sh-stuff to him at a bar. I thought Luke should hear about it."

"What kind of weird stuff?"

"When I asked her to dance, she said she couldn't get near me or her fiancé would go ballistic. I said I didn't see a ring on her finger, and she said it was because they hadn't picked it up from the jeweler's yet." He imitated the expression and body language he'd used that night. "I said, 'It's just a dance.' But she insisted that her fiancé was this insanely jealous animal. I told her I could handle myself in a fight, and she said I wouldn't stand a chance against Captain Luke Trussell."

"Did you know Luke?"

"Not really. I mean, we've played a couple pickup games over at the basketball court, so I recognized the name and had enough respect for him to back off. I mean, I'm not out to force a girl to dance with me if she doesn't want to, you know? But after I moved on, Kalyna wouldn't quit messing with me. She'd sidle past me, brushing her breast against my arm or touching me in some other way. Or I'd catch her staring at me from across the room and she'd give me a 'you know you want me' kind of smile. It was weird. I got the feeling she was trying to tempt me into approaching her again, even though she'd warned me off."

"What do you think she was up to?" Ava asked.

"Playing head games?" he said with a shrug.

"I think she was living out a fantasy," O'Dell suggested. "I saw how she acted with Luke. She's obsessed with him. She'd love nothing more than to be his fiancée and have him care enough to be as jealous as she claimed he'd be. She was enjoying the danger and excitement of flirting with Fewkes as if she really had something to worry about from Trussell."

Knowing Kalyna, Ava could believe it. She expected Luke to return at any moment, so she poked her head out into the hall. But it was empty. She was under the impression that the men in these apartments didn't stay home for much longer than it took to shower and change, at least during the day. They were single and active—this was just a place to bunk at night. "You haven't told Luke about this?" she said, closing the door again.

"I didn't know about it until today," O'Dell said.

"And I didn't see any point," Fewkes chimed in. "If

she was telling the truth, it'd only piss him off that we were flirting with each other. If she was lying, I'm not planning on seeing her again so it doesn't matter. It wasn't until I was lifting at the gym today that I heard O'Dell here talking about how some chick was claiming Trussell raped her. The name jumped out at me—because Kalyna had mentioned it. Made me wonder what the hell was going on. She told me he was her fiancé, yet she was telling everyone else he raped her?"

"Neither is true," O'Dell said.

"She must be a nutcase," Fewkes added.

O'Dell nudged him. "Tell her the rest."

"There's more?" Ava said.

"Wait till you hear this," O'Dell chortled.

"Later that night, when I passed her on my way to the bar," Fewkes continued, "I felt her grab my ass."

Ava couldn't imagine many women being quite that bold. But this was Kalyna, after all. "More teasing?" she said, incredulous.

"I guess, because when I asked her what was going on, she said she wanted me, just didn't dare act on it. So I asked her what would happen if we got caught, and she said her fiancé would kill us both."

"How'd you reply?"

"I didn't believe her. Like I told you, I don't know Trussell very well, but he seems too coolheaded for that. So I said, 'Don't you think that's a little extreme?' And she said, 'Hell, no. I'd do the same if I ever caught him cheating on me.' When I started laughing, she said, 'You think I'm joking, don't you?' I said, 'I think you're drunk.'"

Ava could tell he was leading up to a bigger climax than this. "And?"

"And then she leaned forward to show me a knife she had in her purse and said, 'I've done it before.'"

Chills rolled down Ava's spine. This incident definitely made it easier to believe that Kalyna might've caused Norma's death. "What'd you do?"

"I left. I was done with her."

"Do you think she was serious about having killed before?" Ava asked.

Fewkes's nod was emphatic. "Serious as a heart attack. And I'll testify to that."

His story revealed a frightening cold-bloodedness on Kalyna's part. Because of that, Ava thought Fewkes's testimony might be important to both cases—Luke's and Norma's. "You just might have to do that. Give me your contact information," she said, and after they left she called the Mesa police.

The door opened while Luke was trying to move all his groceries to one arm so he could reach the knob. "Sergeant O'Dell and Captain Fewkes stopped by," Ava announced, stepping back to admit him.

He carried his sacks in and deposited them on the counter. "Who's Fewkes?"

"A guy you've met playing basketball a time or two."

Luke didn't recognize the name. "Why'd he come here?"

"To tell you that Kalyna isn't stable."

"As if that's news." He stowed the milk in the fridge. "How does he know?"

While Ava explained what Fewkes and O'Dell had said, Luke put away the rest of his groceries. By the time she finished, he felt as much relief as concern. The number of people who stood on his side was growing. No court-martial would find against him with the details that were coming to light.

But he still had no idea where this would end. He felt

confident that he could take care of himself, and doubted Kalyna would attack him physically. But obsession-motivated murder didn't happen only in the movies.

You've been seeing her, haven't you!

The accusation ringing through her statement showed that Kalyna viewed them as a couple. And she'd already told him what she had planned for any love interest of his. Was Ava in danger?

He thought she might be. No one even knew where Kalyna was, but if she'd murdered her mother, she could be on a rampage. And she had military training, familiarity with weapons.

"You're quiet," Ava said when he made no comment on Fewkes's story.

He folded the sacks and slipped them onto a shelf in his small pantry. "I'm wondering what to do."

"About what?"

"About you."

"I'm not *your* problem."

Then whose problem was she? He doubted she would've been embroiled in this had she just dropped the case and walked away as she'd initially tried to do. It was her affiliation with him that put her at risk. *She's working for me now,* he'd told Kalyna. He'd all but painted a target on Ava's forehead. What had he been thinking?

That Kalyna was like other people, like him. That she'd respond to the news of Ava's defection by realizing she was losing any advantage she had. That she'd back off. But she *wasn't* like other people. The deeper he got into this, the more he understood that.

"So you'll be safe on the houseboat?" he asked. "I mean, she has no way of finding it, right?"

"No. No way. She knows how to find *this* place,

though. She could come here, shoot up your apartment—shoot *you*—and it would all be over in seconds."

"She's not going to shoot me."

"You don't know that. You can't stay here."

"Where am I supposed to go?"

"To a friend's place."

"My friends have roommates and no extra beds. And I'm not leaving the comfort of my apartment unless I'm happy with where I'm staying."

"Which means what?"

He grinned. "I'm happy at your place."

"No way. You're not coming home with me."

"Why not?" Maybe her clothes were as ugly as ever, but she was pretty in spite of them, far prettier than the day he'd first met her. Why she seemed to have changed so much in such a short time, he couldn't say—except that her personality somehow pulled the entire package together. "You have a comfortable recliner."

Her forehead rumpled. "You're kidding, right? Don't you have to work in the morning?"

"I can make a call, leave a message for my superior officer. I have so much leave coming, he'll give me the whole week. It'll save him from having to think up things for me to do now that I'm grounded."

"So you want to come home with me."

"I think it would be safer." Luke hid a smile. He didn't need to stay anywhere. He had a 9 mm in his dresser drawer. He could protect himself, but the image of Ava in that thong flashed before his eyes for probably the millionth time, and staying home—or anywhere else—just couldn't compete. He doubted Kalyna could find the houseboat, but he didn't want to risk being wrong and seeing Ava get hurt. In his mind, this was more about protecting her, and there was no harm in that. "What do you say?"

"I've used the boat as a refuge for my clients before," she mused. "And I've got an extra bedroom and everything."

You should watch the sunrise from my bedroom... He had no interest in her guest quarters. And he felt it was only fair to warn her. "Just so you know, if you do have me over, it's asking for trouble."

Her eyes narrowed. "What kind of trouble?"

Stepping closer, he lowered his voice. "The kind of trouble that comes with getting naked."

She licked her lips nervously. "You're not attracted to me, remember?"

"I might've overstated the level of my disinterest."

"No, you were right." She backed away. "We're a mismatch. Completely different, ill-suited, worlds apart."

"I keep telling myself that."

"But..."

"I still want you."

She cleared her throat. "Absolutely not. Forget it. I won't be getting naked with you," she said. But when he packed his bag, he took the condoms from his nightstand, just in case.

The woman who'd welcomed Kalyna to Help for Women, a free clinic in Reno that was open twenty-four hours seven days a week, stood in the doorway of the small exam room where Kalyna had been waiting. She was smiling, which boded well. "Great news," she said.

Kalyna's heart jumped into her throat. "Seriously?"

"Seriously. The AIDS test showed no antibodies. You're clean."

But what about the baby? "And the pregnancy?"

Her smile faded. "I'm afraid there is no pregnancy."

No pregnancy! Kalyna couldn't believe it. She'd

never had so much unprotected sex in her life. It *had* to result in a child. When she was younger, she'd gotten pregnant so easily.

"Is something wrong with me?" she asked. "Is there some reason I can't have a baby?" She was feeling the urge to hurt herself again. Why wouldn't God give her a baby?

Because she was bad. But He was the one who'd made her this way. She'd never had anything she wanted, nothing. Why couldn't He at least let her have Luke?

The doctor removed the stethoscope from around her neck and put it in the pocket of her coat. "It's hard to tell with such a cursory examination. You should really see an OB/GYN if you're interested in having a child. And don't worry, even if there are problems, there's so much they can do these days."

But by then it'd be too late.

If only she'd gotten pregnant. Then Luke would've given her another chance. He was that kind of guy. And one more chance was all she needed to prove how perfect they'd be together. No one could be more devoted to him than she was.

"You can go ahead and get dressed," the doctor said, and left the room.

Kalyna slowly stood. What now? It was only a matter of time before Ogitani dropped the case. Her own father would testify against her. So would Ava. That bitch had ruined everything, talking to her mother and her sister and Luke. It wasn't supposed to happen like that....

Ava was the one who'd taken Luke away from her.

I hate her. I hate her with a passion. Kalyna had no hope now. None.

But on the way out they handed her the printed results of the tests they'd performed, and she realized she might've given up too soon. The sheet read *negative,* but that one word wasn't anything a little Wite-Out and a copier couldn't fix.

Luke had asked for proof that she was pregnant. So she'd show him falsified lab results. Granted, the ploy would only buy her a few months. After a while, it'd become obvious that her stomach wasn't growing.

But a few months was better than nothing.

Ava's stepfather had docked the houseboat where she'd left it. Although the smell of his cheap cologne lingered, he was gone—thank God. She didn't want to deal with him. Not when she was going on so little sleep. And not when she had Luke with her.

Well…actually, she never wanted to deal with him.

Once she'd retrieved the key from under her potted hydrangea and let them in, she found a note on the kitchen table, but it was getting dark so she had to turn on a light to read it. "Thanks," it said in Pete's rapid scrawl. Someone else, presumably his new girlfriend, had written underneath: "Thank you so much for allowing us the use of your houseboat. It was a wonderful adventure, one my son won't soon forget."

"Too bad she didn't leave her number," Ava muttered.

"Who?" Luke asked.

"Liz…Smeltzer, if I'm reading her signature correctly."

"Your stepfather's girlfriend? You'd really warn her off?"

"In a heartbeat." She put down her briefcase and took out her laptop.

"Don't tell me you're planning to work some more," he said when she booted it up.

"I'm thinking of doing a few things, like calling Kalyna's sister."

"Any chance she knows where Kalyna is?"

The computer clicked as it ran through its opening

sequence. "She might be in touch with her, but even if she's not, she could become an ally."

"To *us?* How do you figure?

Ava took her seat at the dining room table. "When I talked to her that night at the restaurant, she seemed so different from Kalyna. I got the impression she didn't really want to speak poorly of her mother. Now that this has happened, she might be upset enough to say what she really feels."

Luke put his duffel bag by the couch. "She could also call and report everything you say to her sister."

"I think that's a gamble we have to take, don't you? It's possible she suspects that Kalyna's the one who killed Norma. That might erode some of her loyalty."

"Or she could be afraid of Kalyna," he countered. "Maybe that's why she said what she did on the phone."

"She *should* be afraid of Kalyna. If Kalyna's as narcissistic as I believe, everyone should be afraid of her. But that's why we need to act fast. The sooner the police put her away, the sooner we can all breathe easier."

"You have the number?"

Ava opened her Internet browser and used a search engine to locate the mortuary's Web page. "I don't have a cell number for her, but I can call the business. I'm sure this is how Jonathan came by the number."

"Jonathan?"

"Stivers. He's a private investigator who helps on our various cases."

"He's not Geoffrey."

"No."

"How often do you see Geoffrey?" Luke asked.

"About once a week."

"Why haven't you slept with him?"

She had slept with him, just not recently, and she

wasn't sure she wanted to explain how empty it had felt. "You heard my stepfather. I'm frigid."

"You don't really believe that...."

No, but she hoped *he* would. Maybe that would dilute some of the tension between them. "I don't know anymore," she mumbled.

"How long has it been since you've been with someone?"

"That's none of your business."

"Come on. We're friends, right?"

"No." They weren't friends. That was why she had to change the subject or they wouldn't make it through the next fifteen minutes without taking off their clothes. Then he'd learn for himself that she wasn't "frigid" in the least. Every time she looked at him she wanted to touch him. "We were talking about calling Tatiana."

"Yeah." He rubbed a hand over his face. "Maybe we should wait until tomorrow. She's just lost her mother."

"It sounds callous, but we might get more out of her now. And Kalyna could be dangerous, not only to us but to others."

"It's worth a shot," he said.

Ava dialed the number and waited through the greeting, then pressed "1." No one picked up, but she was given the option to leave a message.

"This is Ava Bixby from The Last Stand victims' charity in Sacramento. I'm calling for Tatiana. Tatiana, could you please return my call? It's very important that I speak with you," she said, and left her number.

She'd just hung up when the phone rang. Caller ID showed the mortuary's number.

Tati paced nervously in her bedroom as she waited for Ava Bixby to answer. She had no business calling her back. She knew what Kalyna thought of Ava, knew her sister would interpret it as a betrayal. But Tati was so confused. She'd been trying to get hold of Kalyna for hours, but either Kalyna's phone was dead, or she'd shut it off. Why hadn't she checked in since they'd talked? She could've used a pay phone and called collect if necessary. Didn't she care that Norma was dead? That their family was ruined?

And what about that picture Mark had e-mailed? What did it mean?

It couldn't mean what *he* said it did. Kalyna had always been aloof. She'd been moody and difficult and, except for a few magnanimous acts like buying Tati those jeans at the mall yesterday, selfish. But she would never murder for the *fun* of it, like Mark said.

I only helped her dispose of the body, Tati.

Why didn't you tell someone?

Are you kidding? I was madly in love with her. And she promised me all kinds of sexual favors if I'd get her out of the mess she was in. It wasn't until she threatened to tell your parents about me and...you know, the corpses, that I gave in. But she liked screwing with the corpses, too. Don't think it was just me. She's the one who got me going. She said she wouldn't sleep with me unless I proved my love for her by—

"Hello?"

Veering away from the sick accusation she was hearing again, this time in her thoughts, Tatiana swallowed hard. "Ava? It's Tatiana Harter. I-I'm returning your call."

"Are you okay, Tatiana?"

Tati hadn't expected to hear such concern in Ava's voice and couldn't help responding to it. "I don't know." She started to weep. "I've never been so scared or...or confused."

"What's going on over there?"

"It's chaos. No one knows anything. Except that my mother is dead."

"Have you heard from Kalyna?"

"Not since this morning when I told her about Mom."

"You don't think she's to blame for what happened, do you?"

"I don't *want* to think so, but...nothing makes sense."

"The police told me it might be a man named Mark Cannaby. That he'd had a few run-ins with your parents, spouted some threats."

"I've talked to Mark several times today and he...he claims he's innocent." And, heaven help her, thanks to that picture she was beginning to believe him.

"Does he have an alibi, Tati?"

"No, he says he was home alone last night. But... Kalyna doesn't have an alibi, either. She said she left at midnight, but that doesn't mean it's true. The ME has indicated that the estimated time of death is anywhere from 1:00 to 4:00 a.m. Even if Kalyna left when she said she did, midnight is close."

"A guy came to see me tonight," Ava said. "He claims he had an interesting conversation with Kalyna in a bar a few weeks ago."

Tati cringed to think what that might be. Kalyna liked to shock people, which often embarrassed Tati. "What'd he say?"

"She told him she's killed someone before. She was convincing enough that he believed her, and after hearing what the police had to say about that hitchhiker...I'm concerned there might be some truth to it."

At this, Tatiana broke down completely. "Oh, God, how can you think you know someone but not know them at all?" she sobbed.

"It happens all the time," Ava said quietly. "Did you ever see or hear anything that might support his story?"

"Not really, but—" Tatiana did her best to recover so she could speak. "Can you give me your e-mail address? I have something to send you."

24

The woman Kalyna had cut off to get into the bathroom at the gas station in Auburn, where she'd stopped to fill up, gave her a dirty look as she emerged, but she merely smiled. After fifteen minutes at the Kinko's down the road, she had a document that appeared to prove she was pregnant, and that was all she needed. At least for the time being. She could hardly wait to show it to Luke. Even if he tried to verify it through the clinic, they wouldn't tell him anything. Places like that kept everything strictly confidential.

Kalyna moseyed down the rows of the gas station's mini-mart. Once he'd had a chance to adjust to the idea, he'd be more receptive, she told herself. She just needed to convince him to forgive her. As soon as she could reach Ogitani, she'd tell her she no longer believed it was Luke who'd raped her, and Ogitani would drop the charges. Then Kalyna would tell Luke she'd come forward with the truth because her conscience and her love for him wouldn't allow her to lie anymore. And while he was feeling relieved and grateful, she'd apologize for her bad behavior and promise him it would never happen again.

She *could* convince him. She could be very persuasive.

Her smile turned dreamy as she imagined them kissing and making up. What she wouldn't give to be in his arms again—

"Watch where you're going!"

"Up yours," she snapped. The near collision was her fault, and the person she'd nearly bowled over was only a teenager, but she didn't care. She'd spotted something that instantly and completely captured her imagination: baby items. There was a whole row of diapers and formula and teething toys, rubber spoons and tiny T-shirts and rattles....

Once she and Luke were back together, maybe she'd really get pregnant. Then she'd finally have what she needed to hold him forever.

She stroked a terry-cloth sleeper. It was so soft. Picturing herself toting Luke's son around in an outfit like that, she couldn't resist buying it. Then, because it made her favorite fantasy feel even more real, she grabbed some diapers and baby food.

"Got a little one at home, huh?" the checker said as she rang up the items.

"I'm expecting," Kalyna replied.

"How exciting! Is this your first?"

"Yes, it is." She took Luke's picture from her purse. "This is the baby's daddy. He couldn't be prouder."

The checker looked up from her work to smile at Luke. "Wow, he's a handsome devil."

"And he's got a really big dick," Kalyna whispered, and walked out, leaving the dumbstruck woman standing there holding thirty-five cents in change.

"So now you're saying I might've impregnated a *double* murderer?" Luke couldn't even look at the screen, didn't want to see that picture of Kalyna. Naked or not, he found her hideous. "What a legacy for my kid."

"We don't *know* she's a murderer. For that matter, we don't even know she's pregnant," Ava said.

Having slept with Kalyna was bad enough. "She said she'd send proof. That makes me fear she's telling the truth for a change."

"You were together *one* time and used a condom."

"But you know what she did with it."

"She could still be bluffing, using pregnancy as another way to get your attention." Ava sat back but continued to stare at the picture Tatiana had sent her. "That's what this has been about from the beginning. She's trying to force you to notice her, to make it impossible for you to move on and forget her."

"She's definitely succeeding there."

"She's so cold, so calculating. I don't think I've ever run up against anyone like her before."

He glanced at the clock. It was only ten, but he was already getting tired. He typically woke early, worked hard and played hard, too. But his usual physical activity was easier on him than what he'd been through this past week. It didn't help that he'd gotten so little sleep last night. "We need to talk to this Mark guy."

Ava leaned closer to the screen. "Look at her smile. It's almost exuberant, as if she holds all the power in the relationship with the person taking the picture and she knows it."

"Mark took the picture, didn't he?"

"I assume so."

"That's another reason we should talk to him."

"But will a necrophiliac be any more credible than Kalyna?" she asked. "He has his own secrets to hide."

"He's already been outed for what he is, so he might not be as defensive. And being a necrophiliac doesn't necessarily make him a murderer."

"True. Especially when it comes to the hitchhiker, Sarah," she said. "We have no proof she even existed. And if she did exist, and she's still missing, they cremated her body so we won't be able to prove that she's dead."

Avoiding a second glimpse of Kalyna's picture, Luke sat across from Ava, facing the back of her laptop instead. "It wouldn't be hard to get rid of ashes."

Ava nodded. "They were in the perfect situation to be able to dispose of a body without leaving a trace."

"True. But Kalyna could be trying to send us scrambling off in the wrong direction. We know how clever she is."

She leaned back. "I say we ask Jonathan to do some checking, see if he can come up with a missing person from New Mexico named Sarah."

Luke rubbed his chin. "Tatiana said Sarah was about fourteen. Is that enough for your investigator to go on? When did this girl supposedly die?"

"Mark worked for the Harters when Kalyna was sixteen and seventeen. That means Sarah most likely went missing right around then, unless she was a runaway who'd already been out on her own for a while."

"At fourteen, I doubt it," he said.

"Not many kids run away younger than that," she agreed.

"But it's been a decade. That won't make tracing her very easy."

"Jonathan's good," she assured him. "The best. But it'd help if we could get some more information from Mark."

Luke stretched out his legs. "He should be motivated to provide any details he can now that Kalyna's pointing the finger at him."

Ava started typing.

"What are you doing?" Luke asked.

"Looking up necrophilia on Wikipedia. This is my first experience with it."

He waited until she stopped keying in information and began to read. "What does it say?"

She summarized it for him. "That most necrophiliacs act out of a desire to 'possess an unresisting and unrejecting partner.'"

"So it's about having power, being in control."

"Like a lot of crimes. And it generally stems from low self-esteem, as one might guess." She paused as she read more, then spoke again. "This is interesting."

"What?"

"In ancient Egypt, they used to leave the dead bodies of beautiful women out to decompose for three or four days before delivering them to the embalmers—to discourage sexual interest." She looked at him around her computer screen. "Who would've thought any civilization would have to resort to such drastic measures?"

"Apparently, mental disorders haven't changed a whole lot over the centuries."

"Thanks to the media, we just hear more about them," she agreed.

Since that picture of Kalyna was gone, he moved to the chair beside hers. "So when do we call Mark? Tomorrow?"

"Why wait?"

"We know he works at the cemetery, but he won't be there at ten o'clock on a Sunday night, will he?"

"People Search will have his home number."

"It's that easy to come up with his personal information?"

"He might be listed in the phone book, but we'll get a

lot more with People Search," she said. "Like his birth date."

"We should be able to get his approximate age from Tati," he murmured.

Fifteen minutes later, she had a number for a Mark Cannaby in Mesa, Arizona. And Luke was certain they had the right Mark. According to his birth date, which was listed as Ava had promised, he was thirty-seven, exactly the age Tatiana had told them when they called her.

A quick check with MapQuest showed that his address was less than three miles from the mortuary.

"I'd offer to let you get on an extension, but all I have is my cell phone," Ava told him.

"I'll lean close," he said, and she dialed.

Mark answered on the first ring. "Hello?"

"Mark? This is Ava Bixby from The Last Stand, a victims' charity in Sacramento, California."

"Why are you calling me?" The suspicion in his voice made him come across as nervous, defensive, maybe even paranoid.

"Tatiana Harter said we should talk to you about a girl named Sarah," Ava told him.

"I didn't kill her!" he shouted. "I swear it. That was Kalyna. It was *all* Kalyna."

"What would Kalyna want with a girl two or three years younger, Mark?"

"She told me she wanted to try a three-way. That was her big fantasy."

Ava glanced at Luke. That sounded like Kalyna. "Where did she meet her?"

"She saw her out front. The mortuary's on a busy road. Sarah was hitchhiking to Tucson. Kalyna convinced her she'd feed her and give her a bed for the night.

But she gagged her, tied her up and hid her in the garden shed."

"Wasn't she afraid her father might find out what she'd done?"

"I was the one who kept the grounds. Mr. Harter never went back there. He spent all his time in the mortuary, embalming and selling caskets. But I was nervous about it. I kept telling Kalyna she should let her go, but she wouldn't hear of it. She kept saying, 'When we're done.'"

"How long was Sarah there?"

"Three or four days."

Ava was gripping the phone so tightly her knuckles were turning white. "It ended in murder?"

"Yes."

"How do you know?"

"I..." His voice faltered. "I helped dispose of the body."

Her eyes troubled, Ava glanced at Luke, and he nodded to encourage her. "That's pretty gruesome, Mark."

Mark said nothing.

"What happened?" she prompted.

"I don't want to remember. I've blocked it out. Otherwise, I wouldn't be able to live with myself."

"You're facing some serious charges. You know that."

Silence.

"I suggest you tell us everything you know."

He muttered something like, "Oh, God." But once he started talking, he seemed willing to spill it all. "She liked making me do stuff to Sarah. She said I had to prove my love, that I had to obey if I ever wanted to touch her again."

"Stuff like..." Ava prompted.

Once again, Luke sensed Mark's reluctance. "You don't want to know."

"I *need* to know."

He groaned. "I knew it was going to come to this someday."

"What did you do to her, Mark?"

"We raped her with objects, sodomized her, you name it."

When Ava shuddered, Luke curled his fingers through hers. This was so depraved he couldn't believe it was real.

"How'd she die?" Ava asked.

"Kalyna got bored with her. I wanted to let her go, but Kalyna said that would be stupid, that she'd tell the first person she saw about us and we'd go to prison for the rest of our lives. So she told me to electrocute her."

Ava's grip tightened on Luke's hand. "In the shed?"

"Kalyna told me to make her stand in a bucket of water, then run the extension cord I used for the edger out there."

This seemed too detailed to be a lie. Luke wondered what Ava was thinking.

"Did you do it?" she asked.

"No. Thank God I drew the line somewhere." His voice dropped again. "But what I did was almost as bad."

"What's that?"

"Nothing. I did nothing to help her."

"What did Kalyna do?"

"When I told her I wouldn't kill for her, she got so angry she started kicking Sarah—in the head, the face. She was handcuffed to the riding lawn mower, and her feet were tied. She couldn't escape. I tried to stop Kalyna, but…"

"But what?"

"I couldn't calm her down. She was so full of rage. I'd never seen anything like it. I was afraid someone would hear and come to investigate, so I left."

When Ava rested her head on Luke's shoulder, he

knew the details were getting to her. They were making him sick, too. But she kept talking. "Then how do you know she died?"

His sigh was long and loud. "Kalyna came and got me later. She said she'd forgive me for being a 'pussy' if I'd carry Sarah inside so we could put her in the crematory. She said it would all be over soon and everything could go back to the way it was before."

"And you did it."

There was a pause, but ultimately he confirmed it. "Yes."

"Then what?" Ava asked.

"Then nothing," he said. "Kalyna took Sarah's necklace before we burned her body. Every time we had sex after that, she insisted on wearing it like some…some trophy. I think she enjoyed making me see it, enjoyed lording her power over me. I actually have a picture of her sitting on my bed—"

"Tatiana already sent it to me," Ava interrupted.

"Then you've seen it."

"Yes."

Silence again. "I'm sorry," he said a moment later. "I wish I'd never met Kalyna."

"Why'd he keep quiet for so long?" Luke murmured in Ava's ear. "Why didn't he come forward?"

When she repeated those questions, Mark laughed bitterly. "You don't know how vindictive Kalyna can be. And she's *such* a good liar. I was older, a man. And her parents thought I was a necrophiliac. I was scared of what might happen if I ever opened that can of worms."

"Are you a necrophiliac, Mark?"

"No. Absolutely not."

"Norma told your girlfriend that she caught you… sexually molesting one of the corpses."

"Kalyna was behind that, too! She set me up, man."

"What do you mean?"

"She liked making me do all kinds of shit that would turn a normal person's stomach. She told me I had to prove my love, but…now that I look back, I realize she just…got off on it. It was an adrenaline rush for her, you know? She'd pick worse and worse things for me to do… I'm not gay or even bi. And I'm not interested in dead people. But…I was so caught up in *her.* I couldn't bear the thought of losing her. I would've done anything. Well, almost anything. I didn't kill Sarah, like I said."

It was all Luke could do to remain sitting with the anger and adrenaline flowing through him. But if he got up, he wouldn't be able to hear the conversation.

"You were ten years older than she was," Ava said. "How could you be at such a disadvantage?"

Luke could hear the incredulity in Ava's voice—and shared it.

"It's hard to explain. I don't have a good answer. She was everything I'd ever wanted. The prettiest girl who'd ever looked at me. And she wasn't so demanding at first. She seemed sweet, even innocent. It was only after I fell for her and she realized I was in love with her that everything changed."

"You said she set you up."

"She did. That's how she got rid of me. I think she was done with me, wanted to get me out of her life. But she'd been telling me I was everything to her, so she couldn't just break it off. I knew about Sarah, for one thing. And Kalyna was getting a lot of attention from some of the football players at the high school. She didn't want to put up with my jealousy, didn't want me in the way anymore. So she convinced me to…you know…do an old lady who'd died earlier that day. She told me I could have sex with her after if I'd do it—she'd started putting stipulations on our time together by then—but she must've told her mother I was up to something, or got her to come to the back some other way, because her mother never went near the preparation area. And yet, suddenly, there she was."

"Where was Kalyna when her mother walked in?" Ava asked.

"I don't know. She ducked out of the room somehow. That's another reason I think she knew it was coming."

"And then you were fired."

"And then I was fired."

Ava turned Luke's hand over and spread his fingers wide. "Did you ever see Kalyna after that?"

"I wanted to. Lord knows I wanted to. I thought I'd die those first few months without her. But she didn't seem to mind the separation one bit. She could've sneaked out to see me, but she didn't. And I couldn't even call. Her parents were determined to keep us apart because of what Mrs. Harter had seen. The few times I called and actually managed to speak to Kalyna, she gave me the excuse that her parents were watching her too closely."

"Where was Tatiana through all of this?"

"Tati's different from Kalyna. She's a real sweetheart. But she's not...I don't know, dynamic, exciting, charismatic like Kalyna. Kalyna knows how to be whatever you want her to be. It isn't until she feels completely safe that her real personality comes out."

"How come Tati didn't see that side of her?" Luke whispered.

"Weren't she and her sister close?" Ava asked.

"Kalyna pretended to be a loving sister, but she's never loved anyone, not really. She'd leave Tati with the bulk of the work and slip away with me. Tati must've known we were having sex, but it was almost as if she didn't want to deal with it, as if it was less upsetting to turn a blind eye. She was loyal enough not to tell. But if she'd thought that what we were doing was worse than fooling around, she would've come forward. Kalyna knew that, knew what to keep from her and what was safe to tell."

"How do you feel about Kalyna now?"

He gave a bitter laugh. "I wish I could tell you I hate her. In some ways, I do but…"

"What?"

"Even after everything that's happened, there are still times I think of her and want to be with her. She was…like a drug for me. I've never smoked, but I've heard people talk about how hard it is to quit, how after years and years of not having a cigarette, they still crave one. That's what it's like for me. But I'd never get with Kalyna again, even if she wanted me. I know she's sick."

"I think she has her heart set on someone else." Ava met Luke's gaze as she said this.

"Oh, yeah?" Mark said. "Well, you should warn him. If he's smart he'll stay far, far away. She'll be everything he could dream of—at first. But then she'll turn on him."

Ava seemed to realize she'd been clinging to Luke and suddenly let go. "Why'd you threaten Mrs. Harter, Mark?"

"That was stupid. I was so angry, you know? I'd finally moved on and was dating a nice girl, someone I thought I could have a serious relationship with. It was the first time I'd cared about anyone since Kalyna. And Norma Harter ruined it for me."

"You broke up."

"She couldn't stand to let me touch her after that, and I can't blame her."

"Have you told the police what you've told me?"

"Yes. I'm going in tomorrow to make a formal statement."

"I have one last question."

"What is it?"

"Why'd you come back?"

"I figured enough time had passed. Kalyna was gone. I'd been in Tucson, waiting tables, and I needed a better job. It's not as if I love the funereal business. It's just...it's all I know."

"I see. Well, thanks for talking to me."

He caught her before she could hang up. "Can I ask you a question?"

"Of course."

"What do you think's going to happen?"

"To what?"

"To me?"

"That depends on the case the D.A. constructs. But if it looks like you're going to prison, you could turn state's evidence and your stay will be a lot shorter than Kalyna's," she said. Then she told him goodbye and disconnected.

"What's your take?" Luke asked as she put her phone on the table.

Ava turned to study him. "I believe him."

"So do I," he said. "Which means..."

"Which means Kalyna is the most evil individual I've ever encountered."

"And she's obsessed with me." He shoved a hand through his hair. "That's always good to hear."

He was being flippant, but she remained earnest. "Normal rules don't apply anymore, Luke. You have to watch your back every second until the police catch her and put her behind bars."

He scowled. "I'm not going to run from a woman!"

Ava got to her feet. "That's exactly the kind of macho bullshit that could get you killed! You realize that."

He stood, too. "But waiting for the police to put Kalyna behind bars could take a long time. There's no guarantee they'll ever be able to gather the evidence they need. I can't let her—or anyone else—disrupt my life indefinitely. *That's* bullshit! If she wants me, she can come and get me. A fight, I can deal with."

"You don't understand. If Kalyna is what Mark's just described, she won't fight fair."

"Doesn't matter."

"Would you quit being so cavalier? She killed an innocent girl for the *entertainment* value! She killed the woman who adopted her—probably for gas money. She's not like any other woman you've ever come across."

"Those victims were both vulnerable to her. They were weaker, unaware that she was dangerous. I won't make that mistake."

"But she has no conscience."

"What do you want me to do? I have a job, Ava. I'll stay here tonight and maybe tomorrow if it'll make you feel better. As long as I stay in the area, I can take some leave. But when that leave is up, I have to report to work whether they've found Kalyna or not."

Anger sparked in Ava's eyes. "You're an asshole, you know that? You're going to get yourself killed!"

Surprised by her harsh reaction, he grabbed her arm. "Whoa, what's going on here?"

"I've dealt with this type of thing before, seen women murdered because they couldn't escape the men who were tormenting them. Do you think I want to see that happen to you? Just because you're a man and feel you shouldn't be frightened of a woman?"

Why was she so upset? Nothing had happened to him yet. "What's the matter, Ava?"

"You're not taking this seriously enough!"

"And I think you're taking it too seriously. Why?"

She glared up at him without answering.

"Are you beginning to care about me?" he asked softly.

"No," she snapped, but she couldn't maintain eye contact. Jerking away from him, she walked out of the room.

A few seconds later, he heard the cabin door slam.

25

Ava had overreacted and she knew it. The lack of sleep, the stress of putting in too many hours and dealing with such high-stakes cases, the knowledge that Jane Burke would be starting at TLS and was ill-equipped for the job, the constant fight not to succumb to her attraction to Luke—it was wearing her down. And what Mark had said about Kalyna... God, it was so dark, so sick, so upsetting—*terrifying.* She couldn't stand the thought of Luke in harm's way.

But Ava's problem ran even deeper.

Are you beginning to care about me?

Yes. She was falling head over heels despite her best efforts to keep some emotional distance. And she didn't want to get a call telling her he'd been killed, especially when they'd had what so many other victims never had—plenty of warning.

The door opened, and Ava heard Luke come out. Hoping the long grass on the bank of the river would hide her, she scooted back away from the water. She needed a moment alone to collect her thoughts and her energy.

I might've overstated the level of my disinterest....

That was hardly an admission of burning desire. She was female and convenient, nothing more. She'd be better off sleeping with Geoffrey again. Maybe she wouldn't see fireworks—she never had before—but she wouldn't be left sad and broken, like her mother.

"Ava?" he called.

She didn't answer. *Go back inside. I'm too emotional to deal with you right now, too tired to shore up my crumbling defenses.* She didn't want to think, be cautious, take care. She wanted to abandon all reservation and grab the pleasure that was within reach. But acting that impulsively was almost always a mistake. And that kind of mistake almost always came with a high price.

"Ava, you might as well answer me. I'll just keep looking until I find you." His footsteps made hollow thuds as he strode to shore on the pier. But when he reached land, he turned the opposite way, so Ava took off her shoes and slipped down to put her toes in the river. It wasn't the cleanest water in the world, but she was tempted to dive in, anyway. She swam in it quite often, and she wasn't alone in that. Water-skiers used it all the time.

Maybe the cold water would act like a slap in the face—give her some more fight.

"Ava! Damn it, don't make me root around like some idiot."

It was childish not to respond. So, as much as she preferred to be left alone, she called out to him. "Go to bed, Luke."

Hearing her voice, he came toward her, eventually dropping down by her side. "What's going on?"

"Nothing, really—just the story of that hitchhiker, I guess. It was so depraved. It brings back the clients I've lost." That was partially true. Bella's situation wasn't the same as Sarah's, but her death felt close right now. So did the fact that Ava could've helped prevent it simply by offering her some support.

"You've got a tough job," he said.

"It needs to be done."

"Maybe it would be better left to someone less sensitive. Someone who doesn't care so damn much about everyone and everything."

She was too intense. She'd heard that before. It frightened people, especially easygoing men who liked to take life in stride and not look too closely at the unpleasant. Men like Luke; men like her father. "I know. But the fact that I care is what drives me. I can't be one thing without the other."

He plucked a blade of grass and put it in the corner of his mouth. "Okay, you're probably doing what you should be doing. But that doesn't make it easy."

The call of the water suddenly proved too strong to resist. It was a way out of the conversation, an escape from his proximity.

Or was it a dare? It had to be a dare because what she was going to do wasn't about escaping from Luke, but getting exactly what she wanted.

Standing, Ava stripped down to her underwear. She would've kept her bra on, but it was expensive and she didn't want to ruin it with river water. She turned away from Luke as she removed it and dropped it in the weeds, then held her hands over her breasts as she waded in.

Luke didn't move, but she could feel his escalation of interest. "How's the water?" he called, as if she hadn't just surprised the hell out of him.

She ducked under, came up and flipped her hair out of her eyes. "Chilly but…refreshing."

"Being able to take a quick dip whenever you want is sort of convenient. With your neighbors off fishing, you don't even have to wear clothes."

"The isolation has other benefits," she said. "Peace. Quiet. Privacy. No roots."

"A lot of women like roots," he said, pointedly.

"Not me. I prefer not to get attached."

"Even to a location?"

"Even to a location." Somewhere along the line she'd lost the ability to grab hold and hang on—to anything. Her father had abandoned her to appease his sexual appetites with woman after woman. Her mother had disappointed her in the worst possible way. Her stepfather had always been too hard to put up with. She'd learned to navigate without anchors and had been doing it for so long she was afraid of taking one on. There was the weight, the confinement, the fear of enjoying some security at last, only to be cut loose when she least expected it. She never wanted to find herself flailing around, trying to regain her bearings. She could tolerate anything but that.

"Are you doing this to me on purpose?" he asked.

She could feel his stare, but she knew the water was inky black. He couldn't see anything except her head—and he could see that only because there was a full moon. "Doing what?" she asked, as if she hadn't known from the beginning how this would affect him.

"Driving me crazy?"

"You can go in the house, if you want." Part of her, the sane part that wasn't sabotaging her future happiness, prayed he would.

"I don't want to go in the house. I want to make love to you. But after what I've been through, I need a very clear invitation. Is that what this is?"

She found the muddy bottom and stood up as far as she could while keeping her breasts submerged. Of course it was an invitation, but it was an invitation she wasn't sure she should be extending. "Maybe," she said.

He got to his feet. "What does that *maybe* depend on?"

"I'm still trying to decide."

"Is Geoffrey the reason you're hesitating?"

"No. We agreed to date other people several months ago. We've just never really acted on it."

Luke moved to the water's edge. "Maybe it's time." He stripped off his shirt and tossed it behind him. Ava could see his muscular torso in the light of the moon and wondered why she'd been foolish enough to provoke him. Soon there'd be no going back....

"Oh, shit," she muttered to herself. But she'd asked for this.

"Would you mind if he was with someone else?" Luke asked.

How *could* she care when she was staring at Luke's bare chest? She couldn't even recall Geoffrey's face right now. "I don't think so."

Luke had already unsnapped his jeans, but he paused before taking them off. "Would you rather be with him?"

Of course not. Or she wouldn't have removed her clothes in front of Luke. But could she really say that?

"Ava?" he prompted when she didn't answer.

"No," she admitted, and that was all it took. The jeans came off, and Luke stood there in nothing but a pair of boxers.

Ava's mouth went so dry she could hardly speak, and yet she had to speak, to fill the silence in an attempt to appease her nerves. "I don't want to hurt him."

"He hasn't made you any promises?"

"No."

"You haven't made him any promises?"

"No."

"Do you want to make love with me, Ava?"

His voice had softened as if he was afraid she'd say no. But a denial would've been the biggest lie she'd ever told, and she didn't even try. "Yes."

Grinning in obvious relief, he dropped his boxers and waded into the water wearing only his dog tags.

As Luke waded closer, Ava's heart began to pound so loudly she couldn't hear anything else. She was excited, scared, hesitant and filled with a driving lust—all at the same time. But fear won out as her most compelling emotion. In a sudden panic, she dove beneath the surface and started swimming as fast as she could in the opposite direction. She had to get away from Luke before it was too late. Before he gave her exactly what she craved and the experience was forever imprinted in her memory....

But he was the better swimmer. Using strong, steady strokes, he quickly caught up with her. He must've been able to feel her shaking because he pulled her close and held her tightly against him instead of touching her in any sexual way. "Hey, don't be nervous," he murmured in her ear. "I'm not in this for a one-night stand. I like you a lot, Ava. You're a good person—stubborn as hell, but a good person. I think we should see where this could lead."

She knew where it would lead. Easy come, easy go. She couldn't trust him. She was too broken, too jaded. How could they start a relationship with her living each day as if she expected him to walk out on her—or turn to the next pretty girl who came along? She was no match for a man like this.

"Let's talk about it later," she said. Presumably when her brain was working again.

"I didn't want you to think this was anything like what happened with Kalyna. I *want* to be with you."

Ava told herself to ignore those words. She couldn't count on them any longer than it took to do the deed. All men talked that way when they wanted sex. Sometimes she wondered if it was a defect in a male's genetic code. "At least you're not drunk, right?" she joked.

He looked at her as if he considered that an odd response, but if he'd expected to hear that she really liked him, too, he'd have a lengthy wait. She wasn't going to fall for this. She was going to enjoy the physical benefits because she craved it as badly—or worse—than he did. But no way would she count on him to be there for her afterward.

"You okay?" he asked.

She nodded.

"You're shaking. You know I'll be gentle, don't you?"

She only knew she'd made her decision and now she could scarcely breathe. Between the cold water moving past her and the heat that threatened to incinerate her from the inside, she was already on sensory overload. "It's been sort of a long time for me," she whispered.

"I know. It's okay."

"Like five months," she added. "And it was several years before Geoffrey came along."

"Just relax."

Impossible. His erection was pressing into her stomach, every bit as impressive as he'd promised at Starbucks, when he'd been purposely provoking her. "What about b-birth control?"

"I've got it handled. Don't worry about anything."

Don't worry? Those were the words any girl needed to worry about! She spoke at high schools on "How to Avoid Becoming a Victim," repeating exactly that message. But his hands were sliding down her back to cup her bottom and his firm, slick body felt so good against hers she couldn't manage any resistance. She was on fire—and quite happy to burn.

He bent his head, but didn't kiss her. He used his tongue and lips on her neck, moving higher until she dropped her head back. But even as she struggled to forfeit her usual control, she worried that her stepfather was right. Maybe she was frigid, in ways. She almost didn't know how to succumb to the pleasure anymore, at least not gracefully. Was that frigid?

"That's it," he coaxed her. "Trust me, Ava."

She was too much of a cynic to trust any man, especially him. But when he lifted her partway out of the water and settled his mouth on her breast, fiery darts of pleasure raced through her, and she knew—gracefully or no—she would succumb. Blanking her mind, she arched into him, and the fear and stiffness began to ease in direct proportion to the rising desire.

He moved to the other breast, and soon giving herself over to him was no longer a struggle. At this point, she couldn't have thought coherently if she'd tried. *Forget. Forget the past. Forget the fear. Forget the future....*

Catching his face between her hands, she brought his mouth to meet hers, and kissed him with all the longing she'd ever felt. He must've liked it because he moaned as his tongue slid against hers. Then his hands found her bottom again. "You definitely know how to kiss," he muttered against her lips. And then he started to remove her panties.

Ava swallowed hard. Oh, no—she was thinking again. She was wondering if she'd regret this. What price would she have to pay for it? Nothing this good came free. Certainly, Luke would become the standard by which she measured every man in the future. Wouldn't that guarantee disappointment? When had she ever met anyone like him?

But then her underwear was gone and she was completely naked. And that made her feel so damn vulnerable.

She gripped his arms. "Do you think this is a bad idea?"

He was too far gone to take her seriously. "I think you worry too much."

Right. No one else seemed to worry about taking what they wanted. She was just being her typical neurotic self.

He threw her panties toward shore, and Ava watched them drop onto the bank. Should she swim off? Head to shore and retrieve them?

"Hey, look at me."

She glanced up at him. He kissed her again, and only seconds later she didn't care about her panties or anything else. Especially when his hand slipped between their bodies.

"Somehow you make it feel like the first time," he said, and gently tugged her lower lip into his mouth.

Ava thought she'd been doing everything wrong. But he obviously didn't mind. "That's it...that's... Oh!" She saw his face, filled with focus and intent, just before she closed her eyes and threw her head back in final and complete abandon. She was close...so close. But she wanted to feel him inside her.

Opening her eyes again, she stared up at him, too hungry to wait any longer. Wrapping her legs around him, she tried to take him inside her.

"Not yet." He stopped her. "The condoms are in the cabin. I'm sorry, I never dreamt we'd do it here."

Torn between practical concerns and a sheer, driving desire, she told herself to be satisfied with less, to enjoy what he could give her short of making love. But somehow, with the next kiss, he was pushing inside her without any protection. They'd stop in a minute, in plenty of time, she told herself.

"That's it," she moaned. "That's what I want."

"It's what I want, too, but don't move," he warned.

She tightened her legs around his waist, driving him deeper.

"Ava, you're killing me," he gasped, his body tensing. Feeling intoxicated, weightless, even *careless,* she raised her eyes to meet his. "Okay, I'm not moving," she said.

"At this point, you might not have to." He drew a ragged breath. "You feel so good. Too good. Let's go in so I can get serious," he said.

Ava didn't want to go in. She didn't want to be the woman who lived in that houseboat, not tonight. She didn't want to be Geoffrey's sort-of girlfriend, the woman who was too preoccupied and practical, the one who was always dependable, who worked too hard and too often. Here in the dark of night with the moon shining on the water, she could be impulsive—someone who would actually do what she was doing. "Leave me here," she said, and pulled away.

He groaned at the loss as if he was once again tempted to overcome his better judgment. "You really know how to hurt a guy," he teased. Then he swam very purposefully for shore.

Ava was still in the river when Luke returned to the edge of the water. He could see her head, but he wanted to see the rest of her, wanted a glimpse of the breasts she'd shielded from his view when she took off her bra. He'd felt them with his hands, his chest, his mouth. But that wasn't enough. She'd surprised him again, making him feel like he'd felt in high school with Marissa. What was it about her?

He waved to her. "Come here."

"Why?" she called.

"I've got plans."

"We were doing fine out here."

"But I couldn't see what I was touching. I want to see you." He dropped the box of condoms so he could arrange the blanket he'd carried out. If he was going to make love to Ava, he preferred to have a comfortable place in which to do it. He wanted this to be special for her.

"You don't need to see me."

He beckoned to her again. "I can do a better job out here."

"A better *job?*" she echoed. "This isn't a performance, Luke. You're not getting graded."

"You know what I mean. I want you to like it."

"I will like it," she assured him, but he wasn't satisfied. This was Ava. He wanted to give her more because she was somehow giving *him* more—something she guarded closely, something she didn't share with just anyone.

"Come on."

"You've seen naked women before. What does it matter?"

Oh, brother. She was self-conscious about her body. That had to be the reason for her reluctance. That was just like her. But it was unnecessary. "I want to see *you,*" he said.

She didn't move.

"If you don't come out, I'll come in after you."

"You'd better not!" she warned, but he swam out there anyway.

She wrestled with him, trying to stop him from dragging her to shore, but he was determined to do it. She had to know that her body was beautiful, and he planned on making that clear.

By the time he carried her out, she was splashing and laughing and still fighting. But she was no match for him.

He was laughing, too—until he placed her on the blanket. Then they both sobered as he pressed her onto her back and held her wrists above her head so he could look his fill.

"Why would you be reluctant to show me this?" he breathed. He remembered when he'd met her, thinking she wasn't particularly attractive. But now he thought he must've been blind. She wasn't big-busted or tanned to a coppery brown like so many of the women who vied for his attention, but there was so much more to Ava. She was...*real.* He liked her just the way she was.

"You have intelligent eyes and a sexy mouth," he told her. "And I love your ballerina body."

"I've never even taken ballet."

"Doesn't matter. Your body's built like a ballerina's."

When his gaze focused on her breasts, she struggled to break his grip on her hands, but he held her fast and bent to take her nipple in his mouth. "Perfect," he murmured as it peaked beneath the thrust of his tongue.

And then everything began to move very fast. Luke wasn't sure he'd ever been in such a hurry before, but he was somehow hungrier for Ava than he'd ever been for anyone. It was probably because he enjoyed the rare spectacle of seeing such unguarded emotion on her face. She was being swept away, swept away despite her attempts to resist it.

When her fingers curled into his shoulders, he knew she was close. The idea that he could get her to respond to him excited him so much he almost couldn't hold out.

"Look at me," he demanded.

Her eyelids lifted. Then her lips parted as her chest rose and fell. She was...there. Throwing back his head, he thrust twice—harder, deeper—and felt her body spasm around him as he let himself go.

26

Luke's car wasn't in the lot, and he wasn't answering his door. So where was he at almost four in the morning?

Was he out with another woman? With *Ava?* Ava had been with him when they last talked on the phone, and it had been late, far later than any appointment Kalyna had ever had.

She stood outside Luke's door and glanced up and down the deserted hallway. It was dead quiet. Which made her even more curious about Luke's whereabouts.

Should she go in? Snoop around a bit? Try to figure out if he was seeing Ava?

She had to. This was the perfect opportunity. She might be tied up later. She knew the Arizona police wanted to speak to her. And judging by the messages she'd received from work, the police had already alerted her superior officer at the base. The gate guards had probably been notified to apprehend her if she showed up or tried to come in. Everyone was looking for her. And she already had half a dozen calls from Tati. She had let them all go to voice mail, but each message was more panicked than the one before.

Kalyna, why won't you pick up? What's going on? I need to talk to you. Please call me.... The police want to ask you a few questions. You should to contact them as soon as possible, tell them what you know about that hitchhiker—before Mark has his say... This is getting so scary, Kalyna. I'm beginning to fear the worst. Where the heck are you?

She was here, right where she wanted to be.

Crouching, she checked under the mat, but the key Luke usually kept there was gone. No doubt he'd removed it in an attempt to tighten security, but that didn't bother her. She didn't need that key because she'd made a copy of it weeks ago. It was in her coin purse.

Seconds later, she was standing in Luke's living room with his door closed behind her. Just in case he'd let a friend borrow his car, which he was prone to do, and hadn't answered her knock because he was sleeping, she crept into his bedroom so she could check. But his bed was empty, perfectly made.

Where was he? He had no business being out this late. Even the bars were closed. Had he traveled to San Diego to visit his family? Or was he in Ava's bed?

What a whore! The mere thought of them together enraged Kalyna. How could Ava turn her back on a victim just to spread her legs for Luke? She came off like such a prude, too.

But of course Ava would do that if she could. Who wouldn't—for Luke?

There was nothing to worry about. It wasn't as if Ava was pretty. If anything, Luke was using her. He'd probably taken her to bed to get her to help him, to flatter her so she'd pose no threat. Once he was out of trouble, he'd drop her like a hot potato.

And Kalyna could make that happen right away. All she had to do was call Ogitani and act a little confused about what she'd already said. Tell her that maybe somebody else had entered her apartment after Luke left, that she was too confused to realize it at the time. She'd say she was remembering more now, and the size of the man was all wrong. Ogitani would drop the case and Luke would drop Ava. Done.

Standing at the window, Kalyna gazed down at the lot. The vehicles beneath the streetlamps were all parked. A moment later she saw headlights on the road and a car drove by, but it wasn't a BMW.

Kalyna told herself she should leave before Luke caught her. But she had good reason to be here. She'd explain that she drove all the way from Arizona, straight to his apartment, to tell him she'd decided to come forward with the truth. He'd want to know as soon as possible. And she'd say the door was open. Since he'd taken the key, he'd have to believe he'd forgotten to lock it.

That would work. And it meant she could stay.

Craving every detail she could glean about him, she searched his entire apartment and even stole a few things. Several pictures of him with his family made it into her purse, along with a T-shirt she planned to sleep in at night. And then she found his hamper. Excited that these clothes had so recently been next to his skin, she scooped out an armful and rubbed her face in them, breathing deep. Short of having sex with him, it was the most private, intimate act she could think of. But the smell only made the longing worse. The desire to be with him grew so strong she was afraid she'd be crushed beneath the weight of it.

Desperate to get close to him again, she stripped off her clothes and climbed into his bed, wearing his boxers. This wasn't as good as being in his arms, but when she closed her eyes and began to touch herself, she could almost believe it was him.

* * *

Ava was physically and emotionally spent. Still damp from their time in the water and their lovemaking, she lay on the bank of the river, gazing up at the stars. Luke was lying beside her. Their hearts were slowing, their breathing evening out. It was over. But she didn't mind. Languid, relaxed, content—completely satisfied for the first time in ages—she felt as if they were floating on top of the water that lapped so close to their bare feet.

"*That* was the best," he told her.

She smiled lazily. It almost didn't seem possible that the person who'd just made love with Luke had been her. She hadn't held anything back. But she didn't regret it. Not yet, anyway. There were too many women in the world who never experienced lovemaking like this. It transcended the ordinary, the mechanical, the casual, to create a once-in-a-lifetime experience.

"How do you feel?" he murmured.

"Fine."

"The temperature's dropping. Maybe we should go in."

She angled her head so she could look at the houseboat. It sat there staring at her, its lights shining through the windows. But she could remain in the shadows, embrace the darkness a little longer. "In a bit."

"You're warm enough?"

"I'm just right. What about you?"

"I'm perfectly comfortable."

She didn't know how long he held her. Drifting in and out of sleep, she made no effort to keep track of time. At one point, she felt Luke shift positions and cover them with a blanket before curling around her again. Soon afterward, she reluctantly opened her eyes to check the sky. They'd been sleeping for some time. But it was still dark.

She could procrastinate for a few more minutes… She'd give herself another quarter of an hour.

But the next thing she knew, it was full daylight and she was blinking up at a third person, who was standing over them, blocking out the sun.

Kalyna was still in Luke's bed. She'd been waiting for him, hoping he'd return so she could surprise him. She planned to offer him the good news about Ogitani and the apology she'd rehearsed. But despite attempting to reenact June 6, she was as unsatisfied as ever.

Why hadn't he come home? He hadn't spent the entire night with *her.* Why would he do that for Ava?

Because he thought Ava could hurt him if he didn't, that was why. He was only doing what was expedient.

Pushing off the covers, she got up to check the parking lot. Still no BMW. She was just turning to get dressed when his phone rang.

She crossed to the nightstand where she could see caller ID. *Edward Trussell.* His father. Or someone from his father's house. That meant Luke couldn't be with his parents. If he was with them, they wouldn't be calling his apartment.

She told herself not to answer. But her hand darted out at the last second. She couldn't help it. She wanted to know these people, be close to them. They were part of Luke. If they liked her, Luke would be more prone to accept her, too.

"Hello?"

There was a brief hesitation. Then a female voice said, "I'm sorry. I must've dialed wrong."

"Not if you're looking for Luke."

"I *am* looking for Luke. This is Robin Trussell, his mother."

"He's not here at the moment, Mrs. Trussell. He was nice enough to let me sleep late while he ran out to get us some breakfast. But I thought it might be you. That's why I picked up."

There was another pause, then she said, "And you are..."

"Kalyna Harter."

"Kalyna?"

She could tell by the affront in Robin's voice that Luke had mentioned her. "Yes. You've probably heard about the mess that's been going on here."

"I've heard a few things that have had me very worried, yes."

"I'm sorry about that. I was...confused. Luke and I were together the night everything went wrong. Then he left, but I was sleeping and didn't know he was gone. Suddenly some other man came in and—" she gulped for breath "—and it was horrible. He beat me and he...he raped me and I thought I was going to die. It all happened so fast, and I didn't remember Luke leaving, so...so I naturally assumed it had to be him. I couldn't imagine someone else coming in so quickly after he got out of my bed."

"But *why* would he hurt you?"

Kalyna sifted through the contents of his top drawer as she talked, studied the songs he'd loaded onto his iPod, fished out some quarters—she always needed spare change for parking or laundry—made note of the other odds and ends he kept. "We'd had a little argument earlier, when he found out I was seeing someone else. Somehow I...connected it all. It's hard to describe how fuzzy my brain was. Have you seen the pictures from that night?"

"No, I haven't."

There was a gun in the drawer, a 9 mm, but that didn't surprise her. Although the guns they used on base had to be checked into the armory after weapons training, a lot of airmen had their own piece, and the 9 mm was the most popular. She'd considered getting one herself; she just hadn't followed through with it. "I was pretty banged up."

"But now you know it wasn't Luke who did that?"

"Yes, of course. It's all straightened out."

"Thank God…"

Kalyna hefted his gun, checked the sights. "Luke would never hurt me like that. We've talked about it since. As a matter of fact, we're back together. So everything's fine."

Robin Trussell coughed as if she'd just taken a drink of coffee or some other beverage. "Back together?"

"Our relationship's been heading in that direction for a while, ever since I was assigned to his flying squadron. But the unfortunate incident of June 6 nearly tore us apart." She pointed his gun at her own image in the mirror. "I feel terrible about what I've put him through. What I've put *you* through. Please accept my sincere apology."

"What we've been through is nothing compared to what you've been through, I'm sure. That must've been a horrible ordeal. I'm sorry for what you've suffered, and I hope they catch the man who did it. Do the police have any idea who that might be?"

Kalyna set down the gun when she found another picture of Luke's family. His mother was a petite woman, slightly overweight, with dancing eyes and a warm smile. "No. They have no suspects. No one saw the perpetrator come or go. Can you believe it? That's partly why it got so out of control. A woman named Ava Bixby, a victims' advocate I contacted for help, kept telling me it had to be Luke, that no one else would've had time to come in after he left. But…you and I both know he's not the type. I won't let Ava pressure me into believing he is, not anymore. That was killing me."

"Did you say Ava Bixby?"

"Yes. Do you know her?"

"Luke mentioned her. He thought she understood the truth and was backing off because of it."

She was backing off because he'd been giving her the ride of her life. "She might've told him that, but only when I started to realize she was manipulating me. She was always saying negative things about him, telling me how he couldn't be as perfect as he seems, that behind his handsome face lies a very twisted man." She lowered her voice. "I think she has some romantic interest in him and sees me as a rival."

Another pause. Then Robin said, "It seems that a lot has changed."

"I know. You wouldn't believe what these past few weeks have been like."

"I'm sorry. And I'm so glad you know it wasn't my son who hurt you. Luke is a good man."

"He's wonderful. I'm deeply in love with him." Kalyna sensed more surprise. "He hasn't told you about us?"

"Not much, but…you know how men are. They don't really talk about matters of the heart. Anyway, I can see why you'd love him. We're very proud of him."

"How's Jenny doing?" she asked.

"You know about Jenny?"

Kalyna laughed. "Of course. Luke talks about her all the time." He'd never actually mentioned his sister to her, but she'd heard other members of their flight squadron ask after his little sister. That was one of the benefits of flying with him. The entire squadron was quite close.

"Then you're already aware that she's giving us a run for our money these days. I'm afraid she's fallen in with the wrong crowd. You know how teenagers can be. But…we're working with her."

"Is she not in a good school?"

"It isn't bad as far as high schools go, but Jenny's so willful. Much more rebellious than Luke ever was."

"Luke's been worried."

"He's protective of her. We all are."

Kalyna pulled out a key that had the BMW logo on it. His spare, no doubt. She put it in her purse. "I'd love to come to San Diego so I could meet you and the rest of the family. Maybe I can talk him into making the trip at Thanksgiving."

"If not sooner. I'm feeling a little left out here. But of course he's been pretty preoccupied the past few weeks."

"We both have. It'll take some time for us to recover."

"Right. Well, it's been a pleasure talking to you, Kalyna. What great news that the charges will be dropped. I can't wait to tell Luke's father."

Robin sounded wonderful, ideal—just like Luke. She'd make a perfect mother-in-law. "Please tell your husband I'm sorry."

"Oh, Ed won't hold it against you. After what you went through, who could?"

Still rummaging through Luke's top drawer, Kalyna found a packaged condom, an Ace bandage and a letter from someone named Phil that'd come from Iraq. This was the only letter he'd kept, so it had to be important to him, which meant it was important to her. "Thank you for your understanding."

"No problem. I'd better go," Robin said. "I have to get to work."

"You work?"

"Yes, once we settled down here I decided to do what I've always wanted to do—teach."

"How do you like San Diego?"

"We love it. It's beautiful here."

"What age group do you teach?"

"Kindergarten."

"Do you enjoy it?"

"I do. Can you have Luke call me at the school when he gets back?"

"Of course. He'll be sorry he missed you." Kalyna sat on the bed so she could read Phil's letter, but she didn't want to let this woman go. It was almost as if she was what she'd said she was—Luke's girlfriend. So she searched for a way to stretch out the conversation, to ingratiate herself further and arrived at the obvious. "We…we have some news I know he'll want to share," she said. "So…be prepared."

"*More* news?" his mother said.

Kalyna toyed with the corner of the envelope she held. "Don't worry. This is *good* news. This is the kind of news that deserves a *celebration.*"

"I hate surprises. Are you really going to make me wait?" she said with a laugh.

Kalyna smiled as she fell back on Luke's bed. She and his mother were getting along so well. It was just one more sign that she and Luke were meant to be together. "I'd tell you, but I think Luke would want the honors."

"I'll act as if I've never heard it before, I promise."

Laughing, Kalyna hugged Luke's pillow to her. "Okay, but mum's the word. Are you ready?"

"I'm ready."

"You might want to prepare for a *small* addition to the family."

"A *baby?* You're expecting a *baby?*"

"Yes. A boy—Luke, Jr.—I hope. Can you believe it? That something so fantastic could come out of what's happened these past few weeks?"

Silence. Then she said, "I…I don't know what to say. I'm going to be a grandmother and I haven't even met my son's, er, my grandchild's mother?"

"He'll bring me to visit. But we might want to get married first. You know, a quick trip to Vegas. Ever since he learned about the baby, he's been in a big hurry."

"His father and I…well, we're a bit old-fashioned," Robin explained. "We'd like the baby to have our name. But we'd also like to be part of the wedding."

"I'll talk to Luke about it."

"Okay."

Kalyna sat up and withdrew the letter from its envelope. "You're not disappointed I can't say *yes* right now, are you?"

"No. I thought this would happen differently, that's all. But…that doesn't mean we're not thrilled. If Luke loves you, we'll love you, too. No question. How far along are you?"

"Just a month."

She counted the months aloud. "So it'll be a February baby?"

"Yes. Just in time for Valentine's Day."

"How exciting."

This woman was so trusting. She believed it all—and so easily. Kalyna supposed it didn't hurt her credibility that she'd answered Luke's phone at a time when ordinary guests wouldn't be visiting. "I'll send you a copy of the ultrasound. I should be getting one very soon."

"I'd love that."

Kalyna ironed out the letter so she could read it.

"Can you give me your address? Or should I just get it from Luke?"

"Who knows if Luke even has it? He drives here, but I don't think he's ever mailed us anything," she said. "Do you have a pen?"

"Just a sec." Kalyna hopped up and dug a pen out of the odds and ends in Luke's drawer. "I'm ready," she said and jotted the address on the envelope of Phil's letter. She finished it off by writing "Mom and Dad" at the top, then told Luke's mother goodbye and stuffed the envelope in her purse. She'd definitely go down and visit them. Soon.

27

It was Geoffrey. Ava stared up at him in shock. He was standing there with a Starbucks cup in his hand and his jaw hanging down to his knees. And she was lying naked with Luke and couldn't get up without sacrificing their only cover. She'd never been at such a disadvantage in her life.

"Is this some kind of optical illusion?" he asked. "Because it looks to me like you just slept with…with this soldier boy."

Luke's entire body had tensed the moment Geoffrey's shadow fell across them. Ava could tell he was reluctant to confirm his nudity by standing up, but if he didn't she'd have to or they'd be stuck cowering on the ground. Either he recognized that, or he didn't want to be caught on his back in case Geoffrey decided to throw a few punches, because he relinquished the blanket to her, got to his feet and pulled on his pants.

Wrapping the blanket securely around her, Ava got up, too. "Geoffrey, I…I—" She felt sick at heart. She was pretty sure she hadn't cheated on him, but some warning would've been nice. She would've appreciated such a courtesy had their roles been reversed. But last night had…gotten away from her. She hadn't thought of what she and Luke were doing as having any impact on reality. It'd been pure fantasy—that was all.

"Geoffrey. That's good. At least you remember my name."

"I'm sorry," she said. "I didn't mean for this to happen. I never expected you to come out here. You hardly ever do. But…if it makes you feel any better, I would've told you. I wouldn't have tried to hide it."

"I can already imagine the conversation. 'Hey, how's work? Excellent. By the way, I'm fucking another guy.'"

"Watch your language," Luke growled.

"You stay out of this," Geoffrey snapped. "You're the interloper here, not me."

Luke's eyebrows shot up. "I'm the interloper who'll lay you out if you don't watch your mouth."

Ava put a hand on Luke's arm to keep him where he was as she addressed Geoffrey. She didn't need this to escalate into a fistfight. "I'm just saying I wouldn't have lied to you, Geoff. I would've felt obligated to tell you that…that there's no point in our seeing each other anymore."

He stepped forward but Luke warned him off with a wave. Luke obviously thought he was protecting her, but he couldn't protect her from her own humiliation. She'd let herself down as much as Geoffrey. Maybe more.

Geoffrey scowled at her. "Who is this guy, Ava? Where'd he come from?"

"He's a client."

"Since *when?*"

"Since…" Dared she say it? Honesty demanded she do so. "…this week."

He cursed, seemed about to stalk off, but immediately faced them again. "You've got to be kidding me!"

If Ava hadn't been so busy holding up the blanket, she would've covered her burning face. She hated being in such an indefensible position. She was never reckless. She was logical, methodical, coolheaded. Until it came to Luke… Apparently, she had a weakness for handsome men, just like her mother.

"This guy doesn't look like a victim to me," Geoffrey muttered.

"What are you doing here?" she asked him instead of responding.

"I flew into San Francisco because all the flights to Sacramento were full. So I figured I'd stop by on my way home and surprise my girlfriend. Isn't that hilarious? Who knew I'd be more surprised than you."

"Geoffrey, I haven't been your *girlfriend* for months."

"I still thought of you that way. Maybe we talked about seeing other people, but I haven't done it. And to my knowledge, you hadn't, either."

"Only because we've both been too busy or too lazy or…something. You told me you didn't want to be exclusive if I wasn't going to continue sleeping with you."

"I told you that so you *would* sleep with me again! Instead, you jump into the sack with this…this G.I. Joe? This guy looks like he stepped right out of a commercial for the marines. Jeez! I know I don't have six-pack abs, but I never dreamt you were *that* shallow."

"I didn't sleep with him for his body."

"Then why'd you do it?" he asked.

Because she was in love with him. Already. She couldn't understand how it'd happened so fast. After starting to date Geoffrey, it'd taken her six months to decide she *might* sleep with him—*if* the planets were perfectly aligned and *if* the timing was right and *if* the mood struck her. Luke had been the complete opposite.

This had to be her punishment for thinking so harshly about her mother's inability to get over her father. "I…" She turned helplessly to Luke, and he took that as an invitation to step in.

"Look, this isn't a good time to discuss it. Why don't you head home and give Ava a call later on?"

Geoffrey's eyes glittered with a passion Ava had never witnessed before. Throwing his coffee on the ground, he stepped up, nose to nose with Luke. "You think you can order me around after—" his voice cracked "—after taking what I want more than anything?"

Luke raised his hands. "I'd rather this didn't get ugly. You don't have to prove yourself to either one of us."

"It's already ugly, so fuck you! *You* leave!"

Luke tilted his head in warning. "Calm down."

"Or what? You'll *make* me?"

"If I have to."

Geoffrey finally turned away. "Would you listen to this cocky son of a bitch?"

"You're provoking him," Ava said.

"And he didn't do anything to provoke me?"

"I've done enough to ruin your day," Luke said, "so let's not make it worse. Go home and call her later. That's what you need to do."

"Tell him to leave instead, Ava," Geoffrey pleaded. "People make mistakes. We'll get past this. Maybe this was the trigger I needed to realize how much I care about you. I should've pushed for more intamacy long ago and…and returned to your bed before someone else could take my place."

No. She was glad he hadn't pushed. Maybe she would've given in and settled. Jonathan had been able to see that she was adrift and susceptible, but she couldn't. Not until now. Now her eyes had been opened. After sleeping with Luke, she wouldn't be able to tolerate Geoffrey's touch. Their relationship had been yanked out of limbo and was suddenly over, because Luke had shown her how dispassionate she really was when it came to Geoffrey.

But she couldn't let Luke know that. Because letting him know he possessed even a piece of her heart gave him power—the kind of power her father had always abused. And she wouldn't become her mother, no matter what she had to do to avoid it.

"I'd like you both to go," she said softly. Then she held her head high and walked back to her former life, knowing it would no longer include either one of them. Geoffrey inspired too little in her; Luke inspired far too much.

Kalyna sat at Luke's kitchen table with her feet propped up on the opposite chair, nursing a cup of coffee as she read Phil's letter.

Hey, Luke—

Yeah, it's me. Surprised? I guess if you've received one letter from me, you've received your quota for life. But, hell, you're no better. I probably wouldn't be writing this if it wasn't for that last phone call. I figured I'd at least try to explain where I'm coming from.

Okay, so you think I'm stupid to agree to another tour. You're right, it's hard on Marissa having me gone. But she knew I was going to be a marine when she married me. And...things between us, they're not so good. I know you don't like to talk about it. (It's true—I can imagine you standing there, shaking your head, but you change the subject every time I bring her up. She's the one thing we can't discuss, not without getting into a fight, which is why I decided to put my thoughts in a letter.) So...basically, I'm hoping the time away will give me and Marissa a break from the constant conflict. We were in love, once. I think.

But I'm afraid that's gone. I can feel it slipping away from us.

So maybe I'm running away from my problems, like you said. Shit, that's possible. I don't want to face what's coming—I'd rather deal with bullets than that kind of pain. That's why you gotta cut me some slack for making this choice, buddy. I'm a marine. I'm good at my job. I feel successful here. But I'm a failure around Marissa. It's not that she isn't a good woman. We're just too different. If you talk to her, tell her I'm sorry, okay? Maybe she'll believe it coming from you. And…I don't know if I should add this or not, but…what the hell. As long as I'm being honest I might as well. I understand the sacrifice you made so we could be together. I've ignored it all these years. I didn't want to feel like I was the selfish one who took what he wanted. But I know you were in love with Marissa, too, back in high school. You stepped aside, and I thank you for that. And for staying out of the way, for giving me a real shot. Now I almost wish it had gone down differently. I'm sure you would've made her a better husband, would've made her happy somehow.

But history is history. We can't change the past. And regret will eat you up if you let it.

Just wanted you to know I'm not a complete prick.
Phil

Marissa… Kalyna glanced at the return address…. *Marissa Hughes*. Phil said Luke had loved her once. But he couldn't have loved her too much, or he wouldn't have given her up.

Her cell phone rang.

Thinking it was probably her sister *again,* Kalyna took her time digging it out of her purse. She was surprised she had enough battery power to receive another call. She'd left her car charger in Jerry's semi and had thought her phone would be dead by now.

But it wasn't dead yet. And the call wasn't from Tati. It came from a restricted number.

The police?

Taking a deep breath, she answered. She had to sound heartbroken, credible. She knew the routine. Only it wasn't the police. It was Major Ogitani.

"Kalyna?"

"Yes?"

"I'm afraid I have some bad news."

Kalyna didn't bother bracing herself. She'd been expecting this. "What is it?"

"I just returned one of many messages I've had from Ava Bixby at The Last Stand."

"Oh, yeah? What did she want?"

"She had some very interesting things to say."

That bitch. Ogitani and Ava were both bitches. Neither of them was any good to her anymore.

"Let me guess. She thinks I injured myself."

"Yes, and she said your father will testify that you've done it before, in violent fits of rage."

Of course her father would testify, in retaliation for Norma.

"She also said she has proof that you showed sexual interest in Captain Trussell long before the night in question."

"So you're dropping the charges?" she said, getting straight to the point.

"That's right."

"Okay."

Her easy acceptance met with silence. Then Ogitani said, "You're not even going to *pretend* surprise?"

"Nope."

"So you were lying, Kalyna?" she asked, obviously appalled. "During our entire interview?"

Kalyna nearly laughed out loud. Ogitani felt like a fool because she'd bought into the act. Even now, she was hoping for something to salvage her pride. But Kalyna had nothing to offer her. Thanks to Ava, Kalyna had been forced to change plans. "Of course not," she said. "But I might've been a little confused."

"I think you need professional help," she snapped, but Kalyna didn't give her a chance to vent any further. She was getting another call, and she needed to have enough battery power left to take it. This was the one she'd been waiting for—from the Mesa police.

Luke was in his car on the way home when his mother called. He'd already noticed that he'd missed several calls from Robin earlier, when his phone was in Ava's cabin on the boat and he was out with Ava on the bank of the river, but he hadn't returned them. It was Monday morning. He'd thought she'd be at work. Besides, he'd been busy confirming his leave. And he didn't feel like talking to anyone about anything personal. The night he'd spent with Ava had ended too badly. He still hadn't completely grasped what had happened. But his mother had tried to reach him so many times he was afraid there might be some sort of an emergency. He had to answer.

"Hello?"

"Luke, why haven't you called me?" she demanded.

He thought of those last few minutes with Ava, when he'd had to get to his feet buck naked in front of the man she'd been dating for more than a year, and shook his head in disbelief. He'd seen better days. "My battery was dead," he said to cut the explanation as short as possible.

Fortunately, she let it go at that. Apparently, she was worked up about something else. "When were you going to tell us?" she asked.

His blinker clicked as he switched lanes. "Tell you what?"

"About the baby."

He turned down the volume on his stereo, which he'd been blasting in an effort to numb his brain. "What baby?"

"Don't pretend you don't know! I just spoke with Kalyna."

"You *what?*"

"You heard me."

"But…how? Why?"

"What do you mean how? I called your house and she picked up."

What the hell was going on? "That can't be true."

His mother hesitated as if she was suddenly as confused as he was. "It *is* true. It was your number. She answered and said you were out getting the two of you some breakfast."

"I haven't even been home since yesterday!"

"Where've you been?"

He really didn't want to go into the fact that he'd been with *another* woman. After avoiding trouble for a number of years, he was suddenly screwing up all over the place. "A friend put me up."

"Oh. So why would Kalyna tell me you were getting breakfast? She said you two were back together. She said you're expecting a baby. She even said you were going to Vegas to get married!"

Dodging traffic, he accelerated. While driving, it was illegal to use a cell phone in California without a Bluetooth, and he'd left his Bluetooth somewhere, maybe at Ava's. He was going to have to risk talking on his cell, along with speeding. If Kalyna had answered his phone, she was in his apartment. How, he couldn't imagine. He'd locked up. He remembered doing it because he'd retrieved his spare key at the same time. It was lying right there, on his console.

"First of all, we're not back together." He darted through the gap between two other cars to get in the fast lane. "We were *never* together, except that one night." A woman honked and flipped him off as he whipped around her, but he didn't care. He was going home, and he was doing it as fast as possible. "Second, okay…there might be a baby. But she's lied about so many other things, I'm not sure. And third, there's no way we're getting married. I'd sooner be castrated."

What his mother had told him wasn't welcome news, but Luke was almost relieved to have an outlet for the surfeit of emotion that had been coursing through him ever since he'd left Ava's. Geoffrey had waited in his car while Luke gathered up his belongings—to make sure Luke drove away. But Luke hadn't waited to see if Geoffrey did the same. He didn't have any problem with Geoffrey, not really. It was Ava who'd upset him. He'd thought they were at the start of something new, something with potential—but she'd acted as if last night meant nothing to her, as if she was happy just to have proved she could make love with the best of them. Now she was done with him.

"Didn't you lock your apartment?" his mother asked.

"I did. I don't know how she got in."

"Why would she act as though she's about to be part of our family? How does that benefit her?"

He saw a highway patrol car up ahead and forced himself to slow down. It wouldn't help him to get pulled over; it would only take that much longer to reach Fairfield. "She'd like to be, I guess. Heck, I don't know. She's not right in the head."

"She told me she's deeply in love with you. And she seemed so sincere. She said she wants you to bring her down to meet us."

Kalyna was trying to infiltrate every aspect of his life. How was he going to stop her? What could he do? Get a restraining order? Maybe, but he wasn't even sure he could prove what he needed to in order to do that. He was in the military. He couldn't imagine the cops being too worried about protecting him from a woman.

He doubted Kalyna would respect it, anyway.

"Don't listen to her," he told his mother. "Don't believe a damn thing she says. Just stay as far away from her as possible."

"I—I won't talk to her again. Of course I won't, now that I know. But..."

She sounded worried. "What?"

"I gave her our address, Luke. She knows where we live. Is that okay?"

He slowed even more. "You *what?*"

"She said she'd mail me a copy of the ultrasound. I wanted to see the baby, so...I told her where to send it."

"No..." he said with a groan.

"I'm afraid so. I believed her. She was in your apartment at seven o'clock in the morning. I assumed you knew she was there. And I'm not used to having anyone lie to me like that, right to my face, and about stuff that's so...so easy to disprove. Why would she do that? What does she have to gain from it?"

"She's obsessed with me, Mom. She wants to believe that what she's saying is true."

"She said she loves you."

"That doesn't make her a nice person."

Now what? he wondered. Why would Kalyna have asked for his parents' address unless she planned on going down there?

His mother was still trying to make him understand. "But she knew so much about you. She was very convincing. She asked after Jenny and my work and…"

A chill ran down Luke's spine at the mention of his baby sister—probably because it brought back what he'd learned about Sarah, that fourteen-year-old hitchhiker who'd fallen into Kalyna's hands. "Listen to me, Mom," he cut in. "You've got to get Jenny and Dad and go somewhere else, okay? I don't know that you're in danger, but you could be, and I don't want to worry about you. Go to a hotel for a week or so until I can figure out what's going on. I'll pay for it. Just pack up and get out of the house, and do it *now*."

"But I'm at work."

He didn't want to frighten his mother, but he thought it imperative she know what Kalyna was capable of. "This person might've killed the woman who raised her. She might've murdered someone else, too—a young hitchhiker, years ago."

She gasped. "How do you know?"

"Ava Bixby found out. She's been working with me."

"But Kalyna said Ava's the problem."

"She's not the problem." Well, she was one of *his* problems, but she wasn't the kind of problem Kalyna meant.

"You're sure?"

"I'm sure." The highway patrolman finally exited the freeway, and Luke punched the accelerator. He had to catch Kalyna in his apartment. This might be his only chance to stop her. If he could arrive while she was still there, he could call the cops and, hopefully, they'd take her in for breaking and entering. And maybe by the time she got off the hook for that, the Mesa police would want her to stand trial and she'd be extradited.

As the needle on his speedometer edged up to ninety miles per hour, another call came through. He told his mother goodbye and hung up so he could switch over. But then he saw that the call was coming from his own number.

It was Kalyna. He wanted to answer—but he didn't want to tip her off that he was on his way, so he set his phone on the console and concentrated on driving.

When her calls eventually stopped, he considered letting Ava know that he'd located Kalyna. He thought she might want to hear the latest. And, if nothing else, it would give him the chance to talk to her. To ask her how she could make love to him as if her heart and soul were involved, only to shrug him off the next morning.

But then he remembered her telling him to leave, remembered her polite, distant nod when he walked out. She'd washed her hands of this mess when she'd washed her hands of him.

Somehow he'd manage on his own. If Ava didn't want him in her life, he'd stay the hell out.

28

The stillness seemed deafening. Ava tried to convince herself that this was the peace and quiet she'd always loved, the reason she lived on a houseboat in the delta, but today she wasn't enjoying it. The place was *too* quiet—in a nerve-racking sort of way. She knew her problem centered on the unsettled feeling she'd had ever since Luke and Geoffrey had left. But she couldn't help that. She could only return to the comfort, such as it was, of her usual routine. Before she screwed up any worse.

With that intent, she'd been trying to make herself get ready for work. If she could immerse herself in her cases, maybe she could forget last night and the terrible scene that'd followed. But she doubted anything could make her forget Luke's touch. And so far, she hadn't been able to get moving. She felt sick. Only she wasn't sure what kind of sick. There were no physical symptoms.

Her cell phone rang, and she glanced at the nightstand, where she'd put it when she'd burrowed beneath the covers a few minutes earlier. It was within reach—but she couldn't summon the energy to grab it. She didn't want to talk to anyone. She wished she could shut out the whole world until she was ready to deal with it again.

The call went to voice mail, providing a brief respite, but more ringing intruded on the silence right afterward.

Someone was trying to get hold of her.

Leaning over far enough to see who it was, she blinked when she saw that the call had originated from Luke Trussell's apartment. That couldn't be. Luke had been gone maybe twenty minutes. The drive took twice that long, especially in rush-hour traffic, which was what he'd face this time on a Monday morning.

What was going on?

Her stomach twisting into apprehensive knots, Ava snatched up the phone and hit the Talk button. "Hello?"

"Ava?"

It was a woman. "Yes?"

"Is Luke with you?"

Kalyna. Ava hadn't immediately recognized her because she'd used such a funny, chirpy voice. But she could tell now. Kalyna was back from Arizona. And, somehow, she was in Luke's apartment.

"What're you doing, Kalyna? Trying to get yourself in more trouble?"

"Just looking for Luke."

"He's not here."

"But he spent the night with you, didn't he? I know he wasn't at home last night."

Images of Luke's larger body covering her own flashed through Ava's mind. "No, he wasn't here."

"Stop lying! I'm carrying his baby, Ava."

Ava couldn't help hoping that wasn't true. Whether she planned to see more of Luke or not, she didn't want to imagine him having a child with this woman. "We have yet to see proof that you're carrying anyone's baby, let alone Luke's."

"We?" Kalyna gave a bitter laugh. "Oh, you got it bad, don't you? You got it bad, just like me. You're no different. Not really. He won't treat you any better. He'll toss

you aside and move on to the next woman. You think he didn't tell me all the same stuff he whispered to you, Ava? Did he tell you how sexy you are? How beautiful? His mouth's been on *my* breast, too. His—"

Ava interrupted; she couldn't listen to this woman cheapening what had happened last night. Maybe she was giving Luke up, but she wouldn't allow Kalyna to destroy the memory. "What do you want from me, Kalyna?"

"I want you to know you're going to lose. I'll get him back. You'll see."

"But you never had him in the first place." Ava had never had him, either. That was the catch with men like Luke and her father, the catch too few women understood. That kind of man was extremely handsome and almost unfailingly pleasant—but didn't know how to love deeply enough to stay with one woman. It came down to whatever or *whoever* was most stimulating at the moment.

"I have his baby, don't I?" she taunted. "That's practically as good. He was only using you—using his body to win you over so you'd help him get out of a rape charge. But Ogitani's dropped the case. As soon as Luke finds out, he'll realize he doesn't need you. And then you won't hear from him again."

After the way their night together had ended, Ava didn't expect to hear from Luke, anyway. "What are you doing in his apartment?" she asked. The fact that Kalyna was at Luke's and wasn't hiding it signified a boldness that frightened her. Did she have a gun? Was she waiting for him to walk through the door so she could make sure he'd never be able to reject her again?

"He gave me a key," Kalyna replied.

"That's not true."

"Then how did I get in?"

"You *broke* in."

"He might tell you he's not interested in me, but that's not what he says to me. You know how men are. I'll be the one with him tonight, gasping and moaning and laughing my ass off that you thought *you* were special."

"Kalyna—"

She hung up.

"Shit!" Her hand shaking, Ava dialed Luke's cell phone.

He answered on the first ring.

"Don't go home!" she cried. "Kalyna's there."

"Is this *Ava?* The woman I made love to last night?" he asked. "How nice of you to call."

He was angry, and he had reason to be. She'd turned on him pretty fast. But this wasn't about them. This was about keeping him safe. "Did you hear me?"

"I heard you. I know she's there. She's been talking to my mother, and she's tried to call me. I'm hoping she'll stay put until I can get home."

"What are you talking about? Luke, no! Don't go there. She could have a gun!"

"If she's been snooping, she has one of *my* guns, a 9 mm. But if she fires at me, she'll go to prison."

"*One* of your guns?"

"I have another one. It's in the trunk."

"Oh, God. This is going to turn into a shoot-out! Don't take the risk that you'll die first. Let the police handle it."

"Come on, Ava. You know what she's like. She'll tell them some bullshit that I invited her in, or she's my girl-friend, or she came to tell me about the baby and the door was unlocked and she thought I was inside sleeping. Unless she's hauling out my TV, what're they going to do? Tell her to leave? I don't think that'll do much to intimidate her."

"At least you won't get shot!"

"Today! What about the next time she's waiting for me? We have to catch her committing a major crime, something punishable by an extended prison sentence, or she'll never leave me alone. I plan to call the police, but not till I feel it will do some good."

"By then it could be too late. You don't have to walk into that apartment. This could be over soon. What about the case in Arizona?"

"I can't count on that. We have no idea how it'll go down. Even if she's their lead suspect, they have to prove guilt beyond a reasonable doubt."

"Maybe she won't be able to make bail."

"And maybe she won't even be charged. How will they prove she was the killer? There's legitimate reason for Kalyna's DNA to be in the house. She lived there. And Mark's as good a suspect as she is. Whether we believe him or not, he did threaten the deceased before she was murdered."

"There's the hitchhiker."

"We have two people pointing a finger at each other, that's all. 'He said, she said.' What jury would convict on that? What D.A. would prosecute?"

"You never know what might happen, Luke. Call the police."

"The hope of someone else solving my problems doesn't feel very real or immediate. I want her out of my life. She just told my mother we're getting married. Then she talked my mother into giving her their address so she could send them a copy of the ultrasound. I can't let this go on. It endangers everyone around me."

"But you could be killed!"

"If she's in my apartment and she fires at me, I'll fire back."

"You want to kill her?"

"I want to put an end to this. And I'm not afraid to defend myself. I'm a soldier, Ava. That's what I'm trained to do."

"She's trained, too."

"That's what makes it fair."

"Damn it, Luke—"

"Hey, what do you care, Ava? This morning was essentially goodbye, right? Isn't that what you meant when you sent me home without so much as saying 'I had a nice time—call ya later'?"

Ava dropped her head in her hand. She opened her mouth but couldn't find the words. What she *wanted* was so different from what she felt she needed. She simply couldn't believe they had a chance, couldn't rely on him for fear he'd be the fool's gold her father was.

"I'll take that as a yes," he said when she didn't respond.

"I *did* have a nice time," she mumbled.

"Yeah, well, let me know when you want to go skinny-dipping again. I'm good for a free fuck every now and then. Ask Kalyna."

Ava stiffened. Luke never used profanity around women. Less than an hour ago, he'd told Geoffrey to watch his language. "I'm sorry if I hurt your pride, Luke."

"My *pride,* Ava? Of course. It would have to be pride, because a guy like me couldn't have a heart," he said, and hung up.

Stunned, Ava sat blinking at the phone. Then she tried to call him back. They had to put their differences aside. Kalyna was dangerous.

But he wouldn't pick up.

With a curse, she called the police. Then she threw on her clothes, shoved her hair into a ponytail and ran out to her car.

* * *

Not wanting to alert Kalyna to the fact that he was home, Luke parked a block from his apartment building. He had no idea what he'd discover when he entered his place, but he was ready for anything. He had the 9 mm tucked beneath his belt. Just handling a gun with the thought of potentially using it might've scared some people, but he was a soldier. It actually felt more comfortable to him than battling unfounded accusations and defamation of character.

He jogged to his apartment building, where he checked the lot for the car he'd seen her drive when she'd come on and off the base. Sure enough, it was parked in one of the five guest spots along the perimeter. He came up next to it and glared in at a bunch of fast-food wrappers, brown-paper sacks and luggage.

What did she think she was doing here?

Taking the stairs two at a time, he strode purposefully to his own door. Then he paused outside to listen. The TV was on. It was so bold of Kalyna to settle into his apartment, he almost couldn't believe she was for real.

"What'd I ever do to deserve this?" he muttered under his breath, and tried the knob. It was unlocked, but…did she have his gun? Would she try to use it?

He cracked open the door as quietly as possible. He could see the kitchen and most of the living room. They were both empty. So where was she?

Another apartment door opened down the hall. Not wanting to be hailed by someone he knew, Luke quickly stepped inside and closed his own door.

A cup sat on the kitchen table, along with a letter—his letter from Phil. The sight of it spread out like that, as if Kalyna had been reading it, made him even angrier. Entering his apartment without permission was an intrusion, but reading his private correspondence was worse. What'd happened between him and Phil was so private. Even his parents didn't really understand the extent of what he'd felt for Marissa.

Gritting his teeth, he headed to the bedroom. In the hall, where the TV wasn't quite as loud, he could hear water running. No way could she be taking a shower, he thought—but the sound grew more distinct as he moved closer.

Although it, too, showed signs of habitation, his bedroom was as empty as the living room and kitchen. His bed was rumpled as if she'd slept in it, a pair of his underwear lay near the pillow and his dresser drawer had been left hanging open.

Luke shook his head in disbelief. Kalyna hadn't even bothered to close it after snooping through his things. But at least that made one detail very clear. She didn't have his other gun in the bathroom with her. He could see the black metal of the barrel in the drawer, along with the box of bullets.

So what now? Did she have her own gun? Or was she unarmed?

The bathroom door stood ajar. Edging over to it, he peeked around the corner, his hand gripping the handle of the gun he'd stuffed into his pants, just in case. But there was no need to draw on her. He could see no weapons in the bathroom, and her naked form was partially visible through the misted glass.

Stepping into view, he said, "What the hell are you doing in my shower?"

She yelped, obviously startled, then slid the door open to poke her head out. She didn't cover up but the sight of her did nothing for him. "There you are!" she said in a relieved voice. "I wondered when you'd get home.

Your mother called while you were gone. She wants you to call her at the school."

Kalyna knew his mother worked at a school? What other details had she learned? His mother had said she'd asked about Jenny… "Get out," he said.

She hesitated as if the coldness in his voice surprised her. "Right *now?* Don't be silly. I've got soap in my hair."

"Rinse it and then get out. I want you to pick up your things and leave my apartment. And I don't want you to *ever* come back."

Her bottom lip protruded in an exaggerated pout. "Is that any way to treat the mother of your baby?"

"Being pregnant with my child—*if* that's the truth—doesn't give you the right to break into my apartment and go through my belongings."

Her gaze lowered to the gun in his belt. "What? Are you planning to shoot me?"

"If I hand you my other gun, will you fire at me first?" he asked.

Her eyebrows drew together. "That's not very nice, Luke."

"You can't blame me for hoping."

"Someone's grumpy. What's the matter, did Ava kick you out of bed?"

Actually, she had—more or less. And it still stung. But he wasn't going to give Kalyna any indication that she'd guessed right. "Why are you doing this?" he asked.

"What?"

"This! Coming into my house! Sleeping in my bed!"

"It's not like I broke in. The door was open—"

"It was locked."

"No, it wasn't. I swear. Look around for yourself. There's no other way I could've gotten in."

Because he lived in a second-story apartment, he couldn't imagine that she'd come through a window. But he'd locked the door. He remembered doing it.

"When you didn't answer, I tried the door," she went on. "I got here so late I was sure you'd be here. I figured you were sleeping. But you weren't, so I waited. I don't see why you're making such a big deal out of it. I had a very long drive yesterday, and it was emotionally draining. I don't expect you to have any sympathy for me, but there's been a death in my family. A murder. Someone killed my mother yesterday, and I think it's someone I used to know. So forgive me if I didn't feel up to going once I arrived."

Leaving his gun in his waistband, he clenched his fists helplessly. "Why'd you come here in the first place?"

"You asked me to. You wanted proof of the baby, remember?"

"And you have it?"

"Yes!"

Hell. The thought of having a child with her made him almost as nauseous as the way she was lathering her body with soap and rubbing her breasts.

"For God's sake, just finish showering," he snapped. "We'll talk when you get out."

Slamming the bathroom door, he stomped into his bedroom and removed the gun he kept in his drawer, as well as the bullets. Then he went to wait for her in the kitchen, where he could pour himself some coffee—and talk himself out of putting a bullet through his brain to avoid becoming a parent with someone who needed an exorcist.

The police arrived while Kalyna was still in the bathroom. She could hear Luke talking to them, assuring them he had the situation in hand. Had he called them? Probably. But he'd sent them away, too, so it didn't matter. At least he was willing to hear what she had to say. At least he wasn't going to have her thrown out of his apartment before she could show him the results of her pregnancy test.

Taking extra care, she added mascara to her eyelashes. She wanted to look good, better than she ever had in her life. Everything she wanted rested on the conversation to come.

He waited for ten minutes or so, but then he threw the bedroom door against the wall. "What's taking you so long?"

Finally. She bent toward the mirror, causing the T-shirt she was wearing to ride up and give him a glimpse of her ass. "As you can see, I'm not dressed."

With a growl of impatience, he returned to the kitchen, which wasn't the reaction she'd been hoping for. But she still had the document from the clinic.

"Come on!" he yelled back to her.

She threw on her jeans without underwear. Her panties were somewhere in Luke's bed. She could probably find them, but since her ploy to entice him back into the bedroom hadn't worked, she didn't want to take the time to look.

When she entered the kitchen, she saw him standing at the sink with a cup of coffee, scowling out at the parking lot.

"Would you like me to make you some breakfast?" She'd offered as sweetly as possible, but his glower only darkened.

"No. I want to see the proof you claim to have."

Silently, she padded over to her purse and pulled out the document she'd doctored at Kinko's. "Here you go."

She stood there while he examined it, but when he didn't react, she moved closer. "It's positive, see? It says so right here." She brushed up against his arm as she pointed and almost couldn't stop herself from slipping her arms around his waist. Just one embrace...

"I want a paternity test," he said.

She'd expected this and had an answer for it. "Of course. But we can't do that now, silly. Not till the baby's born. Otherwise, there are risks. I've already looked into it, since you said you wanted proof."

"We have to wait nine *months?*"

"Well...eight."

Shoving the paper aside, he sank into the chair she'd been using earlier.

"Don't you have anything else to say?" she asked.

His eyes cut to her, and she'd never seen him look quite so malevolent.

She pressed a hand to her throat. "Don't glare at me like that, Luke. It gives me the creeps. It's not *my* fault. The rubber broke."

"Sure it did," he grumbled, and picked up his coffee cup.

She studied the floor, trying to appear contrite. "There's something else you should know."

"What's that?" He didn't sound interested in any more news.

"I told Ogitani the truth. They're dropping the charges."

"And that's supposed to make me happy?"

"I thought it might." She didn't mention the charges that might be filed against her or that there was a detective from Mesa flying out to speak with her tomorrow. She'd deal with that later. One thing at a time....

"Without you, there wouldn't have been any charges," he said.

"I was hurt, Luke. Can't you understand that?"

He sat there for so long she didn't think he'd answer, but he finally said, "Maybe."

"I…I thought we had something together. I've cared about you for a long time, since the first few days after I got assigned to your squadron. When you walked out on me that night, it felt like…like you'd just used me and tossed me aside. And it meant so much more to me."

His chair scraped the floor as he pushed it back, but he didn't get up. Elbows on knees, he rested his head against the knuckles of both hands. What was he thinking? She was pretty sure she was reaching him, but she couldn't be positive….

"I'm sorry," she went on. "I'm really and truly sorry. It was wrong of me to react the way I did. I know that. And then, once I'd said what I did to the doctors, they took it from there and the police came and the situation got out of control. I didn't know how to back out, so…so I stayed mad to keep from thinking about it."

He hadn't showered or shaved this morning. When he rubbed his chin, she could hear the rasp of beard growth.

"I'm just asking for a little understanding," she told him, "for your help in getting through this pregnancy." She wanted to touch him so badly it was almost as if an invisible force kept drawing her hands to his hair. But she fought it, couldn't risk moving that fast. He was trying to be fair. She could tell.

"It's partly my fault," he admitted. "I should never have been irresponsible enough to do what I did." His gaze moved to the letter, then darted away. "Somehow we'll get through it."

"I really appreciate that," she said softly.

He took a deep breath. "And, if this is my baby, I'll do everything I can to support it. I want you to know that."

"Thank you." Her voice was a whisper now. "You're going to be a *great* father."

She thought the compliment might evoke a smile, but his head sank even lower as he covered his face. He wasn't watching her; he was somewhere inside himself. Kalyna lifted her hand. She was just about to risk placing it on his shoulder when a knock interrupted her. "Luke? Luke, are you there?"

It was Ava Bixby.

29

While she waited for the ATM to dispense the three hundred dollars she'd just pulled out of savings, Tatiana rubbed her sweaty palms on her shorts. She was going to do it; she was going to California to see Kalyna. She had to do something. Mark nearly had the police convinced that he wasn't the one who'd killed their mother. He came across as so sincere with all his claims of loving Kalyna, of being wronged by her, that he'd nearly convinced Tati, too. That photo had really thrown her. But she refused to let him persuade her. Now that she'd had more time to think about it, she remembered how creepy he was. He was a decade older. It was partly his fault Kalyna had gotten into so much trouble in her teens. And that hitchhiker? There was no way Kalyna could kill another person, especially at such a young age.

Unfortunately, Detective Morgan didn't seem to view Mark's story with the same suspicion. He was suddenly talking as if it had to be Kalyna. Mark had allowed the police to come in and search the moment they knocked on his door, and because they hadn't found anything belonging to Norma, they were turning their sights elsewhere. Tati had heard Detective Morgan tell her father just an hour ago that he'd contacted the base and asked security to be on the lookout for Kalyna. The second she showed up for work, they'd nab her and hold her until Detective Morgan could arrange a flight out to California to question her.

Tati had to warn her. She'd tried to do it by phone— but Kalyna wasn't answering and, thanks to all of Tati's previous messages, her sister's voice mail was full.

"She didn't do it," she muttered to herself. Tati knew her sister had emotional problems. Kalyna had always been different—impatient to get what she wanted, careless about her mistakes, quick to blame others for whatever went wrong in her life. She could be disappointing and difficult to deal with. But she was the only blood relative Tati knew. Tati didn't want to lose her, especially now that Norma was gone.

The whir of the cash machine stopped. She grabbed the bills, before she could change her mind, and shoved them in the pocket of her shorts while hurrying back to the Oldsmobile. She'd had to take her father's car because she didn't have a vehicle of her own. But she couldn't drive the Olds all the way to California. The hearse was still in the shop; Dewayne would be left without any transportation. So she'd park his car at the airport, where he could have someone help him pick it up. She'd fly to Sacramento, then rent a car.

Doing it this way was costing her almost every penny of what she'd saved so far for the cruise she and her parents had planned to take next summer. It was to be their first family vacation. But her mother was gone, and this was more important, anyway. She owed it to Kalyna to have enough faith to track her down and save her from herself.

Tati hoped she wouldn't miss her mother's funeral in the process. She figured she'd be okay, as long as she could make it back by Wednesday. They hadn't even done the autopsy yet.

The entire car shook as the engine roared to life. Her father was so proud of his eight-cylinder. He was a simple man, a man who worked hard and had few pleasures. Life hadn't been easy for any of them. Why couldn't Kalyna understand that? Why did she think she was the only one who'd suffered?

Being careful not to scratch the car on either side of her, Tati backed out of her parking space and headed toward Sky Harbor International Airport. She didn't want to make this trip, especially alone. She didn't get out much, even around town. And she knew her father wouldn't be pleased when he learned what she was up to. But Kalyna couldn't handle this situation as carelessly as she'd handled problems in the past. This was serious. If she wasn't careful, she'd go to prison for the rest of her life for a crime she didn't commit.

A Verizon store came up on Tati's right. Tempted to stop, she slowed down. She didn't have a cell phone. She'd never been able to justify spending the money. The landline at the mortuary was adequate for someone who worked the hours she did. But now that she was flying to California, she should have some way of staying in touch with her father and Kalyna—if Kalyna ever picked up—shouldn't she?

She thought so, but…how long would it take to buy a phone? If it was more than a few minutes, she'd miss her flight.

A car honked behind her. Then the impatient driver swerved around her, making a rude gesture. She had to make a decision; she was holding up traffic.

Giving the Oldsmobile some gas, she passed the store. She could get by without a phone for the time being. It wasn't as if she needed help finding Kalyna's apartment. Using the address her sister had dictated to her after

Christmas, when Kalyna had called to have Tati mail the hair dryer and shoes she'd accidentally left behind, Tati had downloaded directions from MapQuest before leaving the house.

Willing herself to relax, she leaned back as she drove. Kalyna would be okay, she told herself. Everything would be okay.

She just had to talk to her sister before the police did.

The sight of Ava wearing no makeup and a hastily donned pair of cutoffs with a plain T-shirt and flip-flops should've reminded Luke that he'd been with prettier girls. Instead, it reminded him that she looked the way she did because she'd just been with him on the bank of the river. And that made his heart pound. Why, he couldn't say. A few minutes earlier, Kalyna had all but beckoned him to the bed, and it hadn't affected him in the least. But Ava showed up in some baggy old clothes that did absolutely nothing for her thin figure and he couldn't take his eyes off her.

Wishing he could turn off whatever she did to him just as easily as she'd sent him away this morning, he set his jaw so she wouldn't guess at his true feelings and blocked the doorway with his body. "What do you want?" he asked.

Her gaze shifted to a point behind him, and he knew she was looking at Kalyna. "I was afraid... I wanted to be sure you were okay."

"I'm fine. We're both fine. Kalyna has called Ogitani and told her the truth. They're dropping the charges."

Ava hesitated briefly. "So I've heard."

"That means you don't have to worry about anything. Your job is done. But thanks for coming by. I'll put the donation I promised you in the mail." He closed the door, then sucked in a quick breath to absorb the sting that resulted from treating her so coldly.

"You okay?" Kalyna had moved. She now stood right behind him.

Straightening, he managed a nonchalant shrug. "Of course. Why wouldn't I be?"

Her eyebrows gathered. "I know you weren't in a good mood to begin with, but seeing Ava didn't seem to help. You—you weren't really yourself with her."

"What do you mean? I just told her where we're at with the case."

"I guess. For a minute, it seemed…" She gave an awkward laugh. "I don't know, like you *cared* about her."

"Well, I don't." At least not *deeply,* he told himself. He'd known Ava for barely a week. He respected her; that was all. She was deep and real and concerned about others—and he enjoyed being around her. No other woman he'd met could compare. But if she didn't feel the same, he could walk away. Marissa was the only woman he hadn't been able to forget. He'd feel better in a few days.

"Maybe you're tired," Kalyna said. "Why don't you get some sleep?"

He crossed to the window. Ava was climbing into her bright yellow, rattletrap Volkswagen. Would she ever call him again? He couldn't see why she would….

"I have to go," Kalyna said.

That was a relief.

"But I'll take your laundry. I have to do mine, anyway. And helping you out is the least I can do for…for what I've put you through."

Luke caught only bits and pieces of what she said because he wasn't really listening. He didn't realize she'd asked him a question until she fell silent, then prodded him, saying, "Luke? Did you hear me?"

"What was that?" He turned to look at her.

"I said I'll do your laundry when I do mine today, okay?"

"No. Don't touch it. I'm fine."

"Please? Let me make it up to you. I'm trying to be nice, Luke. Why won't you—"

He raised a hand to stop her. "Fine. Whatever," he interrupted. As long as she left him alone for a while, he didn't care. What did it matter if he let her do his laundry? He couldn't get rid of her, anyway. She was pregnant with his child. She'd be part of his life forever.

"See you later," she called.

He was still staring out the window. "Later," he echoed. Then the door opened and shut, and finally—*finally*—he was alone.

With a sigh, he walked over to the kitchen table and sat down. Phil's letter lay right in front of him. The letter he'd never answered. Why hadn't he written back while he had the chance?

He thought of Marissa. She was trying to cope with Phil's death, not only as his wife, but the mother of his child. Would the situation be different if he'd declared himself before she married Phil? Would she have married him instead? Would they have a kid or two?

If so, he wouldn't be looking at sharing a child with a woman he disliked, and Marissa wouldn't be going to bed alone at night.

He considered calling her. In the past it'd been difficult, painful at times, to hear her voice when he called to talk to Phil. Through the years, he'd missed her smile, lamented the loss of their friendship as much as any deeper relationship. But today…today the only person he wanted to call was Ava.

Picking up Phil's letter, he read it again—but this

time, even though he had nowhere to send it, he wrote his best friend back.

And apologized.

It wasn't easy to tail Ava. Especially once they entered the delta. There wasn't enough traffic to go unnoticed. But Kalyna had two things going for her. As far as she knew, Ava had never seen her car. And she wasn't expecting to be followed.

Actually, Kalyna was pretty sure she had *three* things going for her. She suspected Ava was too preoccupied to notice anything short of an earthquake. Something had happened at Luke's, something to upset her. While they were waiting at a stoplight, Kalyna had seen Ava wiping her eyes, and those tears confirmed what she'd sensed when she'd seen Luke and Ava together—they cared about each other. How, Kalyna couldn't imagine. They'd met so recently. It didn't seem fair. But in the three months Kalyna had known Luke, she'd never seen him treat a woman, or anyone else for that matter, so rudely. Unless provoked, he was always friendly, always smiling.

Except when he'd seen Ava in the hall. Kalyna had felt her own stomach knot with the tension that'd entered the room as soon as he opened that door. His body language, his voice, the look in his eyes—it'd all changed so drastically. And then there was that moment afterward, when he'd ducked his head as if Ava had slugged him. Kalyna had known instantly that he longed to go after her, and she'd barely been able to breathe ever since.

After what she'd been through, she couldn't let Ava get in the way. Not again. She finally had a chance with Luke. He believed she was pregnant, believed it could be *his* child. He was letting her do his laundry. That was a start. Eventually, she'd win him over, prove she could be everything he'd ever want in a woman—if she didn't have to compete with Ava. She didn't want Ava calling or showing up and ruining everything. She couldn't bear the thought of Luke daydreaming about Ava when he was supposed to be thinking of *her.*

As they passed over one bridge and then another, traffic all but disappeared, forcing Kalyna to hang back until she could barely see Ava's car. She lost her when Ava made two quick turns but she got lucky. One road had a sign that indicated it was a dead end, which sent her down the opposite one, and she caught a glimpse of the bright yellow Volkswagen just before Ava parked next to a pickup truck by a pier.

At the end of that pier was a houseboat, but Kalyna couldn't go any closer. After pulling off the road, she hid her car in a copse of trees and got out.

Crying always gave Ava a headache. She hated it— the blotchy face, the clogged sinuses, the swollen eyes. She tried to remain as objective as possible about her work and religiously avoided anything else that might cause tears, like sad books and movies. But she'd thought Luke's life was in danger, so she hadn't been able to dodge coming face-to-face with *him.* And once the tears started, she couldn't fight them.

Finally letting herself go, she'd blubbered during the whole drive home. She cried for her mother, and her father, and Bella, and all the cases that hadn't ended the way she'd hoped since she'd begun working at The Last Stand. Most of all, she'd cried over Luke. Over what she wanted and what she couldn't have. Over her own short-comings and what she perceived to be his. She'd assumed she could stand in her shower and recover for as long as necessary, maybe even take the day off. But when she got home, she didn't find the privacy she was expecting. She found her father waiting for her.

"No way," she muttered as she got out of her car. Although she'd studiously avoided glancing at herself in the rearview mirror because she didn't want to see how pathetic she must look, she knew she wouldn't be able to hide the fact that she'd been crying. She also knew he wouldn't be impressed. He wasn't the type who appreciated displays of emotion; they made him even more uncomfortable than they made her. And here she was, fresh from the biggest crying jag she'd ever had. "This oughta help our relationship."

"You talking to me?" How he'd heard her, she had no idea. The wind must've carried her voice, since he wasn't that close. He was already on the houseboat. When she pulled up, he'd been sitting in one of her patio chairs on the deck, but now he stood at the railing.

"What are you doing here?" she called back.

"I came to see my little girl."

Ava felt the lump in her throat swell again. She wasn't his "little girl" unless he wanted something. What was it this time? Did he need her to dog-sit Carly's spoiled poodle again? She hated that dog almost as much as she hated its owner.

Regardless of what his request might be, she wasn't sure she could deal with it right now. But this was her father. She never got to pick the time or the place for whatever sacrifice he required.

"Everything okay with Carly?" she asked.

"They've been better."

She'd kicked him out. Ava could tell by the sheepish expression on his face. "Where's your luggage?" she asked.

They were only two feet from each other, and he had yet to comment on her tear-streaked face. But that didn't come as a surprise. He'd never been that interested in what was happening in her life. "I haven't packed up yet. She was throwing things. I left before she could cause too much damage."

"I see. Are you going back for your stuff or hoping it'll all blow over?"

He glanced away. "I'm too old to start over again, Ava."

She drew a deep breath. Of course. He'd go back to Carly if he could. That, too, came as no surprise. "Okay. Would you like an iced tea while you wait for her to cool off?"

He didn't answer. "What's going on with you?" he asked.

What? He'd finally deigned to notice?

She attempted what she hoped was a convincing shrug. "Nothing. Just a tough case."

He studied her for a moment, but ultimately nodded. He didn't know her well enough to argue with her. And he wasn't going to argue, anyway. That fell under the category of "dramatic displays of emotion."

"I don't think I've ever seen you cry before," he mused.

Not for years, anyway. Although he and Carly had sat through most of Zelinda's trial—Carly had been fascinated by the whole sordid case—Chuck had been absent the day the verdict came in, and Ava hadn't cried since. Carly had said he wasn't feeling well, that he had a touch of the flu, but he'd been well enough to bring an extra set of keys to the houseboat that night.

Ava had always wondered if he'd missed the culmination of the trial on purpose. They'd all seen the evi-

dence, heard the arguments, knew which way it would
go. Maybe he hadn't wanted to hear the final verdict,
hadn't wanted to face something so negative. Maybe he
feared he'd feel responsible for his first wife's decline.
She'd been a very different woman when she'd married
him.

"Why bother? Tears don't help anything," she told him,
and forced a smile as she unlocked the door to the cabin.

"Your mother told me you want us to move into a
motel, but we're not going to leave our home, Luke. This
woman, whoever she is, has no reason to hurt us."

If Kalyna was as crazy as she sometimes seemed, she
wouldn't need a reason. But Luke wasn't sure whether
or not he should push his father on this. Now that he
knew Kalyna was here in town with him, it seemed a bit
extreme. "She's acting a little more stable than I was expecting. But I'm telling you, Kalyna's unpredictable,
and she has your address. You have to be careful."

"I'll keep an eye out," he said.

Ed thought he could handle Kalyna. He had no idea
how she could twist things in her own mind. But Luke
couldn't imagine her driving down to San Diego to harm
his family without some provocation, and he hadn't given
her any, not this morning. "Mom told you she might've
killed the woman who adopted her and a young teen,
didn't she?"

"She told me. You've really got yourself mixed up in
something, haven't you?"

He had. And he felt he deserved it for being careless
enough to step into Kalyna's trap. "Just do me one favor,"
he said. "If she calls you guys, don't talk to her, okay?
And if she sends you a package or a letter, don't open it.
Call me first."

"I will."

"Good. Let me deal with her."

"I take it you're not going to marry her."

He laughed without mirth. "No, I'm not going to marry her."

"Is she really pregnant?"

He thought of that paper from the clinic. *Positive.* "She showed me the results of a pregnancy test she took yesterday. Looks like she might be. But I'm not certain the baby's mine." He was still holding out hope, although he had eight months to wait.

"Why would she tell you it's yours if it isn't? That's easy to disprove."

"I know." But Kalyna had done enough weird shit where he was concerned that he wouldn't put it past her, not for one second. "She's doing anything she can to hold my attention."

"You don't think you could ever grow to like her?"

"No. Definitely not."

"Okay. Well, I'm glad the rape charges are being dropped, anyway. It was terrible worrying about what might happen to you."

Luke hadn't had a chance to feel very relieved. If that baby was his, he was looking at a life sentence spent shackled to Kalyna. Part of him actually wondered if he might prefer five to ten. But at least he'd been able to call off McCreedy, which meant most of the money he'd put on retainer would be returned to him. "This hasn't been my best week."

"It'd be nice if you could meet someone and settle down," his father said.

His parents told him that all the time. He usually rolled his eyes and tried to distract them with another subject. Today, however, he pictured Ava as she'd been in the moonlight, staring up at him. Her lovemaking had been intense; he'd been completely consumed by it.

"I will. Someday." He hated that he'd been so rude to Ava when she came to his apartment. Maybe he'd expected too much from her this morning. When Geoffrey had shown up, she'd been shocked and embarrassed. Sending him off as if their time together had meant nothing might've been a knee-jerk reaction, a self-defense mechanism snapping into place. She'd been trying to shove him away since the very beginning. But that prickly "I don't need anyone" exterior protected one of the softest hearts he'd ever known. He'd seen that for himself last night.

Had he reacted differently, with more understanding, maybe they'd be planning to see each other tonight.

He wondered what she'd say if he called her....

"Luke?"

"What?"

His father repeated what he'd apparently missed. "I said you're nearly thirty. Don't you want a family?"

"Yes, I want a family."

"Then maybe you should get serious about finding a wife," he said. And, for Luke, that was the deciding factor. He wasn't sure Ava would be the woman he married. But he felt something for her he hadn't felt for anyone since Marissa. He wasn't going to give her up quite so easily.

After hanging up with his father, he dialed her cell number, but it went straight to voice mail.

"Ava, it's Luke. I'm calling because...last night wasn't just another night for me. I'd like to see you again. Will you call me?"

30

"Honey, don't talk like that. Come on, we have a good marriage...I *wasn't* sneaking around. I told her you wanted me to take Buffy to the vet, that I'd have to call her later."

Hearing her father in the living room doing his best to cajole his wife, Ava remained in her bedroom. Her stint in the shower had been much shorter than she'd originally intended, but with her father around, she hadn't felt comfortable taking a longer one. She wouldn't have worried about it if she'd known he'd get into a marathon argument with her dear stepmother, however.

Purposely wasting time, she checked the mirror to see if her eyes were still puffy.

"...I did tell you she called," her father was saying. "It'd already been two days. I felt I should get back to her..."

Fortunately, the swelling had gone down. Now that she'd done her hair and put on some makeup, as well as a blouse and skirt, she didn't look too bad.

"...I can't *ignore* her. I was married to her once. She was part of my life..."

Ava didn't want to walk out and embarrass her father. He had to feel like an idiot sucking up that much. But now that she was finished in the bathroom, she didn't know what to do with herself. She hesitated to go to work today. She feared Geoffrey might've stopped by the office to see her since their run-in this morning and revealed that some cataclysmic event had changed their lives. Even if he hadn't, she couldn't abide the thought of facing Skye or Sheridan or Jonathan, knowing she'd slept with one of her clients. So maybe she wouldn't go in.

Or maybe she would. They'd probably be glad to hear she was no longer seeing Geoffrey. But she was almost as reluctant to acknowledge that as she was to admit the truth about Luke. Her friends had been trying to tell her that something important was missing from her relationship with Geoff. Because she'd clung so stubbornly to the belief that her life was just the way she wanted it, pride wouldn't allow her to admit that they'd been right all along. Not yet. There were too many other emotions swirling around inside her.

"…Boo, stop…"

Boo? Ava grimaced. She didn't want to hear this, didn't want to witness her father begging the forgiveness of a spoiled, selfish woman half his age. A woman who wasn't one-tenth the person Zelinda had been before her fall from grace.

Ava had to distract herself—but with what? She could work from home, of course. She had some of her files here. But most of her open cases required her to place a few calls, and she couldn't do that while her father was using her cell phone. Apparently, he'd scooted out of his house so quickly he'd left his own cell behind. That made it easy to guess what Carly's behavior must've been like at the time. Besides, Ava's laptop was in the dining room, which was on the other side of the living room.

A brief silence gave Ava hope that the conversation

had come to an end. She opened the door to her bedroom, but then her father started again.

"We have a child together, Car. Can't you understand why I'd return her call?...It's not because I'm still in love with her! Neal's getting married. It was nice of her to let me know. It's not like *he* would've told me."

Her half brother was tying the knot? No one had bothered to inform Ava.

God, her family was screwed up. No wonder she worked all the time. She was about to go back into the bathroom to do something really exciting, like repaint her toenails or clean her toilet, when silence fell again. And this time it lasted.

Because there'd been no resolution or even a goodbye, she knew Carly had hung up rather abruptly—probably *very* abruptly. Her father's pleading hadn't been enough to mollify her this time.

"You hungry?" she asked as she walked out.

He was sitting on the couch with his eyes closed, head bowed and resting on the hand that held her phone, but he looked up when she spoke. "Uh, yeah, I could eat." Attempting to conceal his dejection, he smiled.

"I'll make us some lunch. What would you like?"

Standing, he waved her toward the door. "Don't bother cooking. Let's get out of here. I'll take you to my favorite spot."

Ava didn't hide her surprise. "You're going to take me to lunch? Just the two of us?" She knew what that would mean if word of it got back to Carly. He'd be in worse trouble than he was now.

"This place is claustrophobic. Let's go."

She suspected the houseboat only seemed claustrophobic because it was all he had to look forward to if he couldn't patch things up with Carly.

Seeing the cabin through new eyes, Ava drew a deep breath. The houseboat wasn't hers. She'd return it to her father as soon as he and Carly broke off their relationship, which was coming. Ava couldn't see the marriage lasting much longer. They might struggle on for another year or two, but then her father would be on his own—older but none the wiser, if his track record was any indication. And where would that leave her?

She'd be completely free, without anchor or tether, just as she'd always wanted.

But was it really?

Kalyna hid in the trees while she watched Ava come out of the houseboat with an older man. Who was he? A friend? A client? A relative? And was this Ava's place or the man's? Hard to tell….

Ava and whoever he was climbed into the truck next to her Volkswagen and drove off. Kalyna waited for a few minutes, to make sure they didn't come back. Then she walked over to where Ava had parked. The car was unlocked, probably because there wasn't much inside to protect—just a pair of sunglasses. Slipping into the driver's seat, Kalyna tried them on and checked her reflection in the rearview mirror. She didn't care for the way they made her look, but she took them, anyway. Ava wasn't going to be around long enough to need them.

Clipping the sunglasses to her shirt, Kalyna got out of the car and strode down the pier. The door to the houseboat was locked, but the panel felt pretty flimsy. She could break it open. But that would reveal someone had been here, and there was no need to put Ava on alert when surprise would serve Kalyna's purposes so much better.

She took a quick turn around the boat and found a window that was open a few inches. Once Kalyna cut the screen with the knife she carried in her jockey box, she was able to get her fingers through. From there it was only a matter of sliding the window open and climbing in.

She entered through a spare bedroom that looked like any other bedroom. Other than the fact that it sat on the water, the house itself wasn't unusual, either. The kitchen, dining room and living room were joined. There was another bedroom and a second bath in the back, near the spare room.

One thing was obvious, however. This wasn't just a vacation home. Someone was living here on a regular basis, and it was easy to tell who that someone was. Pictures of Ava with various people—a man who had his arm around her on a windy pier, the two women Kalyna had met that day in Ava's office, the man who'd just left with her—graced the shelves above the television. A stack of mail, already opened, waited on the kitchen counter. It was all addressed to Ava at some post office box.

Kalyna thumbed through several bills, pausing when she came to a bank statement. It was gratifying to be able to violate Ava's privacy this way, to paw through a list of her recent purchases and get some idea of where she spent her money.

Judging by the statement, Ava paid her bills on time, but she didn't have much in the bank. The statement showed automatic deposits that totaled quite a bit less than Kalyna made at the base. The stupid woman was facing down rapists, wife abusers and murderers for mere pennies. Why bother?

"Loser," she muttered, and helped herself to a couple of cookies she found in the cupboard while she tried to think. She wanted Ava dead. Gone. Out of her life, and out of Luke's life. But how? She had to be careful.

Thanks to Mark and his recent threats, she'd be able to wriggle out of the blame for her mother's death, but she couldn't be connected to another murder investigation. The cop she'd spoken to on the phone would be arriving tomorrow, but she interviewed well. There was still a chance she could put her life back together without having to leave the country. Losing her mother gave her a good excuse for not showing up at work this morning— she was too emotionally distraught. That wouldn't erase the fact that she'd been absent without leave before Norma died. But her loss should evoke some sympathy in her superiors. Maybe her punishment wouldn't be as serious as it would've been otherwise. Even if they demoted her, she'd have a job, a place to live and Luke, and she could reapply for advancement in another year or so.

Things would work out. If only she could think of some way to get rid of Ava. Ava was the one who'd ruined everything. Seeing that she died a violent and painful death appealed to Kalyna. But torturing her would bring about another investigation. Even if it was just a stabbing or a shooting, the media would get involved and the police would be under pressure to solve the murder of someone so well-known in the area.

There had to be an easier way….

Turning, Kalyna stared out the window—and that was when the obvious occurred to her. Ava lived in a house surrounded by water. It wouldn't be too surprising if she were to drown. Rivers could be dangerous; people died in them all the time. Something as simple as slipping on a rock and banging her head—a freak accident—could have the same result and would warrant only a short mention in the paper.

Kalyna smiled at her thoughts. Better yet, it would be easy to accomplish, especially since she could set it up right now. She'd put the sunglasses back—leave everything the way she'd found it, including the partly open window. She'd smooth the screen so the cut she'd made would only be noticeable if someone was actually looking for it. Then she'd be able to use the same point of entry when she came back tonight.

Excitement brought a rush of adrenaline. As her plan took shape, she walked through the house a second time. She needed to make sure she could navigate the layout without bumping into furniture in the dark, needed to know where to find Ava when she was sleeping.

"She'll be right here," Kalyna murmured as she entered the master bedroom. "And she won't suspect a thing."

Although Ava's room was clean, her bed wasn't made and there was a sweatshirt tossed over a chair. Kalyna could see part of the logo on that sweatshirt—and the familiarity of it made her clench her jaw. Why would Ava own an air force sweatshirt? Especially one so large?

She didn't, of course. The sweatshirt belonged to Luke.

"That *bitch!*" Kalyna screamed, and threw it on the floor. She wanted to tear the place apart, tear Ava apart, too. She wouldn't share Luke; she wanted every tiny piece of him all to herself.

But the only way to get what she wanted was to use her head.

Taking a deep breath, she struggled to calm down. She couldn't get worked up, couldn't succumb to the cutting or scratching or banging temptation that grabbed her when she was upset. *She* wasn't the one who'd be hurt tonight. She'd save her rage for Ava—but she wasn't leaving that sweatshirt behind.

With steely determination, she tied the sweatshirt

around her waist and began to search through Ava's drawers. If she had a weapon, Kalyna needed to know about it, just in case Ava got loose or something else went wrong.

But she found nothing more worrisome than a nail file. Ava wasn't very prepared for what was about to happen.

Kalyna stood at the edge of the room as she imagined exactly how it would go. She'd surprise Ava while she was sleeping and tie her hands and feet. Then she'd drag her to the river—

No, she couldn't drag her. The scrapes would show on the body once it was recovered. She'd have to put Ava on a blanket and use that to get her to the water. There, she'd throw her over the side of the boat and dive in after her, at which point she'd hold Ava's head underwater until she was dead. After Ava's lungs were full of river water, she'd knock her on the head with a rock to make it look as if she'd hit her head and passed out. Then she'd cut the ropes and massage any marks they might've left on Ava's skin.

Kalyna was slightly worried that she wouldn't be able to get rid of the marks completely. She'd never killed in this way before, had no experience to rely on. And it was always the marks on the body that helped the police in those forensics shows. But this would be different. The ligatures wouldn't be on long enough to cause much damage and, provided the body stayed in the water for any length of time, Ava would be too bloated and disco-lored to make them obvious, anyway.

When it was over, she'd take the rock and the rope with her. Then tomorrow, or the day after, or maybe the day after that, someone would find Ava floating in the river. Or, even better, the fish would eat her or she'd drift out to sea. Whatever happened at that point didn't matter to Kalyna, because she'd be back at work with nothing and no one to tie her to such a tragic accident.

And Luke would be hers.

Ava's mind was on the case in Arizona. It was easier to think about Norma's murder, to wonder about the progress Detective Morgan might be making, than to think about Luke. And she certainly didn't want to concentrate on what her father was telling her, or she'd run from the restaurant screaming in frustration. Ever since they'd sat down, he'd been talking about Carly, extolling her virtues and trying to convince Ava—probably himself, too—that she wasn't as bad as she seemed. He actually said she'd calm down and grow up "eventually."

When? Ava wanted to ask. She didn't see Carly's behavior improving in the least. Why would it? There was no incentive for change. If she threw a fit because Chuck wanted to go fishing, he didn't go fishing. If she threw a fit because Chuck was planning to see his daughter, he canceled the engagement. He did anything and everything she demanded.

So why was he lying to himself? Why did he put up with her? That was what Ava couldn't figure out. Could having a trophy wife be that important to his ego? It had to be. What else did she have to hold him?

The reason he stayed with Carly was a combination of pride, ego and fear, she decided. Her father hated the thought of being alone, especially now that he was getting older. But he was still a handsome man. He wouldn't be alone for long. He never had been.

"Ava? Are you listening?" he asked.

She blinked and refocused. Trying to downplay his sudden appearance on her doorstep, he'd said Carly had made him his favorite meal as a peace offering the last time they'd had a disagreement. As if that made up for her petty jealousies and selfishness. And then he'd said something else, but she hadn't caught it.

"Sorry, I—I have a lot on my mind. What was that?" she asked.

"I said, you don't think much of her, do you?"

The resignation in his tone astonished Ava. She wasn't sure how they'd gone from the usual sales pitch—*she means well, she's just high-spirited; her temper gets hold of her, but she has a good heart*—to a comment so blunt and honest.

Ava opened her mouth to lie and say she did. She knew the price of admission into her father's life. She had to pretend to like whatever woman he had at his side because that woman always came before she did. But she couldn't do it today. She was too tired of fighting that battle, a battle she could never win—at least not with Carly.

Tensing, she met his eyes. "No."

He set down his fork. "She's not as bad as you might think, Ava."

"That's what you keep telling me. How many times have you said it just today?" she asked.

"I'm hoping that someday you'll believe it. I'm trying to build a bridge between you."

By making it all *her* responsibility?

"Carly would like to be closer to you," he said. "She tells me that all the time."

Because it sounded good. Because he wanted to hear it, wanted to believe it. But Carly never acted on that sentiment, never put forth one bit of effort. She made it clear that she preferred just the opposite. "Then why doesn't she ever want to see me?" Ava asked.

"She can sense that you don't like her, babe. It makes

her uncomfortable. It would make anyone uncomfortable."

Ava rocked back. "So it's *my* fault?"

"I'm not saying that. I'm just asking you to look a little deeper, try a little harder."

Ava covered her face.

"Are you listening?"

"I'm trying, but…"

"But what?"

She dropped her hands. "It's so hard to watch you making a fool of yourself over a childish brat."

His face flushed red and he shot to his feet. "When you talk like that, you sound as jealous as she claims you are."

"*I'm* jealous? I'm your daughter. I should be entitled to at least some of your attention."

"Don't do this to me," he said. "Not now. I'm going to make my marriage work."

"But don't you see?" she cried. "It takes two. Two *adults*. There's nothing you can do. It's just a matter of time."

"Find your own way home!" he snapped, and stalked out. Then, adding insult to injury, the waitress brought her the check.

It was good to be back in her apartment again. For a while, Kalyna had thought she'd never see it again. While riding in Jerry's semi and envisioning her return to the country of her birth, she hadn't expected to miss it—but she knew better now. She couldn't even remember Ukraine, had no idea where she'd live if she moved there. No, she'd stay here, with Luke.

According to the clock that hung on the same wall as her TV, it was after three. She had a lot to do before tonight. She had to get to the laundry, as she'd promised, so Luke would think she'd been busy with that all day. She had to find an all-black outfit to wear to Ava's and buy some rope. And she couldn't get those items from a store located anywhere in the vicinity. She had to drive out of the area, somewhere the police wouldn't look, in case she was picked up on surveillance video. She'd pay cash and destroy the receipts. Then she'd dispose of the rope by burying it in the woods when she was finished with it.

The entire drive from Ava's houseboat to Fairfield, she'd studied her plan, searching for potential problems, but she couldn't find anything wrong with it. She could improve on it by using someone else's car, of course, but she wasn't close enough to any of the women in her apartment complex to ask that kind of favor. And it would be an unusual request, which would draw attention to her—exactly what she needed to avoid.

Dragging her luggage into her bedroom, she opened it on the floor and pulled out her dirty clothes. As long as she was doing Luke's laundry, she might as well do her own. She wished she'd have time to make them some dinner, too, but she could do that tomorrow or the next night, when Ava was gone.

The thought of Luke made Kalyna want to call him, just to check in. But her cell phone was dead and she couldn't change that until she went to the store to buy a new charger.

Maybe she could do that while she was out getting the rope. She was tempted to buy a few other things, as well—implements she could use to have a little more fun with Ava. If anyone deserved to die the way Sarah had, it was Ava Bixby. But if they found the body, there'd be an autopsy. Kalyna couldn't do anything extra to punish

Ava or it would show up on the body, and the whole point was to make her death look like an accident.

"You're getting off easy," she grumbled. Although Ava deserved more, paying with her life would have to be enough.

31

It wasn't hard to find Kalyna's apartment.

Tati began searching for her sister's car as soon as she drove onto the property, but she didn't see it. Either Kalyna was parked somewhere Tati had missed or she wasn't home. Most likely the latter, since it was only three-thirty on a Monday afternoon, and she was supposed to be at work.

After parking in one of two visitor slots near the rental office, Tati got out and started looking for #132. Built of typical California-style stucco and wood, the apartments were arranged in pods around a pool, all approachable from the outside. Hip-hop music came from a radio near two sunbathers who were enjoying the water and the sunshine. Tati thought it was nearly as hot here in Fairfield as it was in Mesa, Arizona, but there was more grass, not to mention lots more trees.

Kalyna's apartment was in the middle of its pod on the first floor. Tati knocked, but as she expected there was no answer. Hoping she could wait inside, she checked the door.

It was locked and there wasn't a key under the mat or over the door frame. She walked around the building to see if she could find some other way in, but all the windows were closed up tight. She returned to the door to double-check that she hadn't missed a spare hidden in the vicinity but once again found nothing. She was just thinking that maybe she should go to the closest mall or restaurant, where she could while away an hour or two in air-conditioned comfort, when Kalyna's next-door neighbor came strolling out.

"Hey, Kalyna." The woman had her car keys in her hand and would've passed right by, but Tati stopped her.

"Excuse me, but I'm not Kalyna."

The woman peered at her. "Oh, wow. You're not. I can see a few subtle differences now that I look a bit closer."

Tati immediately thought of the weight she'd put on in recent years, but this woman wasn't rude enough to specify *what* differences.

"For the most part you look exactly like her," she was saying. "Amazing."

"We're identical twins." By now that was obvious, but people expected her to confirm what they saw. They liked hearing about twins, enjoyed the novelty.

"No kidding," the woman said. "What's your name?"

"Tatiana."

"It's nice to meet you, Tatiana. I'm Maria. How's your sister doing after the, um, attack?"

"She's okay, I think." With a glance at Kalyna's door, Tati said, "You don't happen to know when she might get home, do you?"

"It seems like she gets off around 4:00 p.m. most days. Is she expecting you?"

Tati didn't want to admit the number of times she'd called Kalyna without a response. "No. I didn't tell her I was coming. I wanted to surprise her. But now that she's not home and the door's locked, I don't know how to get in."

"Oh, I can help with that."

Tati felt her eyebrows go up. "You can?"

"Sure. When she moved in, Kalyna asked me to hold on to a key for her in case she ever locked herself out. It's in the cupboard above my fridge."

"Thanks so much. I'm positive she won't mind."

"It's not as if you could be lying about being her sister," she said with a laugh and turned to unlock her own door. "Just a minute…"

Maria disappeared into her apartment and returned seconds later. "Here you go," she said, and opened Kalyna's door.

Tati stepped inside. "Thanks again. I really appreciate it."

Presumably planning to return it to its place above her fridge, Maria kept the key. "No problem. Have a great time while you're here," she said, and tossed Tatiana a smile as she walked away.

Kalyna's apartment wasn't the cleanest place Tati had ever seen, but it wasn't the messiest, either. Although typically reluctant to go to any extra work, especially if Tati was around to do it for her, Kalyna apparently increased her efforts if she had no backup. The furniture was "secondhand functional," no frills attached, and the dishes and towels were odds and ends at best, but there were groceries in the fridge.

A peek in Kalyna's bedroom told Tati her sister was home but hadn't completely unpacked. Her suitcase lay open on the floor, half-empty with the remaining clothes and shoes jumbled.

Tati wished Kalyna had a landline so she could call Ava Bixby to tell her she was in town. She hadn't done it yet because she knew Kalyna didn't really trust the victims' advocate. But when Tati had talked to her, she'd gotten a good feeling from Ava. It felt as if she could trust her to help with the terrible things going on in their lives. She had more experience with crime and punishment than Tati did. And they needed *someone*. Mark's story was doing so much to discredit Kalyna.

Just as she was curling up on the bed in hopes of sleeping away the wait, Tati's gaze fell on the dresser— and the jewelry box Kalyna had used for years. Kalyna had confessed to having Sarah's necklace, but it'd been a long time since Tati had seen it.

Shaking her hair out of her face, she climbed off the bed and rummaged through the compartments.

Sure enough, there it was—in the bottom drawer, just where it'd always been. Only this time, Tati couldn't bring herself to touch it. That necklace had belonged to a young girl who'd been violently murdered. Who was she? Why had she run away from home? And what about the people she'd left behind? Surely, there were parents, relatives, friends—someone who mourned her.

Tati was so intent on the necklace that at first she didn't see the ring sitting next to it. When she did, the significance didn't immediately register. She stared at it for several seconds, thinking it had to be some trick of her overwrought imagination. But when she picked it up and held it, she knew it was no trick at all.

This was her mother's wedding ring.

The ring that'd been stolen from her purse when she was murdered.

"Oh, God, Kalyna," she whispered, and would've doubled over in anguish if not for the noise at the door. She hadn't heard anyone come in. She'd been too intent on what she was doing.

Eyes blurred with tears, she turned to ask her sister how this had happened. Why had Kalyna done what she'd done to Norma, to *all* of them?

But there was no time to say anything. Spotting the knife, Tati opened her mouth to scream, but her cry was cut off by one quick thrust, and then another and another.

The last thing she remembered was falling to the floor—and seeing her mother's ring roll across the carpet.

Ava stood outside the restaurant in Antioch, wondering how she was going to get home. She knew Sheridan, Skye or Jonathan would come and get her if she asked. It would be a bit of a drive for them, coming from Sacramento, but she could spend the time returning all the calls she'd missed while her phone was off. She'd done so little on her cases this past weekend. She really needed to get in gear, get back to the person she'd been before she met Luke. She hadn't been herself since then.

Her attempt to motivate herself failed, however. She had fifteen new messages waiting for her, and couldn't summon enough enthusiasm to listen to even one.

Tomorrow. She'd start back to work in the morning. Between Luke and Geoffrey and her father...she couldn't cope with business as usual today.

"Hey, ah, you okay?"

The young man who'd served her and her father lunch had just come out of the restaurant. Apparently his shift was over and he was heading home. He'd probably witnessed her father's grand exit and felt sorry for her.

Smiling to cover her embarrassment, Ava planned to tell him that everything was fine. It wasn't as if she had no options. If she didn't want to interrupt her colleagues, she could call a taxi. But when he stepped closer and looked at her with real sympathy, she abandoned the charade she so often used to protect herself.

"I could use a ride," she admitted.

He pulled off the bow tie that was part of his uniform. "What direction are you going?"

She'd intended to tell him she was going to the delta. But she knew that would be out of his way. It was out of everyone's way. Or was that just an excuse to tell him where she really wanted to go? Fairfield would most likely be just as far out of his way. "Covent Garden Apartments. They're in Fairfield."

"Sure, I'll give you a lift," he said, and thirty minutes later she was standing in front of Luke's door.

"I must be a glutton for punishment," she told herself. She'd already ended the relationship and needed to leave it at that before things got any worse. But her heart was thudding so painfully in her chest, she wasn't sure she could move. And now she didn't even have a way to leave. She'd let the waiter who'd brought her drive off with a "thanks for the ride" and a wave.

Maybe, if she was lucky, Luke wouldn't be home. Then she'd be forced to do what she should've done at the restaurant and call a taxi.

Or there was always the chance Luke would tell her he didn't want to talk to her again. He certainly hadn't been happy with her when she'd shown up earlier....

She thought of her father and the fear that immobilized him when it came to Carly. He was so afraid of losing her that he stayed, regardless of the way she treated him. Ava swore she'd never do the same. But she was letting fear control her, too; the difference was, she let fear keep her from trying in the first place.

Refusing to be that big a coward, she threw back her shoulders and knocked.

"Who is it?" Luke's voice rang out above the noise of his television. He sounded bored, so disinterested he couldn't be bothered to answer.

Ava swallowed hard. "It's me."

A second later, the door swung wide, and Luke was there.

"Hi," she said. She expected him to ask why she'd come back or to make her apologize for how she'd behaved this morning, but he didn't. He seemed relieved. Tilting up her chin with one finger, he pressed his lips to hers in a kiss so gentle she thought she'd melt into a puddle on his doorstep.

"Thanks for coming back," he murmured, and drew her inside.

Luke had told himself that if he was lucky enough to get another chance with Ava, he wouldn't take her to bed. Not right away. Last night, they'd jumped ahead and confused everything, which had frightened her. He wanted to slow down and invest the time in getting to know her so he could build up her trust before becoming physical again. With Kalyna pregnant, possibly carrying his child, life was complicated, and he had to acknowledge that. But it wasn't easy to leave Ava's clothes on. Not when their kisses grew so hot that their bodies began straining together.

He'd guided her fingers away from the buttons on his jeans twice. He wasn't sure he could hold out a third time. Not with the way she'd warmed to his touch. Not with the acute pleasure he felt just having her in his arms again. He probably would've given in. He already had her skirt up when a knock made her break away.

With her face flushed and her blouse unbuttoned to reveal her lacy bra, she'd never looked prettier. He grinned at her as she attempted to adjust her clothes, and she flashed him a shy smile.

"Luke? You home?" The voice belonged to Kalyna. He grimaced when he recognized it and wished he hadn't let her take his laundry. She was so damned intrusive. Since she'd transferred to Travis, he hadn't been able to go a single day without running into her somewhere.

"You know who that is, don't you," he muttered.

Ava nodded. "Are you going to answer?"

"Do you think she'll go away if I don't?"

"She's obsessed with you. She'll never go away— unless they put her away."

"Luke?" Kalyna called again.

"Just a minute," he said, and turned back to Ava. "So all my hopes hang on some unlikely conviction? Wow, you really know how to reassure a guy."

"If she killed her mother that might not be as unlikely as it seems."

"Now you've got me thinking I should hire a private investigator to help the Mesa police."

"I can see if Jonathan could squeeze it in," she said.

"You haven't yet? I thought you were going to ask him if he'd try to track down the hitchhiker. Sarah."

"It's been one thing after another today. I haven't even made it in to work, which is unlike me. But I'll get him tomorrow."

That was a step in the right direction. Still, putting Kalyna away wouldn't solve all his problems. He thought of the document she'd brought him, proving her pregnancy. It was still lying on his kitchen table. He needed to tell Ava that Kalyna had been tested and address any concerns she might have about his having a baby with someone else. Especially if that someone was Kalyna... His situation would be a challenge to any relationship— could easily destroy one so new. He wanted to prevent that, if he could.

"Luke, this stuff is heavy," Kalyna complained.

"I'll get rid of her," he whispered.

Ava touched his arm. "Wait. Let me go into the bedroom first. I'd rather she didn't know I'm here. It'll just antagonize her, and I don't think we'd be smart to do that. Not until we find out more about how Norma died, and Sarah."

He waited until she'd slipped past him, then opened the door. He immediately took the laundry, but Kalyna didn't leave.

"Is someone here?" Gone was the solicitous mood with which she'd approached him this morning. Her eyes were narrow and accusing, her jaw hard.

He wanted to tell her she had no right to even ask, but he could get rid of her more quickly if he avoided an argument. "You done already?"

She didn't let him distract her. "I thought I heard a woman's voice."

"The TV's on."

She kept trying to look around him. "If it was just the TV, what took you so long to answer the door?"

Hooking his hands on the jamb over his head, he positioned himself so she couldn't come in. "Maybe I wasn't dressed," he said with a scowl.

She didn't react to the irritation in his voice. The gaze that swept over him was so sexual Luke felt as if he'd been accosted. "I wouldn't have minded."

She'd already made that very clear. Ignoring the comment, he managed a smile. "Thanks for helping out. I'll see you at work."

He tried to shut the door but she stopped it with her foot. "Ava's in there with you. I know it. Don't lie to me."

This time he couldn't keep himself from responding. "Kalyna, I could have as many women in here as I want. You don't have the right to complain."

A feral gleam entered her eyes. "I don't care if you

want multiple partners. I'll even provide them. Just…not Ava. Anyone but her. Don't shut me out, Luke. Let me be number one."

"That's not how a relationship works," he said. "At least, that's not how my relationships work."

"I could be anything you want."

"Kalyna—"

"Just tell me the truth. You've got Ava over, don't you? You're in love with her. You wish she was carrying your baby instead of me!"

Luke said nothing.

"Don't you?" she challenged.

With a sigh, he nodded. "Yeah, I do."

The blood drained from Kalyna's face. He opened his mouth to tell her he'd never made her any promises. What part of "I'm not interested" did she not understand? But she didn't give him the chance.

"You *bastard!*" she screeched. Then she slapped him and ran away.

Ava found Luke standing at his front door, looking a bit stunned. "Are you okay?" she asked.

"To be honest, I'm not even sure I'm living in reality anymore."

"What do you mean?"

He shut the door. "Somehow I've become the protagonist in *Fatal Attraction.*"

"Obsession happens in real life, too."

"To *other* people."

She gave him a sad smile. "Not this time, handsome."

"You've seen it before?"

"More often than you'd think. It's usually a man obsessed with his wife, or girlfriend, getting possessive and dominating, chasing her away while trying to make sure she won't ever leave him. But it can happen in reverse, too."

"But Kalyna and I never had a close relationship!"

"In her mind, you established that the night you slept with her."

His smile slanted to one side as he took her hands. "Did you feel anything that earth-shattering when we slept together?"

"I saw stars..." she said.

He rolled his eyes. "We were sleeping outside."

She laughed. "Um, okay, there were moments I thought I'd drown in desire."

"Or in the river, right?"

She nudged him. "What about you?"

Instead of continuing with more lighthearted banter, he sobered. "I knew it was too early, but I wanted you so badly I couldn't stop."

"We have absolutely nothing in common," she said.

"You're the kind of person I'd like to be with. That has to count for something."

She realized he'd made himself vulnerable with that statement and stood on tiptoe to kiss him.

"Can you tolerate the fact that I might be having a baby with someone else?" he asked.

She preferred not to consider it. "*Might* is the key word there."

He retrieved a sheet of paper from the kitchen and handed it to her. "Looks pretty legit."

Ava felt her muscles tense as she studied the results. She didn't want to see what she saw. "Just because she's pregnant doesn't mean the baby's yours."

"What if it is?"

She had no answer. She hoped it wouldn't bother her, but she was afraid it would. Did she really want Kalyna in her life? "We'll cross that bridge when we come to it, okay?"

His cell phone rang. He glanced at it, then frowned. "It's The Last Stand."

"*What?* Who'd be calling you from there—besides me?"

"We'll find out." He hit the Talk button. "Hello?… This is Luke… Yes, I've seen her. She's right here… Just a minute." He passed her the phone. "It's someone named Skye Willis, for you."

Blinking in surprise, Ava brought the phone to her ear. "Skye?"

"Why aren't you answering your cell?" she demanded.

Ava felt a twinge of guilt. She'd turned it off because she was afraid she'd hear from Geoffrey, or hear from them about Geoffrey. So far, she'd been successful in dodging everyone. "I was having lunch with my father and didn't want to be interrupted."

"Oh." That brought her up short. Skye knew Ava's relationship with Chuck was a difficult one. "How'd it go?"

"We got into an argument about Carly, so he stormed off and stranded me at the restaurant."

"You're kidding."

"Your father walked out on you?" Luke asked. "He left you without a ride?"

Clearly, he wasn't pleased. Ava covered the phone to respond. "He walked out a long time ago. What happened at the restaurant just made it official." She went back to her conversation with Skye but was really speaking to both of them. "In his defense, he was already upset. He and Carly had a major argument."

Skye made a noise of disbelief. "And in *your* defense, that woman's a grade-A bitch. I don't know how you've put up with her this long."

Leave it to Skye to tell it like it was. "True."

"I hope you told him that."

"Pretty much. Same sentiment, if not the same words. That's when he left."

Luke had gone to look out the window at the parking lot. "How'd you get here?"

Ava glanced at him sheepishly. "The waiter felt sorry for me."

"You should've called," he said. "I would've come."

The protectiveness in his voice made her smile, but there was no time to respond, since Skye was talking. "Good," her friend was saying. "Maybe it'll give him something to think about."

"I doubt it," Ava said. "He's so focused on saving his marriage, he doesn't really even notice me."

"I'm sorry about that, Ava. And I don't want to come down too hard on you, but we've been really worried. Geoffrey's stopped by the office twice, looking for you. He told us you're not at home, that he has no idea where you are, and that you broke up with him for someone named Luke. No last name, nothing. If Jonathan hadn't heard you mention a Luke recently, we wouldn't have been able to track you down."

Jonathan was probably laughing his head off. "Tell him he was right about Luke."

"You can tell him yourself in a minute," Skye said. "He's standing here, hovering over my desk, mad as hell that you haven't let any of us know what's going on. You didn't come in to work this morning."

"I don't have set hours. And I always put in more than my forty. So…"

"But you didn't call. You can't just disappear like that, Ava, not even for a few hours, or we assume the worst."

Of course. They weren't used to anything disrupting

her usual pattern. Neither was she, or she would've called out of habit. "I get it. I'm sorry," Ava said. "Is that what you wanted, to make sure I'm okay?"

"No, that's not all. There are some people who've been trying to get hold of you, and it sounds serious."

"What people?"

"A Detective Morgan from the Mesa Police Department in Arizona. And a man named Dewayne Harter."

Ava glanced over at Luke, who was watching her closely. "What is it?" he murmured.

She held up a hand. "Did they say what they wanted?"

"The detective said it was important to reach you. Mr. Harter said it was an emergency."

32

Ava tried to call the detective first. But she was told he was in a meeting and would have to get back to her. So she called Dewayne Harter at the mortuary, who answered as if he'd been waiting by the phone.

"Hello?"

"Mr. Harter, this is Ava Bixby at The Last Stand in Sacramento." She allowed Luke to pull her onto the couch with him so he could listen, too. "You've been trying to reach me?"

"Yes, I…I didn't know who else to call. I don't know anyone in California."

"How'd you get my number?"

"Tati, my daughter, gave it to me before she left town. She said you'd help us."

"I will," she said. "What's going on?"

"I'm not sure. Tati went to California this morning. She didn't tell me she was going to do it. She called from the airport when it was too late for me to talk her out of it."

"Out of what?"

"She wants to reach her sister. Bring her back, if possible, or at least get her to communicate. She's afraid Kalyna's taking the rap for what happened to my wife, and that it's unfair."

Luke shifted and angled the phone closer to him.

"What do you think?" Ava asked.

"It's hard for Tati to be objective. She sees only the best in people, especially her sister. But Kalyna's always been a little...off." Ava caught a look from Luke that said he completely agreed. "I've seen her throw her fits, and I've seen how long she can hold a grudge," Mr. Harter went on. "I think she's capable of anything—even what Mark Cannaby says about her with that...that hitchhiker. God rest the poor child's soul," he added. "But Tati refuses to believe it."

"I can see why you'd be worried, but...what can I do for you, Mr. Harter?"

"I've lost contact with her. Tati doesn't have a cell, and Kalyna won't pick up, at least for me."

"Kalyna was here a few minutes ago. She's fine."

"Tati wasn't with her?"

"No. Did she know Tati was coming?"

"I doubt it. Kalyna wouldn't pick up for her, either."

"What time did Tati leave?" Ava asked.

"About ten. When she called from the airport to tell me what she was doing, she said she'd check in with me as soon as she got there and keep me updated. It's only a short plane ride, which means she's been there for hours, and I haven't heard a word."

Ava covered the phone. "That's weird, isn't it? Do you think she could've been in the car when Kalyna came here?"

"I guess," Luke said with a shrug.

"Would you like me to look into it?" Ava asked Mr. Harter.

"If you could. I'd call the police, but I might be worrying for no reason. I'd hate to send a false alarm."

"I understand," she said. "I'll see what I can find out and get back to you."

Her phone signaled another call. Expecting it to be the detective, Ava said goodbye to Mr. Harter and switched over. She left the phone slanted so Luke could hear, but it wasn't the detective. It was her father.

"Ava? Jeez, *finally* you answer."

Oh, no, not now. Pulling the phone away from Luke, Ava straightened. "What do you want, Dad?"

"What do you think I want? I've been calling and calling. I'm sorry, honey. I should never have left you like that. I went back to the restaurant not long after, but you were already gone. Are you okay?"

Ava didn't know what to say. She'd tried so hard to establish a relationship with this man, especially since her mother had gone to prison. He was all she had. But she couldn't circumvent the roadblock his wife posed. As long as he was with Carly, Carly would come between them, because she wasn't interested in accepting Ava or anyone else in Chuck's life. Carly wanted to prove to herself and everyone else that Chuck cared only for her.

"I'm fine," Ava said. "But…I don't want to hear from you again, Dad. Not while you're with Carly."

The silence that descended told Ava her father was as shocked as she'd expected him to be. "What do you mean?" he asked. "Carly's my wife!"

"I understand that. I know she matters more than anything to you, and that's why I'm getting out of the way. Maybe it'll make your life easier. Since it's what you want, I hope you can hold the marriage together, but from now on, I'd rather not be involved."

"You're upset," he said. "You don't know what you're saying."

Ava laughed, a little sadly. "I know exactly what I'm saying. And I mean it."

"Come on, Ava. Now you're acting like Neal."

"Neal deserves more than you've ever given him. And so do I." She closed her eyes against an onslaught of pain as she hung up. It wasn't easy to sever that tie, not when she'd clung to it so tenaciously. But it was done, and she knew she'd be better off. She couldn't cope with the continual disappointment.

"Hey," Luke said. "You okay?"

The sympathy in his expression as he leaned down brought a lump to Ava's throat. But she didn't regret her decision; she only regretted the fact that she'd let her father put her through so much before making it. "I'm fine." Lifting her chin, she turned her mind to business. "I've got to go over to Kalyna's, see if Tati's there."

"Well, you're not going alone, I'll tell you that much," he said, and pulled her to her feet.

Kalyna's apartment was only a five-minute drive. Luke parked the BMW in a resident's spot because all the guest spots were taken, but Ava wasn't too worried about his car being towed away. They wouldn't be here long enough to inconvenience anyone for more than a few minutes.

"Maybe Tati's flight was delayed," Luke said as he got out of the car and waited for Ava. "And that made her miss her connection."

"You think she had a layover? Phoenix is Southwest's hub. There should've been plenty of direct flights. It's not as if San Francisco is a small, out-of-the-way airport."

"She could've had a stopover in L.A.," he said as they crossed the parking lot.

Ava could've found Kalyna's address in her file, but there was no need. Luke had been here before. That was how everything started... "But even if she missed her connecting flight, there would've been another one by now," she said. "Flights between L.A. and San Francisco run hourly."

"Does she know the area? Maybe she rented a car but got lost."

Once her eyes had adjusted to the bright sunlight, Ava checked the numbers on the doors they passed. "If Kalyna hasn't seen her, I'll have Jonathan check with the car rental companies. If she rented a car, we should be able to find out where and when, which would give us a starting point."

Luke stopped at an apartment on the right and rang the bell. No one answered, so Ava knocked at the door—and was surprised when it swung inward beneath the subtle pressure of her hand. A quick check told her the door had been locked but the latch hadn't caught the last time someone went in or out.

"Kalyna?" she called.

There was no response. Ava started to go in, but Luke pushed her behind him just before he drew a gun from the waistband of his jeans.

"You brought…*that?*" she whispered.

He didn't look back at her. His body was alert, his eyes focused on the inside of the apartment. "Better safe than sorry," he murmured. "Wait here."

Pointing the muzzle at the ceiling, he stepped cautiously inside. But Ava didn't wait. Just as eager to see what was going on as he was, she followed. It was difficult to feel any danger when she was with him.

If Tati had ever reached the apartment, there was no sign of it. There was no sign of Kalyna, either. The living room, kitchen, bedroom and bath were all empty. "She must not have gone home when she left your place," Ava said as they stood in the master bedroom.

Luke frowned at her. "Why didn't you wait in the hall?"

"There was no need. No one's home."

"There could've been someone in here." He returned the gun to the waistband of his jeans. "What about this suitcase?" he asked, touching the edge of it with his foot. "You think it's Tati's?"

"Not necessarily. It could belong to Kalyna. She just got back from Arizona. Maybe she hasn't finished unpacking."

He picked up a blouse that'd been discarded on the floor. "I think it is Kalyna's. I've seen her wear this before."

Ava peered into the closet and found enough sex toys to stock an adult fantasy shop. "Looks like she's got all the tools she needs for her fetishes."

Luke wouldn't even approach the closet. "I don't want to see it."

"Maybe you'd like to see *this*."

When he turned, she lifted an eight-by-ten photograph of him that'd been framed and placed on the dresser.

"What the hell? Where'd she get that?" He took a closer look and cursed under his breath. "That was at the Moby Dick. She had a digital camera that night, kept snapping pictures."

"Apparently she has others." Ava pointed to another one, of Luke in his flight suit; it was displayed on the nightstand.

"I don't remember her taking that one. This is creeping me out. It's like walking in and finding some sort of shrine. All that's missing is the candles."

"It wasn't here the night you came over?"

"I have no idea. I wasn't paying attention to details. And what I do remember I'm trying to block out."

"She needs psychiatric help," Ava said.

"By the time she's done with me, I might need it, too," he joked grimly. "So where's Tati?"

Ava shook her head. "I have no idea. And that concerns me. I'd better get Jonathan working on the rental. This can't wait until tomorrow."

"Can you do it from the car?" he asked. "I'm not comfortable in here."

"Sure."

"Should we lock the door or leave it as we found it?"

"I say we lock it. It was meant to be locked, just didn't latch. She probably wouldn't know that."

"Hey—" he strode over to the nightstand "—that's my watch!"

"Don't take it," she cautioned. "We don't want her to know we've been here."

"I'm not going to touch it," he said with a grimace. "Come on, let's go." He walked out ahead of her. She was about to follow when she noticed a large wet spot on the floor. Shoving some of the clothes and then the suitcase out of the way, she touched it. It wasn't blood, but the carpet was soaking wet—and smelled as if it had just been cleaned. Why?

"Hey, you comin'?" Luke reappeared at the door.

Ava frowned. "Looks like Kalyna spilled something, then scrubbed it afterward."

"It was probably a drink," he said. "Can we get out of here?"

A drink. Ava supposed that was the most plausible answer. People spilled drinks all the time. But because she'd been working with victims of violent crime, her mind immediately went in a different direction.

"Okay, I'm on my way," she said. But she couldn't help pausing at the door for one final glance—and that was when she caught sight of a purse peeking out from under the bed. The way some of the contents had spilled out made it look as if it had been kicked there during a struggle. "Luke? Hang on," she called, and went back to retrieve it.

He returned a second time. "What now?"

Ava knelt on the ground to go through the handbag. Some gum, candy and makeup had fallen out, but the wallet was still inside. She opened it, expecting to find Kalyna's ID and found Tati's instead.

Holding it up, she waved it at him. "Tati's been here."

He didn't come any closer. Arms folded, he leaned against the doorjamb and frowned. "So where is she now?"

Ava said nothing; she was too busy trying not to assume the worst.

"She must be with Kalyna," he said, answering his own question.

Ava's heart began to beat harder as she stared at the wet spot on the carpet. "I hope so," she said, then put the purse and the suitcase back where she'd found them.

After that, she called Jonathan.

The moment Ava saw the Lexus parked next to her car at the pier, she turned to see Luke's reaction.

"Is that who I think it is?" he asked with a scowl.

"It is if you're thinking it's Geoffrey." Ava wasn't any happier to see her former boyfriend's car than Luke was. She was too exhausted to deal with another emotional episode. The last time she'd spoken to him was when she'd insisted he leave this morning.

Luke put the transmission in Park. "Want me to get rid of him?"

She heard the hope in his voice but shook her head. It wouldn't be fair to Geoffrey to have Luke chase him off. He deserved an apology. She just wished she didn't have to deal with him tonight. "I'll take care of it."

As she picked up her purse, ready to get out of the car, Luke caught her arm. "Are you sure you don't want me to make him leave?"

"No. This is my fault. I should've broken up with him long ago. But since I didn't, I owe him the chance to talk. He's looking for an explanation. Some closure."

"That'd better be all he's looking for," he muttered.

Ava arched her eyebrows. Hard as it was to believe, Luke sounded jealous. Could he really be threatened by *Geoffrey?* "If I didn't sleep with him in the past few months, I'm not going to sleep with him now. You know that, right?"

"Of course I know that," he said. "I'm not worried that you'll sleep with him. It's just…"

"What?" she prompted.

"Maybe you'll decide we're a mismatch again. That's what you called us, isn't it? Maybe you'll remember why you were with him in the first place—give him another chance."

"Not likely."

"Somehow, he makes you feel safe, in control, and you gravitate toward that."

Because Geoffrey didn't tempt her into the danger zone she'd always worked so hard to avoid. Being with Luke was a gamble she wanted to take—but one minute she thought she was foolish to risk her heart, and the next she thought she'd rather die than deny herself the chance to love him.

"What you have to offer is completely different," she said.

"What does that mean?" he asked. "What do I have 'to offer'?"

In order to duck out of a real answer, she considered responding with something glib. *The best sex a woman could ask for,* came to mind. But she knew Luke would be offended because he wasn't shallow. Besides, it wasn't fair to cheapen what she felt, or what he had to give, because of her own insecurities. "The moon."

Cocking his head, he narrowed his eyes. "Are you being insincere?"

"No," she said with a sigh. It was a difficult admission to make, but she couldn't regret it when, in the next instant, he cradled her face and kissed her tenderly.

"I'm not like your father, Ava."

She couldn't prevent a silent, "We'll see," but she smiled and nodded. "I'll talk to you later."

"Tomorrow."

"Okay, tomorrow."

Luke had been planning to get up early and head to the base so he could resume his regular duties. He couldn't imagine he'd be grounded much longer, so he didn't want to take any more leave. But he would've gone into the houseboat with Ava if Geoffrey hadn't been there—and not only because he was feeling so possessive. He was uncomfortable with what they'd found at Kalyna's, nervous that Tati's father still hadn't heard from her and it was nearly ten o'clock at night. "You sure you'll be okay after he leaves?" he asked.

"Of course. There's no need to worry. Kalyna doesn't even know where I live," she said. Then she waved and closed the door.

Traffic had been horrendous. There were moments when Kalyna had wanted to scream in frustration. She'd driven to Oakland to buy what she needed, and had managed to get there in record time. It was the return trip that'd taken so long. A semi had overturned, backing up traffic for miles.

But she was home now. And she had everything she needed.

She carried the bags into her bedroom and laid her purchases on the bed. She had a hairnet, latex gloves, a black ski mask, a black turtleneck, black pants and black utility boots. She wouldn't use a single piece of clothing she already owned because there could be hair or other sources of DNA that could get left behind.

Picking up the new boots, she studied them with satisfaction. This was the smartest purchase of all, she thought. They were new, so any footprints wouldn't reveal an unusual tread or the kind of markings that came with wear. And they weren't military issue—important since she was in the military and definitely didn't want to give that away. To top it off, she'd bought the boots in a men's size eleven to mislead anyone who might be looking at shoe size. The rope and the duct tape she'd left in the trunk of her car, along with her knife and a crowbar she'd purchased for good measure.

She pictured Ava's shock. "You won't know what hit you," she said with a smile. The only thing she hadn't bought was a charger for her phone. But she was too consumed with what she had planned to worry about that. She didn't want to hear from anyone right now, anyway. There'd be tomorrow and the rest of the week to squirm out of what she'd done to her mother and to apologize to her superior officer for disappearing without permission. It'd be a lot easier to pull her life back together if she wasn't worried about Ava seeing Luke.

As she stripped down, Kalyna had to decide whether or not to shower. She'd already been in the houseboat and could've left traces of DNA then, so in one way it seemed excessively cautious. But depositing more DNA would only raise the chances of it being found and used in an investigation, so she made herself wash and shave all the hair from her body as she'd originally planned. If she had time after killing Ava, she'd vacuum and dust and do everything possible to erase her earlier visit, too.

Kalyna was still whistling when she finished showering. She was going to enjoy telling Ava that she'd never see Luke again, or anyone else, for that matter. She wished she could rape Ava with her knife. She wanted to destroy the very essence of Ava, what made her a woman. That'd teach her to think she could make love with Luke.

But that would mean blood, and blood was the first thing the cops would look for.

She walked into the bedroom to get dressed—and realized she couldn't put her boots on in the apartment. They might track carpet fibers into Ava's place. She'd have to walk out in her socks and put the boots on in her car, after shaking off the rubber mats.

Maybe she wouldn't have as much fun as she wanted, but at least they'd never catch her. Ava didn't have a chance.

About to pull on the turtleneck, Kalyna walked around the bed—and stepped in something wet that seemed to be spreading out from under her suitcases. Surprised, she pushed it aside and glanced down. It felt as if she'd spilled a glass of water on the carpet. Except that the spot was too big.

She went into the bathroom to see if her toilet had overflowed in her absence, but she'd used it before getting in the shower. And the carpet between the bed and the bathroom was dry. There was only one wet area, and it was right in front of her dresser.

"These crappy apartments," she muttered. "There must be a plumbing leak." But she'd have to deal with that tomorrow.

It was time to go.

33

When the phone rang, Luke was lying on the couch. He muted the TV and answered without bothering to check caller ID. He was hoping it'd be Ava. He hadn't liked leaving her with Geoffrey and had felt a little unsettled ever since—which was why he hadn't gone to bed. He planned to call her if she didn't contact him by eleven-thirty.

But it wasn't Ava. The voice on the other end of the line took him by complete surprise.

"Luke?"

Marissa sounded so familiar and yet so different. Older. Strained. It was as if he could hear the years in every word—the years they'd spent apart, struggling to forget each other.

Suddenly too tense to remain in a prone position, he sat up and leaned forward, resting his elbows on his knees and staring at the carpet. "Yeah, it's me."

"This is Marissa."

"I know." He wanted to ask how she'd been, but there were so many emotions pouring through him he couldn't say anything at all. An awkward silence ensued before he managed a strangled, "I'm sorry about Phil."

"So am I."

Silence again. His mind whirred and his muscles grew tense—he could hear his blood rushing through his ears—but Luke didn't know what to say.

"It's late," she said. "Would you rather I called back another time?"

That was a loaded question if ever he'd heard one. She was asking if he wanted to talk to her at all. And he couldn't decide. He'd stifled his feelings for so many years that he wasn't sure what, if anything, was left. Had she become nothing more than a dream? An ideal? The one woman no one else could compete with?

He had no answers. Neither could he say if Phil would continue to overshadow them. It wasn't as though either of them would ever forget Phil. He and Marissa had been married. They had a son. Luke didn't want to make a move on his best friend's wife and child. That was just too...opportunistic, made him feel lower than dirt. Which was why he hadn't even allowed himself to think about Marissa, let alone contact her. This whole nightmare with Kalyna had made it easier than it otherwise would've been, but now the past was staring him right in the face.

"This is fine." He couldn't hang up. He was mesmerized by the temptation of Marissa and the possibilities.

"Your mother called me earlier today," she explained. "With her regrets. She said I should contact you."

He chuckled without mirth. His mother had no clue what she might've started. "She told me that, too," he admitted.

"Yet you didn't act on it."

"Probably for the same reason it took you this long to call me."

"It's always been complicated between us, hasn't it?" Ever since Phil had declared himself. "Yes."

"Even at this moment, I'm telling myself I'm stupid to ask for more disappointment and pain. But sometimes, when it's late like this, I think about you, and I—" Her voice broke and she didn't finish.

The silence was awkward again. Was she crying? He couldn't tell, but he suspected she was. And that made him feel terrible. They'd been friends. At the very least, he owed her his sympathy. "Don't cry, Marissa. I can't stand it."

"I'm sorry. I'm sorry for everything. That I didn't hold out for you. That I got pregnant so soon and felt as if I was locked in for life. That Phil's dead and we both loved him. Maybe I wanted you instead, but I did love him. I hope you believe that."

She didn't have to convince him. That part was none of his business. "Why didn't anyone tell me about the funeral?" he asked.

"I thought of it. Of course I thought of it." Her voice turned bitter. "But I was so angry at you for—for not taking me out of the situation I've been in for the past few years. And I couldn't mourn Phil, couldn't even think about him, if I knew you were going to be there."

What she'd revealed made him feel guilty all over again. "I couldn't take you out of the situation, Marissa. You were married to my best friend."

"So he meant more to you than I did."

"You were *married*," he said again. "I was waiting to see what would happen with you and Phil. I didn't want to get in the way."

"And now?" she asked. "I'm a widow. Do you still feel anything for me, Luke? Anything at all?"

Of course he cared about her. He'd always care about her. But could he walk away from what he'd just started with Ava?

He rubbed his face. "Too much is happening at once. I need time to think."

"Call me when you decide. I won't make the same mistake twice. I'll wait as long as you need me to," she said, and disconnected.

* * *

Ava was glad when Geoffrey left. She felt horrible that he was taking the disruption of their relationship so hard, but she couldn't even call it a breakup because they'd already broken up. She hadn't expected him to care about losing what was left. He'd been so casual, so preoccupied, so…ready to accept the bare minimum. But he'd stayed for nearly two hours tonight, trying to convince her that she didn't know Luke well enough to choose accurately between them. He said she didn't need to be exclusive with either one, that she should give him another chance.

But she couldn't. She was already in too deep with Luke. For better or for worse, she'd finally summoned enough trust to at least try for the kind of relationship every woman wanted.

Her father had called three times while she and Geoffrey were talking, but she hadn't answered. She felt slightly guilty about that because she knew he couldn't be calling from Carly's house. He wouldn't have dared anger his young wife by showing he cared that much. Which meant Carly must've kicked him out. But even the thought of him on his own didn't make Ava want to speak to him. Why did he reach out to her only when he didn't have anyone else?

"What a day," she grumbled. Hoping to relieve the residual tension from her talk with Geoffrey, she stepped into her shower and felt more relaxed when she got out. She toweled off and was about to put on a nightgown when she remembered Luke's sweatshirt. She preferred to sleep in it, to feel close to him. But she couldn't find it. She thought she'd left it on the floor, the bed or her chair, but it wasn't any of those places.

He must've taken the sweatshirt with him when he

went home this morning. She'd been so humiliated and embarrassed by Geoffrey's sudden appearance that she hadn't watched him collect his things. She'd gone into the kitchen and made coffee while waiting for them to leave.

She checked the clock. Nearly midnight. At this rate, morning would come far too soon.

Finished dressing, she turned off the lights and climbed into bed. She'd cut off her relationship with her father and Geoffrey and welcomed a new man into her heart and her bed, all on the same day. What would tomorrow hold?

Who could say? She fell asleep happy in spite of all that, because she was dreaming of Luke swimming toward her in the river, the moonlight glinting off his bare arms and chest.

Kalyna parked nearly half a mile from the pier where Ava docked her houseboat. It was after midnight. Even with a full moon, the lack of streetlights made this place seem darker than anywhere she'd ever been—except for the inside of a coffin. Not many people could say that with any authority, but she could. Mark had put her in one. It'd been part of their usual game of Truth or Dare. She always chose Dare. Dare got you what you wanted. Truth only got you into trouble.

The ground was too spongy for her footsteps to make any noise. As she got out of the car and went to the trunk to get her tools, a loud chorus of cicadas welcomed her to the delta, along with the fecund smell of vegetation. Using a flashlight to avoid walking into a tree, a ditch, a puddle or a slough, she slung her backpack over one shoulder and kept the beam pointed at the ground to avoid being detected in case anyone else was in the area.

But she'd been here before. She knew there was no one else. No other houses. No other boats. Nothing to worry about.

The darkness felt thick enough to slice with her knife—probably because it was so hot and there was no wind. Beads of sweat rolled between Kalyna's breasts as she hiked to the road and made her way down to the pier, but she didn't think the temperature was exclusively to blame. She had so much adrenaline pumping through her it felt as if her heart would leap right out of her chest.

Ava's houseboat was as dark as the night, but the lapping of the water against its sides helped cloak the creak of Kalyna's footsteps on the wooden pier. She was fairly certain Ava was home, and she was fairly certain Ava was alone. It was a weeknight, her car was where she usually parked it and there were no other vehicles. Kalyna had called Luke from a pay phone only forty minutes ago, and hung up when he answered, just to be sure he was at his apartment.

The boat rocked slightly when she climbed aboard. Wondering how sensitive Ava was to such minute changes in her surroundings, Kalyna snapped off the flashlight and held her breath. But Ava didn't come out to see what was going on. If she was home, she was dead asleep.

Soon, she'd just be dead.

Chuckling silently at her own joke, Kalyna felt her way around the exterior of the cabin to the window with the cut screen.

A splash sounded not far from the boat. Startled, Kalyna froze. The noise had been loud and close, as if something large had dived into the water. But she had nothing to fear from the river. There were no crocodiles in the Sacramento delta. There were some pretty big salmon, though. They came in from the ocean and swam upstream to spawn. She'd probably heard one jump.

Getting back to work, she found the cut in the screen. The window was closed except for a very small crack. Everything was just as she'd left it.

The window squeaked as she opened it, so she had to go slow and do it by inches. There was another splash a few seconds later, but she paid no attention. She was too focused on creating a space big enough to accommodate her.

When she had the window open as far as it would go, Kalyna squeezed her upper body through. The metal rim dug into her hips, but she managed to balance, relieving the pain until she could grab the inside wall to steady herself. From there, she dragged her legs in and was just trying to get down off the dresser when she lost her balance and fell, taking the lamp with her.

A crash woke Ava. She lay in bed, blinking at the darkness, trying to figure out exactly what she'd heard. It'd been loud, she knew that—too loud to be the kind of settling noise that used to frighten her before she'd grown accustomed to the creaks and groans of living on a boat.

She sat up, listening, and heard sounds of movement *in the next room.* Someone was in her house!

As she scrambled out of bed, her mind grasped for a logical explanation. Was it her father? Did he need a place to stay? Or could it be Geoffrey? When he'd left, he'd been pretty upset.

She couldn't imagine either one of them coming into her house in the dark of night, though.

Where was her phone? She'd called Luke to tell him good-night once Geoffrey was gone. Where had she put it? She had to find it. She needed it right away, needed to call for help.

Trying to get her bearings amid an avalanche of adrenaline, she spun in a circle as she struggled to remember. Then it occurred to her. Her phone was in the living room. She ran for the hall, but the person in the next room managed to disentangle himself from whatever he'd broken and came charging out at the same time. Ava almost ran into him before ducking back inside her bedroom and slamming the door.

The snarl that came from the other side as she locked it made every hair on her body stand on end.

"Open this door, bitch!"

Oh, God! It wasn't a *he* at all. It was a *she:* Kalyna. Kalyna was standing between her and her phone—and she was trying to break down the door!

The *whack* of a heavy metal object made Ava gasp involuntarily. She flipped on the light to see the end of a hammer or crowbar come through the wood somewhere near her head. Kalyna was crazy, just as Luke had claimed. And she was violent, just as Ava had feared.

"Kalyna, stop it! You need to calm down. If you hurt me, you'll go to prison."

"I'm not going anywhere, except to Luke's apartment to console him over your death," she said.

She was serious. And because they were so isolated, she could say those words out loud, without risk of anyone hearing or coming to help.

Horrified, Ava stared at the door as Kalyna hit it again. Another hole appeared, close enough to the first to create one large hole.

"Where's Tati, Kalyna? What have you done with her?"

This caused a brief hesitation. "I don't know what you're talking about. She's in Arizona, where she lives."

"No, she's not. She came here, to your apartment. I found her purse in your bedroom. What have you done to her?"

Kalyna smacked the door again. "You're lying! I haven't seen Tati or her purse. And how would you get into my apartment? It was locked when I got home, exactly the way I left it."

Ava measured the distance from the dresser to the door. "It hadn't been closed all the way when we—when I got there. I put Tatiana's purse back under the bed, where I found it. And I locked the front door."

"Shut up! You weren't in my apartment! You're making it all up."

The dresser had eight drawers and a mirror. It was heavy. Would she be able to move it? "Then how do I know about the wet carpet, Kalyna? The spot in front of your dresser?"

Silence.

"Kalyna?" If she could move the dresser so could Kalyna. But it might buy her some time….

"Did *you* make that spot? Did you spill something in my room?" Kalyna sounded bewildered.

Ava had never known a more convincing liar. "*I* didn't put anything there. I saw the spot when I went in, looking for Tati. She's missing and your father's worried sick about her. Call him, see for yourself."

"I'll call him when I'm done here."

"You killed her, didn't you, Kalyna?" She began shoving the dresser toward the door. "You killed her and then cleaned up the blood."

"Stop making shit up!" she screamed, whacking the door again. "I'd never hurt my own sister."

"You killed your mother."

"Norma had it coming. She had it coming for a long time. Tati's never hurt anyone."

The damn dresser moved, but only by centimeters. And it required so much energy. "Then what happened to her?"

"Shut up! Trying to scare me about Tati isn't going to save you."

Scare her about Tati? Could it be true that she didn't know Tati had come to her apartment? Ava didn't see how, but she tried a different tack as she continued to wrestle with the furniture in hopes of creating some sort of blockade. "Luke doesn't want you, Kalyna," she said. "He's never wanted you. You're doing this for nothing."

"Not for nothing," she said. "I'm doing it for my own satisfaction. How dare you think you can take what's mine? How dare you think you can be my friend and then stab me in the back!"

"You were lying to me the whole time, *using* me to punish Luke! How is it that *I'm* the one who betrayed *you?*"

Kalyna didn't answer. She screamed in outrage and started swinging harder. There was no reasoning with her; she was too far gone to respond to logic. And it was only a matter of time before she hacked through the door. The doors on the houseboat weren't solid. They were made with flimsy panels.

Her body clammy with sweat, Ava left the dresser where it was. Kalyna would be inside before she could get it all the way to the door. Instead, she went in search of something she could use to defend herself. But there wasn't so much as an envelope opener in this part of the cabin.

She glanced at the window. Could she get it open and bust out the screen? Probably. But she couldn't let Kalyna catch her partway in and partway out or she'd have no chance whatsoever. She had to finish moving the dresser, create another obstacle while she escaped through the window.

Another blow at the door rocked the whole boat. Kalyna was using a crowbar, not a hammer; Ava could see that now. She could also see that Kalyna was wearing latex gloves and a mask that covered all but her eyes—

Eyes! Dragging large gulps of air into her lungs, she raced to the bathroom and grabbed a can of hair spray from under the sink. When she returned, she held it behind her back. Then she banged on the wall to divert Kalyna's attention from her feverish efforts to get inside. "Hey!" she yelled above the banging. "Hey, you listening?"

The hacking stopped, and Kalyna focused on her through the hole. In another second she'd bring that crowbar up for the final stroke, but it was enough time to give Ava the opportunity she needed. Taking the hair spray from behind her back, she sprayed it right into Kalyna's eyes.

With a scream, Kalyna dropped the crowbar and staggered back. Ava had gotten a clear shot. Now she had to take advantage of what she'd done.

Her only thought on reaching her phone, she threw open the door and shoved past Kalyna.

The hang-up call that awakened Luke after he'd heard from Marissa and then Ava had come in almost an hour ago from a pay phone. A sense of foreboding had hung over him all night, but that last call had made it worse, made it impossible to go back to sleep. Who was it? Why would anyone call him from a pay phone at eleven thirty-five? Although he asked himself those questions over and over, he kept coming up with the same answer: Kalyna. Other than Phil's death, she was responsible for all his recent unhappiness. But if she *was* the one who'd called, why didn't she speak? What was the point of hanging up on him? It wasn't like Kalyna not to have an agenda—not to engage him in conversation, at least.

Using the remote to turn off the television, he went back to bed and tried to sleep, but tossed and turned. He kept thinking about Marissa and Ava—and Kalyna, of course. Why the hell had she called him? What did she want?

Finally, with a curse, he chucked his pillows onto the floor and sat up. He might as well get out of bed and do something, make use of the time.

He polished his shoes and straightened his room. Then he started putting away the laundry Kalyna had done for him. He hated the thought that she'd touched his clothes. More than ever, he wanted her out of his life. But he knew that wasn't likely to happen. Especially if the child she carried was his.

He hadn't even broached the whole Kalyna mess with Marissa. Should he have? Would he tell Ava he finally had a chance to marry the one woman he'd loved since high school and have Marissa move out here so she could be close to him? He was tempted, partly because he was more capable of loving Phil's son than any other man. Maybe this was how things were supposed to go....

But he kept seeing Ava staring up at him as he made love to her on the bank of that river.

Why couldn't anything be easy?

He put away his socks, underwear, T-shirts and gym shorts. Then he came to his air force sweatshirt. He was about to stack it on the high shelf in his closet when it occurred to him that this was the sweatshirt he'd lent Ava.

He smiled as he remembered how tempting she'd looked in it....

But then his smile faded. He'd left this sweatshirt at

Ava's place. So how did it get in his laundry? Ava hadn't brought it to him. When she'd come over today, she'd had nothing with her. Kalyna had delivered this sweatshirt....

His mind reverted to the call that'd troubled him since it came in. Kalyna had delivered the sweatshirt, and she'd used a pay phone to reach him at his apartment earlier. Not because she'd wanted to talk to him. She'd called to make sure he was home.

I'll tell you what I'm talking about. If you so much as look at another woman, I'll kill her....

Suddenly, Luke's blood ran cold. Kalyna knew where Ava lived. She'd been there.

And, if he had his guess, she was going back.

Tonight.

Ava reached her phone but Kalyna was on her before she could press a single button. As tall and strong as some men, with military training to boot, Kalyna probably could've taken her without a weapon, but she still had that crowbar. Coming up on her from behind, she struck Ava in the back with it.

The pain that shot through Ava's body was so intense she felt instantly nauseous. The second blow knocked her to the floor, and her phone dropped—where, she didn't know. Kalyna was hitting her again and again, beating her in a rage.

Lifting her arms to protect her head, Ava turned and kicked her. Kalyna's curse let her know the kick had hurt, but the reprieve didn't buy her nearly enough time. The blows kept coming.

Ava curled up as Kalyna struck her arm, the other forearm, her hand, her shoulder. "I'm going to kill you, bitch!" she screamed over and over again.

Ava believed her. She fully expected Kalyna to keep

swinging, fully expected to be beaten to death in her own living room. *And this from a woman I once pitied,* she thought distantly.

A second later, however, the blows stopped. Why? Did she have a chance to get away?

Gathering her mental faculties, Ava began crawling toward the couch. Her only plan was to get behind some kind of barrier. But then she became aware of another struggle taking place, a struggle that seemed to have nothing to do with her. What was going on?

More confused than ever—and probably a little delirious, as well—she gave up dragging herself and slumped onto her side so she could see what was happening. The only light came from the bedroom—the light she'd turned on herself—but it was enough to make out the silhouettes of two figures.

The second figure was that of a man. He was wrestling with Kalyna, trying to tear the crowbar from her grip. Ava could hear them scuffling, hear him cursing. She didn't recognize his voice, but it had to be Luke, Geoffrey, her father, Jonathan or Pete. Those were the only men in her life. One of them had miraculously come to her rescue, right?

Wrong. It wasn't any of them. She was sure despite the fact that her body was on fire with pain. This man was too short, too bald, too stocky and too unfamiliar.

"What'd I tell you, huh, Kalyna?" he said, breathing hard. "What'd I say?"

"I don't give a shit what you have to say," Kalyna responded. Her voice was still suffused with hate, but there was a quaver in it Ava had never heard before. Kalyna was scared. Why? Why would she be so frightened of this man?

"You should," he said. "Because I made it clear what I'd do if you ever told."

Ava sucked in a stabilizing breath. That voice. Maybe she recognized it, after all. She'd heard it before. She understood what they were talking about, too—remembered what'd happened to Kalyna's mother and that hitchhiker. They were dead. Someone had killed them. Maybe Kalyna. Maybe…

Her thoughts were so muddled she couldn't draw the name of the second person from her memory. She swiped at her face, trying to clear her vision so she could make out the details of the man's appearance, but tears—or maybe it was blood—kept filling her eyes.

Somehow, Kalyna managed to break away. She came to her feet, wielding the crowbar. "Get back!" she cried, raising it high. "You can't hurt me anymore, Mark. You're going soft, you perverted necrophiliac faggot! You might have the police convinced you didn't enjoy what you did with those corpses, but you and I know better. You're probably still doing it every chance you get. A dead body makes you hornier than a live one."

Mark. Mark *Cannaby.* The last name popped into Ava's mind.

"That's right!" With a hungry growl, he stuck out his tongue and waggled it. "Imagine how many times I raped your sister after I killed her."

"No—" Kalyna swooned, and nearly dropped her weapon.

"Yes." He taunted her with a laugh. "But it was good for me."

Searching for her phone, Ava feebly patted the carpet.

"Why?" Kalyna cried. "Tati never did anything to you!"

"I thought she was you when I followed her into your apartment. I should've known you wouldn't let yourself gain that much weight. You've always been too vain."

"I'm going to kill you," she screamed. "I'm going to kill you for Tati."

Ava's movements nearly made her lose consciousness. Where was her phone? How could she find it and get out of here? These people were demented. Two souls so similar they'd briefly joined together—but so narcissistic they couldn't make even that work. Ava knew it didn't matter which one of them came out of this alive. Neither would allow her to go on breathing. They couldn't; she knew too much.

"Like you killed your mother?" Mark taunted.

Kalyna shook her head. "No, more violent than that. Like I killed Sarah."

He pulled a weapon from behind his back. Ava might've thought it was a gun, but she could tell by the way he wielded it that it wasn't a gun—it was a knife. "Take your best shot. You only get one."

34

Fear trickled through Kalyna's veins. She never dreamt she'd come face-to-face with Mark again. He'd been gone from her life for so long she'd forgotten how intimidating he could be. She'd figured she had him, that he'd go to jail for murdering Sarah and Norma, and she'd be able to forget him for good. But he'd come after her, just as he'd promised all those years ago.

Had he really killed Tati? Kalyna couldn't believe it, refused to believe it, even though she had no other explanation for the wet spot in her bedroom or Ava's claim that she'd found Tati's purse.

Thinking of Ava reminded Kalyna of her presence. She was searching for her phone. Kalyna could sense her panic, was surprised she could even move. That crowbar should've done more damage, but she'd been swinging wildly, hitting Ava in places that wouldn't kill her so she could prolong the pain. She wanted to tell Ava with each blow that she was going to die. And she was. As soon as Kalyna took care of Mark. Her plan was ruined, but she'd figure out some other way to dispose of the body.

The knife he held at the ready glinted in the light from the bedroom. Unfortunately, Kalyna's knife was in her backpack in the room where she'd climbed in. She couldn't get to it from where she was. She only had the crowbar. But she wasn't a seventeen-year-old girl any-more. She'd grown up, was at least as strong and smart as Mark. She'd been serious when she said he'd gone soft in the past ten years. She'd felt his rounded paunch when they were wrestling, heard his labored breathing. They'd barely exerted themselves, and he was already winded. The shaved head and the tattoos were just for show.

"You're the one who's going to die, Mark. I should've killed you a long time ago. I should've done it for Sarah."

He narrowed his eyes in derision. "You think you need to avenge Sarah? *You're* the one who killed her! And you enjoyed what we did to her as much as I did. Shit, you thought of half of it!"

There were parts of her that'd enjoyed the power. But Kalyna didn't want to admit it. Mark reminded her of her worst self, of what she could be—or maybe what she was. She didn't want to be around him, didn't want to face the ugly realities he pushed into the light. He was the only person in the world who really knew her. Norma and Dewayne had always suspected the worst; Tati had always seen what she wanted to see. But Mark had em-braced her for who she really was, and she'd hated him for it.

"I enjoyed what I did to my mother, but I didn't even know Sarah," she said. "It was your idea to kidnap her."

His wet clothes clung to him, indicating that he'd been in the river. Those splashes...

"But it was your idea to kill her!" Kalyna shouted. After wrestling with him, her clothes were damp, too.

"What else were we going to do? Let her go? If you think that would've been a better option, you're as stupid now as you were then. We only did what had to be done. And then you did me a favor when you killed your mother. But I'm not taking the fall for it."

"Don't worry. You won't be around to take the fall."
She swung the crowbar, hoping to knock him down before he could use the knife. She had to make her move, had to kill Mark and stop Ava before Ava could call for help. Somehow she'd make it look as if they'd killed each other and then she'd walk away and be done with them both.

But he was quicker than she'd expected. Ducking the crowbar, he slashed up with his knife and caught her on the chin. The sting surprised her, caused her to rock back—and she couldn't recover fast enough. The next thing she knew he plunged the knife into her chest.

"I thought...you loved me. You promised you'd always love me." She attempted to swing the crowbar—but missed. Dropping it, she staggered in an effort to keep her balance.

"You know better than that. Me and you, we don't love anyone," he said as she sank to the floor. "And we don't trust anyone, either. I was crazy to trust you."

Ava had found her phone. Dimly, Kalyna realized she was fumbling with it, trying to dial.

Mark realized it, too. Leaving her where she lay, he yanked the knife from her chest and turned to Ava. Kalyna would die, but at least she'd die knowing that Ava was going with her.

The drive seemed interminable. Luke had called the police as soon as he dashed out of his apartment, but he didn't have an address to give them. He couldn't even remember the name of the town with the bait shop. He highly doubted that his call—saying he thought Ava's life was in danger because he found a sweatshirt in his laundry that shouldn't have been there—was going to convince anyone that this was an emergency. The 9-1-1 operator would probably send a squad car out to drive through the sloughs and waterways of the delta and take a look, but if an officer came across Ava's houseboat before morning it'd be a miracle. Luke knew in his heart that he was Ava's best chance. But he also knew he might be too late. It was after one o'clock. An hour and a half had passed since that hang-up. And Ava wasn't expecting trouble. It would come without warning and end fast.

Frantic to reach her, in case there was still a chance, he took the next corner as if he was at Daytona. The centrifugal force caused his back end to drift, but he'd planned for it. Regaining control, he punched the gas pedal again. "Hang on, I'm coming," he muttered, and prayed that he'd arrive in time.

A second later, his phone rang. Thinking it might be Ava, he snatched it off the passenger seat, letting out a whoop of relief when he saw her number on his caller ID.

"Thank God!" he cried, and hit the Talk button. "Ava, get out of the house! Get out right now and hide. Kalyna's on her way but so am I. I'll be there as soon as humanly possible."

There was no response.

"Ava?" he said.

Again, no reply. Then he heard something. But it definitely wasn't hello.

The knife had plunged into Ava's thigh. Mark would've stabbed her somewhere else, somewhere on her upper body, but she'd rolled to the right, away from him. She'd taken the thrust in a less vulnerable area as she'd intended, but the sight of the blade buried in her leg to the hilt was so surreal she almost couldn't believe this was anything more than a bad dream. She had nightmares occasionally. She saw too much, heard too much at The Last Stand. But she usually woke up once the violence hit.

This was real. But she was probably in shock because there was no pain, just an invading numbness that seemed to be creeping up from her toes.

Fight! her mind screamed, but her body froze as she tried to maintain her precarious grip on coherent thought.

In a hurry to end her call, Mark didn't bother hanging on to the knife. He left it in her leg so he could grab her phone—and suddenly Ava's panic came flooding back. She needed this call to go through. Her life depended on it.

"No!" It'd been too dark to see the buttons, and she hadn't had time to feel her way through 9-1-1, so she'd pressed the large Phone button twice. That was the fastest way to make a call. It redialed her last number. But she couldn't hold the phone to her ear long enough to find out if Luke answered. In the next second, Mark twisted it from her grasp and threw it away from them. Then he went for the knife.

He was going to finish the job, stab her in the heart or cut her throat and be done with her. She could feel his intent as clearly as if he'd shouted it. But she seized the knife before he could.

Kalyna counted to keep herself lucid.

One…two…three…breathe….

One…two…three…breathe….

She was growing light-headed but fought the encroaching dizziness by focusing on a single point—the light coming from Ava's bedroom. She wouldn't give up so easily, would not allow Mark to win after all these years. She'd play dead until he'd finished with Ava and left. Then she'd go, too. She'd drag her bleeding body all the way to her car, if necessary, but she wouldn't let him get away with what he'd done. Not to her, and not to Tati.

She'd have to plan it for another day. But she'd make him pay if it was the last thing she ever did.

The pain didn't hit full force until a second after she'd pulled the knife out. Then, like a wave crashing onto a beach, it nearly bowled Ava over and carried her down, sucking her under, into unconsciousness. Closing her eyes to help her withstand the onslaught, she dropped back, gasping for breath, but managed to wrap both hands around the handle of the knife and held it against her chest, with the point toward Mark. She knew it wouldn't matter. The fight was over. She had no strength left. She couldn't move, couldn't even lift her arms to make the thrust she'd have to make in order to save herself.

Mark didn't try to wrest the knife from her. He probably didn't realize how easy it would be. He didn't need it in any case. He simply turned and grabbed the crowbar.

There were no other cars besides Ava's, at least not that Luke could see. There weren't any lights on, either, except one at the back of the cabin. It reflected off the water as the houseboat bobbed and swayed in the river. Ava's call had cut out only seconds after he'd heard a bloodcurdling scream, but that scream was still with him, echoing in his brain. He wished she was on the line, screaming now. At least he'd know she was alive.

Everything was quiet—*too* quiet.

What would he find inside?

Hesitating for the first time since he'd dashed out of his apartment, Luke swallowed hard. *Please, don't let her be dead. Don't let me be too late.*

Taking his gun, he got out of his BMW and jogged down the pier. "Ava?" The door was locked. He banged on it to see if he could rouse her, but got no response. The houseboat seemed empty, which left him with an ominous feeling to go with the lump of dread in his gut.

Fearing the worst, he used his shoulder as a battering ram and broke the door. As it gave way, it slammed against the inside wall and hung there by only one hinge.

Luke scanned what he could see of Ava's living room. Despite the dimness of the light filtering in through the hallway, he could make out a few details. A chair had been overturned, a lamp was missing from its table and a painting on the wall had been knocked askew. Obviously, there'd been some sort of fight here.

His heart pumping like the pistons of an engine, he flipped on the light and rounded the short half wall separating the entryway from the living room. Then he stopped short. Blood was everywhere. And there was a body lying on the floor, someone dressed all in black and wearing a ski mask.

Sweat made his shirt stick to his back as he stepped closer. Bending, he pulled off the mask. It was Kalyna. She'd been stabbed in the chest.

Relief swept through him as he stood. If Kalyna was dead, chances were good Ava had survived, weren't they? So where was she?

"Ava?" he called again. But then he saw her feet sticking out from behind the couch.

"Oh, God," he whispered, and set his gun on the ground beneath the coffee table as he knelt to roll her over.

Summoning all that remained of her energy and focus, Kalyna opened her eyes. Luke had barely hesitated when he'd seen her. He'd pulled off her mask to identify her, but he hadn't cared enough to feel for a pulse. He'd stepped right over her in search of Ava. But she, Kalyna, was the one who was pregnant with his child. At least, he believed she was pregnant....

She didn't have the strength to laugh out loud, but she laughed inside. She'd done so much to gain Luke's attention. She'd thought he was special. But he wasn't. He wasn't any better than Mark. All men were alike. She'd been a fool to care about any of them, especially Luke, who'd avoided her from the beginning. He hadn't even been willing to sleep with her—until he was so drunk he couldn't think straight.

Maybe that was why she'd wanted him so badly. Because, as much as she preferred not to believe it, he *was* different. Women weren't just a piece of ass to him. People in general meant more.

Seeing his gun below the coffee table not far away, she wondered if she could reach it. She couldn't last much longer—her strength was fading by the second. But if she was lucky, she could take Luke with her.

Or Mark. As soon as Luke's headlights had struck the house, Mark had ducked back, out of sight. She could sense him creeping toward Luke from the kitchen now, hoisting that crowbar....

The creak that came from directly behind him was Luke's first warning that he wasn't alone with the two prone women. He'd been so concerned with trying to find a pulse on Ava, so sure the damage done to both Ava and Kalyna had been the result of a fight between them, that he'd never considered the possibility of a third person. But rapid footfalls made it very clear that someone else was rushing up behind him.

Whirling just in time, Luke managed to duck the metal object that came down hard, aimed at his head. It hit his shoulder instead, which made a cracking sound and hurt like hell.

"What the... Who are you?" he cried.

The man didn't answer. Too intent on killing him, he swung the crowbar again, but he put so much of his weight behind it that Luke knocked his feet out from under him with a well-timed sweep of the leg. The man cursed and fell, but he didn't drop the crowbar. He hung on to it and grabbed something else he found on the floor before scrambling to his feet again.

It took a second for Luke to realize this man now had a knife, as well as the crowbar—a weapon in each hand.

Backing up, he remained half-crouched, in a defensive position, so he could dodge whatever came his way. He could gain the advantage if only he could reclaim his gun, but he couldn't reach it without risking the knife or the crowbar, or both. He dared not even glance in that direction for fear he'd give its presence away. He couldn't let this man become aware of it.

Fortunately, he hadn't set it on top of the coffee table.

"I don't know who the hell you are, but you're in the wrong place at the wrong time," the man breathed.

Luke stepped to the left, drawing him away from Ava. He doubted she was alive—there was so much blood—but he hadn't been able to confirm before this person attacked him. "Why are you here?"

"Unfinished business," came the response.

Suddenly, Luke knew he'd heard this man's voice before. Over the phone. It was Mark Cannaby.

"Kalyna already told the police about Sarah," he said. "They'll get to the truth eventually."

"No, they won't. Their only witness is dead." He

waved toward Kalyna. "Besides, they're not even sure Sarah existed."

"She existed...."

The sound of Kalyna's voice caused Mark to look at her again. His jaw dropped, and Luke blinked in surprise. She was alive?

"But it...won't matter...not to you. I might be dying, but...you're going with me."

Mark didn't appear to be too worried until she raised the gun. He'd missed seeing Luke enter with it—missed seeing him set it aside when he found Ava—but Kalyna hadn't.

She was in bad shape. Unable to stand, she stayed on the floor. It required both hands to lift the gun, but she had the muzzle pointed in their direction and, at this range, it wouldn't be hard to hit one of them.

Mark held the knife toward Luke and the crowbar toward Kalyna as if he could ward them both off at the same time. "Don't do it," he said to her. "You know how I've always felt about you."

"*Now* I know," she said. "Good thing you...explained it to me...."

"Come on, Kalyna. I had to stab you. You would've done it, too. It wasn't easy for me."

"Yes, it was...too easy." Her hands shook so badly, Luke was afraid Mark would dive for the gun. She was certainly vulnerable. Luke would've done it himself, except that Mark was so much closer.

Determined not to let Mark get hold of that 9 mm, Luke edged toward them. If he could grab one of the three weapons, he'd at least be able to defend himself. But a blast rang out just as he made his move, so he lunged to one side instead.

Kalyna had shot Mark.

"That was for...Tati," she said.

The knife and crowbar fell from Mark's hands. "You bitch!" Grasping his chest, he sank to the floor.

Luke eyed the weapons, now only a few feet away from him. They were available but he didn't dare move. Kalyna had the gun trained on him.

"Tell me...you love me," she wheezed. Her hair was matted with sweat. He could see the effort it took just to stay in a sitting position, just to speak. He didn't know how she was still breathing. But it didn't take much to pull a trigger. And she'd proven herself capable.

He stared at her, wondering if he could summon any compassion. But he couldn't. Not after what she'd done to Ava.

"Luke!" she cried. "Say it!"

"I can't." He shook his head. In a world where everything else seemed distorted, he finally understood the one thing that mattered. The decision he hadn't been able to make earlier that night. He loved Ava. He hadn't known her long, had no idea if she was even alive, but what they'd had was fresh and new and every bit as powerful as what he'd once felt for Marissa.

The barrel of the gun wobbled but Kalyna managed to compensate. "I just...want to hear it. Is that too...fucking much...to ask?"

Reaching out one hand, he stepped cautiously closer. "Give me the gun, Kalyna. Give it to me, and let me get you some help."

The shaking grew worse. She'd just killed Mark. She might kill him, too. But Luke couldn't lie to her. Then he really would be as bad as she thought he was.

"Say it!"

"Give me the gun." Dropping and rolling, he grabbed it away from her, but she didn't fire or try to fight him.

She dropped back onto the floor with a gasping laugh. "I'm...pathetic. I couldn't...shoot you. Even now... you're the only man I ever really...loved," she said, and then she was gone.

Luke sat in the waiting room at the hospital, along with Chuck Bixby, Skye Willis, Sheridan Granger and Jonathan Stivers. After making sure both Mark and Kalyna were dead, he'd checked Ava and found a weak but steady pulse. She was so beaten up, he hadn't known how to help her, but he'd figured stopping the bleeding in her leg was a good place to start. He'd tied a dish towel around her thigh. Then he'd carried her to his car and driven her to the hospital. He couldn't have tolerated waiting at the houseboat for an ambulance, could never have sat there, watching her slip away. He'd had to jump into action.

And now there was nothing more he could do except pray. She was in with the doctors. He wished someone would come out and tell him what was going on—he hadn't heard anything for some time—but the minutes dragged on. It was already morning, marching toward ten o'clock.

"She's going to make it," her father said.

Luke didn't reply. He'd used Ava's phone to notify her father, and her father must've called the others, who all worked at The Last Stand. They didn't say much to Mr. Bixby, but they talked a lot among themselves. And almost every time Luke glanced up, he caught one of them staring at him. The women usually gave him a nervous smile and averted their eyes, but Jonathan didn't bother with that. He was curious and he let Luke know it.

Dropping his head into his hands, Luke felt his breath seep out. It had been a rough night. In order to stop

Dewayne Harter from worrying, he'd felt obliged to call him, but what he'd had to say was hard. Both his adopted daughters were dead. The police had found Tati's body in Mark's trunk. Dewayne had lost his entire family in the course of one week. Luke couldn't imagine what that would be like.

"Do you think someone should call Geoffrey?" Mr. Bixby asked.

Skye and the others all answered at once. "No!"

"Why not?" he pressed.

"She isn't seeing him anymore," Skye said.

Chuck jerked a thumb at Luke. "So she's with him now?"

Skye and Sheridan looked at each other as if they didn't know what to say, so Luke spoke up. "Yeah, she's with me."

Jonathan's gaze landed on him again. Luke could feel the weight of it. Irritated by the constant attention, he scowled, expecting the same searching stare he'd gotten before, but this time Jonathan merely smiled.

"I told her you were innocent," he said.

Surprised, Luke let his scowl fade, but a nurse appeared before he could respond. "Ava's going to be okay," she announced. "She needed a transfusion and quite a few stitches. And she has a slight concussion, as well as some broken bones—her collarbone, a bone in her hand and a bone in her arm. But she'll be back on her feet in a few weeks."

"Can I see her?" Chuck asked.

The nurse hesitated. "Are you Luke?"

His eyebrows shot up. "No, but I'm her father."

"That's Luke," Jonathan said, nodding in his direction.

The nurse sent Luke a warm smile. "She's been asking for you. Why don't you come on back?"

Epilogue

A knock at the door roused Ava from a deep sleep. It was nearly nine o'clock on a Sunday morning, but she didn't have anywhere to be, and she was so comfortable pressed up against Luke's naked body, she didn't want to move. Every once in a while, she thought about the violence that had occurred on the houseboat—especially on mornings like this, when the rocking lulled her back to sleep because she didn't have to go to work. But that terrible night didn't seem real, not with so many good memories to crowd out that bad one. It was only six weeks ago that the autopsy performed on Kalyna's body had proved that she wasn't pregnant. Only one week ago that Jonathan and the Mesa police had found Sarah's family, to confirm her existence and explain her disappearance.

Hard to believe… The knock came again. "I think we have a visitor," Luke mumbled.

Ava had been out of the hospital for two months. She had a scar on her leg to show for the knife wound, but there was no trace of her other injuries. Even her cast was gone. "Must be a solicitor."

"That'd be the first we've ever gotten on the boat."

Exactly. Out here in the middle of nowhere, it almost

had to be someone she knew, which meant she had to get up. She started to roll out of bed, but he pulled her back and kissed her temple.

"Want me to answer it?"

"No, I will. I'll make some coffee while I'm at it." They planned to look at wedding rings this afternoon, then go to Skye's for dinner. Luke had asked Ava to marry him a week ago, in San Diego, after she'd met his parents and his sister.

She figured they might as well get moving. She'd been teasing Luke that she was going to choose the biggest diamond she could find, but a simple band would make her just as happy.

"Wake me when you're in the shower," he said. "I don't want to miss that."

She laughed. She knew she wasn't the most beautiful woman he'd ever met, but he made her feel as if she was. "You want breakfast with your coffee?"

"If you don't mind making some eggs."

The knock came a third time, louder.

"I don't mind." She threw on a robe and went to the door. She expected it to be her father. She'd told him not to contact her, but that hadn't stopped him. He'd been coming over more than ever lately, the frequency of his visits directly proportional to the frequency of his arguments with his wife. Ava supposed she and Luke would be getting married and buying a house just about the time he'd need the houseboat. If Chuck could last that long, it would all work out perfectly.

"Ava?" A female voice came through the new door that replaced the one Luke had broken down. "I know you're in there."

Carly.

Tightening the belt to her robe, Ava squared her shoulders. What could her stepmother possibly want? They hadn't seen each other in months; Ava didn't care if she ever saw Carly again.

This was probably about another fight. Maybe she was out looking for Chuck...

Ava opened the door, prepared to tell Carly that her father wasn't there. But Carly didn't ask for him. She handed Ava an envelope.

"We keep getting these," she said. "Every few weeks. Your father tells me to throw them away. I do throw away the ones that are addressed to him. He's remarried and she has no business contacting him. But you're a big girl. I think you should handle your own mail."

It was a letter from her mother.

As Ava stared down at her name and address, written in Zelinda's hand, the sense of loss she hadn't experienced since Luke came into her life reasserted itself. But she refused to let Carly know that passing along this letter had made any kind of impact. "Thank you," she said politely.

"Are you going to open it this time?" Carly asked.

That was none of her concern. Ava raised her chin. "Maybe."

Carly glanced off into the distance before focusing on her again. "I realize we've never been friends, but—"

Luke came up behind Ava. He was wearing jeans and a T-shirt he must've pulled on in a hurry but no shoes. "Who's this?" he asked.

He knew, or he wouldn't have jumped out of bed, but Ava made the introduction, anyway. "This is Carly, my father's wife."

"And you must be Luke," Carly said. "I saw the BMW. Nice car."

The admiration that oozed through her manner bothered Ava, but Luke didn't seem to notice it. "Thanks. It's
a pleasure to meet you."

She offered him a bright smile. "I've heard a lot about
you. Chuck thinks you're great. He says you're wonderful to Ava. But I had no idea…no idea that…"

Once again her stepmother had spoken without thinking. She'd started to say she'd had no idea he'd be so
handsome. It was written all over her face. But she
seemed to realize how rude that would sound and was
searching for an alternative.

"No idea you'd be here," she finished lamely.

Carly had just said she'd seen his car, but Ava didn't
point out the contradiction. She didn't care enough about
Carly to embarrass her. Ava no longer felt quite so injured
by her father's choices; she felt sorry for him. His actions
had hurt others, but he was definitely getting the worst
of it in the end.

"Thanks for stopping by," Ava said.

Carly's eyes darted to Luke as if she was interested in
continuing the conversation, but Ava shut the door.

"What do think?" Ava asked.

"She's not *nearly* as attractive as you are," he said.
Then he motioned to the letter Carly had brought.
"What's that?"

"Nothing important." Forcing a smile, Ava shoved it
in the bookcase and moved toward the kitchen.

Luke seemed to know it wasn't "nothing," but he
didn't push the issue. He followed her into the kitchen
and started the coffeemaker while she scrambled the
eggs.

It wasn't until Ava got home after picking out her
wedding ring and having dinner at Skye's that she re-

trieved the letter. Luke had gone to his apartment because he had to be at the base by seven in the morning, so she was alone. Now she could throw it away without seeming hard-hearted.

Or she could read it....

She thought of the events ahead of her—her wedding on December 5, the birth of her first child a year or two after that, the addition of other children. Was it a life she wanted to live without Zelinda? Could she forgive herself, and her mother, enough to rebuild as much of a relationship as they could have, considering the situation?

No. She couldn't deal with it, even now. Maybe later, she told herself. But that letter beckoned as if her mother was standing in the room with her arms outstretched— and the longing to walk into them, to feel them close around her again, was suddenly too overpowering to refuse.

Her throat tight with unshed tears, Ava slowly opened the envelope. The note was short. She guessed it was basically the same note her mother had been sending for years.

Dear Ava—

I miss you so much. I think about you all the time. I know you need answers. I can't explain what got into me. I was desperately angry and bitter. It ate at me like a cancer. But that's no excuse. There is no excuse. I deserve to be where I am, but that doesn't change the fact that I love you more than life.

I'm sorry.

Mom

Ava stared at those words until they began to blur with her tears. Then she remembered better days—days when her mother would be waiting to pick her up from school or was throwing her a birthday party—and went to the dining room table. Taking out a piece of paper, she began to write a reply.

* * * * *